Tale of the Raptor Men

By

John R. Cobb

Tale of the Raptor Men

Copyright 2022 John R. Cobb
ISBN: 979-8-804065-37-0

Cover designed by Dawn Shain.

Author photo by Heidi S. Cobb.

Printed in the United States of America.

For my Daddy, William Riley Cobb,
and my other Texas Kin.

Contents

Contents

Contents

Prologue
The Fallen

Surrounded by a wide expanse of withered grasses, mesquite, and prickly pear cactus, heat shimmered above the railroad tracks. Beginning in Kansas, Moses Smalls had been walking in a southeasterly direction for weeks and was now somewhere in the hinterlands of Eastern Texas. Months before, he heard from other freedmen that a black man could get a job as a stevedore loading and unloading ships in Galveston. The prospect of regular wages tempted him to risk the expedition rather than continue toiling as a tenant farmer.

When his mule threatened to halt, Moses reached into his pocket for a piece of salt lick to coax the animal along. Thankful for living another day, he wondered how long his luck would last. Moses figured it was by divine miracle he hadn't been killed by now. Texas was full of murderous bandits and Indians, and fatal accidents were always imminent. Rattlesnakes had bitten his mule twice, and scorpions had stung Moses three times. He and his mule were awash with ticks, and itching welts inflicted a terrible suffering.

Having lost track of time, Moses only knew it was the height of summer in the year 1870. Three days ago, he had come across the railroad tracks, which traveled in the same general direction as him. Unfortunately, during the appearance of the first train, a few passengers had fired shots at him. Afterwards, Moses kept a prudent distance to avoid those, who might waylay him, especially suspicious white folk. Although Moses had his musket and knife and could fight, he was alone and far from familiar environs.

From a distance, Moses observed a shape lying on the ground. With little to eat in past days, he hoped for a fresh animal carcass. Buoyed by the absence of buzzards, Moses neared and discovered a creature not of hide and hoof, but of feather and talon. Gazing upon it, his face belied a look of bewilderment. He wiped his brow with a shirtsleeve. His brown eyes squinted under the harsh sun.

"Well now…what sort of birdie did you come from?" Moses spoke in a raspy voice.

Immense wings lie on the ground with a span wider than the mightiest raptor that Moses had ever seen soaring through the skies.

1

A sheath of ashen bone and desiccated tendon held them together. He stroked feathers of mottled colors of gray and black. The tips of his dirty fingers felt oily. Looking around, Angus didn't see a carcass to ascertain the wings source. Several feet away, a railroad pole stood, its lower trunk scorched as if struck by lightning. Lengths of steel chain lay nearby. Many ringlets were malformed, stretched beyond their tensile strength.

"Quite the curiosity, you are. Be shameful leaving yah for the animals to gnaw on," Moses muttered. "Cattle town not too far. Maybe sell 'em?"

Suggesting biblical origins, Moses traded the wings to a young Baptist minister by the name of Jonas Faulkner for jerky, hardtack, and gunpowder. The wings stirred eager fanfare for a church where attendance was usually sparse. At the outset, Jonas allowed his congregation to touch, but after a short while, forbade them to get close, even invoking curses and bodily threats. His longing to spread the gospel waned over succeeding months. One Sunday morning, parishioners found a smoking heap of cinders where the church had been and the minister's charred body with a coil of barbwire around his neck.

Though deacon elders searched the minister's nearby house, they never found the wings. Most folks supposed the fire had destroyed them after Jonas hung himself.

A few years after, a man by the name of Elias Randall, a master leather-smith known for his decorative horse saddles, bought the minister's house. It was an odd dwelling with high ceilings, narrow windows, and dim throughout. So small, it was only suited for a bachelor or childless married couple.

Over the next decades, the Town of Marlboro spread outward as more people settled to ranch and farm. Eventually, streets and neighborhoods developed. Several people owned the house, including a man who had gone insane and murdered his wife and baby son, a recluse woman, who killed herself with rat poison, and a widowed father, who had committed incestuous acts with his daughters.

A later owner was a divorced mother, whose only son died fighting the Japanese at Guadalcanal. Distraught, she had lingered in the house for another decade, rarely speaking with neighbors and only going out for groceries. For reasons unknown, she moved away, leaving behind her red and white Service Flag with Gold Star hanging in the front window.

In 1962, Fletcher and Darla Harlan moved into the queer house on Cobb Street. Fletcher worked a myriad of ordinary jobs from farmhand to school custodian. Darla tended a local laundromat until she bore her first son, Hoyt. After which, she became a homemaker. Over the next five years, she had two more sons, Zane and then Audie. The family was content with simple pursuits. On the weekends, they ran trotlines across the Brazos River, hunted the woods around Marlboro Lake, or watched movies at the Wheeler Drive-In.

Regrettably, hard times befell the Harlan Clan. Fletcher drank often and worked little while Darla came to resent her place in life as a suffering wife and mother. She abandoned her husband and sons, leaving with no explanation whatsoever.

As more years passed, a deepening depression overcame Fletcher. Unable to work, his family's plight worsened. Poverty crept into their home, vanquishing hope and joy. Fletcher became a recluse. One by one, the boys dropped out of school and wandered without purpose.

Hoyt joined the Army and served as a Military Policeman. Zane drove truck, delivering sundry goods throughout the country. Audie remained home to keep his father company, and out of boredom, ventured into criminal activities. For the brothers, romantic relationships were unrealized.

Fletcher died in his bed, his body ruined after a lifetime of nicotine and alcohol addictions, and medications prescribed to alleviate his mental harms. The boys interred their father in a modest grave at *Bell Ridge Cemetery.*

Chapter 1
Fletcher's Legacy

Hoyt fidgeted with his clip-on tie. Although his dress uniform was immaculate with its starched fabric and creased lines, it was uncomfortable in summer heat. The polished brass of his military insignia glinted in the noonday sun. Hoyt's glum expression, ashen and sunken, stared in return from the toes of his polished shoes. His blond hair was close-cropped. His blue eyes squinting against the bright sky, he donned his aviator shades.

Hoyt paid little attention to the minister. Nor, did he really care. The eulogy was the usual homily of loss, redemption, and GOD's ever-loving grace in the kingdom of heaven. Hoyt didn't find solace in the minister's words. He was still in shock about his father's passing. Stationed in West Germany, he hadn't been home for two years.

Zane mingled with cousins, who were the few relatives in attendance at his father's funeral. Unlike his older brother, Zane was more outgoing and liked to talk, especially about himself. Shorter than his two brothers, Zane was more muscular, his blond hair long and tousled, his mustache well kempt. His dark suit jacket contrasted with his blue jeans and cowboy boots. His turquoise bolo tie accentuated his western shirt. Although he exuded good cheer, Zane was depressed. He had been out of state delivering custom auto parts and had not seen his father for several days before his death.

Audie walked the fringes of the cemetery to escape family condolences. His attention kept drifting toward a backhoe covered with a tarp at far end of the graveyard. Not long after this gathering dispersed, a crew would arrive to finish the job of interring his father. Audie leaned over the chain-link fence and bowed his head. He wanted nothing more than go home and sleep, but a tremendous bout of insomnia had kept him up for the past three days. His blond hair was unwashed and greasy. Sweaty strands clung to his forehead. Unlike his brothers, Audie didn't bother dressing for the somber occasion. Besides, he had no formal attire. His shirt and jeans were rumpled and stained. A grimaced expression appeared on his face as another wave of sorrow washed over him. His tears spent after days of crying, he could only shudder.

"Nice ceremony, Reverend. Daddy would have appreciated your kind words," Hoyt said, placing his cap on his head. "If you have a minute, I'll write you a check."

"No hurry, Hoyt, but feel free to get it out of your way," Reverend Lovering replied. "I'm sure you're busy settling your father's affairs and all."

"Not really...other than notifying social security and the bank...and getting the house signed over, but I suppose Zane can take care of that."

"How are you and your brothers getting along?"

Hoyt fumbled with his checkbook as he wrote out the dollar amount and signed his name. "I'd say we're pretty miserable at the moment," he answered. "Audie's taking it especially bad...him being the youngest. Me...I'm heading back to Germany, so I'll have other things to think about. Poor Zane will have to deal with everything at home."

"Well, you may not think so now, but your grief will lessen with time," the Reverend offered. "There will always be a bit of sadness in your heart, but you'll learn to cope with it. You're all young, healthy men. You have a long time to make new lives for yourselves. Yah know...find jobs, meet a good woman, raise kids... In some ways, I envy you boys."

"Wouldn't that be something?" Hoyt said, his mood bolstered by the thought. "Here's your check, sir, and thanks again."

Reverend Lovering's prediction didn't see fruition. The brothers struggled during ensuing years. Hoyt's grief didn't diminish despite deployments to far-flung places like West Germany and Korea. Eventually, he chose not to reenlist, returned home, and lived with his brothers. For a time, he applied for positions at the Wheeler, Timpson, and Austin Police Departments. Although qualified given his military training and experience, Hoyt was never hired. Instead, he took a job with the public works department clearing animal carcasses from the highways.

As time passed, Hoyt became increasingly depressed. He spent much of his time sleeping. When not lying-in bed, he swung on the porch rocker and smoked cigarettes. Despite his many wanderings in life, Hoyt never had a real girlfriend. His only dalliances had been with prostitutes during his occasional forays outside the military bases. Like most healthy young men, amorous thoughts were incessant. However, in recent years, his libido had waned, his need to self-pleasure diminished.

Added to Hoyt's melancholy were peculiar thoughts that materialized as actual voices. Disembodied entities spoke to him, which so disturbed him, he quit his job and stayed in the house, never straying beyond the bounds of the driveway and backyard. One voice rose above the white noise in his head to report the nefarious doings of others.

Evidently, Mr. Hart, an elderly man down the street, was a demon, a killer and devourer of neighborhood cats and squirrels. Mrs. Sanchez from next door was a nymphomaniac, who seduced teenage boys. Mr. Jackson, who lived in the house beyond the backyard fence, worked at the Merrimack Funeral Home as an undertaker and liked to have sex with the dead.

Like creaking boards in an empty attic, the voices came unexpectedly, whispering nonsensical things. Always lurking in Hoyt's restless mind, they spoke about portents of doom, beseeching him to prepare for the coming darkness. For the most part, the voices conveyed observations of those around him, but occasionally, they directed Hoyt to perform innocuous tasks like stacking bricks in a pyramid shape behind the shed or digging holes under the backyard pecan tree with a spoon. However, Hoyt never submitted entirely to the voices, no matter their harsh tone. He refused to kill the songbirds and squirrels that chirped and scurried around the house, and he disobeyed when told to peer into the windows of his neighbors.

Unlike Hoyt's agoraphobic tendencies, Zane drifted in whatever direction his delivery truck beckoned. He crisscrossed the southwest over a latticework of interstates. He became intimately familiar with the byways along his routes. Since he abhorred motels, he oftentimes slept in his truck. It was one of the few instances when he appreciated his modest stature. His life had become a tedious journey down an endless ribbon of gray asphalt. The view through his dusty windshield was a bleak, sunbaked landscape.

Every so often, well past midnight, when the road was barren for countless miles in either direction, Zane would stop his truck and sit cross-legged in the road, eating a sandwich and drinking a cold soda. During those times, Zane savored the isolation, illumined under a canopy of desert stars, lulled by the faraway howl of a coyote and the buzzing of nocturnal insects. Sometimes, he reclined on the asphalt, still warm from the previous day, and rested his aching back. He took care not to doze off, lest another midnight traveler run over him.

Except for a day or two every couple of weeks, Zane seldom lingered home, which was simply a place to take a shower and wash his clothes. Although he left money for Hoyt to pay utility bills and buy groceries, he had no desire to know what was happening with his brothers. At some point, Zane knew he had to put away his wanderlust, but for now, the monotonous road was more sufferable.

Audie was the most restless of the Harlan Brothers. Having dropped out of school, he trolled the nights in search of things to fill his time. Never routine, he might spend a night tending a trotline on the Brazos River. The next, he might hunt raccoons in the swampy pinelands north of Marlboro Lake. On the succeeding night, he might break into a business stealing firearms, ammo, and anything else he could sell.

Occasionally, local police came to the house and asked about his whereabouts on certain dates. As always, Audie was nonchalant in his demeanor and offered practiced answers, not easily corroborated. He was careful to catalog his misdeeds and avoid contradicting himself. Additionally, he stored his contraband in a neighbor's shed two blocks over. For this privilege and Mr. Simpson's continued discretion, Audie mowed grass and did a few odd chores.

Unlike his older brothers, Audie was able to satiate his teenage libido with a bevy of local girls in town. Since he wasn't overly selective, he played the odds until someone accepted his overtures. Audie especially liked older women, who had access to a comfortable bed on which to play. There was an implicit understanding on Audie's part that his partners took care of things like birth control and general health, so he didn't bother with condoms and such. Thus far, he had eluded sexually transmitted diseases and pregnancies.

Chapter 2
Good Fortune My Way

"You're done, Pete!" a man's voice barked from down the aisle. "I'm sick and tired of your bitching and loafing."

"Yah know you can't do that, Eddie. My brother-in-law won't stand for it!"

"Yeah, yeah, I've heard it all before!"

Audie peered around the end of the fishing tackle aisle and watched the exchange near the gun counter. He recognized Eddie Atkins, general store manager of the Marlboro Big Mart, and Pete Gunn, manager of the hunting and fishing section. Eddie was an overweight man with a flattop buzz cut. Attired in a white, short-sleeve shirt and black, clip-on tie, his belly drooped over the front of his black slacks. He always seemed sweaty and breathless. From moment to moment, his face alternated between flush and ashen. Although a taskmaster with his staff, Eddie was always cordial with store customers.

"Well, good luck replacing me," Pete retorted. "No one knows this section better than me."

"Shoot...!" Eddie snorted. "Felix!"

"Yes, sir!" a man called from the next aisle. "Whadda need, Mr. Atkins?"

Audie recognized Felix, an older black man, who worked for Pete and did much of the work in the section.

"You're now in charge of the hunting and fishing section, Felix," Eddie declared. "Mr. Gunn has tendered his resignation as of this moment."

"This is bullshit!" Pete hissed. "No way Randy's gonna stand for this. Mark my words, you fat fuck!"

"Oh...he would, if I told him about you screwing Rosalita in the back lot," Eddie said in a hushed voice. "Better yet, I could mail him a copy of the store videotape. Store cameras usually take a shitty picture, but the one near the dumpster takes really good video."

"Bullshit...you wouldn't..." Pete replied, his indignation diminished. "Randy wouldn't go against me..."

"Oh...wouldn't he?" Eddie said. "Randall may be a lot of things, but he seems pretty close to his sister and all... Even keeps a picture of her on his desk along with the rest of his family. Except…I don't ever recall seeing your smug expression in any of the photos."

"Fine…go ahead, but I want severance…and a letter of reference," Pete demanded, "or, I'm gonna raise a shit storm."

"All right by me, as long as you're outta my store straightaway," Eddie agreed, looking around for customers within range of their conversation.

Audie ducked into the tackle aisle when the manager gazed in his direction.

"Fine…just don't forget to mail my check," Pete snapped, flinging his store vest down the aisle. "Plenty of other Big Marts to work at."

"Uh-huh," Eddie replied.

As soon as Pete disappeared, Eddie turned and said, "Congratulations, Felix. You would have had this job before now, if upper management hadn't foisted numb nuts on me. Anyhow, I know you'll do a good job and all."

"Thanks, Mr. Atkins," Felix said. "You won't regret it."

"I know I won't. Excuse me a second."

By now, Audie figured the whole affair was over, so he returned to the assortment of trotlines at the other end of the aisle. He used his fingers to figure how much money he'd have left…

"Why, Mr. Harlan," a man's voice spoke. "Fancy meeting you here."

"Oh…hello, Mr. Atkins," Audie said with a start. "Yes, sir…just looking over the trotlines. Say…you wouldn't happen to have some stink bait out back, would yah?"

"Forget all that, Audie," Eddie said. "In case you didn't hear already, we have a job opening at Big Mart."

"Oh…sorry about that," Audie said. "I didn't mean to overhear…but you don't have to worry. I'm not much of a gossip."

"The whole store can know for all I care. Pete was a shifty slacker and lucky he lasted as long as he did," Eddie said as he mopped his head with a damp handkerchief. "Well…are you interested or not? You've filled out enough job applications, and you're practically here all of the time anyway."

"You're offering me a job?"

"Well yeah… Whadda you think I'm doin' over here? You better get a clue."

"Yeah...sure," Audie answered. "When can I start?"

"That's what I like to hear," Eddie said. "Job comes with a six-month probationary period and pays minimum wage. After that, we'll parlay some more about pay and benefits. Come to my office, and I'll set you up with some paperwork to take home and fill-out. Then, come back tomorrow morning at six o'clock sharp, and I'll put you out back on the dock. Oh...wear clean slacks and a shirt with a collar. You do have some decent clothes, don't yah?"

"Well...not really... I suppose I could borrow something from my brothers..."

"Screw that," Eddie declared. "Come with me, and we'll get you something off the rack. First outfit is on me, but the rest will come outta your paycheck—minus your employee discount, of course. Oh yeah...good hygiene is a plus around here, so use some soap on something other than your pecker when you take a shower. Got it?"

"Uh...yes, sir."

Elated by his good fortune, Audie barely noticed his walk home. He recalled having submitted several job applications since dropping out of school, but never called back for an interview. Big Mart was the big employer in town, and openings didn't come often. He was thankful for his luck. A few minutes sooner or later, he might have missed Pete's firing. For the first time, Audie thought about his good fortune.

***

A cigarette ember glowed in sultry shadow. A narrow shaft of sunlight streamed through a small hole in the window blind, smoke and dust drifted through the stale air. Hoyt's tee shirt and underwear were damp. He wiped sweat from his high forehead. A tickle in his chest summoned a long coughing spell. Burning and piercing pain crept from his trunk and settled in the back of his throat...

There was a knock at the door followed by a woman's voice, "Hoyt, are you home?"

"Uh...yeah..." Hoyt called out as he felt in the darkness. "One sec..." His mind struggled to register several thoughts at once. *Who's at the door? Where were his pants and shirt? Was he presentable?*

Blue jeans and boots in hand, he raced for the kitchen at the back of the house. Hoyt stumbled about as he pulled up his pants and inserted bare feet into his boots. As an afterthought, he turned on the

10

tap, splashed water on his grimy face, and wiped his brow with a mildewed dishtowel.

Shit...that stinks!

After a quick glance in the mirror, Hoyt pushed through the backdoor and loped around the side of the house. Regina Nash stood on the front porch. She lived across the street with her two daughters, Sarah and Sandra, and a nasty husband, Nate. Hoyt's neighbor was a pretty woman of Mexican descent with raven hair, tan skin, and a shapely figure. Like Hoyt, Regina was in her late twenties. Her husband was middle-aged with a potbelly and flabby biceps and an unpleasant temperament. Regina and Nate were an unlikely union of unknown circumstances. Hoyt liked Regina and her girls, who always waved and said hello. Too often, Hoyt had romantic and lustful thoughts involving Regina. He figured he shouldn't have such fantasies given her kindness and marital situation, but he couldn't help himself.

"Hey there, Regina. What can I do yah for?"

"Oh, Hoyt..." she said with a start. "I'm so sorry for knocking on your door, but I'm desperate... Nate's out of town, and I don't know any other neighbors, who could handle this..."

"What's the matter?"

"There's a snake in my house. Big water moccasin...I think... I have no idea how it got in there, but the girls are hysterical...trapped in their room with that thing coiled up and hissing outside in the hallway. It lunged at me when I tried to shoo it away. It stinks really bad. Could you get it out of my house?"

"No problem...I'll be right back," Hoyt said as he backtracked to the shed. Straightaway, he found what he wanted leaning against the studded wall on his left. He grabbed a long dogwood staff. At one end was a two-prong fork with two branches sawn to stubbed points, a fitting tool for securing the dangerous end of poisonous serpent. Hoyt retrieved a burlap croaker sack, a pair of thick leather gloves, and an oiled machete.

"Lead the way, Regina."

Hoyt walked fast to keep pace with his neighbor. Arriving at her house, Hoyt's heart pounded. He breathed deep to catch his wind before asking, "Where was it last?"

"End of the hallway...see?" Regina replied, pointing through the picture window. "Be careful, it may be anywhere now."

"Okay," he said. "Just stay outside the screen door."

Eyes scanning the living room, Hoyt tried to distinguish a snake hidden amongst the furnishings of a family home. The brown carpeting, beige couch, and chairs were perfect camouflage for a moccasin painted in shades of olive, brown, or black.

Frightened cries carried from the end of the hall, "Mama, help us!"

"It's okay girls! It's me...Hoyt...from down the street. You mama fetched me to catch that nasty snake. Just stay in your room, and don't worry, okay?"

"Okay," pitiful voices answered.

A noxious smell wafted through the air. Musky and skunkish, Hoyt recognized the odor of a water moccasin. A loud hissing issued from the gloom. A lamp lay on the floor where it had fallen from a stand. Hoyt observed a shadowy mass at the threshold of a doorway to the right. Hoyt flipped the light switch on the wall, but the overhead bulb didn't work.

Damn!

The narrow hallway was gloomy with little room to maneuver. Although many snake species were shy and prone to flee at the slightest danger, water moccasins were notoriously aggressive, especially the big ones. Hoyt has seen many as big around as his bicep and several feet or longer. On his many forays into Texas wetlands, he had come across many a serpent. Oftentimes, the smaller ones slithered away so fast, he wondered if he had imagined their blurred forms fleeing through the underbrush. Sometimes, the larger ones remained coiled and ready to strike. As boys, he and his brothers trekked to the bottoms at Marlboro Lake with long sticks and sought them out. Backs broken and heads stove in, they slew hundreds if not thousands during their hunts.

The one in Regina's house was huge. Black as coal and quivering with muscle, it was more than capable of injecting a toxic dose of venom. It may not paralyze the heart of its victim like a rattlesnake, but its poison could destroy tissue with a bacterial-laced bite. Spoiled flesh and amputated limbs were common injuries if not treated posthaste.

Need more light... Now where...?

An upright lamp stood behind a recliner next to a pedestal ashtray. Hoyt repositioned it to illumine the hallway. Sure enough, a large serpent lay coiled, angular head raised above the floor, forked tongue flicking, and fanged maw opening and closing as it hissed and spat. So black, Hoyt barely discerned the snake from its shadow. For a moment, he felt anxious, but he dismissed the feeling.

"All right...enough of this happy horseshit," Hoyt mumbled, donning his gloves. "You're not welcome here, yah ugly bastard. Back to the willy-wags with yah..."

Hugging the left side of the hallway, so he didn't block the light, Hoyt approached with forked staff in his left hand and machete in the other. He focused on the snake's head seeking to fathom its intentions. Unlike mammals like raccoons and opossums, reptiles were entirely unreadable. Hoyt believed all creatures had souls, but he wasn't so sure about serpents. Purely instinctual creatures, dead eyed and unfeeling, he likened them to psychopaths of the animal kingdom.

Hoyt held his breath against the snake's odorous assault. He leveled the staff as he neared. He estimated the distance and angle...

Suddenly, the serpent's body quivered, its tongue flicking. Hoyt thrust the forked staff, pinning the base of its head against the paneled wall. The serpentine body thrashed, thumping against the doorway. He dropped his machete and maintained a two-handed grip as he inched up the staff. The snake wrapped around his leg. Hoyt felt repulsed as it writhed and constricted against his upper thigh. Undeterred by the sensation, he willed himself forward. He braced the staff in the crook of his left arm, reached out with his gloved hand, and clamped his fingers behind the snake's head.

His arm quaking from the struggle, Hoyt lay the croaker sack down and inserted the moccasin's head. At once, the snake relaxed, its body uncoiling from around Hoyt's leg. As soon as he released the serpent, it slithered in without further resistance. When the last of its stubbed tailed disappeared, Hoyt cinched the ties and hefted the weighted sack.

"It's okay, girls. You can come out now," Hoyt beckoned. "Your mama's outside waiting for yah."

A shaft of light penetrated the dim hallway as the bedroom door opened. Sarah asked, "Did you get it, Hoyt?"

"I got 'em, Honey. Big ole mean water moccasin, but he's harmless as a butterfly in this croaker sack."

"It stinks awful," Sandra said. "Like a skunk..."

"It sure does," he agreed, "Your mama's gonna have to open the windows and mop the floors with some Lysol to cut the smell. You girls go through the living room, and I'll take this thing out the back."

Using both hands, Hoyt carried the sack through the kitchen and into the backyard. He laid it on the ground under a shaded oak. The burlap material moved as the moccasin shifted inside, then became still. Hoyt wondered how such a large snake slithered through half a mile of residential neighborhoods and made its way into this particular home. He looked around. Straightaway, he noticed a vent for a clothes dryer protruding from the rear of the house. Spring-loaded flap jammed with lint and stuck open, the hose connecting the vent cap to the dryer had come undone.

There yah go.

"Thank you, Hoyt...so much," Regina said, rounding the corner of the house with Sandra on her hip and Sarah by the hand. "I didn't know who else to get with Nate away... He doesn't like anyone coming around the house..."

"No problem, Regina. I'm just glad you and the girls are all right," he replied. "It'll make a good story to tell my brothers."

"Are you gonna kill it?" Sarah asked, and then suggested. "You should smash it with a rock or something."

"Well...I probably would have whacked its head off if it gave me too much trouble, but I might call someone at Tyler University. This one's so unusual...it being so big...and black as coal. Seems a shame to kill it, but you won't have to worry about it no more."

"How do you suppose it got in?" Regina asked. "I keep the doors closed and locked."

"I'd say he crawled through your dryer vent."

"Oh...Nate moved the dryer the other day," Regina said. "Hose must have come loose."

"Here...I'll dig out the lint and reconnect the hose," Hoyt offered. "Shouldn't take but a few minutes."

"No need... Say...Hoyt, mind if we keep this to ourselves?" Regina asked. "It's no secret my husband can be mean with the neighbors, and as much as he should be thankful for your help, he might get mad anyway."

"Not a problem, Regina. I understand," he said. "I'll just grab this beast and head home."

Smiling and waving to the girls, Hoyt lifted the heavy sack and walked back to the house. He placed the burlap bag in his broken-down truck and searched for a bucket of paint. In little time, Hoyt placed a board across the truck bed with the words *Danger Snake!* He went inside and searched for a phonebook to lookup the number for Tyler University.

***

"What cha doin', Sweetness?" a woman asked as she sat across from Zane in the booth. "Looks like you've been on the road for a spell. Where yah headed?"

She was a tall, gangly woman, who looked years older than she probably was. Her dirty blond hair was long and stringy and framed an angular face thick with rouge, mascara, and lipstick. She reeked of stale cigarettes and cheap perfume. Zane recoiled from an unsavory musky scent wafting from her body.

"Hello, yourself," Zane replied. "I'm heading back home by way of Denton and Wheeler."

"You are, huh?" she said. "My name's Nikki. What's yours?"

"I'm Zane."

"Well, Sweetness… How about buying me lunch and giving me a ride to Denton. I'm real good company when I'm fed and comfortable."

Most times, Zane was more discriminating, but it had been a long trip, and he was feeling horny. "Sounds like I'm in luck," Zane said. "It'll be nice to have company for the last leg of my trip."

After a hurried lunch, Zane led his guest to his truck. "Oh…wait a sec'," Zane said climbing into the passenger side of the cab. "I'm not much for housekeeping since I usually travel alone."

While his new traveling companion waited, Zane stowed his bag behind the seat and collected trash from the floorboard. It was sweltering inside the cab. Zane regretted not starting his vehicle beforehand and turning on the air-conditioner. Sweat beaded and flowed down his face. In the restaurant, he was dry and comfortable. Now, body odor exuded from his grubby shirt and pants. He longed for a shower and a clean bed.

"Sorry, for the wait," he offered. "I should have done this before bringing you out."

"Don't mind me, Darling. I'm probably smelling a little ripe myself. Help a lady up, kind sir?"

15

Zane took Nikki's hand and hoisted her up. Her short skirt rode up revealing a long bare leg. He imagined her legs wrapped over his shoulders as he pounded... Zane shook the image from his head when he realized he had been staring. Nikki didn't seem to mind.

Zane started the truck and cranked the air conditioner. After a minute, cool air filled the cab. He wiped his brow with a handkerchief and asked, "So, where are you from, Nikki?"

"Me...? Everywhere," she answered, looking at her reflection in the rearview mirror. "My father was in the Army, so we moved a lot."

"Was he ever stationed at Fort Hood?"

"Texas?"

"Yeah...largest military base in the Free World..."

"I don't think so...his last post was in California," she replied. "I ended up running away to Los Angeles when I was old enough."

"Really...?" Zane said. "Did you ever meet any movie stars?"

"A few celebrities," Nikki said. "They're all over the place out there."

"What did you do...for a living? Did you try acting?"

"Who...me?" she said as she primped in the mirror. "No...that's a pipe dream for anyone going out there. I worked odd jobs...mostly...and shacked up here and there. Unfortunately, I got turned on to drugs, and eventually, turned tricks to make my way. Yah know...became a hooker. That's why I'm goin' to Denton. I have a friend there to set me up."

"Well...that's quite a story," Zane said. "Not really sure what to say to that...?"

"You don't have to say anything at all, Honey. In spite of your southern boy ways, you've been around, I'll bet."

"Yes, ma'am...I have...I guess," Zane said, his face growing flush.

"Now...look at you," Nikki said with a laugh, her hand caressing his leg. "All embarrassed like... Since I'm so tired and dirty, let's say you find us a nice motel to spend the rest of the day and night. While you go get us a pizza, beer, and condoms, I'll take a hot shower. After you get clean, I'll give you an erotic massage and see what happens.

***

16

"There you go, Sweetie," Nikki said pulling off Zane's cowboy boots. "Water's nice and hot, so get cleaned up. Don't bother shaving. I like a man's whiskered face."

Nikki wore a towel around her lanky body. She swept long, wet hair back over her shoulders. Face cleansed of makeup, shadows appeared under her eyes. Her skin was blemished and pimpled. Scabs and bruises covered her skeletal legs—some recently inflicted.

Undeterred by physical imperfections, Zane savored her nearness and willingness. He longed to shed a long run of sexual frustration. Aroused by the prospect of sex, Zane hurried to the bathroom. Even though he was distracted, he had the forethought to stow his wallet in the truck.

"I'm gonna have another beer and get myself ready."

"I hear yah," Zane called out as he turned on the shower. "I won't be long."

Zane scrubbed hurriedly but thoroughly, taking care not to bathe his nether regions too long. After he toweled off, he brushed his teeth and took a quick look at his reflection. As usual, his image in the mirror didn't quite match the likeness he had of himself in his mind. However, his wet hair slicked back and his naked body flush after a hot shower, Zane was ready.

"Oh…look at you," Nikki said tilting her head back and finishing off her beer bottle. "Come over and let me…"

Dispensing with pleasantries, Zane offered himself, his body moving in cadence. He reached under the bedspread. His fingers ran across Nikki's chest. Finding no purchase, Zane pinched her nipples. Heavy breathing and groans filled the room. He moved his hand past her muscled belly and pelvis. For the briefest moment, Zane tried to associate tactile senses… He stumbled backward.

"Nikki?"

"Come on, Lover…don't be like that," she said, pulling back the covers and revealing her own engorged manhood. "I'll do you better than any woman ever could…"

"Aw…hell," Zane sighed, his excitement waning in an instant. "…sorry…didn't know…"

"Whadda doin' now?" Nikki asked. "Get back here."

"I gotta go," Zane said, struggling to pull on his pants. "Sorry…really…"

17

"So, that's it?" Nikki said, her voice becoming indignant. "Yah know, I've done all kinds of men…straight…gay…doesn't matter as long as you let yourself go…"

"Guess, I'm kinda ole fashioned that way," Zane stammered. "Look…I don't blame you, and I don't wanna make this all weird…"

"Well, go ahead then! You're probably an asshole anyway! Waste of horse cock on a pussy like you!"

"Yeah…probably right about that, but at least, I'm not raging about it. I'm sure some fellas get awful mad when they find out."

"Fuck you! Get out before I start screaming rape!"

"Now…no need for that," Zane said, pulling a thin fold of bills from his sock. "Here's a little something to smooth things over. There's a bus depot a couple blocks down the street. Should be more than enough to cover a ticket to Denton. Again…I'm sorry and good luck to yah."

"Yeah…well, you can still go fuck yourself!"

Closing the door, Zane hurried along the walkway, keeping his head down. Despite his anxiety, he resisted the urge to bolt. Only when Zane pulled away from the motel in his truck did he relax. Although he had heard of such encounters, Zane assumed many were just stories. He never actually knew anyone, who had experienced that scenario…until now…

"…never happened…" Zane sputtered. "…to the grave…"

18

Chapter 3
Heartbreak Cafe

It was a long drive between Wheeler and Port Lavaca but making the trip with a broken air conditioner on a hot summer day made it even more wearisome. Zane licked his chapped lips and wiped his sunburned face before jumping from the truck cab. A sharp pain flared up his back as his boot heels landed on the asphalt.

"Oh, shit!" Zane groaned without thinking. Leaning side to side to stretch his back, he noticed an elderly woman sitting in an idling car. She stared at him with a disapproving look.

"Oh...sorry ma'am," he said with a wave. "My back hurts some awful today."

Instead of offering an empathetic reply, she fixed her gaze elsewhere as if he wasn't worth acknowledging. Most days, Zane might have taken offense at the woman's snub, but he was too tired to bother. For a moment, he thought about getting takeout from Church's Chicken and just going home. Instead, he stuck with his original plan to have a sit-down meal at the Marlboro Cafe.

A cool blast of air greeted him as he walked through the door. Zane went straight to the restroom. Though the tap water wasn't refreshing and had a slight odor, he always felt better cleansing the day's sweat and grime from his face. He studied himself in the mirror, not expecting his face to look any different. A man with thinning blondish hair, piercing blue eyes, and an unkempt mustache stared back. At twenty-four years old, his skin was much too weatherworn and furrowed. He ran his fingers across deep, parallel lines running from temple to temple across his high forehead.

Damn! I'm gonna be as bald as Uncle Buddy by the time I'm thirty-five. Better find a girlfriend before I lose my bloom entirely.

Zane reckoned he'd never be asked to model for a JC Penny catalog. Even so, he thought a woman somewhere might consider him handsome enough—at least, in the right lighting and from a distance. He hoped so. Still, his short stature was an impediment he could never overcome. Occasionally a woman was interested in bedding him, but his timidity hindered most opportunities for a sexual dalliance. The few he met were too depraved, too young, too old, and or too married.

However, there was a waitress at the Marlboro Cafe that Zane had liked since he was a teenager. An unassuming girl in high school, Francine Grover never socialized with a particular crowd. Pretty and smart, blond and curvy, she was diminutive, which Zane found especially appealing. He was drawn to her reserved demeanor when she waited on customers.

At school, he had watched her every passage down the hallways and sitting in the cafeteria. Though Francine oftentimes ate alone, Zane never approached her. Instead, he had let his fantasies substitute for reality. He figured she would be alarmed to realize how many places they had been together, or how many times they had made love or had raucous sex. Zane had never spoken of Francine to anyone outside of his own mind, so his imagined affair was safe from ridicule.

Alas, he never had the nerve to speak to her. Since he had been in the vocational program learning about air-conditioning and refrigeration, and Francine attended classes for college-bound students, their academic and social paths rarely crossed. During junior year, her family had moved to Wheeler. Zane often wondered if her absence had bruised his heart. Every morning before he went to school, a chill coursed through his gut. Sometimes, he cried, and sometimes, he picked fights with the football players, so he felt something other than the sadness twisting his insides. After junior year, he dropped out of school.

Some years later, Zane had gone to the cafe, and there she was serving tables. Other than looking a bit older and curvier, she had changed little. Francine's hair was shorter and blonder, but the bobbed style made her look even prettier. Most noticeable, she wore no gold band on her left ring finger. Most likely, she already had a boyfriend, but Zane hoped, nonetheless. Regrettably, he didn't sit in her section, so Francine hadn't served him on that day. Three or four times a week, Zane went to the diner. As usual, he didn't speak to her except to order a meal. So far, there had been no recognition. They hadn't spoken of their time at the same high school and what they had been up to since. In Zane's mind, theirs was an unrequited love he hoped might still develop.

"What'll you have today?" she asked, her slight voice tinged with a southern dialect, and her blue eyes looking everywhere, except at him. "The special today is country-fried steak, mashed potatoes, and corn-on-the cob. Would you like a drink to start you off?"

"Oh, I'll have the special and an iced tea, please," Zane replied. "Oh, extra gravy too."

"Not a problem," Francine said, heading to the kitchen counter to finish scribbling his order.

And that's the way it had been for the past several months since Zane found her again. Not quite the reunion he had often thought about, but it was more of a relationship than they had had in high school. For now, his thrice-weekly excursions to the cafe were enough to keep him from pondering a final desperate act. More than a few times, he had careened down highways on his motorcycle with thoughts of swerving headlong into an oncoming tractor-trailer. A split-second decision was all it would take, leaving no time for doubt, no more misery... Immersed in their own miseries, Zane figured his brothers would take little notice of his absence.

***

"Come on, Dude, you owe me," Jimmy Ireland said, stamping his foot on the ground. "Don't I pay you reliable when you sell me stuff?"

"Yeah...but that's the usual way when you're buying and selling, isn't it?" Audie stated. "Not like we've ever had a lay-away plan, and I wouldn't sell you anything without cash in hand."

"Whadda mean? I'm always payin' yah top dollar for your shit. In fact, I'm your best customer. Seems you could return a favor."

"I don't know what the hell you're talking about, Jimmy," Audie said, "and you're nuts if you think I'm goin' on a drug deal with you...especially out to Pima. I hear that man is crazy in the head...and I've seen lots of crazy in my life."

"Luther isn't all that bad," Jimmy said, staring into the canopy of the pecan tree in Audie's backyard. "Nice enough, when you get to know him...and he'll like you."

"Uh huh... I'll take a pass, Jimmy. I'm not doing anything to get myself busted."

"Right...you're quite the bigwig at Big Mart, huh?" Jimmy sneered, his gaunt face growing flush. "Think you're better than me now?"

"Nah, man," Audie countered, "but I'm done taking chances. I kinda like my job. Pay isn't great, but it's a steady check.

21

Anyhow…I'm almost through my probation, so I'm buckin' for a raise."

"Big fuckin' deal… If they knew how big a thief you are, they'd…" Jimmy was saying before collapsing to the ground with a thud.

"Oh shit," Audie uttered, looking at his fist with a fresh gash in the middle knuckle. "Guess you pushed the wrong button there, Jimmy."

"Whad dah fuck?" Jimmy said as blood coursed from his nose. Struggling to his feet, he wavered as if balanced on a slick river rock. "Not cool, man…not cool at all… Fuck it then, I'm goin' home."

"What you boys doing out there?" Mrs. Sanchez called through her kitchen window. *"Sin peleas, por favor."*

"Lo lamento, Mrs. Sanchez," Audie offered. "Just a misunderstanding. My friend is just leaving."

"Yeah, yeah…" Jimmy said, holding a shirtsleeve to his nose.

"Always something with you *ninos*," Mrs. Sanchez exclaimed.

"I know…seems like it," Audie agreed.

Chapter 4
Big Box Payday

"Audie, I'm moving yah to sporting goods," Eddie announced from behind his cluttered desk. "Normally, I wouldn't give that section to someone who's only been here a short while, but most of the supposed male employees around here are a bunch of Nancy-boys, too squeamish to handle crawlers, or too damn English illiterate to make change for customers. Besides, you seem to be the only twenty-something in Feral County, who hasn't been pinched by the police for something or another. Apparently, you're the only honest young man around here, or yah just too clever or plain lucky. Still…from where I'm sitting, you have the look of someone who doesn't put his balls in a vise unless there's a good chance of a big payday."

"Well, I'm not sure what to say to that, Mr. Atkins, but I really like working here, and thanks for the opportunity," Audie said. "You won't regret it."

"Damn right I won't!" Eddie snapped, his shiny baldpate growing flush. "You might have made it through your probationary period, mind yah, but you better not start pilferin' tackle, or fantasizin' about the mannequins in women's apparel, or you'll have to give me a urine sample. If that chem-strip looks a smidgeon off-color, you'll be out the door and banned from workin' or shoppin' at another Big-Mart anywhere in the country. Do I make myself clear?"

"Uh, yes sir, crystal clear, Mr. Atkins."

"Damn right, crystal clear. Now go report to Fred Sanford and do what he tells yah to do," Eddie directed as he pulled his clip-on tie from his shirt collar and unfastened the top button. "When he says you're ready, you'll be put in charge of the nightshift. *Comprende*?"

"Uh, Fred Sanford?"

"Yah know…Fred…the old Redd Foxx looking sonofabitch," Eddie said, mopping his sweaty forehead with a sodden neckerchief.

"Oh…you mean, Felix."

"Chrissakes, Audie! Should I draw yah a picture of him while I'm at it? Because I'm none too good at drawing pictures. Go on already!" Eddie barked, spittle flying from his mouth. "Jesus Henry Christ Almighty!"

"Uh…yes, sir," Audie said, rising hurriedly from his chair.

Audie disliked going to the manager's office. The air was always stale and humid in there, and Eddie's cheap cologne did little to mask the big man's body odor. However, the promotion was worth being near the boss, who had transferred from another store branch in New Jersey. Eddie personified all the ugly stereotypes that southerners held of northern city folk. Audie could only imagine what Eddie thought of Texans, especially of the laidback residents of Marlboro, whose kin were descended from the region's farmers and ranchers.

***

Later in the afternoon, Audie inventoried a box of fishing lures. Like the contents of a treasure chest, he marveled at the myriad gold and silver blades, bodies of every imaginable color, and feathered treble hooks. He had never seen such an assortment of lures, new, sparkly, and needle-sharp. Audie inhaled a scent of fresh plastics and cardboard…

"I know you," a woman's voice said. "I used to go to middle school with you."

"Oh…hello there," Audie replied, looking up. "You're Kaneesha, right?"

"That's what the nametag says," she spoke, her voice sharp. "How come you got bumped to sporting goods? I've been here a lot longer than you."

Kaneesha Mack was a tall young woman, who towered over most women and many men, including Audie. Her skin was like dark caramel. She was stunning, exotic looking with her high cheekbones, wide nose, and plump lips. Plucked eyebrows highlighted a piercing stare. Cornrow braids dangled from her head. Audie's mind gave thought to a mixed-race Cajun woman borne from the murkiest depths of a Louisiana Bayou.

"Are you listening to me?" she repeated, her annoyance palpable. "Damn…boy…are you high or what?"

"I'm sorry, Kaneesha. I couldn't help but stare… I mean…you're real pretty and all. I remember you running track in school. You had the longest, sexiest legs I ever seen."

"What…what's that, you say?" she said, placing her hands on her hips and standing askew. "Are you messing with me or something?"

24

"No...not at all," Audie sputtered. "I thought you were a real beauty in school...even from a distance and everything...but being so close to you now...I mean...wow..."

"Um-hum..." she said and paused as if searching for a proper response. "I come over here to give you the what for, but now... Just remember...I'm keeping my eye on you, white boy."

"I hope so. I know I'll be watching you." Audie returned, his attention distracted by the sound of a bell dinging from the service counter. "Excuse me, Kaneesha. I gotta tend to business. Really hope we can talk again. See yah."

Sensing watchful eyes on his backside, Audie maintained a cool facade, walking casually. As he rounded the aisle, he recognized the customer lingering at the counter.

Willy Gallison...

William "Willy" Gallison was an old acquaintance of his father. Living a hermit's existence in a dilapidated trailer along the eastern shore of the Brazos River, Willy worked little, except for occasional jaunts to town with his carpet-cleaning machine. He spent most of his time traipsing the clay banks of the river with rod and gun in hand. Since Willy was an elder and a longtime friend of his family, Audie was always polite but maintained a distance. Audie thought there was something off with the man.

"How do, Willy?"

"Audie! I heard tell you was working at Big-Mart, but I didn't believe it. Before long, you'll be running this place, won't yah?"

"I don't know about that, but it sure beats working outdoors."

"I bet," Willy said, removing his grimy cap and running gnarled fingers through a clump of thinning red hair. An ample belly hung over a straining belt. "Say...there must be a gaggle of ladies working here, huh? Lots of young ones..."

"A few," Audie answered, his mind forming an image of Kaneesha's long, lean body. "For now, I'm just trying to make a good impression. I'll wait a while before I start chasing tail around here."

"Probably, a good idea," Willy agreed. "Hey...point me to the trotlines, will yah."

"Over here," Audie replied, leading the way. "We got a new shipment in yesterday. Really good price for such quality line and hooks, but it's a new company outta Austin making the rigs, so they're probably discounting their product to get a toehold on the market."

"Listen to you, why dontcha," Willy said as he handled the trotline. "You got the whole sales spiel down pat."

"Aw…don't give me any grief, you old poacher, or I'll call the game warden on your ass."

"Now, now…that's no way to talk to the customer," Willy retorted, a wide grin appearing on his weathered face. "I'll take two of these here fancy trotlines. Big-Mart still givin' discounts to seniors?"

"Yeah…come over to the counter, and I'll ring you up."

"You still mourning your daddy?"

"A little, but not nearly as bad as before," Audie replied, his mind puzzling over the odd question. "It's been hard…on all of us. I guess the hard part isn't knowin' if we'll ever see him again… I have a hard time squaring with GOD and heaven and such. Seems like a bunch of fairy tales to me."

Willy seemed to stare into an emptiness beyond the grid of fluorescent lights above and said, "I don't know much about GOD either, but I've seen your daddy since he died."

"Now…whadda you mean, Willy?" Audie asked. "Have you been drinking homemade hooch again?"

"I know it's queer sayin' such things—it's true though," Willy said. "He comes 'round every so often askin' about you boys. Even though he's in another place—much better than here—he still worries. He visits me by the river…at night…usually. He's always preachin' to me 'bout this and that…like I need that… Gets a little frustratin' having him point out all the bad things I've done."

"Chrissakes, Willy. Why you wanna bring up stuff like that around me. I might be grieving less, but I still hurt about my daddy."

"Sorry, Audie... I thought you'd wanna know."

"You did, huh. Well, tell me this. Why you? Why doesn't he visit his own sons?"

"He can't go far from the other side for too long…and even then, only certain people can see and hear him. I reckon it's me because I nearly drowned in the river when I was little."

"You did?"

"Yeah, I was too little to remember, but my mama said I went wadin' and stepped into a drop-off. She turned 'round one sec', then

26

poof...I was gone," Willy recalled. "Took a while before they found me lyin' on the bottom. Anyways, I was white as a sheet...not breathin' or nothin'... No amount of shakin' could wake me, so they gave up. Funny thing is...when my daddy was carryin' me up the bank, he dropped me. Drunk as usual, I suppose. Anyhow, Mama said I rolled several times, then I started throwin' up and coughin'."

"So, you died and came back," Audie asked, his curiosity roused, "and you don't remember anything at all?"

"Guess not... Wish I remembered something, but I was too little," Willy answered. "Anyways, your daddy keeps goin' on 'bout dead bodies nearby, and there bein' a crack between worlds where he squeezes through every so often. Maybe, I nearly slipped through the same crack when I was little? Did your daddy ever tell you about bodies buried down by the river?"

Audie ripped a paper receipt from the cash machine and slipped it into the bag. "Buried bodies? Nah. It's a helluva story though," Audie said. "They should put you on TV. Get a news crew from Wheeler to interview you. Maybe, my daddy could give you next week's lottery numbers. Now...that would be something."

"You don't believe me. I get it. I probably wouldn't believe me either... Anyways...he wanted you boys to know something's coming...something momentous... Sorry...he's always pretty vague. Can't get much out of him. Mostly wants to know about you boys."

"Momentous, huh? That's a big word for something so vague," Audie chuckled. "Anything more than that?"

Removing his cap and scratching his head, Willy pondered for long moments, then said, "Something about the kitchen...above the kitchen. Sorry, Audie. I'm usually pretty buzzed when he comes around, and I can't 'member much after his visits. I suppose I should write things down..."

"It's all right, Willy. I'm not mad or anything. I hope what you're saying is true. Knowing death isn't the end all would be real comforting."

"I swear it's true...on my mama and daddy's graves."

"Okay," Audie said, feeling this conversation had lasted long enough. He looked around in case his manager was eavesdropping from afar. "Tell yah what. You come back around if my daddy says anything real interesting. Oh...tell him we miss him and love him, and we're getting by okay."

"Will do, Audie, and I'll be sure to start writin' things down. I'll pick up a pencil and notepad on the way out."

"All right then," Audie said. "Good luck with the new trotlines and stay out of the snags. Oh...and don't go tripping over dead bodies."

The box of lures beckoned again. As he sorted, Audie thought about Willy's odd ramblings and his penchant for telling yarns, many of which included ghosts and other supernatural visitations. No one, including his daddy, ever took Willy seriously, but he always seemed genuine.

"Above the kitchen?" Audie mumbled. "What the hell does that mean...above the kitchen?"

After a while, Audie forgot Willy's revelation as he stocked shelves and tended customers. Within a few weeks, he mastered many of his new duties, requiring less and less oversight from his immediate supervisor.

Chapter 5
Darkening Skies

"Fuckin' Clyde Rush!" Zane seethed in his mind. "What the hell is he doing here?"

Clyde was a tall, muscular brute in his early forties. He had a wide face and a jaw so square, a carpenter could use it to plumb a doorframe. Clyde kept his dark hair close-cropped, though it was difficult to tell with an ever-present Stetson atop his head. His skin was bronzed, but not from days toiling outdoors. Zane had seen his enormous Dodge Ram pickup a few times parked outside a tanning salon in Wheeler called Sun Delight. Like many male Texans looking to impress the ladies, he wore shiny cowboy boots, a western shirt, tight jeans, and a thick leather belt with a big silver buckle.

Zane loathed the man. Thrush mufflers rumbling, Clyde pulled his black truck alongside Zane's little Ford Ranger. Before turning off the ignition, Clyde gunned the vehicle's powerful engine. When he entered the diner, an invisible cloud of cologne followed. Zane's nostrils recoiled. Clyde had numbed his olfactory sense after countless spritzes of Aqua Velva, so he had to apply more and more to smell it himself.

"Good afternoon, folks!" he called out in a booming voice to no one in particular. "I'm so hungry I could eat an armadillo enchilada with a side of mesquite fries!"

Sitting at the counter, Clyde had not bothered with the menu board. When Francine came over, he declared, "Well, hello, pretty lady! You must be the new waitress I've been hearing about."

"Um, yes…" she answered. "What would you like?"

"What would I like…?" he replied, eyeing her slight form with no subtlety whatsoever. "While I think on that, I'll have a big steak, mashed potatoes and gravy, and fried okra. Oh…and a pitcher of iced tea with lemon, Sweetie."

A wan smile crossed her face as she turned to place the order. Clyde's eyes followed her backside. Zane's fingers clenched the glass mug he was holding. He felt an overwhelming desire to bash the man's thick skull with a mallet. The thought evaporated when he noticed Clyde looking at him.

"Something on your mind, little man?" Clyde asked, his voice loud and abrupt. "You seem to be eyeballing me."

"No, no… Just admiring your Stetson…" Zane sputtered. "It's a fine one."

Unmindful of it, Zane supposed he had been staring, most likely, with a surly expression. No doubt, the man was justified calling him out. If only he had kept his anger in check.

"Is that so?" Clyde replied. "You seem to have an unfriendly look about you."

"My pardon…no offense meant," Zane said as he felt other diners looking in his direction. "Unfortunately, I have a naturally pissed off expression…I guess."

"Well, you should work on that, Little Hoss," the man said sharply and turned away, "or someone's liable to wipe that look off your face."

Ice swirled in the bottom of his mug as Zane sipped the last of his tea. His face was flush. He masked his feelings and stared out the window, letting his thoughts wander until he calmed. The other patrons drifted back to their own business. All the while, Clyde kept talking up Francine. Though Zane didn't look in her direction, he heard her giggling at the man's flirty remarks. Instead of going to the register, Zane paid for his meal by leaving cash on the table along with a twenty percent gratuity.

Halfway home, Zane pulled into a gravel lot behind the laundromat and parked. Windows open and air conditioner off, summer heat filled his truck cab. He closed his eyes and breathed in the super-heated air. Disjointed thoughts flickered. He heard Francine's laughter as Clyde talked her up. Zane imagined storming back into the cafe and beating Clyde Rush to death with a tire iron.

Chrissakes, what's the point of living when I feel this awful all the time?

For several minutes, Zane endured the Texas sun. He wondered how long it would take before he passed out. Would his brain parboil from the heat? How soon before death arrived? Would his consciousness continue in another form…another place…free from heartache? Or, would he endure an even worse fate…

A shadow fell upon him as angry, cumulous clouds blotted the sun overhead. Zane felt a noticeable drop in temperature and a change in air pressure. A slight breeze lifted and swirled dust from the gravel lot. The incessant white noise of buzzing cicadas ceased in the surrounding treetops. Zane heard a sound like muted applause approaching from the west. His body trembled as the first droplets pelted his windshield. In an instant, a torrential downpour engulfed his truck. Heavy raindrops pounded the cab roof. The raging thunderstorm replaced Zane's puny, depressive thoughts. He breathed in the cool, moisture-laden air. Then, marble-sized hail plunged to the earth. The sound was terrible and deafening inside the truck…

"What's this all about, Mr. Atkins?" Audie asked as he looked around his boss' office. Two men sat to his right. He knew Randall Greaves, the regional store manager. Attired in a dark business suit, he stared at Audie with a blank expression. The other man, Audie wasn't familiar with, but he recognized the man's bearing.

Store cop! What the fuck?

"Audie, have a chair," Eddie ordered, his voice terse. "You know Mr. Greaves. This here is Bob Rich. He works for corporate security."

Sitting and turning his chair to face all three men, Audie said, "My curiosity is piqued, sirs. What's this all about?"

"Audie, it's come to our attention that you have a criminal record," Eddie stated. "Normally, this wouldn't be an issue, but I erred when I assigned you to manage our sporting goods section. Evidently, I didn't investigate as well as I should have…" Eddie paused, clearing his throat and tugging at his collar. His thick neck bulged over his shirt's top button. His face was sweaty.

"Mr. Atkins made a big mistake having you oversee firearms and ammo," Bob interjected. "ATF would be crawling up our asses if they caught wind."

"Unfortunately, Audie, someone reported you to corporate, and we have to act on it," Randall said. "Bob made it known that Eddie and I are liable if circumstances come to light."

"Who exactly reported me, Mr. Atkins? Seems, I should know that."

"Anonymous call, and I couldn't tell you anyway," Eddie said. "You'll have to guess on your own."

Watching his managers fidget, Audie comprehended his situation straightaway. Employed at Big-Mart for most of their working careers, their jobs were in jeopardy. Although Audie didn't care for

Eddie when first hired, he came to appreciate his employer's gruff management style. He had worked hard to gain Eddie's trust and respect, and most days, he liked his job and his co-workers, and he liked serving his customers...his friends and neighbors. Even if it was just selling fishhooks and shotgun shells, it was honest work. Big-Mart was clean and air-conditioned. Otherwise, he might be shoveling asphalt or pig manure for minimum wage.

"First of all, I've been arrested a few times for piddling things, but never convicted, and I've never done anything unlawful since working at Big-Mart," Audie attested. "Of course, Eddie—Mr. Atkins—didn't know any of that, and I didn't exactly volunteer it. So, do what you gotta do with me, but I wouldn't be too hard with Mr. Atkins. He's a good manager...a good shit."

Eddie sighed. "Like I said, Randy, this whole thing was an honest oversight, and obviously, the background check didn't pick it up either. It's your call, but I suggest we let this go. I could transfer Audie to another section..."

Eddie's boss cut him off with a wave of his hand. "Like you, I would prefer settle this matter here and now," Randall said. "What do you say, Bob?"

"Uh, usually, I would handle something like this in-house, but I'm in as deep as you fellas," Bob replied. "Chrissakes, I only have two years before I'm eligible for company retirement. Regrettably, the boy must go. We best make it an official termination."

His mind wandering, Audie let out a deep breath, waiting for the end of this meeting. At this point, he wanted to take off his Big-Mart shirt and trudge home.

I wonder if I can finally get my truck running... Drive west, maybe... Nah...starter solenoid hasn't come in yet... Just wanna go home... Where did I put my 10-gauge? Still under my bed? I think Zane took it to the tank, duck hunting. Hoyt's pistol is his bureau somewhere...

"Audie," Eddie interrupted. "Sorry to say, but we gotta do this. Since it's technically a firing, we can't offer severance, but Randy has a company dispensation fund for special situations...like this. He'll give four-weeks net wages—off the books. Understood?"

"Yes, sir, I understand," Audie answered. "I'm sorry for the trouble and appreciate how you're handling it and all."

Randall stood and fixed his tie knot, "I'll leave the rest to you, Eddie."

The men brushed past the back of Audie's chair and departed Eddie's messy office. Beyond the open doorway, it was quiet. He sensed his coworkers—soon to be ex-coworkers—cloistered somewhere whispering about Mr. Randall's unexpected visit and pondering Audie's situation. He thought of likely suspects, who may have called corporate. Audie wondered if Kaneesha had done it since she thought the night manager job should have gone to her.

***

The sweltering heat added to Audie's misery as he began the long walk home. Air laden with humidity, sweat sieved from every pore. He turned down Gray Street staying in the shade offered by a line of oaks along the sidewalk. Audie fumed about the anonymous person, who caused his termination.

"Fuckin' asshole," he seethed under his breath. "If I ever find out who, I'm gonna beat him sideways."

At the sound of thunder in the near distance, Audie noticed the darkening sky. Clouds so heavy with moisture, Audie wondered if he should pick up the pace. Instead, he slowed and hoped for a downpour to wash away his depression. Hail streaked downward.

"Fucksake!" Audie barked as marble-sized pellets hit his head and face. He ran to the leeward side of the nearest oak and clung to its trunk. The sound was deafening as hail lashed the rooftops of cars and homes. Branches cracked and fell. Striking the asphalt pavement, ashen balls of ice bounced upward.

Within a minute, the aerial assault subsided. An odd silence descended. Audie looked around. Nearby vehicles had dimples in their hoods, and a few had cracked windshields. Leaves and branches covered the ground. In the next instant, rain pounded. Lightning streaked through the sky followed by a thunderous concussion.

Audie left the shelter of the oak and trudged home. The storm did little to dampen his sour mood. He shivered as cold rain dribbled down his face and backside. Sticking his hands in his pockets, Audie hunched his shoulders and lowered his head against the downpour. In the distance, he heard a wail of sirens massing somewhere ahead. Audie quickened his pace.

***

33

"Dammit…" Hoyt sputtered, scratching his arm for the umpteenth time. Though it was a balmy day, he shuddered from an incessant chill coursing through his lanky frame. Sweat dribbled down Hoyt's brow and coalesced on the tip of his nose. His brothers hadn't been around, even though Audie was supposed to bring home groceries. With no soda or iced tea in the fridge, all he had to drink was lukewarm tap water that smelled rank and had a metallic taste, not even fit to flush a toilet.

Dammit, Audie…Zane!

Huddled on the shaded side of the front porch, Hoyt lit a cigarette and watched heated air radiating above the asphalt street. His hands clenched and opened. In past days, he had been unable to sleep, and it felt like a swarm of hornets had built a nest inside his skullcap. So agitated, he had punched holes in his bedroom wall when he couldn't find his lighter. The heat was unbearable outside as the sun blazed overhead.

Feral kittens lounged under Mrs. Sanchez's rose bushes to escape the scorching sun. Hoyt hadn't seen their mama in days, so he had been giving them water and tuna. Originally, there were seven. Now three felines remained—a calico, a yellow, and gray. The calico was Hoyt's favorite since it was the friendliest—though none came within arm's length yet.

A clanging noise approached. Hoyt recognized the sound of the old Plymouth Fury that belonged to his neighbor, Nate Nash. Sections of twisted fence wire held the car's rusted muffler and tailpipe in place. Noxious exhaust belched noisily. Oily smoke hung in the humid air.

As the car approached, the kittens became frantic. Tiny ears laid flat and tails bushed, the felines shrank into the bushes. While Zane made sounds to soothe them, he heard fragments of a nasty argument carrying down Cobb Street.

"You sure…like you were eyeballing him…!" Nate yelled. "Damn lucky…asshole…beat down."

"That's not true…" Regina said in her defense, and then uttered something unintelligible. "… know better…"

"You lying, bitch!" Nate raved. "You wait until…home. You'll be sorry then."

Nate gunned his engine and squealed the tires. In response, the kittens scattered. The calico ran into the street as the behemoth car

34

sped past. With nary a sound, the little feline disappeared beneath the car's undercarriage. For a moment, Nate stopped to look in his rearview mirror.

"Oh, shuddup, it's just one of those stray cats," he snapped at his crying girls. "Nothing to get all upset about. Their days are numbered anyway."

Nate started to go when he noticed Hoyt staring. "Well, retard...are you gonna start crying too? If you're so fond of those cats, maybe you should keep a better..."

Hoyt rose from his chair and approached. Sensing he overplayed his hand, Nate drove away. Hoyt knelt on the sidewalk and stroked the dead kitten. Blood seeped from the feline's mouth. Limp as a wet rag, Hoyt lifted the calico and carried it to the backyard where the Harlan's had interred generations of pets. Hoyt's face grew flush as he fought to contain his tears. The sun disappeared behind ominous clouds high in the atmosphere. Darkening skies sullied an already foul mood.

"Get your asses in the house...right now!" Nate growled at his wife and daughters. "You're all in trouble now, especially you, Regina!"

"Come on, Nate, no need to be so angry," she said, scooping Sandra from the backseat. "It's okay girls. Daddy's upset. He'll be all right...like..."

Nate rounded the car and slapped his wife in the face. Regina fell to the lawn with Sandra still cradled in her arms. Faraway thunder sounded. A slight breeze kicked up a dust devil. A great silence descended.

"It's your fault!" Nate raged. "Always gettin' me riled up with your bullshit!"

"Daddy, no!" Sarah screeched, running to her fallen mother. "Mama, get up!"

"I told you girls to get in the house!" Nate hollered, pushing her away. "Regina, get your ass up!"

"Chrissakes, Nate!" Pete Vose called from across the street. "Leave 'em alone, will yah!" Elderly and bone thin, Pete looked like a gentle breeze could topple him. He held a garden hose, water dribbling on the hot sidewalk.

"Mind your business, Pete, or I'll come over there and whip the shit out of yah!"

35

"Well…you don't need to be so hard…is all I'm saying," Pete said with a tremor running through his voice.

"You keep talking, big man!" Nate said, turning back to his wife. "Regina, I told you to get in the house…right now!"

"Nate, enough already!" Pete called out. "I'm callin' the police!"

"You do, and I'm comin' over there next!"

"You come on my property threatening like that, and I'll shoot you!"

For a moment, Nate paused, and as if making up his mind, he grabbed his wife by her ponytail and dragged her across the yard. Regina screeched and kicked, all the while holding tight to her daughter, who wailed. Still stunned from the openhanded slap across her face, Regina couldn't make words. Instead, she moaned. Spittle ran down her chin. She clawed at Nate's arm.

"All right, you fuckin' bitch!" Nate yelled and raised his fist. "You have it coming!"

Nate suddenly bowled over in agony. Waylaid from behind with a kick to the groin, he grabbed between his legs with both hands. Nate gasped and sputtered on the ground. "Please…don't!" he grunted to no one in particular.

Not saying a word, Hoyt kicked the man full in the chin with a booted foot. An audible crack sounded as bone and teeth shattered. He straddled Nate, who was now senseless and incapacitated. Hoyt clamped a thumb and index finger around the bridge of Nate's nose and twisted. Blood gushed…

"Hoyt, don't! That's enough!" Pete called out. "He's done! Stop it before the police get here!"

A spray of cold water from Pete's garden hose brought Hoyt to his senses. As he staggered to his feet, icy pellets stung. A deafening sound followed like applause. He lifted his arms, smiled, and turned. Soon, the rain came, lashing him with a barrage of cold droplets. Through the downpour, Hoyt spied Regina and the girls huddled together on the porch and crying. Dazed and wounded, their expressions belied conflicted emotions at what their unassuming neighbor had done to their patriarch. A siren sounded from far away, drawing nearer. Hoyt cleansed his hands. Crimson rivulets cascaded from his fingertips—blood of feline and man. Tears flowed down his grizzled cheeks. In this moment, he longed for his daddy. Hoyt was scared.

Chapter 6
After the Reckoning

After arriving at the VA psyche ward, days passed before clarity returned. Sedated with heavy tranquilizers and dosed with anti-psychotic drugs, memories were hazy and confused. Unintelligible voices, fluorescent lights, and hospital noises added to his anxiety. Hoyt was helpless and subject to the whims of hospital staff. His only comfort was fleeting glimpses of his father, who gazed upon him with a passive countenance.

Hey, Daddy. Where you been? Are you all right?

"*I'm okay, Son. I've been around...watching mostly...hoping you boys might find your way,*" his father answered without actually speaking. "*Feeling lowdown about now, aren't yah, Hoyt?*"

I suppose...but I can't really remember the last time I wasn't. I reckon I'm afflicted like you. Why are we like this, Daddy? Why are we so miserable?

I don't know, Hoyt... Even from here, I don't rightly know.

I can't stand feeling this way. It's too much. I really hate myself.

"*Now, now, Hoyt,*" his father soothed in low, gentle tones. "*Just remember how I love you. You'll always be my little boy.*"

Then, can I come with you?

"*Not now, Hoyt,*" he replied. "*Your time will come, but not now...*"

A pallid ceiling replaced his father's ghosting image. Paint flaked from the farthest corner. Hoyt shivered from a draft of cold air blowing from a vent above. He breathed deeply, trying to clear his mind. After hours of hazy contemplation, he tried to sit upright, but restraints pinned him to the bed, which was just as well since his entire body hurt.

"Hey..." he croaked, his throat parched, his lips cracked. "Hey! I gotta pee real bad..."

He longed to empty his aching bladder and have a cool drink of water. Conflicting physiological urges battled until he could no longer contain himself. Hoyt relaxed and urinated. He loathed wetting himself, but the relief was immediate. Now, he hoped someone would tend to him sooner than later. Hoyt closed his eyes.

***

"Up and at 'em, Mr. Harlan," a deep male voice said. "Looks like we let you lay here too long. You feeling okay? You wanna take a shower and put on some scrubs?"

"Yeah...sorry 'bout the mess," Hoyt croaked. "I'd be glad to cleanup if you give me a mop or something, but could I have some water first?"

"Let's get you loose, then I'll walk you to the fountain."

"What are you doing, Louis?" a nurse spoke from the doorway. "This one's under strict supervision. You can't just let him up without authorization."

"Dammit, Irene, you're not gonna start playing Nurse Ratchet again, are yah? Man's been hogtied since he was brought in. Did you leave him all night in wet drawers? I hope not cause I have to write that shit up!"

"Calm down," Irene scolded. "Just don't go far, and keep an eye on him. Don't need him acting out. The ward's crazy enough as is."

"We'll be fine, won't we, Hoyt?" Louis said as he thumbed through a clipboard.

"No... I mean, yes, sir," Hoyt answered. "I'm usually pretty mild. I expect I'm here for what happened to Nate Nash. Honestly...I don't remember much. Is he okay? Are Regina and the girls okay? He was doin' a job on her... I had to help..."

"Says here, you're here for a psychiatric evaluation, Mr. Harlan," Louis replied again referring to the clipboard. "Seems you beat the shit outta your neighbor. Your brothers insisted you be sent here...the V.A. that is. Otherwise, you'd be sitting in jail."

"Nearly killed the man," the nurse opined. "It's fortunate you're a veteran."

"All right then, let's sit you up," Louis offered after undoing the restraints. "Slowly now...you've been under heavy sedation. That's it."

"Whoa..." Hoyt uttered. "My head's spinning..."

"Close your eyes and breathe," Louis said, placing his hands on Hoyt's shoulders to steady him. "Irene, could you get Mr. Harlan a glass of water? I'd do it myself, but he's liable to fall over."

"As a lead ward nurse, I don't do that," she said sharply. "That's your job."

"Would you rather handle, Mr. Harlan, yourself? Cause it's six o'clock in the morning, and no one else is around for a while.

Again…I'd rather not have to write-up that he's been restrained throughout your entire shift."

Without another word, the nurse left and returned with a cup of water, which she handed to the orderly. Louis then handed it to Hoyt, who drank in a single gulp. The water was refreshing, going a long way to quench his thirst.

"Much appreciated," Hoyt said, and then coughed to clear the rasp from his throat. "I don't know when I've been so dry in the mouth."

"Medication might be contributing to that," Louis suggested. "Now, let's get yah some scrubs and a breakfast tray."

* * *

The stars shone brighter than Zane had ever seen in his life. Desiccated desert air magnified their brilliance unlike the usual pinpricks of pallid light in the night sky back home. Celestial objects winked and pulsed as if powered by an ageless heart. Zane understood the luminance observed was millennia old.

Zane urinated in the middle of the highway. Well past midnight, he hadn't seen another traveler for hours. Tired of the incessant journey, he had pulled over into the dusty median to stretch his legs and take a nap. The nighttime vista was endless with no visible landmarks, except for a blur of mountain peaks beyond the horizon. Zane was accustomed to the woodlands of Eastern Texas not the boundless expanse of desert, sand, and scrub of New Mexico.

The silence resonated in his ears as a loud ringing. Zane breathed the air, still laden with heat from the previous day. He figured there were times of the year when the desert renewed and flourished. Passing many dried arroyos along his route, it made sense that rain wasn't lacking entirely. Presently, Zane couldn't envision a lush landscape.

Walking down the road, Zane lifted a water jug and drank until satiated. He set the empty container on the broken centerline. Back at his truck, he fingered a blank panel on the bottom left of his console and released a hidden latch. Behind was a recessed storage space. He pulled out a leather belt and holster with a single-action 22-magnum pistol and a box of ammo. Zane had it for obvious reasons. Although those in his profession were generally a friendly lot, bandits still roamed the asphalt byways. It was illegal in many states to carry a concealed handgun and discovery could land a person in jail with little prosecutorial effort. Zane figured jail was preferable than being murdered over a load of home appliances.

Stark moonlight brightened the nightscape. Though colors were absent, Zane could see the water jug...at least, a distinct silhouette. He unlatched the pistol's cylinder to ensure he had chambered eight rounds. Zane holstered the pistol and buckled the belt around his waist.

Standing in the middle of the road, Zane looked around for signs of approaching headlights. Satisfied, he faced his intended target, his right-hand hovering above his holster. Suddenly, Zane drew his revolver, thumbed the hammer back, and pulled the trigger. Although he hadn't quick drawn in some time, his technique appeared smooth and practiced, albeit not as fast and accurate as those, who competed regularly. The water jug hadn't budged, though Zane figured the bullet would have pierced flesh if a person had been on the other end. In succession, he holstered, drew, and fired several more times with increasing rapidity, adjusting his aim as the jug rocked backward and to the left.

One at a time, Zane ejected the spent shell casings and replaced with eight fresh rounds. A curl of grayish smoke hung in the dead air. Once again, he drew repeatedly, firing until his pistol clicked on a spent cartridge. Although too gloomy to see, Zane reckoned several or more bullets had found their mark. He reloaded and holstered the revolver.

A sheen of cold sweat coalesced on Zane's forehead. A droplet dribbled down the bridge of his nose. Tilting his head back, Zane opened his mouth wide and screamed for the longest time. There was no reply to his declaration of anger and frustration. His cry went unanswered, no echo from a distant mountain or anxious shriek from a nocturnal creature. He may as well have been shouting into a vacuous cave. So alone, Zane slumped to the road with his hands on his knees and bawled. Tears splattered on the warm asphalt.

What's the sense when you feel so miserable all the time? Chrissakes, I've been hanging on for years now...waiting and hoping...for what? So tired...so sick and tired...

Zane cocked his pistol and placed the barrel to his temple, his finger caressing the smooth trigger. Eyes closed, Zane's face grimaced. After a few seconds, he stuck the barrel under his throat above his quivering Adam's apple. Changing his mind, Zane placed it against his chest where his heart pounded. His breathing rapid and shallow, his finger exerted gradual pressure. Shoulders slumping, he opened his eyes.

He stared at the desert highway bathed in moonlight. Dark fragments of rubber covered the asphalt. Zane figured a truck had blown a tire. The same had happened to him on a few occasions. At least, that's what he thought before noticing hundreds of objects moving across the highway. When one crossed within arm's length, Zane understood.

Unfazed by Zane's presence, desert tarantulas marched past. A few arachnids stopped to touch his knees with forward legs, and then kept walking. Cloaked under night sky, a soundless migration proceeded. Holstering his pistol, he reclined on the warm pavement. Zane stared at the stars until they faded...

***

"Hey there!" a man spoke. "What're you doin' in the middle of the road? You tryin' to get killed?"

Lifting from the pavement, Zane observed a crimsoned tinge in the eastern horizon as sunrise approached. A tractor-trailer idled on the road, its diesel engine clattering. The highway was empty of hairy tarantulas.

"Sorry, mister," Zane answered. "I got out my truck earlier to lay down and rest my back. I must have fallen asleep."

"Sure you're not drunk or high?" the man asked as he combed his long white beard with his fingers. "You shouldn't be driving otherwise."

"No, no...just a bad bout of white line fever and an aching back."

"You're okay then?"

"Yeah...yeah," Zane said, standing and stretching his arms. "I appreciate you not running me over."

"No worries," the man said. "I know all about white line fever and achin' backs. I tell yah...if I could do something else for a livin', I would. I get awful tired of bein' away from home. How 'bout you?"

"Suits me fine...for now. I don't have anyone back home, so I'm never in a hurry to get anywhere."

"That's good..." the man said, stretching his arms high and arching his back. "My name is *Jesús*."

"Like Jesus?" Zane asked.

41

"The same," he said. "My family are devout Catholics of Mexican descent, so not an uncommon name for us."

"I understand," Zane said smiling and holding out his hand. "Nice to meet yah, Jesus."

***

"Just look like you belong, and try not to say much," Jimmy Ireland instructed from the passenger seat. "In and out... Luther's okay by himself, but his guys make me awful nervous...like they're gonna beat on me if I look the wrong way. So, you may wanna move slower than usual. Yah know, try not to look threatening."

"I hear yah. Speak when spoken to and don't make eye contact... I got it," Audie replied. "I've never seen you this riled up."

"Sometimes, you just can't read people, especially when they're all hopped up," Jimmy said, looking into the mirrored visor and combing back his mullet. "I keep wondering if I should have told Teresa where I was goin'—just in case. You didn't tell anyone, did yah?"

"Nope, and you said don't," Audie answered, his eyes never wavering from the roadway. "Your new Supra drives real nice."

"Yeah, it's a nice ride. I'm glad you decided to come along. You stand tall, maybe, you'll earn enough to get a sweet ride of your own. Slow down and turn right here."

"I've been down most every dirt road in Pima County, except for this one."

"No shit," Jimmy said pointing to *No Trespassing* signage. "The Hadley's were never welcoming. Whole spread is fenced and gated off for miles around. I wouldn't be surprised if they have cameras hidden in the pucker brush too."

"Is that it up ahead?"

"Yep," Jimmy replied peering at a wrought-iron gate illuminated in the surrounding darkness. "Just pull up slow and be cool."

Audie turned down the high beam lights and eased up to a brick-and-mortar pedestal. A stainless-steel enclosure housed a speaker, call button, and keypad. Audie depressed the lighted button and sat back, so Jimmy could speak.

A gruff voice spoke from the appliance, "Who's your driver, Jimmy? We've never seen him before."

"Hey there, Eloni. This here is Audie Harlan. He's a local boy from Marlboro. His family's known around these parts."

42

"I've heard of 'em," another man spoke in a voice tinged with curiosity. "Bunch of reprobates…thieves and poachers, I hear. Isn't that right, Mr. Harlan?"

With no hesitation, Audie answered, "Well, I can't argue that, Mr. Hadley. My family does have a lawless reputation. Just wish they were more ambitious. Yah know, like robbing trains and banks and such instead of petty stuff."

A chuckle issued from the speaker, and the heavy gate swung inward as if powered by ghostly motors. Down the long driveway, a series of lights flickered on, lighting their approach to a mansion— still unseen.

"Thanks, Mr. Hadley," Jimmy said. "We'll be there in a few."

Beyond the gate, the roadway was paved with new asphalt, blacker than night. On either side, Audie could see nothing but a backdrop of withered grasses and an occasional clump of cactus. Even the stars above were invisible. During a fleeting moment, he thought he saw a possum dragging a buzzard carcass. Moments later, he thought saw a fox carrying a limp snake in its jaws.

Usually, animal sightings caused Audie to slow for a looksee, but he figured this wasn't the time and place to exercise his curiosity. Taking deep inhalations to steady his breathing, Audie's anxiety grew; a slight tremor coursed through his body. He focused on driving and maintaining a bearing down the precise center of the road, lest he swerve into the shadowy void where nocturnal creatures and other things lurked.

"Up ahead…pull up to Luther's truck," Jimmy instructed, "not too close though…wanna be able to get around it in a hurry…yah know…just in case."

"Truck, hell…that's a freakin' tank," Audie exclaimed, staring into the front grill of the behemoth truck. "Where would you drive something like that?"

"Luther Hadley can drive anything, anywhere he wants," Jimmy said. "Remember…just be cool. He's gonna be curious about you, so he'll be asking questions. Don't bullshit him. You're just a good ole boy like I said. Easier to tell a line of truths than lies."

"I hear yah."

Before Audie killed the engine, a large man loomed outside his car door. Untucked shirttails covered a set of wide hips. A beefy hand held a heavy revolver. Audie looked up to see the man's face, which appeared descended from Polynesian relatives. He stared with a baleful expression.

"Outta the car, runt...slow like."

Even if the mumbled directive wasn't intelligible to Audie ears, the man's tone was clear. For a moment, Audie considered ramming the door into the man's groin. Instead, he steeled himself and exited. Instinctively, Audie turned toward the car and raised his arms.

"Thatta good boy," the man said in a deep voice. "You know the drill."

Audie tried to relax as big hands patted him thoroughly. The man lingered between his legs, fingers slid up and down his inner thigh, palmed his scrotum, and trailed up his butt crack. Audie felt the man breathing down his neck. The man removed Audie's wallet from his back pocket.

Keep it up, asshole! You're about three seconds from a cut jugular...

"He's clean, boss!" the man called out before flipping through Audie's wallet and taking out his driver's license. "Uh, Audie Harlan...twenty years old...lives at 26 Cobb Street...Marlboro. Looks legit, Boss."

"Very good, Eloni."

Audie recognized the voice heard earlier through the gate speaker. On the other side of the car, another man wearing sunglasses similar in stature and ethnicity to Eloni patted down Jimmy, who appeared accustomed to the procedure. Audie felt his wallet sliding into his rear pants pocket.

"Please excuse my associate, Audie, but it's standard routine, especially for those unfamiliar to me. Isn't that right, Jimmy?"

"That's right, Mr. Hadley," Jimmy answered. "Quite understandable...no offense taken at all..."

"Well, that's very fortunate," Luther replied. "What about you, Audie? Any offense taken?"

"No, sir," Audie said. "Eloni...was it? Eloni was very gentle. I wish my girlfriend was as sweet."

"What dah fuck..." Eloni sputtered.

"Easy, big man," Luther said, waving a thin hand. "Audie's just being a cutup. I can tell he's quite the jokester, but he doesn't seem mean-spirited. We could all use a bit more levity around here."

Wearing slippers and a shimmering robe, Luther turned and ascended a stairway leading to the mansion's columned portico. Given Luther's delicate manner and swishy walk, Audie couldn't help but make assumptions about the man's sexual preference.

Another man, who resembled the others, followed Luther. All told, there were three bodyguards. Eloni wore sandals, baggy shorts, and a Hawaiian style shirt with a floral pattern. The other men were similarly attired, except they both donned sunglasses. All carried large caliber revolvers in leather shoulder holsters.

"Samoans?" Audie wondered to himself though he didn't really know, except for their hulking stature and Pacific appearance.

"Come, come, gentlemen!" Luther called from the porch. "Eloni, bring Jimmy's satchel."

Audie and Jimmy trailed Luther up the stairway while the two unnamed guards followed. Audie looked around the mansion, studying every detail, while conveying a curious facade as opposed to excessive interest in the trappings. When Jimmy stopped at the threshold to take off his boots, Audie did the same. He was thankful he had taken a bath earlier and put on clean clothes, including a pristine pair of white socks. The other men replaced their sandals with slippers.

In his mind, Audie catalogued many pieces of artwork and a myriad of antique objects, but there were few items he could fence like cash, guns, or collectables. Not to say such things weren't lying about, but he didn't see them now. Instead, Audie contented himself with the experience of peering inside Luther's opulent home.

"Here, Audie. Have a seat on the divan," Luther beckoned with a sweep of his hand. "Jimmy, help yourself to the bar, you know where everything is. Audie, would you like some iced tea, or something stronger?"

"Iced tea sounds good," Audie answered as he sank into the lush sofa.

"Eloni, take charge of Jimmy's satchel and ensure everything is in order," Luther ordered. "Togo, Lolo…go see to our other guests, and tell Angelina to bring an iced tea for Mr. Harlan."

"Yes…Boss," both replied.

Eloni paused and asked, "Sure you don't need us around?"

"No," Luther shooed them away with a wave. "We're all friends here. Isn't that right, Audie?"

"Sure enough…I'm glad to be here," Audie said, trying not to fidget in response to Luther's leering stare.

"Have you known Jimmy long?" Luther asked, his gaze never wavering. "He usually does bring a friend along during his visits, so he must have been keeping you all to himself."

"Well…we've known each other since we were boys," Audie answered, "but kinda dropped out of touch in past years."

A knock on the door preceded the appearance of an older woman of Hispanic lineage. She delivered a glass of iced tea directly to Audie.

"Thank you, ma'am," Audie said, accepting the glass.

"Yes, thank you, Angelina," Luther said. "Close the door on your way out."

Head down and not making eye contact, the housekeeper departed without a word.

"All here, Boss," Eloni said, closing the satchel. "Same amount as before?"

"How about it, Jimmy?"

"Uh, yeah," Jimmy answered. "Prices are steady at the moment, but I'd let you know otherwise."

"Eloni, pay the man," Luther ordered. "Jimmy, I assume you can double my order next month. I have company coming, and I want to be a good host."

"Double your latest order, or do you want more of some and less of the other?"

As Luther and Jimmy haggled, Audie feigned looking around the parlor as if admiring the antiques and art. However, his attention was on a walnut cabinet with a set of glass doors. Audie figured that from Luther's perspective, his guest was studying an assortment of knickknacks. Although Audie made a mental note of antique fishing lures behind the glass panes, he watched the reflection of an ornate framed mirror in the other room. Tilted downward at a shallow angle, the mirror reflected the wide backside of Luther's henchman, crouched in front of a stone fireplace. Eloni pressed a low gray stone on the fireplace wall. For several seconds, nothing happened, and then with no sound, hydraulic pistons lifted the front edge of a heavy slab that acted as a hearth in front of the fireplace.

Underneath was a vault with a keypad embedded in a steel and asbestos-lined lid. During the several tries it took Eloni to key the correct combination with thick fingers, Audie memorized a simple sequence of numbers—six, nine, six, nine, six, nine, six, nine. At least, that's what he had deduced. More surprising was a view of the vault's contents reflected in the mirror. Revealed were reams of paper money along with a hodgepodge of gold and diamond jewelry and assorted drugs.

Holy shit! Tens of thousands of dollars, at least! Who the fuck keeps that kind of...?

"Jimmy said you have an unusually large cock," Luther said unexpectedly. "Is that true?"

In an instant, Luther's comment vanquished other thoughts from Audie's mind. Every conceivable scenario raced through his head, but Audie couldn't fathom a proper response. Being in Luther Hadley's presence was uncomfortable enough as is.

"Uh...I'm not really sure what to say to that, Mr. Hadley," Audie replied truthfully. "I don't remember ever being asked such a thing."

Luther glanced at Jimmy, who cringed.

"Jimmy didn't familiarize you?"

"Evidently not," Audie said. "What exactly, don't I know?"

"Well...in addition to our usual business arrangement, Jimmy solicits sexual prospects for me," Luther revealed, his voice quaking. "For the sake of expediency, I won't bother with subtleties. We're all adults here, and I'm quite sure this conversation will never stray beyond this room. You see, Audie...I have an insatiable appetite for delicious young men, and I must say I find you very appealing. Your naivety...your light hair, fair skin, and blue eyes... I'm very aroused at this very moment just being so close to you."

"Wow...yeah...you're right. Jimmy didn't tell me anything of the sort," Audie said. "I guess I should feel flattered somehow, but I just don't go that way, Mr. Hadley. I'm sorry if Jimmy gave you other ideas."

"Luther, I'm—," Jimmy uttered.

"Shut your mouth!" Luther barked. "You sit there and stay quiet!"

"Uh, sorry..." Jimmy mumbled.

"Yes, you are a sorry son of a bitch," Luther hissed. "Bringing this sexy stud into my home with no assurances."

Luther's Samoan bodyguard had reentered the parlor without a sound. He stood in proximity to the doorway. There was no leaving without a physical altercation. Audie was thankful that Luther hadn't yet summoned his other protectors. If this situation played out, he would have to do it straightaway.

"Now, Audie, I'd rather you stay under your own accord. I usually have sadist proclivities, but in your case, I would be very pleased to do whatever you desired," Luther said his voice trembling. "What say I offer you a generous stipend for your services?"

"I'm sorry, Mr. Hadley, I can't do that," Audie answered calmly. "If I swung that way, I'd probably be happy to take you up on your offer, but..."

"If you wanna play hard to get and up the price, then your plan is working. Eloni, get me five-hundred dollars," Luther directed.

"You sure, Boss?"

"Just do it!" Luther stammered wiping spittle from the corner of his mouth with a quivering hand. "Mr. Harlan, I am very gifted with my mouth. I'll wager I could satisfy you in under a minute. If not, I'll get down on my fours, and let you go to town. I promise you'll love it. What do you say, Stud? How about showing me what you can do?"

"Uh...no, sir."

"No? You're actually saying *no* to me?" Luther snapped. "Why...you little cock tease. I've been very gentile and patient with you. Haven't I, Jimmy?"

"Yes, Luther...very gracious," Jimmy agreed. "Audie, just do it...it's not like Luther's expecting you to be on the receiving end. Why you might even enjoy it. If not, Luther has always got a couple of hot Latinas around for fun. Why, they'll clean you up good afterwards, and make you sparkly clean."

"Fuck that shit!" Audie replied. "You go to town on him, why don't yah! I'm done here."

"How dare you speak like that in my home!" Luther yelped, spittle flying from his mouth. "You're not done here! No...not at all! I retract my previous offer! *You* will be the receiver now! Why, I'm gonna break you in good. After that, my boys are gonna take a turn or two. By the time we're through, you'll be wiping blood for days..."

In a motion so unexpected...so swift, it even surprised Audie. He flew from the sofa, grabbed Luther by the silky scruff of his robe, and pulled him close. Audie unsheathed a squat dual-edged knife hidden in his belt buckle. Designed with a single finger hole and shallow handle, Audie palmed the bladed weapon expertly. He jammed it into Luther's throat just shy of puncturing his carotid artery. For good measure, he released the collar of the slippery robe, inserted the middle and ring fingers of his left hand into the man's mouth, and clasped his cheek. Luther screeched as Audie threatened to rip his face. Eloni bounded into the parlor with his revolver drawn.

"Back the fuck away, or I'll slit his throat!" Audie threatened. "He'll bleed out before you can do anything!"

The large Polynesian man stopped in his tracks. Unsure what to do, he looked to his employer for direction.

"Shoot!" Luther bawled painfully as he struggled to break free. "Do…it!"

With a quick, stabbing motion, Audie drove the tiny blade into the muscle of Luther's outside thigh. Luther shrieked and recoiled from the painful wound, drool ran down his chin and hung. Eloni took a tentative step, leveling his revolver.

"Go ahead!" Audie barked, pressing the blade tip into Luther's neck. "Try it!"

"No…no…" Luther bleated, waving his hand.

"Jimmy, open the fuckin' door!"

"What…whadda mean? I ain't gonna do that."

Audie spoke into Luther's ear as if imparting a secret, "You have my blessing if you tell Eloni to shoot Jimmy in the gonads."

Before Luther could offer a pained reply, Jimmy opened the door wide.

Audie held the man close and whispered into his ear, "Don't you call out. I see one of your dudes, you're dead."

Luther didn't say a word and submitted entirely. Audie wasn't swayed. He knew Luther would try to retaliate, if not tonight, then later when the immediate threat was over. Audie didn't relish the thought of killing *anyone*, but that possibility weighed on him. He hoped to find a way out before he had to resort to a desperate act.

Before stepping into the foyer, Audie peered in both directions. Luther's other henchmen were nowhere to be seen. Unfamiliar sounds carried from the hallway. Audie wasted no time trying to discern their context. He pressed the blade into Luther's neck and spoke, "Once we're past the gate, I'll set yah loose. Until then, you're in real danger. Now, signal your man to stay in the parlor. I see, hear, feel anything at all…"

"Uh…" Luther waved his hand.

Understanding his employer's command, Eloni shut the parlor door. Audie had no doubt the man was ready to act.

"Put your hands in your pockets," Audie whispered into Luther's ear and pressing the blade against the man's neck for further effect. "Keep in mind, I've abandoned all hope of gettin' outta here alive, so that makes me very dangerous."

The night air was heavy and balmy. Audie's eyes darted about as he shuffled down the walkway with Luther under his control. Drool flowed down the underside of Audie's forearm as Luther moaned and frothed.

"Open the passenger door and go 'round the other side, Jimmy."

Audie detoured to the massive truck in front of the Jimmy's little car. With a flick of his knife, Audie slit the valve stem. Pressurized air whooshed out. Audie breathed in an odor of vulcanized rubber. Fortunately, the tire stem was at a convenient height, so he didn't have to force Luther to his knees.

Turning back to the car, Audie paused for a moment thinking, *"How am I gonna pack this asshole into this tiny car?"*

Audie piled into the passenger seat on top of Luther. It was a clumsy maneuver, leaving a weak defensible position. Audie prodded Luther to pull his legs back until he was half kneeling over the seat. Luther grunted in protest, but Audie didn't relent. Never removing his fingers from Luther's mouth, Audie placed his left knee into the man's back and half straddled the leather seat. He didn't shut the door. Instead, Audie his kept knife-wielding arm free. Jimmy hovered outside the driver side door, as if deciding to get in or bolt.

"Get in!" Audie roared.

"I dunno if I should."

"You think you're gonna walk outta here if I skin him right here?" Audie posed. "They'll probably rape you with a broken bottleneck before they finally put you down."

"All right…all right," Jimmy said. "I'm really sorry, Luther. I didn't see this coming…"

As soon as Jimmy got behind the wheel, Audie gestured with the knife and warned, "You decide to speed up or swerve, I'll stick you in the fuckin' eyeball. Now, move!"

With a grinding of gears, the Supra lurched ahead as Jimmy struggled to shift and accelerate. "Sorry…" he uttered.

The passenger door slammed closed from the sudden momentum. Except for a mewling noise, Luther was silent and motionless. For Audie, it was a long, anxious drive to the gate. Glancing up often and looking through the narrow rear window, he could see nothing, but a plume of dust bathed in red taillights. He had no way of telling if Luther's men were following, or if they had gotten ahead of him. The car slowed as Jimmy neared the gate.

"It's closed…" Jimmy said before the gate swung open. "Never mind…"

"Turn right and gun it."

Beyond the gate, Jimmy seemed more comfortable as he shifted and accelerated.

"Stay right at the fork coming up."

"Where we headed?" Jimmy asked, peering in his side mirror. "We…"

"Shuddup!" Audie snapped, whipping his head to fling away a bead of sweat from the tip of his nose. "Just drive!"

After a mile from FM 1246, Audie closed his left eye and pointed to a nameless dirt track, "Turn up there," Audie ordered.

Without a word, Jimmy turned. The Supra's low-slung frame grazed prickly scrub that grew thick in the middle of the lane. A stick jumped up, gouging at the undercarriage. Washboard surface caused the car to shudder and rumble. Luther grunted as his injured thigh spasmed. Thickets grew dense on both sides. Skeletal branches scratched at the car body and windows. Jimmy mumbled, presumably displeased with the treatment of his new sports car. Audie ignored his ex-friend's frustrated mutterings.

Thankfully, his vague recollection was accurate. Sure enough, the moon illumined an open space ahead. They drove past an open gate hanging askew on a steel post. Tufts of dried grasses blemished the crushed ashen limestone that surfaced the lot. On the far corner, a cylindrical tank silhouetted the starry sky. On the left, rusty girders perched upon a concrete platform. Years ago, Hadley and Sons Incorporated had drilled this isolated patch of ranchland and constructed a derrick that pumped crude oil. Now wild and isolated, it was an ideal place.

"Stop here," Audie spoke, "and shut it down."

With the engine and headlights off, a faint ringing filled Audie's ears. Moon shadow created an army of gloomy shapes until Audie opened his left eye. His night vision improved at once—a trick learned from his father.

"Take your keys, come 'round my side, and open the door," Audie directed. "Just one more thing before I drop you off here, Luther."

Swinging open, the passenger door creaked on its hinges.

"Aw, man..." Jimmy whined. "My car's gonna be a rattletrap by the time you're done with it."

"Quit your bitching and step away," Audie instructed. "Come on, Luther."

Joints and ligaments protested as Audie exited the car. He imagined Luther felt even worse, but Audie didn't much care.

Audie removed his wrinkled fingers from Luther's mouth and shoved him hard with the heel of his foot. Luther lurched ahead several feet, then crumpled to the ground. In the same instant, Audie reached under the passenger seat where Jimmy kept a snub-nosed revolver. He raised the weapon just before Jimmy lunged in his direction.

"Don't do it, Jimmy!" Audie warned. "Pretty ballsy, but you're no fighter. Take a walk while I have a talk."

"What about my car?" Jimmy whined. "I don't wanna..."

A loud percussion from the revolver was Audie's answer. Visible under the bright moon, a curl of smoke wafted from a bullet hole in the Supra's rooftop.

"Oh, fuck...man!" Jimmy exclaimed. "What you do that for?"

"Start walking before I put one in your kneecap!" Audie roared. "Move it!"

Staggering backwards, Jimmy turned and ran across the abandoned lot, stumbling on uneven ground. Audie turned his attention to Luther, who lay on his back with a hand on his wounded leg.

"What now, my boy?" Luther asked. "Surely, you're not going to hurt me further, are you? As is, your situation is dire enough already. Things would go much easier for you if you simply leave...Texas, that is. Perhaps then, I'll let this matter drop..."

"Listen here, Luther. Just because your family is well heeled, doesn't mean you can do whatever you want. This whole thing is your doin', and you left me no way out."

Standing silent and resolute, Audie stuffed the pistol under the waistband in the back of his pants. Placing his hands on his hips, he stared at the moon, his eyes squinting against its unnatural brilliance. All the while, he watched Jimmy's vague form shuffling at the far end of the fenced lot. Audie pondered various scenarios and courses of action until deciding and acting.

"I'd be doing the world a favor if I just put a bullet in your head, right here...right now." Audie opined. "Hell...everyone in Pima County would probably give me a medal. Hell...moms and dads would probably offer up their virgin daughters for putting you down."

"Why...you little shit! You will regret what you have done tonight. I'll have your scrotum hacked off and stuffed down your throat, then I'll find your family and come after—."

As soon as Luther's indignation escalated into threats against his family, Audie lost it. He kicked and cursed without regard of bodily harm to his tormentor. Dirt and dust flew as he pummeled with his booted feet. Luther's shrieks were shrill as he tried to crawl away across the coarse gravel. At the edge of Audie's enraged mind, he heard Jimmy calling out, but he paid him no mind. Too winded to continue, Audie ceased his attack. Seeing Jimmy pacing but not having come closer, Audie straddled Luther's back and yanked his ponytail, pulling his head up.

"You stupid fucker!" Audie hollered. "You're so full of yourself, you don't even have the commonsense to keep your mouth shut! Are you naturally stupid, or maybe your family's just too inbred?"

All Luther could do at this point was moan. Audie pulled the pistol, placed it against the back of Luther's head. A tremor flowed throughout his entire body as his index finger hovered above the trigger. All the trials and tribulations of his short life led to this singular moment. As if it was his destiny to destroy a truly bad—.

"Audie, don't do it man!" Jimmy called out his hands raised high. "He gets it already. Luther overplayed his hand, and someone finally called him on it. Killing him won't do any good. Just get yah thrown into Huntsville, is all."

"I can live with that," Audie said, never wavering. "Rid the world of someone really wicked."

"I dunno, man," Jimmy said. "No redemption in killing someone."

"Shit, Jimmy, I wouldn't be in this situation if not for you. What the fuck you care if I shoot this asshole?"

"Man, I'd like to keep living around here. Otherwise, I gotta move. You...you have your family to watch your back. You're right...if it wasn't for me..."

"Damn right, if it wasn't for you...pimping me out to some rich pervert, who'd kill me on sight if he didn't get his way. You're dealing with sick, dangerous people, Jimmy. You saw those Samoan sons of bitches...turn you inside out with one word from him," Audie said, leaning down to make sure Luther heard him clearly. "I don't care for being at someone's mercy, especially this fucker."

"Speak with him...come to an understanding then."

"There ain't no understanding with people like him," Audie growled. "At least with the devil, you can bargain, but not with psychopaths. Isn't that right, Luther?"

"At the moment, I'm amenable to terms," Luther croaked. "I'd like nothing better than go back to my dear home and forget about this unpleasantness, even if I have to set aside my vanity and not pursue retribution. Point of fact, I'm willing to go abroad until emotions settle."

"Hear that, Audie?" Jimmy said as he lowered his arms and stepped closer. "We can push through this ugliness without doing something drastic."

"Step back and keep those arms up," Audie ordered pointing the pistol. "This here conversation is between me and Luther. I'm not parlaying terms to help you. You'll have to make your own deal."

"Right...whatever you say...sorry, Dude," Jimmy replied, raising his aching arms and stepping back. "Just tryin' to help."

"You realize how close you were, right?" Audie murmured. "How you can't always control others, especially the desperate ones."

"I understand completely, and I won't intrude on you," Luther said. "I only have one demand of my own."

"And, what's that?"

***

54

Jimmy wasn't pleased when Audie drove away in his car. "Come on, Luther!" he pleaded "This isn't cool man."

"Quiet...!" Luther roared, his body racked with pain. "You're not excused for your part in this fiasco."

***

For several days, Audie remembered little after that night, just the numbness of waking in Jimmy's crashed Supra, and the cloying odor of radiator steam. He didn't know how he made it home. Zane had been there, which was unusual for him lately, but instead of taking Audie to the emergency room, Zane had cleaned him up and put him to bed, not allowing him to fall asleep until the next day. In the Harlan Family, there were few, who could afford hospitals, and Audie was in no shape to explain away a car accident.

Just in case he didn't pull through, Audie explained to Zane what had happened, and the pact negotiated. He had bested Luther and his Samoans, but Luther insisted on some form of reparation. It was an unconventional covenant, but Audie accepted the terms to prevent reprisals. He figured Luther needed something to maintain his ruthless reputation, so Audie deliberately crashed the car and injured himself.

Eventually, Audie recovered from a concussion, though for some time, an incessant ringing sounded in his left ear. He had suffered numerous contusions and lacerations. After several weeks of hidden convalescence, a girlfriend of Jimmy's had come to the house asking about his whereabouts. Jimmy had disappeared, and she was worried. Given her gaunt appearance, agitation, and nail-biting, Audie figured she was more concerned about her next fix than her boyfriend's welfare. Audie told her nothing. Instead, he gave her money and said he would let her know if he heard anything. Thankfully, she never returned.

Zane made discreet inquiries among a network of trusted kin. Veiled stories spread through the family grapevine about Audie's encounter with Luther Hadley and his minions. Precise details weren't forthcoming, but it seems Audie was beaten for an unknown slight. An enemy of the Harlan Clan was afoot. Watchful eyes prowled dusty back roads and withered pastures for further signs of retribution, but none came. Luther had gone—South America, it was supposed. For Audie, it didn't matter, just as long as the man was elsewhere. In his absence, reticent employees maintained Luther's unseen estate, and kept his businesses operating.

Chapter 7
Coming Home

Though hot and humid, Hoyt breathed deep and let the Texas breeze wash over his face through the open window. He smelled a faint aroma of manure blended with green grasses and clover from thousands of acres of cattle pastures. Hoyt hadn't smoked a cigarette since leaving the VA hospital, but he didn't want to replace the pleasant scents. After several months in the mental ward, a transport van now ferried him home.

Staring into the blueness above, hazy thoughts meandered. Hoyt thought back to that day in his neighbor's yard and shuddered. Like seeing a nightmare through another's eyes, Hoyt recounted what had happened in the aftermath. Blue sirens blaring and police barking orders, Hoyt fought. The harsh physical treatment did nothing to make him submissive. He punched, kicked, and grappled for a long while. It took four cops to pummel him unconscious with batons. Incensed by Hoyt's capable defiance, the police spared no blows.

In the end, Hoyt convalesced through multiple concussive injuries, broken bones, and contusions. He had no recollection of his time in the intensive care unit, and awareness was slow returning as he adjusted to a varying regimen of drugs to treat his psychosis. He had acclimated to the routine of the ward, which demanded little of him except compliance. Most times, he slept and watched television in the community room.

Once the van exited Interstate 35 and passed through Wheeler, he recognized landmarks along the Route 6 corridor. An anxious feeling twisted his insides as Marlboro drew nearer. Since leaving the Army, Hoyt no longer had plans of any sort. The thought of going home weighed on him. He set a goal for himself.

If my life doesn't change for the better by next year, then I'm cashing it in. No way I'm gonna keep living the shitty life I crapped out for myself. Nope...I'm done.

"Here yah are, Hoyt," the driver said. "You need any help with your bag?"

"Nah, I'm good Earl. Thanks for giving me a lift."

"Good luck then," Earl returned. "Hope we don't see yah again too soon."

"Me too."

All was quiet on Cobb Street, but not surprising given the hot summer day. Heated air shimmered above the asphalt. Hoyt shouldered his knapsack. Cicadas buzzed from high in the treetops. Dust kicked up as Hoyt trudged down the crushed limestone-driveway. Sticks and debris were scattered about the yard, and bags of trash were stacked high. The back lawn was a mosaic of wilted grasses and patches of dead soil. Fire ants trundled in and out of dozens of low mounds dotting the yard.

"Hello, there," Hoyt announced as he opened the kitchen door. "Anyone home?"

"Hey! He's here!" Audie called out. "Hey there, Big Brother!"

"Hey, yourself," Hoyt said, unshouldering his knapsack. "Hot as a skillet out there."

"It is," Audie replied. "Come into the living room. The air conditioner's goin'."

Except for the glare of a large television, the curtains were drawn throughout the house, keeping out the raging sun. Having grown accustomed to the antiseptic smells at the hospital, Hoyt winced. Masculine odors, ripe garbage, and stale cigarettes assaulted his olfactory sense. Though Hoyt wasn't much of a housekeeper himself, at least, he had kept the place somewhat clean. Surrounded by the clutter of two men, who didn't mind living in squalor, his absence was apparent.

Guess I'll be picking up around here for a few days.

"Welcome home, Brother," Zane said. "We made up the living room just for you and put in an air conditioner and a television to boot. Just take it easy until you get squared away."

"Sounds good to me," Hoyt said, his expression vacant, his words slurred. "I'm glad to be outta of the loony bin."

"What was it like in there?" Audie asked. "Any buggery goin' on in there?"

"Why…thanks for asking. Well…none I know of, but compared to other folks in there, I was only a little crazy." Hoyt replied. "At least, after a couple days of meds."

"Well, I'm sorry we didn't visit as much as we should have," Zane said. "I've been driving all the way to Alabama and back for the last three months, and Audie's been laid up."

58

"So, Hoyt…you sure yah didn't get buggered in the loony bin?" Audie inquired again.

"For Chrissakes, Audie!" Zane snapped. "Stop goin' on about that shit. I'm sure Hoyt puckered up tight in the shower."

"Well, Uncle Buddy was always going on about fighting to keep from getting ass-raped by the queers," Audie retorted. "Those crazy sons of bitches were probably hearing voices telling them to go after Hoyt."

"Audie, for Chrissakes!" Zane barked.

"Never mind me," Hoyt said. "What's this I hear about Audie getting waylaid? Zane, why didn't you take him to the emergency room? What the heck's been goin' on since I've been gone? Not like me being here would have made a difference, but damn…"

"Hey…don't badger me," Zane defended. "You weren't here…remember? If I thought Audie was in real danger, I would've got him to the hospital. Besides…no tellin' what he would have said with his head all screwed up. As is, I lost four days of work holed up in the house looking after him and making sure no bad dudes showed up in the middle of the night."

"It's all right, Hoyt…no harm…I'm nearly mended," Audie said. "Just a few aches and pains, is all."

"That's good… Sorry for pestering," Hoyt said, rubbing his eyes. "Any word of Hadley and his boys wanting payback?"

"Nah, he's gone," Zane said. "From what I hear, he's known to disappear for long stretches at a time. Our cousins and cousins' cousins are keeping an eye out. If one of them Samoans show up, we'll hear about it soon enough."

"Sounds like you been doing the right things," Hoyt said. "If I wasn't messed in the head, I would have done the same. I haven't been much of a big brother…I'm afraid…"

"Not your fault," Audie said. "Trouble seems to follow me around like stink on a turd."

"That's for sure," Zane chimed. "The family fuckup…"

"You're one to talk," Audie said. "No tellin' what you get yourself into on the road…"

"All right, stop sniping like a couple of rim jobs at an ass convention," Hoyt interrupted. "We've all messed up time and again. Maybe, we can wipe the chalkboard and start fresh. I know I could stand a change."

"That's good to hear," Zane said. "Fresh start..."

"I could go for that," Audie concurred.

"All right, boys. How 'bout letting me go lay down for a nap," Hoyt said yawning. "I can barely keep my eyes open."

"Go for it," Zane said. "We'll wake you up for supper. Audie picked up some pork chops and corn on the cob. We'll have a good ole homecoming for yah."

Hoyt considered himself fortunate the police hadn't prosecuted him for assault. Circumstances leading up to the act and the sympathetic testimonies of his neighbors, Pete and Regina, lead to a dismissal of charges. He had suffered a psychotic breakdown, and the Veterans Administration was now treating him with heavy doses of Clozapine. Instead of the chronic depression and the odd voices in his head, Hoyt now felt like a zombie of sorts. Monochrome thoughts and incessant fatigue sapped his desire to do anything but sleep.

His time in the mental ward had been a hellish experience for him. Taken from home where he felt most comfortable, he was imprisoned in a world of infinite madness. Heavily medicated, many patients just shuffled around all day, while others sat and stared at walls of blue cinderblock. And, there were those, who screamed and ranted day and night. Hoyt was curious why the insane fixated on religion, and why some claimed to be Jesus reborn.

One night, a man named Bruce Giles had tried to strangle Hoyt in his sleep with a leather bootlace. Fortunately, Hoyt had slipped his fingers between the lace and his trachea before the man pulled tight. During the nearly silent struggle, the man whispered of killing those, who claimed to be angels. How lowly men could never hope to occupy blessed ranks. Hoyt broke free when he knuckled the man across the bridge of his nose. Afterwards, the man was isolated from other patients.

At home, Hoyt felt relief, but knew he was trapped in a muddy narrow between drug-induced stupor and madness. Before, there was hope, albeit faint, that his melancholy might dissipate like a noxious cloud against a stiff wind. Box spring creaking underneath, Hoyt reclined on his bed and closed his eyes. In his mind, the noises of the psyche ward still sounded: a shuffling of feet in the corridors, voices shouting from the community room, announcements over the paging system... In little time, his thoughts diminished as he fell asleep.

***

Wind whipped at his face, stealing his breath. His body somersaulted in midair. A chill permeated his body. A starry night sky swirled in a sickening display. There was no earth below, just an inky void. The rush of air deafened, except for shrill screams all around.

Just a dream, Hoyt. Wakeup...just a dream...

It was dark and quiet in the house. The digital clock showed 2:15 a.m. Hoyt stared at the bright crimson numbers. A swell of nausea roiled in his abdomen. His mouth salivated. Falling to the floor on his knees, Hoyt crawled to a wastebasket on the other side of the room and emptied it. For long minutes, he vomited. Bile spewed from his mouth and nostrils. Acidic and burning, the taste made him gag and heave more. When it was over, Hoyt spat into the wastebasket. Cold sweat coalesced on his forehead, flowed down the bridge of his nose, and dripped. An awful feeling pervaded his mind and body. Lying on his side and curling up, Hoyt sobbed, not knowing if his brothers were in the house.

A rustling sound roused him from his misery. Hoyt listened. A wash of silence filled his ears with a loud ringing, but somewhere above, something stirred. A foul stew churned in his abdomen. Rolling to his knees, Hoyt crawled to the bathroom. His physical agony overwhelmed any thoughts of what might lurk above the ceiling.

Chapter 8
Attic Oddity

Even at midday, the kitchen was gloomy. Pulled blinds and grimy walls made it impossible for sunlight to enter. Dirty dishes, brimming ashtrays, and empty soda cans cluttered the table. At night, the pantry was dark and suffocating, filled with grotesque things that rustled and stirred as rodents and cockroaches scoured the floor and countertops. A larger nocturnal denizen roamed the house.

Audie had considered traps and poisons, but he was bored. Since he didn't have a BB gun, he used the next best thing in his arsenal. With Zane on the road and Hoyt holed up in his bedroom, Audie removed an old Winchester 1890 rifle from his closet. Loaded with .22 short bullets that disintegrated on impact, Audie figured he wouldn't do much damage if he missed, and the small caliber shouldn't make enough noise to rouse his neighbors.

With a section of whitewashed plywood acting as a backstop, Audie placed a piece of cheese on the counter near the sink. Certain he would see the rat's silhouette, Audie took a seat behind a wall of furniture and boxes in the kitchen. When twilight faded, the rodent would appear.

Come on you little fucker. I gotta surprise for your ass. Teach you to munch on my donuts...

Before long, a shape flitted from the pitch dark near the kitchen closet. The rodent searched, beginning with the cabinet under the sink, and then to the tabletop. The creature was a blurred shadow. Audie marveled at its speed and stealth, and he recalculated the odds of a kill shot. For a moment, Audie deliberated taking aim, but the table was too muddled to make out his quarry. With all foodstuff stowed away, the rat would eventually make its way to the counter and find the cheese. Sure enough, it climbed a hanging dishtowel and scurried to the bait. Audie took careful aim as the rat strained to dislodge the cheese nailed to the counter. Exhaling silently, he squeezed the trigger's smooth surface until nothing...

Dammit! Didn't cock the rifle...

Slow and silent, Audie pulled back the hammer with his right thumb. He winced when the mechanism creaked. The rat didn't take notice as it worked on the bait. Using his vast hunting experience and much guesswork, Audie lined the rifle's front and rear sights on his target in the darkness. He squeezed the trigger. A muted snap, dull flash, and wisp of smoke followed. Audie observed the rodent twitch and tumble to the floor. Flipping a wall switch, a florescent fixture hummed, illuminating the kitchen.

Audie pumped the rifle, ejecting the spent cartridge and loading a fresh round. A sharp smell of burned gunpowder tickled his nose. Another scent wafted in the stale air, warm, metallic, and gamey. A length of tablecloth and a chair blocked his view. Audie circled, eyes searching the gloom. A trickle of dark blood trailed from the countertop to a small pool on the floor. From there, droplets formed a line disappearing under the table. Audie stooped...

Hissing and screeching, the rat launched from under the table. Audie jumped back, kicking. The rodent attacked, scratching and nipping at his pant legs. The rifle was useless against such an assault. Audie flailed his arms and legs to keep tiny teeth and claws from sinking into flesh. Suddenly, the creature stopped and crouched as if preparing to jump. Audie pointed his rifle with one hand and jerked the trigger. The rat convulsed and became still. Audie discharged another round at pointblank range.

For fuck sakes!

Taking deep breaths, Audie took a minute to let adrenaline stream away. He heard snoring from the bedroom where Hoyt still slept. Audie turned on the sink tap and let the water run for a minute. He filled a cupped hand and drank enough to wet his mouth. His face grimaced at the liquid's lukewarm temperature and unpleasant taste.

A thought flitted through Audie's mind, *"Now, where did that rat come from?"*

Flipping the wall switch, Audie's eyes squinted against the sudden radiance as he probed the kitchen closet. On the left side, a stack of narrow shelves rose from the floor. The uppermost shelf was inches from the ceiling. Sundry items crammed the sills. Food tins, pots and pans, and miscellaneous clutter threatened to avalanche. Beside the rear wall, a thick hemp rope hung from a nail affixed to the uppermost shelf. Knotted at irregular intervals, the line ended near the floor. A familiar feature throughout his life, Audie's interest was never piqued, and he never questioned its purpose. He had no doubt the rat was expert at scaling a rope.

Where's your den, Rat?

Reaching up, Audie pulled a string attached to a dangling fixture. An incandescent bulb cast a yellowish glow. The plank shelves seemed sturdy enough under his hands. Audie raised a leg and tested his foothold on the lowest shelf, which didn't protest under his full weight. He took hold of the higher sills and slowly ascended. Shadows fluttered when his shoulder brushed the light. Pausing at each shelf, Audie looked for the telltale signs of a nesting rodent but found no mass of shredded papers and fabrics.

Several feet above the floor, he reached the final shelf. A rivulet of sweat trickled down his backside. Unable to raise his head higher, Audie probed with his hand. Tactile senses could not discern what his fingers felt. One by one, he withdrew various things, including an empty thread bobbin, a marble, and a desiccated mouse. Reaching in farther, Audie felt a waft of warm air. Fingers traced the ragged edge of a hole big enough for a rodent to squeeze through. Pulling his hand back, Audie's knuckles lifted a board embedded into the ceiling.

A scuttle hole?

Another odd facet of their house came to mind. Immediately outside was a shallow roof gable with a tiny windowpane. Like the hemp rope, Audie never gave it any thought. Now, he envisioned a crawlspace big enough to stow a box or two. Curiosity stoked, he pried and pulled to dislodge the upper shelf.

Suddenly, the shelf on which he stood buckled. Audie felt his stomach lurch as he dropped feet first. Subsequent shelves pancaked under his weight. So abrupt and violent, Audie barely registered what was happening. Like an out of body experience, he could do nothing to stay his fall. Somehow, he landed feet first. Food cans rained down pelting his head and shoulders.

"Shit!" Audie yelped, blood spraying from his mouth and splattering against the wall.

In an instant, it was over. Audie stumbled from the closet. He winced as his ankle flared with pain. Shaking, he checked himself for injuries. A ripped fingernail on his right hand bled profusely. Upper lip gashed, a metallic taste filled his mouth. Small lacerations peppered his arms. Audie hobbled to a mirror. Blood welled in his mouth, turning his teeth black in the gloom.

Audie turned on the faucet and cleansed his swollen finger. He scooped water with his other hand and rinsed his mouth. He spat blood for a long while. His hands and body quaked. He bowed his head and sobbed. Throughout Audie's mishap, his eldest brother still slumbered.

***

After clearing the closet, Audie buried the rat in the backyard. He looked under the house, which was perched atop wood posts and blocks. Several feet from the moonlit edge, a wooden ladder hung from rusted nails. Undaunted by the pitch-black recesses, Audie crawled underneath with nothing more than a penlight clenched in his teeth. Spittle flowed down his chin. Though he wasn't sure, Audie imagined a swarm of cockroaches scuttling beyond the border of the penlight's dull luminance. He shied away from a black widow spider clinging to a web and swatted away a scorpion glowing green under the light.

The ladder was stout, heavy, and long, so Audie crawled farther under the house to unlatch the far end. It fell to the packed clay ground with a thud. He grappled with the ladder, dragging it inches at a time. Audie felt the night air on his sweaty backside. He snorted and spat, trying to purge the musty odor from his nostrils. He clawed at unseen cobwebs stuck to his face.

Laid upon a sawhorse, droppings and dirt fell from the ladder as Audie cut it to a manageable length. It was a chore to bring it into the house and stand it upright in the narrow closet, which left little space between the shelves and wall. During the maneuver, he smashed a fluorescent lamp and upended the kitchen table. Still, his oldest brother slumbered, oblivious to Audie's nocturnal stirrings.

Audie's heart pounded as he ascended the ladder. Brushing against the dangling bulb, shadows danced. He lifted the board, his penlight barely penetrating the darkness. Audie envisioned a series of rafters and roof-planking. Thick with dust, hot air wafted downward. Narrow and rectangular, the opening was just large enough to squeeze through. Audie suckled the penlight and lifted himself. Unlike the humid coolness under the house, it was hot in the attic crawlspace. He took care not to graze dozens of rusted nails protruding through the roof. There was little room to move around.

Stacks of newspapers disintegrated at the slightest touch. Affixed to a rafter was an antique glass fire extinguisher. Filled with toxic chemicals, Audie avoided the glass globule. After a few seconds, his fading penlight shone on a nondescript wooden box secured with a

65

heavy padlock, which was unlocked. His penlight sputtered and went out.

Shit!

For a moment, Audie considered rummaging through the box with his bare hands but decided against it.

Could be full of rusty razorblades and shards of glass for all I know.

The moon shone through the grimy windowpane. Audie shucked his sweaty tee shirt and wiped the glass, allowing more moonlight to filter through. He pulled on a leather strap riveted to the box. Audie expected resistance, but it slid across the planking like a pat of butter on a warm griddle.

Fuck... Way too light... Probably nothing inside but dust bunnies...

He uncoupled the open lock and lifted the cover. "What the...?" Audie uttered as his mind struggled to comprehend.

Animal hide...fur coat? Not fur...feathers... Birds...mounted? Nope...leather straps and buckles... Folded? Holy shit...they're bird wings!

Straining to see, Audie moved to the side to allow more lunar radiance to reveal the contents within the box. The giant wings trembled and unfurled.

"Hey...hey!" Audie yelped, backing away on his knees and scrambling through the scuttle hole and down the ladder.

Chapter 9
Under a Pale Moon Sky

"Chrissakes, Audie! What yah do now?" Zane snapped as he appraised the damage. "Always a mess waiting when I get home from the road."

"Easy, Brother," Hoyt soothed. "Nothing we can't fix…"

"Say again?" Zane retorted, eyeing his older brother. "The way you all carry on when I'm on the road… Why I have a good mind to get my own place…"

"Oh, stop pissin' and moanin'," Audie said.

"Yeah…but at least, I'm bringing money home," Zane sputtered. "You haven't cashed a check in months…gettin' fired like yah did… And, you, Big Brother, you're as shiftless as they come. Unless you start bringin' in more money, you're good for nothing."

"Aw, go stuff it!" Hoyt snorted. "You're not cock of the walk around here. At least, I did something…went places…"

"Well, you haven't been anywhere lately, have yah?"

"You all stop sniping at each other…and me too," Audie interrupted. "I didn't call you out to the kitchen to argue."

"Then, what?" Zane asked. "I'm tired and wanna go to sleep."

"Did you see the scuttle hole in the kitchen closet?"

"Yeah," Zane replied, tilting his head and looking upward. "So, what of it?"

"Never knew it was there," Hoyt said.

"Found it last night when I killed the rat," Audie answered. "Damn shelves buckled on me."

"So, you went rat hunting last night?" Hoyt asked. "In the house?"

"You were sound asleep," Audie said. "Shit…I fired a gun and everything, and you still didn't wake up."

"Really…fired a gun in the house? Oh, never mind," Hoyt sputtered. "Did you find anything interesting?"

"Just a bunch of newspapers and an old wooden box," Audie said. "Just enough room to crawl around a little."

"What's in the box?" Hoyt probed. "Is it full of gold bullion or what?"

"Yeah, it was full of something but not gold," Audie said, scratching his head. "The box had birdwings inside…"

"You're shittin' me," Zane said. "Birdwings…like clipped wings from a dove or something?"

"Nope, big wings," Audie said. "Like a man could wear."

"That's the dumbest shit I've ever heard," Zane cracked. "You must have split your skull for sure."

"Don't have to take my word for it!" Audie barked. "Get up there and look for yourself!"

Zane looked in the closet. Shelves removed and stacked on the kitchen table, a rickety wooden ladder leaned against the wall inside, barely room enough to climb. Any other time, Zane would have been intrigued by a mystery box.

"I can't imagine there being anything valuable up there," Zane said, "but how is it we missed it all these years?"

"I dunno," Hoyt said, "but this house is built so odd, you wouldn't know there was a crawl space. Then again, we're not the most industrious bunch."

"Again, with the big words," Audie scolded. "Get up there, Zane."

"Shit! You go up there?" Zane challenged. "You found it. You've already been up there…unless you're scared…"

"I ain't scared on nothing, nimrod!"

"All right, enough of this happy horseshit! You all sound like a couple of angry twats with yeast infections," Hoyt interrupted. "Outta the way."

"Help yourself," Zane offered. "No tellin' what's livin' up there. Hell…Jimmy Hoffa could be up there for all we know."

"Jimmy Hoffa…that's a good one," Hoyt chuckled. "I'm holding out for something worth a few bucks."

Lifting his leg high, Hoyt attempted to find a foothold on the ladder, which was jammed into place at a very steep angle. Hoyt reached up, grabbed a higher rung, and pulled. It was a clumsy maneuver. The ladder shifted, scraping the wall and bumping the light pendant. Hoyt waited for the light to stop swinging.

"Here," Audie said as he knelt. "Stand on my knee. It'll give you a lift."

Sure enough, it gave Hoyt a better position to get his footing. He ascended, taking care to test each rung. The ladder held. The access

68

hole was now within reach. Once painted shut, Hoyt observed where his brother had broken the seal. He pushed. The plank lifted. Heated air wafted down. Hot and musty, Hoyt breathed in attic-baked timbers and stale air. It was pitch black above.

"Flashlight," Hoyt beckoned. "Like a mineshaft up there."

"Here," Audie said, stretching his hand upward. "Fresh batteries…"

The crawlspace was cramped. The roof pitched steeply to his right. Ahead was a narrow alcove several feet long. Old newspapers were stacked on either side of a rectangular box.

Given the confined space and airless environs, Hoyt had no desire to crawl inside. He considered other options to retrieve the box before deciding he had no choice. Grasping the lip of the scuttle hole on either side, he hoisted himself. Hoyt regretted the move straightaway when his head grazed a nail protruding from between the rafters.

"Dammit!" he sputtered, his fingertips tracing a gouge on his scalp. He wiped his hand on his tee shirt, knowing he left behind a trail of blood.

"You all right?" Audie asked. "I forgot to tell yah about the nails sticking out everywhere."

"I should have figured," Hoyt replied as he repositioned himself and tried again.

This time, Hoyt lowered his head and clambered inside. Penlight clenched in his mouth, he used his forearms and knees to belly crawl. Hoyt grabbed a leather strap on the side of the box. He snorted to expunge a cloud of dust disturbed in his passing. The box shifted as if empty. It moved across the rough planking with no effort.

What the?

Hoyt's feet dangled as he searched for a rung. Soon, he felt someone take hold and guide his foot. Hoyt's head grazed a rafter and scuffed his scalp wound. He angled the box to fit through the scuttle hole. Hoyt lowered it to Audie.

Placing the box on the kitchen table, Audie backed away, and said, "Help yourself, Zane."

"Me?"

"Yeah, you…" he answered. "Just let me get out of the way first."

With his brothers around the table, Zane lifted the cover. Inside was an apparatus constructed of a multitude of interwoven feathers resembling a set of impossibly large wings. Mottled colors of gray and black, the feathers were disheveled and malodorous after decades of interment in the attic.

"What the hell?" Zane exclaimed. "What…how?"

"I'll be darned," Hoyt chimed. "Who would've thunk it?"

Audie was mute, gazing at it from the side. "Take 'em out…let's see…" he said.

Zane scooped the wings into his arms. "Set the box on the floor, will yah?" he asked to no one in particular.

"Got it," Hoyt said, taking the box down with some physical effort. "Weighed a lot less before?"

"Let's see," Audie said, lifting the box. "What dah? Thing's heavy as a car battery now."

"Really?" Zane asked, a puzzled expression crossing his face. "Why this contraption doesn't weigh anything at all. A slight breeze would send it airborne."

The brothers studied the wings under the fluorescent lights. Having plucked and skinned thousands of mourning doves after their many hunting forays, the brothers recognized the wings' genuine qualities. Skin sheathed the bone framework from which thousands of quills grew, beginning with the wispiest downy to the largest primary feathers. An unusual lattice of bone and tendon interlocked both wings. The physiology was alien to the brothers. A skilled leather smith had woven an elaborate harness in and around the bony mesh, creating a girdle that encircled the chest and abdomen of the wearer.

After a few minutes of handling and examination, the wings had transformed, now pliable as if living just seconds before and having yet lost their elasticity. Even the leather materials were supple with no sign of age.

"How that happen?" Hoyt asked. "Things were ready to fall apart a minute ago. Now, they're like new?"

"That's strange," Audie said.

"Try 'em on, Audie," Zane suggested. "You found 'em."

"I'm not trying 'em on," he replied. "Weird things goin' on with 'em."

"I'm game," Hoyt said with no hesitation. "Maybe you guys could help me figure 'em out."

"They're pretty wide. May have to go outside to put 'em on," Zane observed. "Come on, Audie, grab hold."

"I got it," Audie replied. "Take care with 'em. Might fall apart if we're not."

"See here, Hoyt" Zane said, nodding to a girdle of sorts. "Stoop down and push up."

Hoyt threaded his head and shoulders through. Struggling at first, he slipped easily through the leather garment, which wrapped around his chest, abdomen, and back. Afterwards, Hoyt palmed a set of round leather grips affixed to the underside of the wings near the second joint of its midsection. Zane and Audie cinched and buckled a thick waist belt.

They stepped back and stared at their brother, who now appeared like a demigod of sorts. The veins in his arms and neck swelled, and his biceps now appeared toned and muscular. His paunch disappeared under the snug girdle. Hoyt placed his hands on his hips and struck a pose.

"Look at you!" Zane declared. "You look pretty good in that contraption."

"Yeah, Mrs. Sanchez would get all hot and bothered if she gotta look at yah," Audie rejoined. "Hell, we outta take you to Piggly Wiggly and let you stroll the grocery aisles."

At first glance, it was a simple apparatus, but it appeared custom-built for Hoyt's gaunt frame. The back girdle fit snug and comfortable. Tough and supple like the finest Chamois lambskin leather, the material molded and stretched with every bodily motion. Hoyt palmed the leather grips and stretched his arms outward. The wings swept wide, enveloping Zane and Audie in a cloud of dust. Flexing his elbows inward, the wingtips closed. Hoyt opened and closed the wings several times. His brothers marveled.

"Holy shit!" Audie blurted. "That's no ordinary pair of costume wings."

"That's for sure," Zane agreed. "Chrissakes, makes you wonder if you could actually…"

The brothers fell silent as if considering the possibility.

"Nah, that's just stupid," Hoyt said, shaking his head. "Anyhow, let's go outside and air 'em out, at least."

The wings closed tight when Hoyt brought his elbows to his side. He turned sideways and squeezed through the kitchen door. Shaded from the streetlights, the backyard was dark. Branches of the high oak and clouds blotted the moon and stars. For Hoyt, an unusual glow bathed the yard. Beady eyes shone from the tall grasses near the back fence where a flying squirrel foraged on the ground. Nocturnal sounds filled his ears.

"Why's it so bright out?"

"Whadda mean?" Zane said. "Back light bulb's been burned out since last week. Dark as a coalmine out here with no moon."

"Yeah, it's dark," Audie concurred. "Maybe when my eyes adjust, but I can't see anything yet."

"Funny? I can see and hear everything," Hoyt said, his eyes flitting around. "Like...right after the sun goes down, and before the first stars appear."

"You mean twilight?" Zane offered.

"Yeah...twilight...that's it."

"Never mind that shit," Audie interrupted. "Flap your arms and see what happens."

The wings spread wide as Hoyt extended his arms. Zane and Audie stepped back without thinking. Even in night shadow, their eldest brother cast an impressive silhouette.

"Hot damn!" Zane exclaimed, his voice quavering. "I can't describe it. Like a picture in a bible book...or something. Quite the sight, isn't he, Audie?"

"Gives me the heebie-jeebies," he answered. "Maybe you oughta take 'em off until morning? That getup is freaking me out some."

"Nope...feels good...like...I dunno...?" Hoyt said as he drew the wings in and out. "Damn, it's tough to describe."

"Do it," Zane said.

"Do what?" Hoyt asked.

"You know...try 'em out," Zane answered. "Flap your arms like a bird."

"Stop that, Zane," Audie whispered. "We don't know what that thing is. We should wait for morning."

"I'm gonna do it," Hoyt said, crouching slightly.

"Yeah, do it," Zane prodded. "Stand back, Audie."

Before Audie could speak, Hoyt suddenly launched a dozen or more feet into the air. Tree branches snapped as he flew into the oak canopy. In a panic, Hoyt flailed his arms blindly, propelling himself into the tree trunk with enough force to drive the air from his lungs.

72

Hoyt fluttered to the ground like an autumn leaf. Zane and Audie rushed in and caught him in midair. Light as a balsawood airplane, they set him down, taking care of the wings. Hoyt wheezed painfully, trying to breathe.

"Easy now…it'll pass soon," Audie soothed. "Relax."

Within seconds, Hoyt took shallow breaths. An ache emanated from somewhere below his ribcage. "I hate it when that happens," he shuddered. "Nothin' worse…"

"Did yah see that?" Zane said excitedly. "Even a professional basketball player couldn't jump that high… Need to take you out to a pasture somewhere and let you play. We should do it now."

"Hold on now," Audie said. "Tomorrow maybe…somewhere private. Don't need anyone seeing."

"Yeah…tomorrow…first light," Hoyt agreed. "Let's go back inside."

"Me next," Zane insisted. "I wanna try 'em on for size. Then you, Audie."

"All right," Audie said, "but I'm not keen on this. No tellin' what's gonna happen. I mean…magic wings for Chrissakes! We don't know what we're doin'."

"Aw, don't be a pussy," Zane rejoined. "When are you gonna have this much fun without gettin' the clap?"

Chapter 10
Birdmen

Waking was a gradual happening filled with nonsensical dream imagery. Zane stared at the yellowed ceiling with no recognition. A long crack made its way across an expanse of nicotine-stained surface, ending near a corner adorned with a cobweb. Zane yawned, clearing his mind of muddy thoughts until he recalled the events of the previous evening. He turned his head and studied the clock on his nightstand.

"Shit!" he sputtered, wiping bleary eyes. "We overslept! Get up!"

"What?" Audie said, swinging his legs over the side of his unkempt bed. "What are you goin' on about?"

"Where are they?" Zane asked as he hiked up his blue jeans. "Do you have 'em?"

"Have what?" Audie answered, looking around the bedroom. "Oh yeah…the wings. Hoyt!"

"Don't yell! I'm up," Hoyt called from his bedroom. "I have 'em."

"How are they?" Zane said, peering in from the kitchen.

"Not the same…not alive…" Hoyt replied. "They're stiffened…like a roadkill buzzard."

"What did yah do with 'em?" Zane demanded, his fingers caressing the feathers and leather harness. "Stiff as a barn board… How's that…?"

"Dunno?" Hoyt said as he gently pulled a wing's leading edge. "They were okay when I nodded off."

"Daylight," Audie said without a doubt. "They only come alive at night."

Hoyt and Zane exchanged looks, their expressions haggard and pale.

"What now, I wonder?" Zane asked.

"Put 'em back and wait 'til later," Audie answered. "I don't think sunlight is good for 'em."

"Hurry and get the box," Hoyt directed. "Keep the shades drawn."

"Here," Zane said, bringing the box into the kitchen.

Hoyt placed the wings inside. He smoothed the disheveled feathers before closing the lid.

The box was heavy and cumbersome as Hoyt and Zane lifted from inside the narrow closet. After minutes of fumbling, Hoyt slid the box into the farthest recesses of the crawlspace and replaced the cover to the scuttle hole.

"Let's hope that does the trick."

The day was hot, but instead of sweltering inside, the brothers did chores. Hoyt picked up debris around the yard and built a cairn. Afterwards, he untangled a snarl of weathered garden hose and wrapped electrical tape around several cracked sections. Hoyt raked leaves and sticks from around the pile and wetted the surrounding ground. He sprinkled the remains of an old gas can and stepped back. In many residential environs, neighbors didn't appreciate someone burning trash. Usually, a permit would have been required, but the Town of Marlboro had relaxed attitudes.

Hoyt inhaled the last of his cigarette and sent it sailing through the air with a flick of his finger. For a moment, the butt smoldered, smoke curling around dried leaves, sticks and timbers. He sat back in a creaky lawn chair and waited. With the heat of day to aid in combustion, it was just a matter of time… A sudden whoosh preceded an eruption of flame. Hoyt flinched as superhot air buffeted his whiskered face. He grinned as he doused the fire with a mist of water to keep the flames from reaching too high. Within minutes, the smoke subsided as heat funneled upwards above a bed of embers.

Inside the house, Zane bagged garbage, washed dishes, and scrubbed the counters. Audie gathered dirty clothes and bedding to feed their antiquated wringer-washer machine. It was a tedious chore given the volume of laundry, but with several hours until sunset, Audie needed to pass the time.

Hoyt couldn't help but wonder about his sudden enthusiasm. It had been years since he had risen before noon and toiled around the house. For some inexplicable reason, it felt good to straighten up. Hoyt cataloged a list of jobs to tackle. He dragged out the pressure washer and scoured mildew from the house siding. He replaced the rotted doorsteps. He cleared kudzu from the backyard.

"Hey, come on in," Zane called. "We should eat before going out. Say…you've been working, all right. I can actually see the ground."

"Yeah, what time is it?"

"Suppertime," Zane answered. "It'll be dark in an hour or so. We'll wanna get goin' before long. You coming?"

"As soon as the fire's out...not much longer," Hoyt said, stirring the steaming embers with a stick.

"Audie, enough with the clothes," Zane said. "Just mac' and cheese... Not much, but it'll do. Tomorrow, I'll get groceries."

"Shit...already?" Audie asked. "Where the day go?"

"I dunno?" Zane replied. "One minute, it's ten o'clock...next thing, it's after six. I got so busy I lost track. Probably just amped about trying out those wings."

"Wow...did you do all this?" Hoyt said, shuffling into the kitchen. "Cockroaches are gonna leave for the neighbors."

"Yeah... like I was on autopilot or something," Zane said. "Kinda like driving down a long highway and daydreaming. Before you know it, you're coming to the end."

"Same here," Audie added. "I must have done a dozen loads...bedding too."

"Just as well, I suppose," Hoyt said. "We would have gone stir-crazy waiting for sunset. Anyhow, let's eat and get washed up. I'm anxious as hell to see what we're dealing with."

***

"Next left," Audie pointed through the dusty windshield. "See the gate?"

"Yeah," Zane said. "And, you're sure no one's out here tonight?"

"Chrissakes, Zane! How many times are you gonna ask me that?" Audie snapped. "Mr. Gallison's been laid up for the last two years, and he hasn't bothered to lease his land to anyone yet. Besides...we got an understanding. I can hunt and trap all the feral pigs I want as long as I don't shoot any deer or fish his tanks. Of course, that was a while back, and he may have been drinking around that time...probably he was..."

"Well, I feel better already," Zane snorted. "If we get pinched by Joe-Law, then you can do the explaining."

"Enough, both of yah," Hoyt interrupted as he shifted between his brothers in the little pickup. "Like a couple of hens scrapping over a cricket... Damn! Gate's locked!"

"No worries," Audie said. "Douse the lights, will yah."

Before the truck rolled to a stop, Audie hopped from the cab and raced ahead, his feet kicking up dust in the glow of running lights.

With no hesitation, he hopped the metal gate and disappeared into the nighttime murk. After a minute, he appeared and fumbled with a heavy-duty padlock. Soon, he pulled on the gate, hinges creaking. Audie beckoned with a wave. As soon as the truck passed through, he closed and locked the gate, and then pocketed the key. Audie jumped in the truck bed and tapped the cab roof.

Standing up, Audie held tight to a makeshift roll bar adorned with spotlights. He glanced at the wooden box wrapped in a packing blanket and strapped to the truck bed. Audie breathed deep, savoring the night air. Countless points of light pierced the inky sky. The moon was full and shone with an unusual brilliance.

Audie tapped the cab roof and shouted into Zane's open window, "Take a left at the end of this road and straight to the end!"

Lined with crushed limestone, the ashen road reached a cul-de-sac. When the truck halted, a cloud of dust wafted past. Zane shutoff the truck and sat. Darkness enveloped the brothers while they waited for their eyes to adjust. Silhouetted against a starry sky, Zane made out a tree line that wrapped around a large pasture.

"At least forty acres...no fences, gullies, or rocky outcrops nearby. Ground's soft, and there's thick grass...no burrs, brambles, or cactus," Audie spoke. "Good place to get airborne."

"I'd take real care," Hoyt chimed. "We still don't know what we're dealing with here."

"You're right," Zane agreed. "That's why I volunteer you go first."

"What?"

"You're the expert...being in the Army and all," Zane offered. "Besides...you're the only one, who's done it so far."

"Just because I rode in helicopters doesn't make me no expert," Hoyt countered, "and I could get killed for all we know."

"Well...that's a chance we'll have to take," Zane joked, "and you've actually flown already."

"I don't think catapulting into an oak and nearly breaking my back really counts," Hoyt returned. "This is the dumbest idea ever."

"None of it makes any sense, does it?" Audie added. "I mean...are we really gonna fly like birds?"

"Enough jibber jabber. Let's do this," Zane said as he unstrapped the box. "Audie, lower the tailgate, why don't yah. Hoyt, break out the Coleman."

A match flame illumined the darkness followed by a whoosh. The lantern wick glowed white, casting an intense light in a ten-foot radius. The brothers' faces looked ghostly and gaunt. Hoyt lifted the lid and unpacked the box, revealing the wings. The feathers trembled under the moonlight.

"They're alive," Audie said. "They're really alive. The moon…"

"Yeah, I'm thinking so," Hoyt said. "They're a lot more lively."

"It was overcast last night…real dark under the oak and everything," Zane explained. "Here, let me…" He grabbed the harness from the rear and held the wings out.

Hoyt shucked his tee shirt and hunched, threading his arms, head, and shoulders through the girdle. The supple leather yielded easily, flowing down his bony frame. Like before, the chest harness constricted and hugged every feature of Hoyt's upper torso—snug, but comfortable. Coming alive, the wings spread wide and quivered. Hoyt's senses suddenly intensified. Nighttime surroundings became visible. Twilight enveloped the open pasture and tree line. Nocturnal eyes glowed as a red wolf loped along a distant fence line. A myriad of sounds and scents threatened to overwhelm his senses. Hoyt closed his eyes and breathed deep.

"Look at that," Zane said, stepping back. "If that isn't magic, then I don't know what is."

"It's amazing…wonderful…" Audie said, his eyes glistening in the darkness. "I'm not saying you're one, but you sure look like an angel…like something out of a Bible story or something. Makes yah wonder where these things came from."

"Never mind that now," Zane interrupted. "I wanna see what these puppies can do. How about it, Hoyt, you ready?"

"As ready as I'm gonna be. Feels good…like being high. I can see everything…hear…smell…" he replied. "Here goes nothing."

Hoyt palmed the thick leather grips. Bending at the elbows, the feathered appendages opened and closed. He took his time, growing accustomed to strange sensations. When he swept downward, his heels lifted until he balanced on his toes. Hoyt repeated several times until the basic mechanics felt natural. However, it was one thing to flap while earthbound and another thing altogether should he actually take flight.

"Slow and easy," Audie cautioned as he stepped back. "I wouldn't go all Superman. You're not all powerful and shit."

Hoyt pumped his arms faster until he lifted. Suspended several inches above ground, he maintained a steady rhythm. Hoyt drifted side to side and back and forth but kept a semblance of control. Changing the pitch of his arms and favoring one over the other, he steered in a general direction. Learning to fly was more instinctual than trial and error.

His confidence growing, Hoyt stroked his arms more powerfully. Ascending twenty feet or higher, he straightened and flew, his legs pulling rearward like a tail rudder. Once he achieved momentum, he glided easily and didn't have to propel himself with as much effort. Hoyt scanned his surroundings. Aware of the littlest details, he anticipated movements in advance of course changes. Trees, fences, and utility lines came into focus allowing him opportunity to circumvent potential hazards. For now, it was enough to fly around the pasture, acclimating to new sensations.

Despite the sheer enjoyment, a sudden fatigue forced Hoyt to abort after several minutes. Ascent came more naturally than the reverse. He vacillated as he considered how best to slow his trajectory and land. Hoyt stroked his arms less powerfully and glided. As the ground neared, he stroked his legs to come to a running stop. Unfortunately, he lacked experience in this feat. Hoyt tumbled across the grassy pasture. Instinctively, he folded the wings to protect them and rolled several times.

"You okay?" Audie shouted as he sprinted over. "Did you hurt yourself...the wings?"

"I'm all right," Hoyt said. "Just dusted up is all."

The brothers hoisted Hoyt to his feet and stood back. Hoyt unfurled the wings and shook off bits of grass. Amazingly, the appendages appeared pristine under the moonlight. The feathers gleamed as if oiled, impervious to wet and dirt. The underlying downy feathers were thicker and more luxurious than before the flight.

"Like flooring the gas pedal and blowing out the carb," Zane said. "Just needed to be taken out for a ride."

"Yeah, like new," Audie agreed as he caressed the quivering feathers. "How do you feel? You winded?"

"I got tired...sudden like..." Hoyt wheezed, sweat running down his face. "Not surprising...too much of a couch potato... more conditioning...last longer... here...one of you go..."

"Hell, I'll give it a try," Zane said. "You okay with that, Audie?"

"All right by me," he replied. "I'll learn more if you two get banged up first."

After several minutes, the wings adorned Zane's back. The fit was perfect, adjusting to his shorter frame as if custom made for his body. Spreading his muscled arms, the wings opened, revealing a latticework of feathers underneath, vague bands and spots covered their mottled surface. So intricate, it seemed impossible someone could have created the apparatus by hand.

Unlike his older brother, Zane didn't hesitate. He swept the wings downward with a powerful stroke and propelled skyward. The sudden ascent caused him to exhale. For unsettled moments, Zane couldn't breathe. Adrenaline flowed. Without thinking, he slowed his arms into a rhythmic motion. He propelled ahead and flew a wavering path. His organs floated in his abdomen causing a rash of belly bumps. For a mile, Zane made small adjustments, turning in the direction from which he came. Rather than enjoying the newfound experience, Zane focused on the simple mechanics of flight. He had not forgotten Hoyt's injurious landing, so he tried to learn as much as he could before that eventuality.

Like his brother, Zane tired after several minutes and succumbed to the temptation to remain aloft. Steering in a general direction back to his brothers, Zane slowed his approach, hoping to lose altitude gradually and alight as gently as possible. As the ground neared, he pedaled his feet. For several or more teetering steps, Zane remained upright. He fanned out the wings to create drag to slow himself. Unfortunately, he couldn't adjust to the abrupt change in momentum, and he pitched headlong, sliding across the grassy field on his belly. Zane let out a grunt.

"Pitiful…absolutely pitiful!" Audie jeered as he ran over. "I may not have seen either one of you in the dark, but I sure as hell heard both of you crash landing."

"Okay, numb nuts, you'll get your chance soon enough," Hoyt rejoined. "How was it, Zane?"

"Pretty awesome…scary…but awesome," Zane replied, rising to his knees. "Really takes the wind outta yah…." He bowed over and spat. His spittle had a metallic taste. He closed his eyes and drew slow, deep breaths until his head cleared. Sweat poured down his face and dripped from his nose and chin. He winced under the beam of a flashlight.

"Too...bright..." Zane wheezed. "Need a minute to catch my breath."

"Sorry, Brother," Audie offered. "Drained yah, huh?"

"Yeah, but worth it," he said, rising to his feet. "Here, let's get you outfitted."

"Damn right!" Audie said. "I'm ready to go."

"Remember...go slow," Hoyt cautioned. "It's gonna take some gettin' used to."

"Screw that!" Audie remarked. "I'm goin' balls out."

"Okay..." Hoyt answered, knowing it pointless to advise his littlest brother, who learned most things by cause and effect. "Just don't kill yourself first time out."

After donning the wings, Audie shouted and sprinted across the pasture in a loping run. He flapped wildly like a chicken chased by a fox. Once, he lifted several feet from the ground but came down hard and bowled head over heels. Before his brothers could run to his aid, Audie jumped to his feet, swept the wings down, and leapt skyward. An abrupt ascent left his innards lurching. He peed his pants, but he didn't take notice as he flailed every which way. After a short while, he found a rhythm that stabilized his flight.

When he looked around, Audie noticed how high he had climbed. He barely recognized the terrain below in the twilight glow. Audie observed a patchwork of pastures, dirt roads and fence lines. The few houses seen were separated by miles of ranch and farmland. Audie searched for his brothers, but he was disoriented with no landmarks to navigate. Although he wasn't much into maps and such, he soon spotted the Brazos River and a familiar bend flanked by a steep bank of red clay. From there, he flew an erratic course to the road junction leading back to his brothers. Along the way, he felt more weighted with each stroke of his arms. Audie steadily descended, too fatigued to maintain altitude.

Shit!

Audie glided downward in a steep trajectory. Light as a bird at the outset of his first flight, he was now laden like a lead brick. Just missing the jagged edge of a barbwire fence, Audie careened into a field overrun with saw grass and brambles. He slid across the ground. Razor sharp grasses and prickly plants grazed his face. Momentum spent, he came to rest inches from a cactus patch covered in thorns. Audie struggled to his knees and unslung his arms. The wings folded. He stood, his body trembling. Audie recognized the side road that led to the pasture and his brothers. He trudged.

Man...so...tired...

The night air was heavy and warm. Sweat ran down his brow and into his eyes. Audie mopped his face with the back of his hand. For long minutes, he slogged down the road. His sneakers kicked up dust in his wake. Surprisingly, he could still see well, though the twilight glow was fading. Audie's other senses felt heightened. A white noise of nocturnal insects filled his ears, and musky scents pervaded his nostrils. He tasted honeysuckle. Voices nattered from far off. Shortly after, Audie heard Zane's truck approaching. So sure, it was his brothers, Audie stood and waited. Otherwise, he would have jumped a fence and hid in the mesquite.

Squinting against yellow headlights, Audie dropped to his knees and placed his hands on the ground. A taste of bile added to his misery as he vomited. Truck doors opened and closed. Hands patted his back. Audie spat, phlegm dripping from his nose. A water bottle appeared before his face. Condensation coalesced on the cool plastic. Audie gulped until the bottle collapsed.

"You okay?" Hoyt asked. "We were gettin' worried."

"I'm...all right...just shaken up..." Audie panted. "Takes the wind outta yah."

"Yeah, it does," Hoyt said, patting his brother's back. "Pretty awesome though, wasn't it?"

"Yeah..." Audie said before another wave of nausea overwhelmed him.

"He's okay...just reckless as usual!" Zane snapped. "Nearly broke 'em before we had another chance."

"I'm sure Audie will take it slow next time," Hoyt soothed. "I don't know about you, but I don't have strength for another go tonight. How 'bout you, Zane?"

"I wish..." Zane replied. "I can barely stand as is..."

"Let's get goin' then," Hoyt suggested. "We'll rest up and try again tomorrow night."

Chapter 11
Gravity Be Damned

"Couldn't ask for a more pleasant evening," Hoyt said, breathing in the night air. "Clear skies...low humidity..."

"So, who's first?" Zane asked, opening the wooden box. "How about rock, paper, scissors?"

"Nah, you go first, Zane, and Audie can go after," Hoyt offered. "We'll rotate as we go along."

Audie shrugged his shoulders. Although impatient to go, he agreed with the sequence since he had almost wrecked the wings the previous evening. In the meantime, Audie watched and learned from Zane's experience.

Before donning the wings, Zane stretched. His body ached from the night before. Though he went through various repetitions throughout the afternoon, the stretches seemed to inflame muscle and tendon even more. Anticipating further discomfort, he had taken a double dose of aspirin, eaten a plate of pasta, and drank lots of water. Only during the last hour did he stop to let his stomach settle. Bending forward at the waist, his legs trembled.

"Oh, come on," Audie mocked. "You're not a ballerina. Just suit up already."

"You should do the same, Little Brother." Hoyt chided. "Do what you need to do, Zane. This is serious business."

"All right," Zane said, lifting his arms. "I'm ready as I'll ever be, but I'm still sore as hell."

The supple leather girdle slid over Zane's head and trunk much easier than last time. He palmed the handholds. Hoyt and Audie cinched the belt and tucked in loose clothing. Audie held a water bottle aloft for Zane to take a sip and wet his throat.

"How's it feeling?" Hoyt asked, stepping back. "Too tight...too loose?"

"No, feels good...feels real good," Zane answered. "I'm not as lame. Hardly any soreness in my muscles now. Say...did you notice how bright everything gets? Like...right just after sunset. I can see everything."

"Pretty amazing, but good thing though," Audie offered, "or we'd be flying blind. Lots of stuff to watch out for…power lines, trees, and such."

"Well, here goes again," Zane said. "Hopefully, a better landing this time."

He pushed his arms downward in a deliberate motion. Immediately, Zane lifted from the ground. Raising his arms, the wings adjusted with lessened drag. Sweeping downward again, he climbed even higher. Around a hundred feet or more in the air, he angled the wings to propel himself forward. Purely instinctual, Zane made small adjustments in wing pitch to execute purposeful flight. His speed increasing, his legs hung behind like tail feathers, which he used to rudder and brake.

Adrenaline coursing, Zane's senses magnified. Thoughts flickered through his mind at a quickened pace. Ahead and below, he observed numerous hazards like branches and utility lines, and he adjusted his path. Once, he banked left and narrowly missed an owl that had taken wing at his approach.

He needed no map or bearing to stay on path. Zane knew he could retrace his flight, never doubting which way to go. Occasionally, when he felt an updraft, he held in place, hovering for minutes at a time far above the ground. More than once, Zane was tempted to tuck his wings and dive earthward. However, this being his second flight, he figured he should exercise some discipline. Zane was also wary of undue stunts that caused him a motorcycle accident two years ago. He considered himself fortunate to have survived that mishap with only scrapes and a few contusions. With that incident in mind, Zane maintained as smooth a flight as possible.

He luxuriated in the experience, trying not to exert himself unnecessarily to prolong his flight. Fatigue came knowingly this time, so he reversed course and ascended in a shallow glide. Zane recognized the L-shaped field from far-off along with his truck and two brothers, who appeared as specks on a twilight horizon.

For the first time, Zane marveled at the heavens. The moon shone so bright, his eyes squinted against its glare. Cratered and scarred, the lunar surface was visible like no other time in his life. Celestial forms appeared from the murk of an infinite universe. So distinct, he observed the greater planetoids of the solar system and distinct galaxies of countless stars. Every color of the visible spectrum was plain, and others he had never seen before now. Pinpoints of light orbited.

"Satellites," he thought, except a few didn't circle in a predetermined path. Some appeared to move under their own influence—not piloted from afar like unmanned spacecraft. These flew a circuitous path, as if unmindful of fuel dispensation. As if...

"Oh, shit!" Zane sputtered before skimming the upper canopy of oak trees on the far side of the field.

With tremendous effort, Zane swept his arms downward, trying to overcome inertia coursing through his tired limbs. "Come on, you fucker, climb!" Zane ascended slowly, grazing a few more branches along the way. Sweat poured from his face as he attempted to backtrack by turning starboard. Zane aimed for a gap that appeared between a stand of cedars along a barbwire fence line.

Oh shit!

Zane's right leg grazed a rusted point, shearing through denim like a razor. At the last second, he turned his forearms upward creating a windbreak. Zane's body went from horizontal to vertical in a split second. With his legs underneath, he came to halting stop on the ground. Amazed by the birdlike maneuver, Zane looked himself over for injuries, but thankfully found none. Unsheathing his arms, he bent and felt his leg.

Nasty scratch, but won't need stitches... Tetanus shot?

"All right!" Audie called as he came running. "Didn't look good there for a second, but you pulled your dick out just in time!"

"Yeah, gravity be damned," Hoyt said. "Impressive move...like a kestrel lighting on a fence post."

"Did yah see me flying?" Zane asked, his voice quaking, adrenaline still rushing. "It's like...like I knew what to do without really knowing how... And, the stars in the sky...so bright...so beautiful. I could see everything. I saw you all from miles away. Audie was racing back and forth, and you, Hoyt, just standing still, gazing up..."

"To hell with all that hippy dippy talk," Audie said, his impatience growing. "Shuck those wings already; I'm ready to go."

Chapter 12
Wing and a Prayer

"Oh shit," Zane grumbled, his entire body aching. "Hoyt, we got any aspirin?"

"Kitchen cabinet," a deep voice mumbled. "Leave the bottle out, will yah?"

"Me too..." another voice muttered.

Zane didn't know who said what. Tired and sore, he only wanted a shower and breakfast and nap until nightfall. For now, his life revolved around the wings and the thrill of supernatural flight. All other matters would wait until things settled, except there was a stack of unopened mail on the kitchen table. Unpaid bills and notices were piling up, and it wouldn't be long before the electric company dispatched a technician to remove their meter.

Hell! I don't wanna go to work...not now anyway...

Zane opened the fridge and observed a half-empty bottle of ketchup, a jar of desiccated mustard, and a tub of moldy potato salad. In the door were two eggs—cracked—and a tube of ointment for anal itching.

Oh, you gotta be kidding me!

Finding no water or anything else, Zane drank from the sink tap. Though the water was shy of lukewarm and had a sulfur taste, he drank from cupped hands, satiating a great thirst. He usually shunned the town water supplied from a murky reservoir, tinged green with algae during summer and reeking from manure throughout the year. This morning, he could have drunk muddy water from an old man's boot. His thirst slaked, Zane downed three aspirin and left the bottle on the table.

"Hoyt...Audie...got any money? We need fresh jugs for the water cooler, or we're gonna have to keep drinking from the tap. And, we need groceries...and pay some bills."

"Fuck sake!" Audie groaned, plodding into the kitchen. "All I got is three dollars and some loose change."

"I got a five and two ones," Hoyt called from the bedroom. "I bought groceries and cigarettes with my VA check a couple weeks back, but nothing else coming in until end of month."

"Well, you two are pathetic!" Zane snorted.

"Whadda you goin' on about?" Audie retorted. "At least, Hoyt and me have a tenner and change between us."

"Yeah…well, that's not gonna go far now, is it?"

Looking pale and disheveled, Hoyt came into the kitchen and plopped into a chair. He fumbled with the aspirin bottle a long while, trying to remove the childproof cap. After a minute, Audie grabbed the bottle, popped the cap with his thumb, and poured several ashen pills onto the tabletop.

"Thanks, Brother," Hoyt said, placing three aspirin in his mouth and chewing.

"Chrissakes, Hoyt," Audie said. "How do you stomach that? Drink some water, will yah?"

"I guess…" Hoyt replied, pushing up from the table. He rinsed a dirty coffee cup and filled it. After gulping several cups of water, he handed it to Audie, who did the same.

"Bone dry this morning," Hoyt said, smacking his mouth. "Some cold, clean water would be nice."

"How about taking me to the redemption center," Audie said. "I got a pile of bottles and cans we can sell. Probably get close to twenty bucks. And, Billy Tremont's been eyeing my carbine rifle. Might get eighty for it."

"I was hoping to nap today, but we gotta do something," Zane said, pausing. "Yah know…maybe we should figure something out?"

"Figure what?" Hoyt yawned.

"Well, we got these magic wings now," Zane began. "Maybe, we could make some money with 'em?"

"What…put on a show…give rides to the kiddies?" Audie opined. "Yah know the government would take 'em and put us away for shits and giggles."

"No, nothing like that, but maybe, we could do some stealing or something," Zane suggested. "It's not like you aren't a thief already."

"Hey! I don't steal from honest folk!" Audie countered. "I take shit from assholes, who probably stole it from someone else. I'm just taking stuff back, is all."

"Which by definition is stealing, isn't it?" Hoyt offered. "Anyhow, I'm not comfortable with the idea. As is, we're just learning to fly without crash landing. How are we gonna get away? And, how would we fence our stuff without drawing attention?"

"I can take care of that," Audie said. "I've been dealing with Earl Pomeroy at the pawn shop for years. He's got a lot more to lose if he got caught. Besides...I haven't been pinched for anything serious yet, so I'd get off light as a first offender."

"I wouldn't count on that, Little Brother. Except for the magic wings, we have the lousiest luck," Hoyt said. "All right, just suppose...hypothetically...this is a good idea, what's our preferred merchandise? Cash...jewelry...? Remember, the wings don't allow us to carry much more than our own weight."

"Drug money," Zane said matter of fact. "Lots of dealing goin' on in Wheeler nowadays. I know of a dozen boys thereabouts, always carrying around a shitload of cash. Not like they're gonna go to the cops or anything."

"It's a terrible notion," Hoyt disputed. "Most likely, we'd get caught or killed. Worse yet, we'd lose the wings somehow."

"That would suck," Audie concurred. "I couldn't abide that."

"I wouldn't toss my idea in the crapper just yet," Zane said. "Just sayin'."

The brothers fell silent to ponder. Drinking tap water, Hoyt's face grimaced. Zane stared into the refrigerator, his haggard face illumined by the lamp. Audie's stomach rumbled. Suddenly, the house went dark. The utility company finally lost its patience.

Well, I suppose we can't argue with that. We try it out, and see what happens," Hoyt said, his countenance cloaked in gloom. "Not like we have better things to do."

"Good," Zane said. "I have a plan."

"Already?" Hoyt asked. "We just decided..."

"Wesley Bethel...he's our mark," Zane said. "Heard of him?"

"I know about him," Audie answered. "Black dude...big time dope dealer in Wheeler. He's got a storefront in the rundown mini mall off Luke and Bryant Streets. Lots of rich kids buying off him."

"That's the one. He's got retail space at both ends of the mall. Two kids always posted looking out for cops. Cameras everywhere..."

"Yeah, I've seen 'em in action," Audie said. "Customer pulls up behind the mall. Dealer checks 'em out. If they look okay, he tells 'em where to go. Never the same place... Bunch of teenagers ... First time offenders, if they get pinched. And, they never deal with Wesley, so no way to connect him."

"Yeah…instructed to lawyer up and keep their traps shut…or else," Zane said. "If they man up and do their penance, Wesley pays a bonus and retires 'em. If they go out on their own and deal anywhere near Wheeler, they usually disappear."

"Disappear, my ass," Audie said. "I hear his daddy raises hogs in Golinda. Big ole nasty hogs with a taste for meat."

"I wouldn't doubt that," Zane said. "Wesley's a mean bastard with smarts…deadly combination."

"Then, we take our time and plan this right," Hoyt said. "No jumpin' the gun on this one."

***

"I still think this is a dumbass idea," Hoyt said, staring at the nighttime scenery outside the truck window. "We're still not strong enough to stay airborne long, much less flying through a city landscape. Too many things can go wrong."

"Calm down, Big Brother," Audie soothed, gripping the steering wheel and maintaining a prudent speed. "Not like we have other options. Hell…the fridge is empty, and we ain't even got running water to flush a toilet. It's time we did something."

"Maybe…but I still don't like it," Hoyt mumbled. "Dammit, my clothes are gettin' awful rank."

"Tell me about it," Audie said. "Still, it's an awesome plan…you playing a hobo and all… I wish I was doing more than driving. You'll be right there in the thick of it."

"Not my idea of fun," Hoyt said flatly. "Not like I've ever been in a shootout before. I just hope I don't piss myself, or get Zane killed. This could go bad…awful quick."

"Hey, keep your voice down, will yah. Don't get Zane frettin' about this."

"I can hear everything you say!" Zane called out. "Keep talking shit, and I'll just fly away with the money!"

Huddled in the truck bed, Zane was antsy to reach their destination. For the past week, the brothers had reconnoitered Wesley Bethel's operation from afar. During the day, they spied on the strip mall through high-powered binoculars from a Piggly-Wiggly parking lot a couple blocks away. At night, Zane alternated between a dilapidated billboard and adjacent rooftop overlooking either side of the mall. Despite Wheeler's bright streetlights, Zane was a phantom, blending into the murky night like the blackest raven.

Even his brothers couldn't see him. Many times, he just circled above, shrouded in a smog of city lights.

Zane loved the nighttime outings. After much bickering, the brothers agreed that he should wear the wings in preparation for this raid, so he could increase his skill and endurance. After all, it had been his idea, and no one had offered a better scheme with a bigger payoff.

Last evening, Zane overheard a phone conversation—another benefit of the wings was a heightened sense of hearing. Wesley spoke with a man named Angie, who was scheduled to pick up a bag of *rags* tonight at eleven o'clock. Zane guessed *rags* was street slang for money. It seemed reasonable since he hadn't noticed a currency exchange yet.

With information in hand and their fortunes waning, the Harlan Brothers decided this was an opportune time. Unfortunately, they knew few details about Angie. Would others accompany him, and how many? Were they armed? Would Wesley have guards on his end? All Zane understood was that this was a routine handoff. He had sensed no tension in the conversation overheard.

***

The abandoned lot was empty as usual. Overgrown with weeds and strewn with trash, the industrial park was rundown. Once occupied by active businesses and warehouses, the place was a ghost town, especially at night. A few lingered like an auto body shop, a carpet cleaning company, and a metal recycler. A few buildings stored material for other outlying businesses. Others were nondescript with no signs or placards to give evidence of their purpose. Zane suspected a few illegal enterprises conducted their trade behind false facades, and the brothers steered clear of those establishments. The abandoned lot was an ideal place on the periphery. No traffic or security cameras were present to record their comings and goings.

"Here," Zane said hoisting the shopping cart out of the truck bed. "You all know the plan by heart. Just stick to it and keep your heads down."

With those few words, Zane shucked a blanket that concealed the wings. The appendages spread wide, trembling under a gray moon. Hoyt and Audie stood back and marveled. Hands on his hips and his chin out, Zane was an imposing figure despite his unshaven face, wrinkled tee shirt, and ragged jeans. He palmed the leather handgrips, crouched, and leapt. Zane disappeared into the night with nary a sound.

"That's, that," Hoyt said still staring into the inky sky. "Be ready, Brother."

With that remark, Hoyt loaded his cart, pulled his grimy sweatshirt hood over his head, and trundled away. Hoyt had spray-painted the plastic cart dark gray, oiled the wheels, and secured rattling parts. It rolled noiselessly over the rough ground. Beneath a pile of plastic bags full of rags, Hoyt had stowed his M14 rifle with scope and silencer. Under his jacket was a .45 caliber semi-automatic pistol.

For past days, Hoyt had pushed his cart along the streets. Dressed in dirty clothes and muttering unintelligibly, his outward appearance was that of a homeless man—not an entirely uncommon sight. Hoyt blended into the cityscape as if he wore a cloak of invisibility. People avoided eye contact. Only once, a police officer had stopped and warned him not to loiter long in one spot. Paying heed, Hoyt wheeled aimlessly, never lingering, searching for a position with a good line of sight.

Most likely tonight, Angie would come from Bryant Street, which was one-way, and park at the rear of the mini mall. Hoyt didn't expect the courier to dawdle—probably in and out. At the far corner of the mall was a dumpster near a cluster of oak and cedar. Hoyt wheeled into the trees, side stepping a large fire ant mound and a patch of thorny cacti. About one hundred and fifty feet away, Hoyt had a good vantage point with cover and protection. Nothing to do now but set up and wait.

Circling high above, Zane observed his older brother taking position while Audie parked nearby. He circled several times looking for police and bystanders. Except for Wesley's street dealers and a trickle of cars streaming down Luke Street, nothing appeared out of place. Dark cumulous clouds approached from the west. Zane sensed a thunderstorm from far off and hoped the courier kept to his schedule. Although the brothers had no way to communicate directly, they had discussed their plan at length and knew their specific roles, even what to do for contingencies.

Zane wavered on his approach to the billboard but held steady. At the last moment, he pulled up and hovered above his intended perch. His confidence buoyed after several nights of successive flights, Zane lighted on a narrow catwalk atop the placard. He crouched until his equilibrium stabilized. Grounded firmly, Zane relaxed and unclasped his hands. He checked a revolver secured to his chest holster. The hardwood grip was comforting in his palm. Although his heart pounded, Zane was calm. Holding out his arms, his hands and fingers were steady. Not a tremor stirred.

All right, you know what to do. Swoop in, wallop the courier, take the cash, and fly like hell. Hit and run...hit and run...

Zane fished a watch from his pocket. Nearly eleven o'clock, he observed a car turning onto Bryant Street. He recognized the long body of an Oldsmobile Delta 88 approaching unhurriedly. Zane reckoned its daytime color was dark crimson, but after sunset, it was a much darker shade like dried blood. Even from three blocks away, it was plain the owner took good care of his vehicle, which glinted under passing streetlamps. The car had a vinyl roof, ivory colored and newly polished. As if trying to arrive at a precise time, the driver crept along.

Zane palmed the leather grips and knelt in the lower corner of the billboard. Once emblazoned with an advertisement for Penelope Whiskey and Spirits, its backdrop was once charcoal gray. Now, the surface was tattered and sun-bleached but still dark enough to camouflage Zane's form. He noticed slight movement in the trees behind the dumpster. Hoyt had spotted the vehicle and was readying himself.

The car slowed by the trash container and lingered. Soon, it moved past and pulled alongside the curb outside a rear entrance to the mall. After a moment, the driver placed the vehicle in park and shutoff the engine. For several seconds, the car engine continued to diesel before stopping.

"Motherfucker," a man's low voice growled from inside the car.

The driver, presumably Angie, unlatched the door, which opened quietly on oiled hinges. Oddly, the car's interior light didn't brighten. Angie was a hulking form, broad and tall. He wore a fedora hat and a tan suede overcoat that looked uncomfortably warm on a summer night. His dress pants were crisp. Patent leather shoes glistened. Angie's dark face was clean-shaven. Large, black-framed eyeglasses set atop his wide nose. He held an attaché case in his right hand. His car keys dangled from his left.

"Gotta wait for the exchange," Zane whispered, his mind racing through varying scenarios. "Just wait."

The man looked in Zane's direction, seeming to stare directly at him. Zane froze, but didn't flinch, confident in his concealment. Angie was just checking his surroundings like anyone carrying around a bag of illegal drugs in a seedy neighborhood. Zane's vision was so keen he could see the man studying the billboard's faded advertisement. Angie turned and walked to a nondescript door— gunmetal gray with numerous dents. A single heavy-duty deadbolt stood out in contrast with its plain surface. Angie rapped the steel door with his knuckles and waited. A voice called out, words unintelligible, even for Zane's acute hearing.

"All's well on this summer's eve my brother," Angie said in a singsong manner.

The heavy door opened outward several inches, kept in check by a thick chain. An indistinct figure shuffled. The voices of two men, Wesley and Angie, spoke hushed words, but no pleasantries. There was an exchange of two cases of similar size and shading. Angie lingered a moment.

"Don't stand there, fool...do your thing!" the man barked from behind the door. "And, don't lose it, or you'll be a sorry muthafuckah."

"I hear yah," Angie replied. "Your green is safe and..."

The door closed on stout hinges. Wesley had not bothered to watch his courier return to his car. So routine a transaction, the men had become complacent, despite the amount of drugs and cash involved.

Zane didn't hesitate. Launching from his perch as silent as a great-horned owl, he glided downward, arms spread wide. At the last moment, he pulled up, his booted feet bashing the courier in the head. Zane stroked his arms downward and lighted on his feet. Releasing the hand grips, the wings folded against his back. Zane spun around, unholstering his pistol in a fluid motion. His eyes darted around, his other senses seeking movement and sound. Except for a drone of distant traffic from Interstate 35, it was quiet. No alarms had been raised.

Zane knelt, ready to grapple if his quarry was combative. The big man was prone and still. Zane pulled on the case, but it didn't yield since it was handcuffed to the man's wrist. Zane thought back to

Angie lingering at the door and an odd clicking sound, not realizing what the courier had done.

Oh, you gotta be shittin' me!

Thoughts raced through Zane's mind like a torrent. Adrenaline surging and heart pounding, he took a deep breath, never letting down his guard. His attention remained focused on his prey and his immediate surroundings. Straightaway, he calmed, and an obvious solution came to mind. Zane holstered his pistol and scooped a set of keys on the walk next to the man. Although he had never owned a set of handcuffs himself, Zane observed a stubby tubular key. Within seconds, he removed the case from the courier's thick wrist. Zane strapped it around his abdomen.

Glancing around, Zane crouched and launched skyward. He pumped his arms harder to offset the added weight. Soon after, he heard voices shouting in his wake but fading as he climbed higher and increased his distance. Zane adjusted course and circled high. He spied Hoyt making his way back where Audie waited in the truck.

Behind the strip mall, several young men raced up and down Bryant Street in search of Angie's assailant. Zane couldn't make out words, but he recognized Wesley's enraged voice barking orders and issuing threats. Zane felt a fleeting pang of sympathy for the courier. He leveled out and glided, trying to conserve his waning energy.

Far below, Hoyt threaded his way along a rehearsed path to his rendezvous point. As soon as his brother was aloft, Hoyt had retreated from his makeshift sniper position. He left nothing behind to reveal his identity, but the shopping cart, which he had wiped clean, and its load of anonymous rags.

Following a weaving periphery of vacant lots and wooded clusters, Hoyt avoided open areas and streetlamps. He appreciated his improved night vision. Each successive flight with the wings left remnant abilities such as heightened mental acuity, strength, and senses. Hoyt knew his brother wheeled high above, watching his back trail. Coming upon a narrow lane, he looked in both directions. Satisfied the way was clear, he whistled. Headlights appeared from across the way.

Pulling alongside, Audie said in a hushed voice, "I didn't hear shooting, so I assume we're good to go."

"Seems so, but we better hightail it," Hoyt replied, placing his gear in the back. "Streets are gonna be crawling soon."

94

Hunched over with his hands on his knees, Zane spat into the dust. He hung his head and closed his eyes. Drool spilled from his mouth as a wave of nausea caused his innards to churn. An immense exhaustion overwhelmed him. Unable to contain himself, Zane vomited. His abdomen tightened into a painful knot. He abhorred the sensation. Once triggered, there was no stopping it. Zane grunted and groaned in agony. Soon, the sickness subsided, and sweat oozed from every pore of his body. He straightened, his head clearing. As much as he coveted the wings, he was ready to relinquish them—probably Audie, since his turn was long in coming.

At the distant sound of tire tread on crushed limestone, Zane retreated to the brush and brambles alongside the dirt road. Soon, he recognized the vague outline of his truck and the familiar silhouettes of his brothers behind the windshield. Zane stepped out and waved his hand.

"There he is!" Audie called out, jumping out of the truck. "You all right? Did the big man put up a fight? Did yah get the money?"

"Yes…no…yes," Zane answered. "Here's the case. I haven't had a look yet."

"Well, let's take a look see!" Audie chuckled.

With the truck shutoff, darkness shrouded them. Hoyt retrieved a Coleman lantern. He pumped a knob to pressurize the fuel tank and turned a lever. A hissing sound issued. Hoyt ignited a wooden match by swiping it along the inside seam of his pant leg. He held the match to the wick, which ignited immediately. A harsh glare pushed aside the darkness.

Audie laid the leather carry bag on the hood and unzipped it. Atop a pile of stacked bills was a chrome-plated automatic pistol with walnut grips.

"Fancy pistola, huh?" Audie said, taking out the gun and two magazines. "Look at that moola!"

"Looks like Wesley had a good week…until tonight, that is," Hoyt observed. "Can't say I feel too bad about his loss though."

"Yeah…fuck him," Audie snapped. "Son of a bitch is lucky he just got fleeced. Save folks a lot of trouble if we just shot him instead."

"Lots of mixed bills here," Zane said. "Need to count this out on the kitchen table, but there's gotta be at least twenty-grand."

"More than enough to get square, and then some," Hoyt said. "Need to pay some bills and get groceries tomorrow."

"Yeah, I'll take care of the utilities, and you and Audie can go to the grocery store."

"Sounds good," Hoyt said. "Looks like someone needs to handoff the baton."

"Yeah…that little jaunt took the wind outta me," Zane agreed. "Audie, looks like you're up. Give me a hand, will yah?"

"Sounds good to me," Audie said, assisting with the wings. "I've been hankering to go flying."

"Still a while until sunrise," Hoyt said. "Go have some fun."

"Take care not to go far," Zane cautioned. "Really wears you down quick."

"No worries," Audie said, taking hold of the handgrips. "Should I take the money for safekeeping?"

"No need. We'll toss the cash if we run into trouble," Hoyt answered. "Besides, you don't need the extra weight."

"Okay then, see yah before sunrise."

Before he could reply, Hoyt's youngest brother disappeared. One moment he was there, and then, gone the next. "Damn! I'll never get used to that," Hoyt said, peering into the starry sky. "Like a banshee…"

"Can you drive, Hoyt? I'm not feeling so good."

"My driver's license expired a while back."

"Yeah, so didn't my truck tags," Zane replied. "As long as you remember how to drive a manual shift, just check your speed and watch where you're goin'."

"Will do," Hoyt said, still searching the sky.

Chapter 13
Raptor's Delight

Rain parted as Audie flew headlong through the storm. Hoyt had advised against tonight's flight, but Audie was having none of it. It was his turn, and he wouldn't be dissuaded. Besides, Zane had flown in worse weather and was barely wet afterwards. The wearer of the wings was impervious to the elements. Heat and humidity, rain and damp, inclement conditions didn't bother, not even pounding rain or pelting hail.

At the outset, the rush of air stole the flyer's breath, but after multiple flights, centrifugal forces lessened, allowing the brothers to arc, dive, and somersault with little affect. No belly bumps or rushing of blood to the extremities. Fighter pilots of the world's most sophisticated aircraft would have been envious.

Bolts of lightning brightened the night sky. Audie had a close-up view of an awesome natural spectacle. He hovered as black cumulous clouds boiled in the farthest reaches of the atmosphere. The hair on his head and arms stood on end as another volley of lightning streaked past. Audie was unafraid, certain of his invincibility, protected by powerful supernatural forces bestowed by his magic wings.

Audie spied a banshee. Formless and aimless, the shape appeared as a coal-black bed sheet lifted skyward by a gust of wind. Most times, they remained far off, but occasionally, one crossed his path. Circling far below, it rose, raised by a vortex of currents. Audie floated in the stream as he gauged the entity's progress. He would make no physical contact, but he wanted a closer look. Soon, it whipped past and continued rising. Audie pursued in widening circles. Silent and aloof, the thing stayed out of reach as he tried to overtake it.

It's aware of me but won't let me near. Lightning doesn't show anything. What the hell are they? Wait a sec'.

The shape hesitated allowing Audie to close the distance. Fifty feet away, he matched its speed and observed a quivering black mass. As if a miner excavated a solid piece of darkness from the deepest mine and brought it above ground, it reflected or absorbed no light as it undulated, one moment, spreading wide and thin like a ragged blanket then coming together.

Audie experienced overlapping emotions of fear, loathing, and sorrow. Heart pounding, adrenaline streaming, Audie wanted to flee from the powerful feelings, but he stayed his course. He wanted to know what the banshee was—of its purpose. Was it an exiled soul left to wander in the clouds pondering an immoral life from long ago? Did it interact with others of its own kind? Could Audie send it a simple mental greeting?

Hey there. My name is Audie.

The entity answered with a rapid procession of images. It was a masculine presence, a man, who had lived more than a century ago. Audie envisioned a hardscrabble existence, murderous Indians and banditos, laborious farm work, raising pigs... Audie felt the searing heat of endless Texas days. A widower with several daughters raised in frontier desolation. An incestuous father condemned to a cloudy purgatory with an abundance of time to contemplate.

Suddenly, the shape darted upward at an impossible speed—faster than Audie could ever achieve, even in steep dive. The banshee disappeared into the high cumulous. Audie looked for others but saw none. The emotions and images stopped entirely, leaving Audie slightly ill. He folded the wings and dove.

Cool air caressed his face. Before the ground drew too near, Audie opened and turned his arms. Feathered appendages caught the air and slowed his descent as efficiently as falcon wings. Leveling off, he scanned the fields for interesting sights. A herd of cattle huddled along a length of barbwire fence. Water sieved off soaked hides. Tails twitched at imagined flies. An armadillo forded a shallow creek bed that was dry much of the year. Thousands of roosting birds hardly noticed as Audie skimmed the treetops.

Ahead, he recognized the blue tin roof of the Bell Ridge Baptist Church. He lighted atop the church steeple and hunched. Audie stretched his arms and flexed his forearms and biceps. With no prompting, the wings raised and spread, creating a canopy. Water repellent feathers deflected the downpour. Except for a mild dankness, Audie was warm and comfortable. He shivered at the sensation of being sheltered from the violent thunderstorm inches away. Though fierce, the wind scarcely buffeted.

The cemetery below and beyond the church was a surreal landscape of tilted tombstones, hoary cedar, and ancient oak. The wind whipped through the thick branches. Horizontal sheets of rain blew. Heavy droplets pounded muddied puddles. Audie gazed at his Daddy's grave. A brown stone was set in a concrete piling. A simple epitaph, *Loving Father*, was etched below his father's name. A rivulet of rain dribbled down the stone face and spread across the sodden ground.

Unexpectedly, the pall diminished as a ghostly mist, imbued with the colors of infinite stars, wafted through the air. Though Audie could see through the darkest nights, a strange twilight permeated the cemetery, like a theater projector showing a film against a rainy backdrop. A fathomless melancholy came over Audie when a slight figure emerged from the dark fringes. The silhouette of a petite woman sauntered above the ground. She stopped at a gravestone. Carved into the marker was the name, *Kelsey A Blanchard, Beloved Husband and Brave Soldier*, and his birth and death dates, *January 19, 1895 – October 13, 1918*.

The lady wore formal attire, suited for church services. A dark, tight fitting jacket accentuated a long skirt. She had swept her hair into a bun and covered her head with a wide-brimmed hat. She knelt near the earth and bowed over as if weeping. Audie sensed grief and loneliness. Her emotions once so powerful in life that a daily sojourn to her husband's grave played out again and again.

No living human had ever witnessed her mourning ritual. A hollow in the ground marked where *Kelsey A Blanchard*'s casket had collapsed years ago. However, the gravestone lacked a name for the heartbroken woman. Perhaps, she had remarried and raised a family and was now interred elsewhere. Regardless of this woman's circumstances, her sorrow had carried from The Great Beyond. Audie felt pity for her later husband. There was little doubt in his mind she had pined for her first love even as her post-widower life played out to its fruition.

For many, grief was a creek flowing a moderate distance to an endless sea. Once arrived, the mournful feelings dissipated. For others, the creek meandered, taking longer to reach the ocean, with time, their grief becoming more dissolute. And, for a few, sorrow was a desert creek sieving into a briny lake. With no other place to go, unrequited emotions simmered. If fortunate, a springtime flood might soften, but the sun always came back and returned the lake to a salt plain. It was a pitiless cycle.

Plagued much of his young life, Audie was intimately familiar with despair. The emotion infused his every breath. So pervasive, people had shunned him. He had hated his pitiful life. So much so, he had considered death a cure for its unrelenting stranglehold. Except now, he had the wings, which gave him power and purpose— though he had yet to figure out exactly what to do with them. For now, his apportioned nighttime flights were enough to experience what others could only dream of.

***

Thunderstorms relenting, the moon hung overhead peering through thinning clouds. The wings had shorn the rain. Preened and oiled, the feathers glimmered in the moonlight. Audie was a vague silhouette against a starry backdrop. The bright lights of Wheeler came nearer with each stroke of Audie's muscular arms. In recent months, there had been a crime wave of sorts due to gang activity. Illicit drug dealing was rampant, spawning other criminal acts. Local police were seemingly powerless to stem the epidemic.

Most disturbing was the recent disappearance of Becky Zephyr, a young woman, from Marlboro. Hoyt had gone to grade school with her. She was the seventh victim in a series occurring in Feral County over the past three decades. Since the abductions had taken place years apart, and the victims' bodies never recovered, the police had only recently considered the possibility of a serial killer running amuck. Now, Texas Rangers were dredging up records, canvassing the region, and interviewing family members.

The Harlan Brothers made a pact to help, but they didn't really know how to use their supernatural abilities in this endeavor. For now, they searched rural byways, read the thoughts of solitary travelers, and sniffed the countryside for unmarked graves. At the same time, they thought it prudent not to ask questions of others, lest suspicions point in their direction. The brothers sought to avoid the scrutiny of police since they already had a dubious reputation. It was best that law enforcement focus on a lone murderer instead of three odd brothers.

Audie alighted atop a billboard sign that advertised big deals at the *Double Decker Pawn Shop* located at 2061 Alexander Avenue. Although it seemed a conspicuous place for a man wearing wings to perch upon, the lights cast upon the placard created a shadowy void above and behind the sign. Audie wondered if anyone would take notice of him even in plain sight. Another of the wings magical traits was the ability to camouflage the wearer. Audie had taken dozens of Polaroid photos of his brothers donning the wings, and not one showed a clear image. In fact, his brothers were nothing but smudged reflections.

It was three o'clock in the morning, and except for an occasional hum of traffic on Interstate 35, it was quiet on Alexander Avenue. The street wound through a mile or more of dilapidated warehouses on its west end, cloistered neighborhoods in between, and rundown storefronts closer to the highway. Audie watched a particular house.

Sided with salt and pepper colored asbestos shingles, it was an ordinary looking dwelling. Unlike neighboring homes, its windows were shaded. The only light was a yellowish bulb illumining the front stoop and a doorbell button. If the owner had a vehicle, it was parked in either the attached garage or elsewhere.

Closing his eyes and tilting his head, Audie listened. A murmuring of voices carried from the house. He couldn't discern actual words. A blaring television masked intelligible conversation. Audie heard muffled sounds from the back of the house. His mind filtered out the ambient noise, isolating the sounds he wanted to hear. He heard heavy breathing, grunts, and curses.

Someone's having a good time…

Audie felt a feminine psyche, who was an unwilling participant—someone subjugated into submission by feeding a heroin addiction. Fear, loathing, and shock reverberated through his inner being as he empathized with the poor woman held in this place for several days now.

"You done with that bitch yet?" a man called from the living room. "I'd like to rip me off a piece before I make this drop. Angel's gonna be pissed if we're late again."

"Yeah, yeah, hold your dick, I ain't done yet," another man replied from a bedroom at the back of the house. "Besides, you may wanna wait until she's awake. She could use a shower."

"Oh, fuck that shit, man! I'm outta here. Maybe, you could get Rita back here. She's good for blowjobs too, unlike that bitch."

"I hear that."

A minute later, the garage door rose on noisy rollers. No lights revealed the interior, but Audie discerned the shadowy form of a large man. In one hand, he held a paper grocery bag. He stepped into the driveway and sauntered to the street. He looked around and then headed north on foot.

Audie searched the street for others, but he saw no one else. He vaulted from the billboard and swooped down in pursuit. Perhaps, sensing someone following, the man turned in time to see a work boot slamming into his face. Audie straddled the big man's inert body and reached for the bag. As expected, it was full of cash—stacked in thousand-dollar bricks.

Jesus...must be twenty thousand or more!

Wasting no time, Audie cinched the bag to his waist and donned a pair of leather gloves. He turned and ran to the house in exaggerated leaps. Audie heard two men laughing inside. Looking overhead, he followed the electric service entrance cable. In a single leap, Audie landed near the corner of the house and ripped the meter from its socket. The home's interior went dark. Back at the front entrance, Audie tore a flimsy screen door from its hinges and kicked the main door with the flat of his heel. The wings opened instinctively providing balance. The reinforced metal door buckled but didn't open straightaway. Audie kicked twice more. The deadbolts shattered, and the heavy door flew inward. The wings closed against Audie's back as he entered the house.

"What the fuck!" a man's voice roared.

Two men scrambled in the darkness. One man wearing nothing, but underwear brandished an automatic pistol, pointing in the general direction of the front door. From Audie's perspective, the men moved with an unnatural slowness. Audie stepped aside as the gun discharged. He saw the bullet, even its spinning rifling as it sped past. Not hesitating, he rushed ahead and kicked. The armed man crashed into the wall. Audie reached out with his right hand and covered the other man's face with splayed fingers. With surprising strength, Audie lifted the much larger man from the floor and threw him down against a heavy hardwood coffee table that cracked and splintered.

In the aftermath, it was silent, except for Audie's pounding heart. He listened for the sounds of others and heard someone in a back room, fearful and cowering. Audie also sensed a buzzing outside the house as neighbors roused. He hurried to the bedroom.

"It's okay, ma'am," Audie called out in a low voice. "These assholes aren't gonna hurt you anymore. I'm gonna come in, okay?"

Chapter 14
Wicked Creatures

"Twenty-eight thousand and change," Zane said, tallying up the money absconded by Audie. "Pretty good haul, huh?"

"Like taking candy from a dead baby," Audie added. "Assholes scrambling around in the dark and bumpin' into shit. I laid into 'em real good. Didn't know what hit 'em. Big guys too... I couldn't believe how easy it was."

The brothers milled around a rubbish barrel in the backyard feeding broken branches to the flames. An odor of burning plastics clung in the balmy air.

"You actually saw the bullet in midair?" Zane asked. "That must have been something."

"If it wasn't for the poor girl you rescued, I'd say it was a fool thing to do," Hoyt interrupted. "In case you haven't noticed, we're not bullet proof. We're still mortal."

"Aw...don't go pissin' on my parade, will yah. It was a good score. Except for those assholes gettin' the beat down they deserved, no one got hurt. And, that poor girl couldn't have been more than sixteen. They would've killed her for sure," Audie defended. "Besides, the police got nothin'...no witnesses, no evidence. They'll never pin this one on us."

"I wouldn't say *never*," Hoyt cautioned. "Police have all kinds of forensics nowadays. Boot imprint on the door you kicked in...a strand of your blond hair...a droplet of blood...even sweat... I need you to do something."

"Yeah, what's that?" Audie snapped.

"Gather and burn everything you wore last night—boots included," Hoyt said. "I know it sounds pointless, but I'm not asking."

"All right, all right," Audie conceded. "I'll toss everything in the rubbish barrel."

"Anyhow, I can't fault you for what you did, but you gotta be careful," Hoyt explained. "You're too quick on the draw. You just can't go kicking in doors without thinking it through. Maybe in this case, you should have called the police?"

"Maybe…but I don't think the girl would have thought so," Audie said. "For her, I think a minute in that place felt like forever."

Rubbing his shaven face, Hoyt reconsidered his brother's rationale. "I understand, Audie," he said. "I guess I would have done the same."

"Damn right, you would have," Zane spoke. "I can't say what we're doing is right, but we have to do whatever we can, whenever we can. Otherwise, we're just low life thieves not deserving of such powers. As far as I know, angels are supposed to do good."

"Well, that's not necessarily true all of the time," Hoyt said. "Since we still don't know the providence of the wings, I've been reading at the library."

"You actually got a library card?" Audie chuckled.

"Yeah, I gotta library card. I'm not illiterate, yah know. I like to read."

"Shuddup, Audie, will yah," Zane scolded. "What did you find out, Big Brother?"

"Seems there's all kinds of angels. Good ones, bad ones, and some in between," Hoyt explained. "From what I've heard and read, GOD made 'em before humans to do his bidding. After a while, some of 'em got jealous because HE gave us more attention. Even the devil was once an angel before he started mouthing off, and GOD threw him outta heaven. There are others, not as well known as Lucifer but still awful in their own way. They're kinda stuck on earth, so they mess with us like whispering in our ears and filling our heads with wicked thoughts. Although humans are inherently good…mostly…we're prone to sin. Yah know…envy, greed, wrath. Now imagine some archangel inside your head swaying you to act against your better judgment."

"If that's true, imagine the world without those sadistic bastards?" Zane said. "I know I've heard those voices."

"We should take care not to blame them entirely," Hoyt supposed. "Otherwise, it would excuse all of our bad behaviors."

"Like you finger bangin' Sue Curley in the backyard, Zane!" Audie laughed. "Man…that must have been one wicked angel!"

"Shuddup, Audie!"

"You shuddup!"

"Fuck you, Audie!"

"No…fuck you!"

"All right, boys, calm down the both of you... You all are like two possums fightin' over a chicken bone," Hoyt interrupted. "Anyhow, Audie tell us what you saw at the graveyard."

"Like I told yah earlier, I've been seeing weird things," Audie explained. "Spirits and such."

"You've been seeing 'em too!" Zane exclaimed. "I thought I was just seeing things but didn't wanna say anything until I knew for sure."

"Yeah, yeah," Audie said. "Sometimes, it's shadow people flying through the air. Scared the shit outta me the first time one of 'em flew across my path."

"So, we've seen disembodied figures during our night jaunts," Hoyt said. "Sometimes, ghostlike and human, and sometimes, like a black mass."

"Yeah, that's right," Zane replied. "First time for me was at Brazos Falls. I lighted on the sandbar below the Falls, and there he was...a black boy standing on the spillway."

"Yeah...so?" Audie said. "Someone's always fishin' off the spillway at night."

"This was earlier in the spring," Zane explained. "Remember the storm mid-April that flooded the bottomlands?"

"Yeah."

"It was the third night into the storm...about two or three in the morning," Zane said. "Wind blowin'...riverbank overflowin'. Well, here's this boy, probably about eight...seven years old...up to his waist. Just sorta wading through the river like he was ankle deep in a puddle, except the current was strong enough to bowl over a locomotive. Well hell, you know how the Falls are when there's a flood."

"He's right," Hoyt said. "There's no wading across the Falls even after a sprinkle. What happened?"

"I just reacted...thinkin' this kid was gonna drown for sure. I flew over to him not knowin' how I was gonna haul him out. Anyways, I'm hovering in front of him flapping my arms really hard hoping he might grab hold, and he acts like I'm not even there."

"Maybe, it was too dark?" Audie surmised. "Middle of the night, and it was stormin' hard."

106

"That's what I thought until he walked right through me," Zane said. "I'm not ashamed to say I pissed myself. Like a winter chill seeped into my body. Took me all morning in bed to warm up again."

"Where the boy go?" Hoyt asked.

"He kept walking across the spillway and vanished. One moment, he's there; the next, he's gone."

"Yeah, spirits don't seem to take notice for some reason," Audie opined. "It's like watching someone in a movie. If you go to Jellison Park about two o'clock in the morning, you'll see a guy walking a dog."

"What's so strange about that?" Hoyt asked.

"He's not so much walking but kinda drifting along, his feet not touching the ground at all. He and the dog both. Seen 'em six times, same place, same time. Last time, I was so close I could have reached out and tapped him on the shoulder."

"What did he look like?" Hoyt asked, "Did you recognize him?"

"A white man dressed in a fancy suit and bowler hat from olden days," Audie offered. "The dog was a terrier like Toto from The Wizard of Oz. They kinda shimmered…colors all washed out. I suspect they'd be invisible in daylight. Probably why most ghosts are only seen at night… I don't think they're really aware of us at all."

"Residual hauntings," Hoyt said. "I think that's what they call it." "Yeah, that's right," Zane chimed. "No intelligence, or maybe, we're not interesting enough to take notice of."

"Well, that's a big relief for me," Hoyt said. "I've had a clear head these last few months, so I was worried about my mental health."

"No worries, Hoyt," Audie assured. "Zane and me noticed how well you been doin'."

"Yeah," Zane concurred. "Smart as a whip…"

"Thanks for saying," Hoyt said, scuffing a fire ant mound in the dusty grass. "Anyone seen the other things?"

"The Tasmanian Devils?" Audie spoke. "The critters that scuttle from shadow to shadow?"

"Tasmanian Devils?" Hoyt asked.

"Yeah, that's what I call 'em," Audie answered. "They kinda move like whirligigs when they get upset."

"Yeah, I've seen those," Zane replied. "I give 'em a wide berth."

"Mostly when the moon isn't as bright, or when there's lots of cloud cover, huh?" Audie said. "My last time out was real bad. I was flying over the Brazos near Hart when I landed on a sandbar to take a leak. Real gloomy that night. So, there I am with my cock hanging out, trying to prime my bladder when a black shape appears on the far bank."

"Any outline?" Hoyt asked.

"Not really," Audie answered. "Mostly a black smudge...blacker than night."

"Anything happen?" Zane asked.

"At first, it just hung around—that is, until it sensed me staring at it," Audie said. "It's tough to explain, but it was fidgeting like it wanted to attack but couldn't get a full measure of me. It kinda paced side to side making a sound like a cat clawing a scratching post. Made the hairs on my head stand up straight, I'll tell yah."

"Did it come after you?" Zane probed. "I had one come right at me."

"Not then," Audie replied. "I was so surprised, I ended up pissing on my pant leg. When that happened, I got real angry and started cussing and throwing rocks at the thing. Must have spooked it because it hightailed into the mesquite. I winged it outta there in a hurry. Haven't been back to that stretch of the river since. Still have no idea what the hell those things are, and it makes me uneasy knowing they've always been out there—unseen, unheard... Sometimes, I wonder if I would have been better off not knowing at all."

"Whatever they are, I agree they're wicked creatures," Hoyt surmised. "Like you, I can't even guess their purpose, but it's gotta be sinister. It's obvious humans aren't supposed to know of 'em. Probably best not look at 'em straight on until we learn more."

"Sounds reasonable," Zane said. "We should keep track of everything out of the ordinary and report back."

"You mean other than strapping on magic wings and stealing from drug dealers," Audie retorted. "I don't know about you, but I don't think we'll be seeing *ordinary* again anytime soon."

"All right then, just report anything that could be dangerous," Hoyt said.

Chapter 15
Birth of the Thinker

The house was calm and quiet given the lateness of the morning. Although the air conditioner had not run through the night, the air felt cool and clean as if still shrouded in nighttime shadow. Hoyt swung his long legs over the side of the bed, stretched his arms, and yawned. He wiped his whiskered face and reached for his cigarettes. Realizing the pack was empty, he sighed, but his nicotine addiction did not flare. Hoyt's stomach growled from hunger pangs, and his mouth salivated at the thought of bacon, eggs, toast, and coffee.

After breakfast and reading the morning paper, Hoyt took a shower. He lingered as hot water coursed down his back. Having been on anti-psychotic drugs for the past several months, his mind had been languid, no focus of thought, just an overwhelming sense of mental and physical fatigue, and sexual urges had ceased altogether. As he stood under the showerhead, blood flowed. Hoyt stepped back letting the water spray against his stiffening member.

Carnal thoughts flickered in his mind. He thought of Regina and imagined her lithe body lying on his rumpled bed, her luscious pelvis thrusting in unison with his own. She moaned and whispered hoarsely in his ear, telling him to pound harder and faster. Hoyt touched himself with a soaped hand.

"Regina…you're so beautiful…" he panted. "I could love you all night… Oh…!"

With that single bodily release, it was as if a switch had been flipped in his mind, innumerable circuits bridging at once. Random at first but coalescing in logical sequences, a torrent of thoughts streamed. Hoyt wondered how Regina and her girls were doing, and if her no good husband was gone from their lives for good. He thought about the possibility of a cracked distributor cap in his old truck. Hoyt speculated how the phases of the moon affected the wings vitality, how cloud cover didn't diminish their strength, and how he could document this phenomenon. In his head, Hoyt graphed the correlation of physical conditioning and lunar pull…

"Gotta get a pencil and paper," he muttered, toweling off. "Full moon next time out for me."

After hours of manic scribbling, Hoyt settled back in his chair and stared at the sheets of paper littering the kitchen table. A multitude of geometric patterns and complex formulas rose from the pages, theories and inventions that could help humanity if someone other than him could explain to the right people…someone credible with a sterling academic background…

"Aw, hell…" Hoyt muttered. "Maybe if I think on it some more."

As an afterthought, Hoyt rummaged in his bedroom closet. In the deepest recesses, he found an heirloom of sorts. Hoyt hefted a short sword. Rumored to be a Confederate Calvary sword from the Civil War, the Harlan Family had passed it down for generations in a deteriorating condition. The brass pommel and hand guard had a patina like an old penny. The wire-wrapped leather handle was weathered and cracked, the blade pitted and corroded, and its edge dulled and gouged in several places. Most noticeable, the sword was broken two feet from the hilt.

The sabre lacked any value as a collectable. Hoyt's daddy had also brandished it over the years clearing brush around the yard, further diminishing its worth. Since his father's death, Hoyt acquired the antique with hopes of refurbishing it. Regrettably, the sword was beyond salvaging as a relic. Instead, Hoyt mounted a steel vise to the kitchen table and positioned the blade between the jaws with wood blocks. He grasped a file and commenced a long, arduous chore.

Hours later, a passable sword tip emerged. Hoyt changed files at regular intervals until he reached the finest one in his box. Metal filings and oily rags covered the kitchen table. Such a task was extremely tiresome, but for Hoyt, it had been a relaxing exercise—a chance to clear his head and meditate. Although there was little he could do with the gouged blade, he intended to restore a sharpened edge. It wouldn't be pretty, but it would be a deadly implement worthy of winged men. Hoyt held the weapon aloft and looked down the length of the short blade.

"Look at that," Audie said, walking into the kitchen. "Sounded like cicadas buzzing in here all morning."

"Yeah, I needed something mindless to do," Hoyt said. "Seems like I've been inside my head a lot lately."

"Haven't we all," Audie replied. "Probably a good thing though, don't yah think? We're usually runnin' off at the mouth more than listening."

"Where's Zane at?"

"Oh...he's buying a new outfit," Audie said. "He wants to look his best for the ladies tonight. You should go with him."

"Nah...I don't wanna," Hoyt said. "I'll just hangout here in case you have trouble."

"You gotta get out there, Big Brother. You haven't done much since the Army. These wings are gonna make us rich, so you better get used to being fat and happy."

"I don't know about that. I'm awful scared for us," Hoyt cautioned. "We're up to our noses in filthy water, and something bad is gonna speed past in a boat and make waves."

"To hell with that... I'm gonna have fun for as long as it lasts," Audie snapped. "You need to get out there and enjoy it too. Otherwise, Zane's gonna bring home a couple of ladies to pop your cherry."

"Aw...I took care of that long ago."

"Your hand don't count, Hoyt. You need to have nooky with an actual girl."

"You're full of shit," Hoyt sputtered. "You should get ready. It's nearly twilight."

"Seriously, we're not done talking about this," Audie said as he climbed a custom-built ladder in the kitchen cupboard. "I know you love to fly—we all do—but you gotta do more. We need a business of sorts."

"Business? What are you goin' on 'bout now?"

"Earl's Pawnshop," Audie said. "Yah know...the one where you bought your Marlin rifle."

"You mean the dingy place in Wheeler off Biloxi Boulevard?"

"Yeah, that's the one. Seems Earl's gettin' decrepit and wants to sell. We could buy his building and inventory at a steal if we move fast. Yah know...make him a cash offer."

As he helped his little brother don the wings, Hoyt deliberated about the pawnshop. He and his brothers were flush with cash, and a small business could offer legitimate cover. Besides, the Harlan Brothers were collectors—a hereditary trait of their father. Unfortunately, their treasures were generally of little worth and usually traded up or sold for quick cash. Many of Audie's items held dubious provenance, increasing the likelihood of arrest and incarceration.

"Yah know, Audie, that isn't the worst idea in the world. Better than most of your other money-making schemes. Have you floated it past Zane yet?"

"Not yet," Audie said. "He's quick to shoot down my ideas before I even have a chance to explain."

"Yeah…Zane could be more open-minded," Hoyt concurred. "Anyhow, I'm sure he'd consider the idea. If you like, we could sit him down and make a case. Between the two of us, we could convince him. If not, we could beat the shit outta him until he gives in."

"Yeah, let's do it! Beat the shit outta him…that is…" Audie said. "Well, I'm off. Don't wait up for me."

Turning off the back light, Audie peered outside, searching for curious eyes. Fortunately, most of their neighbors were elderly and not prone to go out after sunset. Many were settled in dim living rooms with curtains drawn, watching television. Other than the sound of dogs barking from the next block, it was quiet. After a hot summer day, the evening air was balmy, uncomfortable for sitting out. Audie's heightened senses indicated no attention in his direction. Leaping across the yard, he paused in the shadows before launching skyward.

After cleaning up the kitchen, Hoyt grabbed a pitcher of ice-tea and sat on the front porch swing. Except for the distant sound of a barking dog, Cobb Street was silent. Since the incident with Nate Nash, the town's animal control officer had gathered up the feral Calico cat and her kittens from under Mrs. Sanchez's porch. Hoyt missed the felines, but recognized it was the sensible thing to do, especially with the countless strays already wandering the streets of Marlboro.

"Not too bad of an evening," a thin man spoke from the sidewalk, spectacles glinting in the dull moonlight.

"Pleasant evening, actually," Hoyt said. "How are you, Pete?"

"Pretty good," he replied. "Just mindin' my business."

"That's tough to do around here. Want some ice-tea? I'm sure I have a clean glass somewhere."

"Sure, if it's no problem."

"Pull up a lawn chair and relax," Hoyt said. "I'll be right back."

Pete Vose settled into a rickety chair and looked around as if noticing the fresh paint and new gutters on the front of the house.

112

"Here yah go," Hoyt said, filling the glass from a pitcher. "Sun-brewed this afternoon."

"Thank you much."

"Say…we haven't really talked since the dust up, have we?" Hoyt inquired.

"Nope…we haven't," Pete replied.

"I've been meaning to make amends with the neighbors."

"I've seen you out and about. You're doing a lot better."

"I am," Hoyt said, rocking on the porch swing. "Can't say I remember much from that day, but I recall you conducted yourself well…standing up to Nate and getting me to stop wailing on him. I shouldn't say this, but I really wanted to kill him. If you hadn't sprayed me with the hose, no tellin' what might have happened."

"You, me, and a whole lotta other folks," Pete said. "Nate's a terrible bully…an all-around American asshole. Neighborhood's glad to be rid of him. Just too bad Regina and the girls got caught up in it."

"Yeah, it's tough to see the *Auction* sign on the lawn," Hoyt sighed. "Any idea where she and the girls ended up?"

"You don't know?"

"Nah…I figured it best to leave her be, but I'm still curious," Hoyt said. "Nate's still in jail, I hope?"

"He is, but no tellin' how long. The judge was way too lenient in my opinion, but the son-of-a-bitch hadn't ever been arrested before—surprisingly. Hopefully, he'll leave 'em alone," Pete answered. "By the way, she and the girls are living in Timpson. Not sure where exactly. I hear she's working at a laundromat."

"That's good to hear," Hoyt said. "Just wish I knew how I could atone for what I did…how to help…"

"You did more than you think. He was always raging at her and the girls. I think it was a matter of time before he killed her," Pete said. "If you think you need to do more, I'll keep my ears open about Nate. He's supposed to keep away, but I doubt he'll mind a restraining order."

"You have a way to keep tabs on him?"

"I know someone, who knows someone else…but reliable info," Pete admitted. "I could even find out when Nate last took a shit."

"If you don't mind, I'd like to know when he's supposed to be let out," Hoyt said. "Between you and me…"

"I'll do that," Pete said, looking around. "Mrs. Sanchez still visiting relatives in Port Lavaca?"

"She is, so say what you want."

"There's something I've been wondering about."

"What's that?"

"Since you've been back, you and your brothers are different somehow. I've never seen your house and yard look so good. Whole street's been noticing too," Pete confided. "We think it's great, but real curious why."

Hoyt took a moment to consider a plausible reason not involving magic wings. "As you probably guessed, I was suffering through serious mental health issues. Keeping to myself...never goin' out...speaking gibberish... Anyhow, my trip to the loony bin shocked me back to reality...along with antipsychotic drugs... Since then, I've been more motivated. Seems to have rubbed off on my brothers too. I'm drawing VA disability, Audie's been doing ranch work, and Zane got a pay raise. Not perfect, but we're trying."

"That's good to hear. You boys deserve to get your lives on track. Too much melancholy goin' 'round," Pete said, then pausing. "I hear you boys helped settle a few squabbles."

"Well, Audie got Henry Luce to stop mowing his grass at five o'clock in the morning, which Mrs. Anderson appreciated. Let's see...Zane got Reggie Folsom to stop peeling rubber and racing up and down the street. Larry Wiley's boys stopped bullying the other neighborhood kids," Hoyt said, listing from memory. "In Larry's case, it took firm persuasion on Audie's part to get him to deal with his boys."

"Larry's always been difficult," Pete said. "How did Audie convince him to control his boys?"

"Audie was courteous and patient. He explained how being bullied damages a child's self-esteem, and how they can carry those feelings into adulthood."

"Really?" Pete said unconvinced. "I've known Larry Wiley for a several years, and I have a hard time thinkin' he'd be swayed by psychology talk."

"Probably not," Hoyt confessed. "Maybe, because Audie threatened to haul Larry into the street, pull down his pants, and take a switch to his buttocks."

"But...Larry's like six foot two and well over two-hundred pounds?" Pete said incredulously. "Audie's tough and wiry, but probably, a hundred pounds lighter."

"Well...it must have been psychology talk then," Hoyt said with a wink. "Doesn't matter as long as nobody got beat up and spanked in public, does it?"

"No, guess not..."

"Are you havin' any issues with someone?"

"Uh...well...Rick Sherman's been making nasty comments. Saying things about my manhood... I don't deny being a confirmed bachelor, if you know what I mean, but I mind my business...pay my taxes...try to be a good neighbor and everything," Pete stammered. "Hell! I'm a retired Marine... Got shot up at Guadalcanal for Chris sakes! I don't think Rick Sherman of all people should be calling me such names, especially with other people around. I may be too old and decrepit to use my fists, but I still got my pride. GOD knows I killed enough Japanese during the war, so I wouldn't have any problem whatsoever putting him down with my Colt, and prison wouldn't bother me in the least!"

"Geesh...I've never seen you so worked up before," Hoyt said. "Mind you, all your neighbors think kindly of you, including me and my brothers. Folks on Cobb Street don't judge others, at least, be outright rude. Rick Sherman's just a redneck asshole, who hasn't done anything since his high school football days, except empty dumpsters."

"I'm glad you said that, Hoyt," Pete said, taking out a handkerchief and wiping his nose. "That means a lot."

"No worries, Pete," Hoyt soothed. "Rick Sherman will mind his manners after tomorrow. Polite talk should take care of it, but if he's insincere, I'll know it."

"Thanks, Hoyt. I'd appreciate that."

"Here's to the United States Marine Corps," Hoyt toasted, raising his glass, "and fuck Rick Sherman, and the horse he rode into town on."

Chapter 16
Pawnshop Blues

"So, are we agreed on price?" Zane asked. "Building and stock, per the current inventory list?"

"You got it," Earl concurred. "As soon as we settle up and sign the paperwork."

"And, we can keep the store name for as long as we want," Audie iterated.

"As long as you boys run a reputable business, you can keep my name on the placard as long as you want. I don't wanna bother redoing the paperwork, so we'll make it a gentlemen's agreement."

"Sounds good," Audie said. "Store name has a long memory in these parts."

Earl Pomeroy was the proprietor of Earl's Pawnshop, which had been in business longer than many Wheeler residents could remember. Fortunate for the Harlan Brothers, Earl's health had declined to the point where he had to sell. He was familiar with the Harlan's since they were regular customers—buying and selling guns, jewelry, and varied antiques. The brothers were collectors, who recognized the value of things that people threw away without a second thought. Except for the odd item, their merchandise was aboveboard—at least had a stated provenance that couldn't be proved otherwise.

"And, we've confirmed all taxes have been paid in full. Our accountant audited your books, Earl. You're gettin' paid well above market value...and in cash, so we're not comin' good for any undisclosed debts."

It's all good, Zane. My recordkeeping is a little sloppy, but the numbers add up—more or less. You can count on it," Earl stated. "And, you boys have been squirreling money away all these years? Cause the IRS might be askin' questions at some point."

"Fuck 'em! Let 'em prove different!" Audie retorted. "We've been living in a hovel all our lives...never been married...got no kids. Between the three of us, and the little our father hid away, we saved enough."

"Yeah...not like we've been keeping our money in a bank neither," Zane added. "Don't have a paper trail to follow."

"I'm not saying otherwise," Earl replied, igniting another cigarette. Clear plastic tubing ran from below his nose to an oxygen tank.

"Chrissakes, Earl, you're gonna set yourself ablaze smoking around that O2," Audie chided. "At least, turn off the tank."

"Oh, never you mind that!" Earl growled. "I'm gonna do what the fuck I want until the BIG MAN upstairs snuffs me out."

"All right, all right," Zane soothed. "No disrespect meant, Earl. Isn't that right, Audie?"

"Yeah...yeah," Audie said. "My apologies for speaking outta turn, Earl."

"I accept your apology," Earl said. "And, the firearms?"

"Yeah, I'll buy those not deemed antiques on my own dime," Zane said. "Once we have the necessary licensing and such, I'll sell back to the store."

"Keep your dicks clean, if you wanna deal firearms," Earl reminded, "or the ATF will be so far up your assholes, you'll be shitting out your ears."

"Thanks for that visual," Zane replied. "We just wanna run an honest business, is all."

"You decided on moving in yet?" Earl asked. "I need to vacate soon."

"Yeah...me and Audie will move in first thing tomorrow."

"All right then, boys. I'll see yah tomorrow."

The brothers left the store—now closed until the business had formally changed owners. From the sidewalk, they stared at the storefront. Zane inhaled deep and let out a slow breath. Although bordered by a depressed industrial park and a patchwork of modest residential homes, the brick-and-mortar pawnshop building resided on a busy thoroughfare with ample parking.

"Who knew we'd actually own a business?" Audie said. "You psyched?"

"Nah... I'm more worried how we'll get along," Zane answered. "Never get anything done if we're always squabbling."

"We'll figure it out," Audie said. "We'll find our own niche. Maybe, Hoyt will take care of things behind the counter...keeping the books and tracking inventory. With your knack for talking, you can deal with customers and handle sales. Me...I can find stuff to buy."

117

"And, scrub the toilet and mop the floors…"

"Whoa! Not so fast. I'll do my share, but we're all doing that," Audie said as the handle of the passenger side door snapped off.

"Chrissakes, Audie!"

"Chrissakes, yourself!" Audie returned. "If it weren't for Bondo and duct tape, your old truck would fall to pieces on the highway. We need to stop sitting on our money and buy a few things…like reliable transportation."

"I know, but we gotta be careful. Just can't start buying stuff, or folks are gonna get curious. Don't need the assholes we're stealing from gettin' suspicious."

"I know, but we can't keep living like hoboes. I wanna get my own truck someday."

"We will," Zane said. "As soon as we earn some honest cash, we'll buy a new truck and write it off as a business expense. Then, we'll start drawing a paycheck…health insurance…all that stuff."

"Soon, I hope!" Audie said, crawling through the truck window. "I'm not gettin' any younger."

Keying the ignition, the truck engine turned over several seconds before finally starting. The engine knocked and idled roughly. A gray cloud of exhaust plumed in the air.

"Whadda say now, numbnuts?" Audie countered. "You think we're gonna make it home in this heap? I don't think so."

"Shaddup…"

***

"Well?" Hoyt asked. "We all set?"

"Ours tomorrow," Zane answered. "You'll need to come out and sign paperwork."

"Audie will stay at the house, right?"

"Yeah, we'll shuttle you and Audie back and forth, so someone's always here," Zane said. "Pain in the ass but can't be helped."

"We're gonna have to keep fixin' this place up too," Audie said. "If it wasn't for the wings, I couldn't stand staying here anymore."

"At least, it's clean with fresh paint," Hoyt said, "but I hear what yah saying. Place needs more work, all right. Updated electrical…new appliances."

"Fuck yeah!" Audie concurred. "And, a color TV and cable…and a VCR for fucksakes! Zane, if you don't open the fuckin' pocketbook, I'm gonna beat the shit outta you!"

"Okay, okay, enough already. I'll go to Big Mart this afternoon, but just a few things," Zane said. "What's priority?"

"I kinda agree with Audie about a new TV and VCR. It'd be nice to rent a few videos once in a while."

"Shit yeah!" Audie said.

"Hoyt, any life left in your truck?" Zane asked. "Mine's limping to the bone yard. Engine's sieving oil...valves rattling...starter's grinding."

"I looked my truck over the other day. Needs a new distributor cap, plugs, and oil. Oh! Needs to be registered."

"I'll get the parts today, and we'll go to the town office first thing tomorrow," Zane said. "Move a few things to the apartment tomorrow afternoon."

"Lots of stuff to do going forward," Hoyt said. "We're gonna work real jobs now. You all are up for it?"

"Fuckin' A right!" Audie said. "No more answering to *The Man*."

"I'm ready," Zane said. "No more driving all over the country for me."

"No more livin' like hermits," Hoyt said. "Now, if we don't kill each other."

Chapter 17
Love is All Around Me

It had been months since Zane had gone to the Marlboro Cafe. Instead, he had been frequenting places like Lucky's Lounge in Wheeler. With Tyler University nearby, the lounge was popular with students. When it wasn't his turn with the wings, Zane dressed in his favorite western-style shirt, blue jeans, and snake-skin boots. He accessorized his attire with a big silver belt buckle and cowboy hat. Usually, Zane might have felt somewhat self-conscious in such a place, but he was relaxed. Much had changed about his sense of self.

Flush with monies, Zane had no problem passing a crisp twenty-dollar bill to the bouncer for entry. Until recently, he had been oblivious when a woman may have had a sexual interest in him, but now, Zane had become attune to female subtleties: mascara-lined eyes following him, aroused bodies turning in his direction, delicate fingers touching his arm. However, the most reliable tells were physiological. Zane was grateful for heightened senses gifted by the wings. Now, he could detect when a woman's heartbeat quickened, blood flowing and coalescing in her nether regions, exuding a faint musky fragrance laced with perfumes and lotions. The female biological cue was a powerful aphrodisiac.

For Zane, these new tools were invaluable, sparing much anxiety from sexual overestimation and rejection. He could now sidestep disinterested women in a moment's glance and refocus his attentions elsewhere. More than a few times, when his gaze returned to those women he had passed by earlier, they had become aware of his indifference and tried to stoke his interest.

The lounge was busy this evening. The country music was loud, and people shouted above the din. Cigarette smoke hung in the humid air. An odor of stale beer and liquor permeated the floor and furnishings. Zane removed his hat and wiped his head and brow with a neckerchief. He considered going home early since it was his turn to open the shop tomorrow morning. Hoyt had been lecturing about keeping better track of their receipts and staying atop inventory. Recently, Audie had purchased stolen jewelry that police confiscated later. Hoyt was right. He and his brothers had to be more attentive to the business, or they would end up stealing again.

At that moment, Zane discerned two women seated on the other side of the lounge. He didn't see them immediately through the gloom, but he sensed their interest in the handsome little man with the mustache. Though deliberate and disciplined with their drink, they had been there for a while and getting more inebriated and bored. Zane had no reason to know this, but these young women were the daughters of devout Christian families and sexually immature, except with each other. Paired as roommates and away from home for the first time in their adult lives, their friendship was emotionally and physically intimate.

Both women were taller than Zane, but not towering. One was auburn-haired. Zane suspected a layer of makeup hid a few freckles on her milky skin. The other was raven-haired, her skin brown. Both were beautiful and sexy. Zane could not help but imagine their ashen and tan bodies entwined and grinding against each other, guttural, breathy sounds, and whispered curses...

Before Zane realized it, he was standing before them. "Hello ladies," Zane said, as he handled a wristwatch with a cracked glass lens. "Would one of you have the time? I dropped my watch earlier."

"Why, that's too bad. Looks like a nice watch," the auburn-haired woman said, her voice tinged with a southern dialect that Zane couldn't place straightaway.

"Yeah, a family heirloom," Zane replied, "but no problem, it can be fixed." It was a quality timepiece acquired after its former owner pawned it and never returned. Unfortunately, Audie had dropped it on its journey from the backroom to the display case.

"Waunita always knows the time, even without a watch. Don't cha, girl?"

"Yes, I do, Lily. It's quarter past eleven," Waunita answered without hesitation.

"Are you from around here?" Lily asked. "You look like you know your way around here."

"Why, I am. My name's Zane...Zane Harlan," he said, extending his hand and shaking Lily and Waunita's with a firm but gentle grip. "Born and raised in a little town called Marlboro twenty miles east of here. I still live there with my brothers. We own a business in Wheeler."

"Are you a real cowboy?" Waunita asked. "You look like the real-deal."

"Well, I'm from a family of ranchers and farmers, but most everyone in Feral County can say the same," Zane revealed. "Can't say I own a big spread and a herd of cattle, but I can saddle and ride a horse though."

"You don't say," Lily said, her interest piqued. "Waunita's family is part of the Attacapan People."

"She is?" Zane said. "Sunrise or Sunset?"

"Why...Sunrise...Western Atakapa," Waunita said as if taken aback. "How do you know?"

"Oh...I know a little about indigenous peoples from around Eastern Texas," Zane replied. "Not too many of you folks around, are there?"

"Not many," Waunita said. "My family now lives among the Alabama-Coushatta Tribe."

"Oh, congratulations!" Zane said. "It's about time the government restored federal recognition to your Tribe."

"Uh...thank you..." she said. "Would you like another beer? Our treat..."

From that point on, their conversation was comfortable and free flowing. Lily and Waunita asked many questions. Flattered by their attentions, Zane realized their friendly interrogation was to get a better measure of him. He recognized a past inclination on his part to embellish his personal story, so he made every effort to come across as honest and humble. In due course, Zane tried to buy them a round of drinks, but they declined his offer and bought him a fresh beer instead.

For the next hour, the women edged closer speaking just loud enough for their exchange only. Zane relished the intimacy of their conversation, their physical closeness, and their perfumed scents. Even if he ever could decide, who he liked better, Zane never played favorites. He maintained a delicate balance between the two women, fixing his gaze on the one speaking and always including the other in his responses. At one time, it would have been an impossible task for him, but now, it was instinctive.

On one occasion, two men sauntered up to their table and interjected, "Hey, cuties! I'm Frank, and this is my friend, Charlie. Whatcha drinking?"

Tall and strapping, they towered above Zane from the other side of the table. In the past, Zane would have bristled. Instead, he grinned and listened. Unflustered, he lifted his beer glass and drank. Other times, such an intrusion may have escalated with insults, shoves, and fisticuffs. Never one to cower from a fight, even with the biggest opponent, Zane usually ended up with cuts and bruises to his face and ego and a swift rebuff from the woman he had tried to impress. In this instance, he was certain of a favorable outcome.

"Hello, gentlemen," Lily said without looking, her fingers caressing the back of Zane's neck. "Thanks for coming over, but we're with our boyfriend."

"Yes, we are," Waunita laughed, her hand lighting on Zane's leg, "so why don't you two go fuckoff."

Lily and Waunita leaned in and whispered together, lips caressing his ears, "Don't pay them no mind. They're just a couple of roughnecks with tiny peckers…yeah, real tiny…"

"What the fuck!" Charlie retorted, veins rising from his stout neck. "You rather be with this twerp than us!"

"Couple of lipstick wearin' lezzies…" Frank said. "If you girls want a real man, give us a shout!"

As much as Zane wanted to get up and pummel these men, his anger paled in comparison to his companions. Their bodies stiffened as they prepared to launch from their seats and tear into these men. Zane clasped and kissed their hands. "I feel your anger," Zane soothed, "but I got this." Rising from his chair, Zane tilted his head back and fixed his gaze at Charlie, who appeared on the verge of throwing punches.

"What's this?" Charlie barked. "Little man gettin'…"

Before Charlie could finish his remark, Zane propelled his beer mug across the table into the big man's crotch causing him to pitch forward. In a blurred arc, Zane slapped the man across his face. The resulting sound drowned out all other noise. The lounge fell quiet as Charlie tumbled sideways over an adjacent chair. Zane redirected his attention toward his other adversary projecting potent emotions through unseen mental frequencies. First, he made his anger known toward those attempting to ruin his encounter with two beautiful, lusting women. Next, he hurled thoughts of violent retribution and cruel bodily injuries. Lastly, Zane instilled dread into the men. After a brief stare down, Frank's face became ashen. He stumbled backward and bowled over another chair. Patrons gawked in shocked silence.

"Are you two done?" Zane said, rounding the table.

Three large bouncers appeared from the murk. The one wearing a Stetson hat, quickly assessed the situation and pointed. "Pick these two off the floor, will yah," he directed his colleagues. "What the hell is goin' on here, ladies?"

"These drunken men came over and started bothering us...groped us and called us cunts," Waunita said without hesitation. "Thankfully, our boyfriend was here."

"Is that so," the bouncer replied. "Is that what happened, Zane?"

"That's what happened, Shane," Zane answered. "They weren't acting very gentlemanly to the ladies."

"Very ill-mannered," Lily said. "We should tell our girlfriends to avoid this place."

Shane understood the gist of Lily's comment. He looked at the two hulking men assisted from the floor and at Zane and rendered swift judgment. Removing his cowboy hat and placing it across his chest, he said, "Ladies...Zane, please accept my apologies for not being on top of the situation. Allow me to show these lunkheads the door and tender a lifetime ban from our establishment. And...offer you all a round of complementary drinks."

"Is that acceptable, Zane...Waunita?" Lily asked.

"I'm okay if you ladies are," Zane said. "I just don't care for rudeness."

"I guess so, but I'm not usually so forgiving, but we accept your apology, good man," Waunita said, and then added in a faux English accent. "Now...away with these swine."

"Here, here!" Lily added with a similar dialect. "Our delicate sensibilities abhor such brutish behavior!"

Still numb from Zane's physical and mental assault, Frank and Charlie shambled away amidst a chortle of laughter and ridicule from the crowd. "That's what happens when you mistreat women...Get the fuck outta here...Dumbasses..."

"Drink up, folks!" Shane called out, trying to distract the crowd. "We're collecting glasses and bottles in twenty-minutes!"

"You wanna keep visiting?" Zane asked, offering chairs to the women. "I hope this business didn't upset you ladies too much."

"Zane, what did you do?" Waunita asked, taking a seat. "It was a blur."

"Yeah, one moment you're sitting, and the next, the bigger of the two is on the floor," Lily observed. "You slapped him hard, and I don't even know what you did to the other. Like he saw a ghost or something."

"Nothing really…surprised them is all," Zane said. "I didn't give the first one time to react, and the other just backed down."

"I'm not buying that," Waunita said. "You're holding back something."

"No…really," he said as Shane arrived with drinks. "Anyhow, looks like last call."

"No need to call it a night yet, is there?" Waunita asked, stroking Zane's forearm. "I'm so fuckin' horny."

"I know how she feels," Lily said as she draped her own hand across Zane's other arm. "So, Waunita and I are not only roommates, but we're really close friends."

"Really close," Waunita said, leaning in closer. "Lily is a lustful slut. The things she does with that sweet mouth of hers, no one can resist for long. I should know."

"She's one to talk," Lily said into Zane's other ear. "There isn't an orifice in me her tongue hasn't thoroughly explored."

"Shut up, you little bitch!" Waunita hissed, her hand clamping onto the inside of Zane's thigh. "As good as I am, Zane, I can only do so much. Poor Lily hasn't been deflowered yet, and there aren't any real men around here worthy of the job. Are you man enough for that?"

"Yeah, are you, Zane?" Lily repeated as her own hand found and fondled his stiffening member. "Goddamn, Waunita, I don't know… He's big…and hard as a tree limb. It might hurt too much my first time."

"You're not backing out of this, Lily. I'll make sure Zane does you proper."

"Okay, okay, Waunita," Lily said excitedly. "How about it, Zane? Do you have your own place? If not, we could sneak into our dorm room."

"Damn," Zane sputtered, clasping their hands. "Ladies, most likely, I'll never have such an offer again, but I have to beg off."

Zane regretted making that pronouncement before the women had relinquished their grip. Long fingers wrapped around his manhood from both sides and polished nails dug into his thighs.

Beautiful, angry eyes stared at him. In that instant, Zane felt tremendous empathy for a wayward young woman, who found herself in an isolated place with lusting men.

"Waunita…Lily, you are the hottest women I've ever met, but I just don't know you well enough… I need more *familiarity*."

"*Familiarity*?" Lily asked. "What does that mean exactly?"

"Yah know… Get to know each other better," Zane struggled to explain. "I might seem like a nice guy, but for all you know… Anyhow, maybe it's my Baptist upbringing, but I'm old-fashion about certain things."

As Waunita and Lily exchanged glances, their grasps lessened, but not completely.

"We're sorry, Zane. I guess we got caught up," Waunita said. "We know better, but we're drawn to you."

"No harm done," Zane said. "I'm not saying I wouldn't jump at the chance at a more opportune time though."

"There's a long weekend coming up, and Waunita and I don't have plans yet. We could go out and become more *familiar*."

"I would like that," Zane said, his mind racing. "I'd like that a lot."

***

"So, you'll pick us up tomorrow evening?" Lily asked again as they walked across the dusty parking lot. "We would be quite upset if you stood us up."

"Well, I don't doubt that," Zane said, removing his hat and combing back his long hair with his fingers, "but there's no chance of that."

"Good," Waunita said as she grabbed a handful of Zane's blond hair and pulled him close. "When you're jacking off tonight—and you will be—I want to you to imagine pounding Lily's sexy ass, and then me finishing you off, because that's gonna happen the first time."

Waunita wasted no time getting acquainted with a tentative goodnight peck. Lips parted and mouth open, her delicious tongue darted and swirled. Zane gasped when her hand reached below and massaged his throbbing member. Without thinking, he ran his fingers down the back of her tight jeans and kneaded her shapely derriere. He pressed her close and ground his pelvis into hers.

"Don't be a selfish bitch, Waunita!" Lily hissed. "Outta the way!"

"Goddamn!" Zane thought, his body and mind feverish. If his first sexual experience was magnified a hundredfold, it would never compare to the intensity of this moment. Feeling exposed, he tried to ease Lily into the shadows.

"Chrissakes!" a female voice called out. "Get a room!" Laughter erupted as a group of women walked by.

"Mind your own fucking business, cunt!" Waunita hollered. "No one asked for your opinion!"

"What did you call me, bitch?" a woman shouted in return, her stout form breaking from her group. "I know you ain't talking to me!"

Instead of getting into a pissing contest, Waunita leapt and landed a fist to the side of the woman's head. She fell to the ground in a heap. As her friends stared with astonished expressions, Waunita screeched and advanced on them. They bolted in a flurry of screams.

"Dammit, Waunita!" Zane yelped. "Bit of an overreaction don't yah think! Chrissakes, I hope she isn't dead."

"She should have kept quiet! No one calls me a bitch and gets away with that shit!"

"Yeah, fucking whore needs to keep her mouth shut!" Lily chimed. "No one talks nasty to my bitch, except me."

Zane knelt beside the woman. Though the parking lot was dim, he observed a nasty welt rising on her head. She moaned, and her hands flailed. Lily and Waunita's shrill insults nattered in his ear.

"Thank goodness," he said. "Girls, you better get goin' before the police show up."

For a moment, Lily and Waunita stared at him as if unaccustomed to demands.

"For chrissakes, the police will haul you off, and you'll have lots to explain to your families!" Zane barked, and then softened his voice. "I'm not trying to order you around, but you'll wanna trust me on this."

"Okay, Honey," Lily replied matter of fact. "We'll see you tomorrow then?"

"Yeah…for sure," Zane answered. "Now, please go."

He remained with the injured woman, cupping the back of her head with his hand, and trying to keep her calm. Paramedics arrived before the police, so he explained the situation before merging into the growing crowd of onlookers. Fortunately, the incident had been cloaked in darkness, and the woman's friends didn't recognize him being in the company of the attackers. He pulled out of the parking lot just as a Wheeler Police cruiser arrived.

"Crazy ladies," he sighed, knowing he should run, but unable to resist an opportunity that most men could only imagine. "I'm probably gonna regret this."

Chapter 18
Into Thin Air

Audie's grinning face ached as he somersaulted through the sky. The straps on his new goggles held fast. Having acclimated to the unnatural sensations of flight, Audie's stomach no longer lurched with every abrupt dive, and he no longer needed to straighten and level his path until his vertigo subsided. Flying had become a visceral experience of aerial mechanics.

In the beginning, the tremendous rush of air deafened him, but with time, he discerned more sounds from the ground below, especially when gliding just above the treetops. He heard televisions droning from a thousand living rooms, and the breathless grunts and moans of dozens of fornicating couples. On more than a few occasions, he lighted upon branches and rooftops and peered into bedrooms where curtains weren't drawn. Most times, the carnal viewings were far from seductive as hairy, rotund bodies writhed on sweaty bedspreads. However, a few domiciles offered viewings of lithe, attractive couples fucking without inhibition.

He observed many nocturnal creatures during his jaunts. Countless water moccasins slithered along the Brazos riverbanks. Hundreds of feral pigs rooted lush farmland with impunity. Red wolves unnerved cattle herds slumbering uneasily in moonlit pastures. Darkness no longer impeded his vision, even when he wasn't the wearer of the wings. Nighttime was akin to civil twilight when the sun had descended below the horizon, but artificial light wasn't yet needed. Though still gloomy, Audie held an extreme advantage over earthbound humans. Occasionally, he felt sorry for their physiological limits. Other times, he felt them inferior, though that feeling was pointless given the clandestine use of his new powers.

Tonight, Audie wanted to test the bounds of high-altitude flight. Until recently, it had been enough to stay within a thousand feet of the terrain below. Even after months of physical conditioning, direct ascent without pause was still exhausting. Usually, Audie employed a circular arc, climbing at shallow intervals to catch his breath. During an earlier outing, he stopped when a great thirst overwhelmed his resolve to continue.

Lighting on the ground, Audie urinated on the withered grass and studied the full moon overhead. His newfound avian sight could discern many more features on the satellite's gray surface than the keenest human eye. Zipping his fly, he repositioned a canteen strapped to his waist with a short length of tubing. He suckled the end for a quick swig of water. He swished his mouth and spat. Audie palmed the wing's leather handholds.

Kneeling, Audie closed his eyes and breathed in the balmy air. The day's summer heat still radiated weakly across the pasture. Always present, a cloying odor of manure masked other smells like a rotting cow carcass and a fresh discharge of skunk musk. He concentrated to discern a pleasing scent from the thousands that suffused his olfactory sense. Soon, a wisp of honeysuckle vanquished all else.

Extending his arms, the wings spread wide. The entwined feathers rippled. With a blur, Audie folded his winged arms and leapt skyward several feet or more. At the apex, he unfolded the immense wings and swept downward, propelling himself higher. Audie controlled his breathing and exerted a sustained rhythm as he stroked the air like an Olympian swimmer crossing a calm millpond. Audie flew a direct path toward the bright moon, his eyes never wavering.

After an appreciable time, sweat dribbled down Audie's forehead despite the cooling atmosphere. Continuing upward, inhalations became rapid and deep as the air thinned. The moon was impossibly large and bright. He observed countless shadowed craters and large expanses of waterless seas pockmarked by meteor impacts. Audie's beaming face expressed elation at being untethered from the peopled earth. Tears flowed and evaporated.

Reaching the end of his physical limits, a myriad of bodily ills overwhelmed him. Pain flared in his elbows and wrists. Audie's head pounded. His mouth watered as a surge of gastric juices threatened. Just as he leveled his flight and began a gentle downward glide, Audie vomited. His abdomen squeezed painfully to purge his bowels. Struggling to breathe, a great blackness enveloped him.

Twisting and turning in different directions all at once, Audie roused. A bitter chill permeated his body. The moon spun as he tumbled through the air. Spreading his aching elbows, Audie straightened his path but dove headfirst at an impossible velocity. He extended his arms slowly, lest the wings rip from his body. So disoriented, he couldn't distinguish landmarks below, but observed the earth racing toward him. Adrenaline flowing, Audie swept the wings outward slowing his fall and maneuvering into a steep glide. Just as he leveled off, he careened across a canopy of high trees. Thin branches gave way but slowed his momentum and forced him lower. Audie plowed through stouter branches. Without thinking, he brought his arms forward to protect his head and face. Audie slammed against a tree trunk. He fell through branches and brambles. Landing on his back, he struggled to breathe for agonizing moments, and then blacked out.

***

Carried across moonlit fields, Audie shifted painfully on a makeshift stretcher. Blurred stars wavered in the night sky. Audie felt for the wings. For a moment, anxiety caused excruciating injuries to flare until he sensed Hoyt's presence above and behind him. His brother wore the wings, appearing like a dirty, disheveled archangel. Near his feet, he observed Zane's backside.

Though laborious and unending, Audie's brothers conveyed him effortlessly and silently across wide expanses of field, meandering creeks, and over barbwire fence lines. Somehow, they had sensed what had befallen and searched for him. His mind clearing and his physical shock subsiding, Audie suffered the full brunt of his injuries. His entire body ached. The fingers on his right hand traced multiple abrasions on his face and scalp. He closed his left and right eyes one at a time to test his vision and wiggled his toes. For the most part, he was intact, but a splint and wrappings bound his left arm to his side.

This is bad...really bad...

Finally, they reached Zane's truck, parked in the depths of an unfamiliar forest of oak and cedar. Audie breathed. A scent of morning air flooded his nostrils. A dim glow touched the fringes of the eastern horizon.

"Too late to fly back, but just as well," Hoyt observed as he removed the wings. "Open the box and get my long coat, will yah, Zane. I'll ride in back with Audie."

"We need to get our stories straight before we get to the hospital," Zane said. "Falling out of a tree will do, huh?"

"Yep, that'll do all right. Night hunting, shot a raccoon in a tree, climbed to get it…slipped and fell," Hoyt said. "Isn't that right, Audie?"

"If you say so," Audie groaned. "How's my arm?"

"Pretty bad," Zane answered. "Open fracture, broke in a couple places. Pins and stitches, most likely. Hate to say this brother, but your daredevil horseshit finally caught up with yah. You're gonna be grounded for a while."

Clenching his teeth, Audie hissed. "Well, don't sound so fuckin' happy about it."

"Sorry, Little Brother," Zane said. "It sucks, but you're goddamn lucky you're still alive. That was an awful spill."

"Yeah, nearly killed us getting out here as quick as we did," Hoyt agreed. "Let's get Audie to the emergency room before he passes out. He's gettin' shaky."

"Fuck man…" Audie gasped. "I really messed up."

"What happened?" Hoyt asked, making a bed for his brother. "Zane and I both felt something awful. I saw the moon spinning."

"I ached throughout my body and got sick," Zane added. "I was almost out the door and booking it home when Hoyt called."

"The moon…" Audie said. "Nearly touched the moon, then wham…all at once."

"Altitude sickness… You got the *bends*," Hoyt said. "You must have been flying really high, boy."

"I suppose," Audie said. "Never had a chance to tell… Man, I'm not feeling so good…"

"Try to stay awake," Hoyt coaxed, as he removed Audie's sneakers and elevated his feet.

"I'll go slow as possible, but we have a few miles of bumpy road ahead," Zane warned. "Take it easy, Little Brother."

Despite his brother's appeals, Audie couldn't tolerate the pain for long. Eyes rolling back into his head, he lost consciousness. Audie journeyed elsewhere…beyond the here and now…an ephemeral state between life and death. The experience wasn't an empty blackness forgotten when he awoke. Audie was wholly aware and curious.

"How are you, Son?" his father spoke without speaking. "I didn't foresee your visit?"

"Hey, Daddy," Audie said. "It's good to see…feel you. I mean I sense you, but I can't see you."

"We can take care of that," his father said. "Just imagine the sandbar below *The Falls*…where you caught the monster alligator gar."

"I know where you mean," Audie said.

The sandbar appeared in twilight. The brown river flowed, but imperceptibly like time and space had slackened. Silent and peaceful, it was an ideal place to converse.

"There you are," his father said, standing on the shore. "You look good…bigger…stronger."

"We miss you, Daddy," Audie said, embracing his father. "We nearly fell apart after your passing."

"I'm sorry to hear that, Son. I expected your grief to lessen with time, so you and your brothers could get on with your lives. Alas, you have discovered the root of our family curse."

"Root of our family curse?"

"Yes…the thing that has disheartened all those living in our odd little house on Cobb Street."

"Not the wings?" Audie said. "The wings have been a divine gift…our salvation…"

"For now, maybe," Audie's father said, "but they were never meant for humans."

"That may be, but so far, so good…"

"Then, how are you here?"

"Uh…well, nothing's perfect, but nothing ever is, is it?"

"You were always good with doublespeak, my boy," his father replied. "You're not here long, so you should make haste with questions. Regrettably, you may have no recall of the answers I'm allowed to offer."

"Then, I'll just try to enjoy the moment," Audie said. "What's this all about?"

Audie's father guided him through an infinite, timeless universe illumined by endless galaxies. The cosmos was teeming with inestimable souls of all, who had once lived a corporeal existence and had passed, now residing in this realm. The alien psyches of plant and animal intermingled, conveying fantastical memories, ancient and new, all the while retaining singular consciousness. Millions…billions…innumerable psychic beings approached him, all yearning to know his story. At first, Audie resisted the onslaught of mental voices, but soon surrendered to the joyous din.

"They're especially curious about you," his father said. "They sense you don't yet belong. They wonder if it's possible for you to return messages on their behalf."

"I would," Audie said. "Is it allowed?"

"Not a matter of being permissible, but each place has its own rules of nature like linear time, gravity, and the speed of light. *Here*, it's nearly impossible to journey back."

"Nearly impossible," Audie probed, "but not impossible?"

"That's my boy! Always lookin' to bend the rules. Always lookin to poke holes in the dark and let in the light," his father exclaimed. "You're right. Nothing is impossible, but it's highly improbable."

"But...you've done it," Audie realized. "You've gone back and spoke with Willy Gallison."

"Yes, I have, but don't bother yourself about him," his father admitted. "In fact, don't go around Willy Gallison. You hear me?"

"Why, Daddy?"

"I can't say. Just promise me you'll steer clear of him."

"Okay...but, that's just odd."

"Never mind all that. Just enjoy the moment."

"So, this is it...*The Great Beyond*?" Audie asked. "It's pretty awesome." "It is awesome...for most," his father explained. "In this place, you can know everything...go anywhere...be anything. It's difficult to describe...even when you're already here."

"I guess there's a reason we don't know what happens after death," Audie said. "Otherwise, people back home would be jumping off bridges left and right."

"I never thought of it, but that sounds logical," his father agreed. "The course of mortality is linear...never predetermined...always evolving. There's a natural flow for all. Even *here and now* is transient. Eventually, we will travel beyond here."

"You're blowing my mind, Daddy."

"Is that so?" Audie's father chuckled.

Cold and pain supplanted the warmth and joy. Audie shivered. His eyes cringed against the brightness overhead. "Hospital?" he croaked.

"Yes, Baby," a woman's voice answered. "You lay still; you hear?"

134

"Yeah...don't feel much like movin' no how."

"I'm Nurse Hill, but you can call me Ida. What's your name?"

"Audie...Audie Harlan."

"Okay, Sweetie. Who's the President?"

"Reagan...unfortunately. My apologies, but my family has been voting Democrat since *The New Deal*."

"Thank goodness for that, but don't tell anyone I said so," Ida said, looking into Audie's eyes with a penlight. "Lots of Republicans 'round here, especially the doctors."

"No worries, Ida. I won't tell no one."

"Do you know what day it is, Mister Harlan?"

"Uh... Thursday, unless I've been laid up for some time," he replied. "Are my brothers here?"

"One of 'em is in the waiting area. The shorter one took off somewhere, but said he'd be back."

"So, what's the prognosis, ma'am? How banged up am I?"

"Well, the doctor's still waiting on x-rays, but I'd say you're gonna live. No spinal or neck injuries, so you'll walk outta here, all right. Except for some nasty contusions, your left arm is the most serious. Doc' Carver is the best bone doctor around. He'll patch you up good."

"Guess I won't be flying for a while."

"What's that, Baby?"

"Oh, nothing... Just talking to myself."

"On a scale of one to ten with ten being the most unbearable, excruciating pain ever. Yah know, like Jesus spiked to a cross... What's your pain level?"

"Given that comparison, I guess I'm feelin' somewhere between seven and eight."

"All right then, we'll get you something for the pain," the nurse replied. "Don't you go anywhere."

"No chance of that ma'am."

135

Chapter 19
The Price to Play

"Don't stop, Zane!" Waunita cried, her voice breathless and hoarse. "Keep going!"

Rapid and forceful, Zane pounded against Waunita's wonderful backside. Lily reclined aside her girlfriend choreographing his motions and whispering obscene instructions. For Zane, the sexual experience surpassed his most lustful imaginings.

Oh, man...I can't believe this!

Unable to hold back any longer, Zane doubled his efforts, his hips a blur of motion. Suddenly, his body slackened and shuddered for long seconds. Feeling his partner tremble, Zane penetrated deeper. Waunita groaned. Not wanting the sensation to end, he maintained a firm grasp and savored the moment. Zane pulled out and fell upon Waunita's sweaty backside. He wrapped his muscular arms around her slender waist.

"Shit...that felt so good!" Waunita sobbed. "I love you so much, Zane!"

After such a tremendous sexual release, life's ills disappeared from Zane's mind and body. As Waunita and Lily showered together, he lounged and meditated, waiting for his pounding heart to subside. Not long after, carnal thoughts intruded once again. Zane imagined Lily's milky backside, the curve of her hips.

Waunita returned with a hot, moist towel and scrubbed. Afterwards, he was thoroughly aroused. Zane whispered, "Do you think Lily is up for it again?"

"Damn!" Waunita exclaimed. "You just did it, and I've lost count how many times already. Are you sure? I know I'm feeling a little chafed."

"Only if you and Lily don't mind," Zane soothed. "You two are so hot I can't help myself. I'll make it quick if you want."

"It's okay, Zane. We'll do you as long as you want," she answered, applying a dollop of lubricant on her palm. "Lily, get your hot ass in here! You're not done just yet."

***

"Doing all right this evening, ladies?" Audie said, holding the door open for two women entering Ray's Snack Shack.

"We're just fine," the taller woman replied. "You stayin' outta trouble, Audie?"

"I was until I saw you two foxes driving up. You dining in or out?"

"We're dining in tonight. Ain't that right, Maxine?"

"Sounds good to me, Aubrey."

"Are you meeting anyone?" Audie asked.

"Who...us?" Aubrey said. "We're just driving around. Why...you got something goin' tonight?"

"Nah, I was gonna eat by my lonesome," Audie said with a mournful tone. "It's an awful feeling...sitting by yourself with no one to talk to... Just hopin' somebody will give yah the time of day... Why I'd be more than glad to buy someone a meal for the company."

"All right, all right, that's just sorry," Maxine laughed. "Come on, White Boy, we'll take pity on you if you're gonna pay."

"Well, come in, Sweethearts," Audie said, holding the door open. "How 'bout a deluxe platter with all the fixin's?"

"And, a pitcher of beer," Aubrey added. "Come on, girl. I gotta pee."

"Back in a sec', Audie," Maxine called over her shoulder. "Make sure you get us a clean table."

"Will do, Honeys!"

Ray Bean, proprietor of the Snack Shack, said in a low voice, "Gonna get some brown sugar this evening, I see."

"Now, Ray, that's just downright crude," Audie scolded. "Besides, I like all women...no matter size, shape, color. In fact, I should have gone after them a lot sooner. Hell...I've known 'em since grade school."

"More power to yah, Boy. You're gonna need it with those two," Ray said. "Probably wear your cock to the bone."

"Real romantic, Ray. Quite the ladies' man, aren't yah?"

"Well sure... I've had plenty of tail in my time. Fucked my way to China and back during the Korean War. Why yeah, I've had my fill. Yellow, brown, black...all taste the same to me. Why there was this one time..."

"Chrissakes, Ray! Shut the hell up, will yah? I'm not gonna make any headway with your bigoted stories. How 'bout you go cook me some catfish and hush puppies."

"No need to be rude, Audie. Just tryin' to help yah out."

137

"Yeah, yeah…get," Audie snapped, waving his hand, "and don't skimp on the tartar sauce either!"

"Everything all right?" Aubrey asked. "Ray being crude and foolish again?"

"No worries… Just his usual self," Audie said. "Let's grab the booth by the window."

"Don't you all start without me?" Maxine called out. "Aubrey, you leave me some hush puppies."

"Dontcha worry none, skinny bitch. Audie's gonna feed us real good."

"Um-hum…" Maxine replied as she slid into the booth on the other side of Audie. "I assume you're talkin' about our meal."

"Dontcha worry now," Aubrey assured. "We'll get our dessert sure enough."

"Um-hum…" Maxine said, her long fingers gliding along the inside of Audie's thigh. "Ooh…glad to see me?"

"Audie's been holdin' out on us," Aubrey said, peering down. "I ain't never had vanilla. Is it hard like they say, Maxine?"

"As a rock," she answered, her voice quivering. "Goodness! Long and thick too."

"Slow up, girl, or he's gonna give it up right here," Aubrey cautioned, slapping Maxine's hand. "There's people 'round…"

Brushing against Audie's member, Aubrey's hand lingered, fingers feeling its entire length. Audie casually looked around. Thankfully, there were only a few patrons, and they sat on the far side of the cafe. Two cars pulled into the gravel parking lot.

Maxine pulled a compact mirror from her purse and applied lipstick. "Hard…isn't it?" she whispered, her voice nonchalant. "Like to wrap your mouth around that, wouldn't yah?"

"I would…" Aubrey replied, wiping away spittle from the corner of her mouth. "I'd do it right here…right now…"

"Here's your order, ladies…Audie…" Ray said, depositing a large brown bag on the table. "If you don't mind, I packed your food to go. You can pay me next time you're in…get my drift?"

"Loud and clear," Audie said. "Girls, let's take our patronage elsewhere?"

"Um-hum," Maxine said. "We know when we're not wanted."

"Come on, Audie. We'll take yah home with us," Aubrey said, sliding out of the booth and pulling her skirt down her ample derriere. "We got a twelve-pack in the fridge and fresh sheets."

"Thanks, Ray," Audie said. "See yah in the funny papers."

"Um-hum…" Ray grumbled, holding open the door.

***

Nearly midnight, Hoyt hunkered on a shadowed rooftop. He peered through veiled curtains into the gloomy interior of a bedroom. Regina and her daughters now resided in a modest neighborhood in Timpson. Their house was a single level rental with few frills but had a fenced-in backyard. Varied smells permeated the summer air, including the tangy aroma of a recent barbecue. A faraway dog barked.

Incarcerated for spousal abuse, Regina's husband no longer terrorized his wife and daughters, at least for the time he had remaining on his sentence.

Although their lives were uneventful, Regina and her daughters appeared to have adapted. Regina worked at a laundromat, and the girls went to school. Both places were within walking distance, so Regina sold her car to pay overdue bills. Hoyt wanted to speak with her and apologize for what happened, but in the end, he thought it best to do nothing. Hoyt remembered the horror on her face when he lost control and pummeled her husband into a bloody pulp. He planned to give her money once he figured how to offer it without protest.

Any fantasy Hoyt ever had of a romantic relationship with Regina was long gone. He could only check on her to make sure she and the girls were okay. Hoyt was determined that Nate would never threaten his family again. Now, it was a matter of deliberation and execution. Earlier this evening, Hoyt had heard Regina speaking to someone over the phone about a work furlough. She had been upset. Regrettably, Hoyt had been unable to piece together snippets of her conversations enough to understand.

A figure walked down the street, coming closer. Though vague and misshapen, Hoyt recognized the hulking form. Sending his consciousness outward, Hoyt sensed malevolent intent. He winced from a bitter stench that came from the shadowy man. Nate Nash was out of prison and walking toward Regina's house.

Work furlough… Makes sense now, except you're supposed to be in your cell at night. Packing a gun and knife in your jacket, eh? No need to ask about your intentions. Couldn't leave well enough alone, could yah?

Hoyt probed his surroundings for waking thought and sensed someone else. A vehicle approached. Just before it appeared around the corner, Nate disappeared behind a row of hedges to his left. A floodlight combed the sidewalks as a policeman patrolled the neighborhood. For a moment, the light's glare swept past Hoyt's face. He didn't shy from the luminance. He closed his eyes to safeguard his night vision, confident he would remain unseen unless he willed it.

Timpson Police know you're out, don't they, Nate? Maybe I should fly down there and beat on you some…toss you into the street after…?

A loud percussion sounded. Thoughts erupted in Hoyt's head as sleeping minds awakened with a start. Two more shots followed. The police car swerved, its floodlight exploding from a bullet impact. Nate stalked toward the car firing as he approached. Hoyt observed the police officer trying to take cover but struggling with his seatbelt. Several feet from the vehicle, Nate stopped and fumbled to reload his revolver.

Swooping down soundlessly and lighting beside his nemesis, Hoyt asked, "What exactly did you have in mind coming here tonight, Nate?"

"Huh?" he replied, looking around with a shocked expression. "It's you!"

"Yeah, it's me… Retard from across the street," Hoyt said, the wings unfurling. "I was conflicted about how to protect Regina and the girls. Then you happen along tonight with murderous intent…"

Hoyt didn't have a chance to savor the moment. Nate lunged, sweeping his heavy revolver downward. Hoyt's mental and physical reflexes were much faster as he turned deftly and evaded the attack. With a blurred motion, he drew and plunged his stunted sword upward, piercing Nate's chest cavity. Hoyt twisted the blade and splayed the man's heart. A torrent of heated blood spewed.

Even in the throes of death, hatred crossed Nate's grimaced expression as he grunted, "Wha…are you…?"

"Still the same...just different," Hoyt answered, bewildered by his own admission. "I'll be seeing yah in hell."

Nate collapsed to the pavement, inky blood spreading outward. The corpse expelled a vaporous shadow. The shape lingered. Abruptly disconnected from his body, Nate's soul was fully aware of his newborn essence but still malevolent and fearful. Suddenly, it flitted away as if something terrible followed in pursuit. Lights flickered on throughout the neighborhood. Voices carried. Dogs barked. A man moaned.

Hoyt approached the police cruiser and peered inside. He discerned wounds to the officer's left shoulder and arm. Shallow lacerations crisscrossed his face from imploded glass. Bullets shredded his uniform shirt in several places. Gray fibers protruded from his Kevlar vest. The policeman stared, unable to speak. His face was ashen and damp. Etched into the plastic nametag on his chest was the name *Bates*.

"Hang in there, man," Hoyt said, reaching through the window. "All survivable injuries."

"Shooter...?" the policeman asked. "...down...?"

"Down for the count," Hoyt said, pulling the radio mic from its cradle. "Hello there, I'm calling from Patrolman Bates' police car."

"Who is this?" a stern voice answered. "Where's Patrolman Bates?"

"A concerned citizen... Listen here... There's been a shooting near the corner of..." Hoyt said, looking for the street signs, "...Nutt and Gallison. Patrolman Bates is okay, but he's injured and needs help. The shooter is down. Did you copy that?"

"Corner of Nutt and Gallison, over?"

"Yes, please hurry."

"You stay put. Officers are responding, and EMTs will be onsite shortly. What's your name again, over?"

"I never said," Hoyt said. "Just hurry."

Dropping the radio mic, Hoyt disappeared into shadow and ascended into the night sky. He circled overhead, masked by the glare of city lights. Neighbors congregated along the sidewalk. A few people approached the patrol car. Soon, he spied flashing strobe lights followed by a piercing caterwaul of sirens. Satisfied that aid was in route, Hoyt banked and flew a circuitous route home.

Chapter 20
The Vaqueros

"I'm laid up at home, and you're all flying on my dime!" Audie blustered. "It ain't fair!"

"Take it easy," Hoyt said. "Maybe Zane can have one of his lady friends come over and keep yah company."

"I don't want his skanks! I wanna fly, goddammit!"

"What are you gonna do? Strut around the kitchen and preen your feathers?" Hoyt asked. "No need for 'em to go to waste. At least we can do something with 'em while you're mending. Maybe scout out the house and property you've been goin' on about?"

"The Hadley Estate! That's my baby! I'm the one who should be goin'!"

"Chrissakes!" Zane called out from the bedroom. "Shuddup, before Mrs. Sanchez starts hollering out her window!"

Hoyt and Audie fell silent. Not that Zane had a natural commanding presence, but anyone who adorned the magic wings assumed an air of authority. Zane relished the opportunity to fly every other night. Their supernatural influence gave him more insight, strength, and abilities. He had fleeting thoughts of absconding with the wings, but familial devotion overcame the urge. Other times, he thought about dropping in on Waunita and Lily in full regalia and having his way, but he doubted that would be prudent. Waunita might castrate him with a razor and steal the wings for herself.

"Maybe we wanna beg off tonight?" Hoyt suggested. "We could check out Audie's scheme instead?"

"Nope," Zane replied. "We're goin' after Romero. Big exchange tonight. Enough cash to last us a long while. After Audie's accident, we're lucky the wings weren't wrecked. I'd just as soon get us set up before we piss away the magic. We need to keep our eye on the ball."

"But, is it worth risking our lives?"

"I'm not goin' back to my old life!" Zane barked. "No way I'm gonna live and die in this damn house like Daddy. I have plans. I wanna be someone and dip my wick in every woman I can before I go crazy like everyone else in our family."

"Zane, there's no guarantee that'll happen."

142

"It is if we stay here. I may not have heard voices in my head like you, but I've been miserable my whole life," Zane spoke, as the wings' feathers ruffled. "I've lost count how many times I've wanted to stick a shotgun in my mouth and be done with it. Mark my words! I'll burn down this fucking house and everyone fool enough to stay in it before I'm done."

"Let's hope it doesn't come to that," Hoyt soothed. "I'm with you…we're both with you. We'll stop screwing around and focus on business."

"Just be there tonight," Zane instructed, as he opened the kitchen door. "I don't wanna be out there with my dick in my hand."

Peering into the night, Zane looked for prying neighbors, but observed none. He sensed their next-door neighbor, Mrs. Sanchez, cloistered in her living room, watching television. He stepped outside, closed his eyes, and listened. Within the fenced-in backyard, Zane heard a cavalcade of nocturnal insects emerging from hidden nooks and crannies to begin their nighttime wanderings. A juvenile snake slithered on its scaly underbelly, flicking tongue tasting the air and homing in on crickets chirping under the pecan tree. Zane sent his auditory senses beyond the yard. The usual early evening sounds carried from the neighborhood: blaring televisions, squealing tires, screeching kids, barking dogs, and slamming doors…

The wings trembled whenever the moon shone on their glossy feathers. Zane pulled his goggles over his eyes, and as effortlessly as taking a shallow breath, he bent his knees and lunged skyward. Zane swept his arms downward and flew away silently. Although sunset had long passed, twilight hues bathed the earth below. Beautiful and ethereal, Zane commanded an enviable view. Nothing escaped his avian vision as his eyes focused narrow and wide.

Maintaining a southwesterly course, Zane piloted toward the familiar skyline of Timpson. He and his brothers had never attempted to clock their speed in flight. Zane guessed eighty miles an hour when flying level at a comfortable pace. He figured a hundred miles an hour or more was possible if he exerted himself, and there was no telling how fast in steep descent. In little time, he banked left and paralleled Interstate 35 to the south until he reached Socorro. Heading farther west, Zane followed a creek of the same name. The narrow creek snaked through wasted fields and scrubland.

After several miles, Zane came upon a rudimentary bridge at an intersection of dirt roads crisscrossing the landscape. Maintaining a prudent altitude, he flew around the meeting spot in widening circles, studying every shadowed place below for someone hunkered in an ambush position. Zane detected no one. On the northwest side of the creek, he lighted upon a sturdy oak.

The stout branch on which he perched barely bowed as if he was no heavier than a mockingbird. Wings still extended, he balanced for a few moments testing his footing. Zane felt the rough bark through the soles of his new rock-climbing shoes, which clung to the branch like Velcro. Hoyt had purchased three pairs of the specialized footwear after Audie's near fatal mishap. Although he preferred well-worn cowboy boots, Zane appreciated the shoes.

Figuring he had a couple hours, Zane relaxed. He unhitched his arms and stretched before unzipping his fly to relieve his bladder. As scalding urine rained through the tree canopy below, Zane tuned his senses outward. It was still quiet in the distance.

He and his brothers reconnoitered the area by truck, foot, and wing in preceding days. An hour behind him, Hoyt and Audie were making their way from Socorro to a cul-de-sac at the end of an old access road, east of his present position. Once there, Hoyt would walk a footpath that paralleled the creek with his M14 rifle with night-scope and bipod. Three hundred feet downstream, Hoyt would take a position at the crest of a limestone outcrop overlooking the bridge. Since Audie's arm was still lame, he would stay with the truck, but ready to help if needed.

From the north, the Romero Crew would approach with a satchel of cash. From the south, another group of men would arrive with a case of cocaine. Zane wasn't familiar with the others, but the name *Castro* peppered the conversations overheard from a tree overlooking the backyard of Angel Romero's home. Sometimes, he heard Angel and his associates discussing business affairs as dozens of kids frolicked in the swimming pool. Regrettably, Zane didn't know the precise meeting time, but he suspected sometime past midnight. If necessary, he and his brothers would wait until first light.

Other than beer and smoking marijuana on rare occasions, Zane didn't care for the harder drugs, and he had no desire to risk his freedom selling the product, regardless of its profitability. He craved cash, and tonight, Zane expected a windfall.

An hour later, Zane heard a familiar footfall approaching from a half mile away. Though Hoyt usually lumbered when walking, a lifetime of hunting with his father and brothers honed his ability to stalk silently through the woods. As the wearer of the wings, Zane's five senses were heightened far beyond those of normal humans. Once his brother settled into his ambush position, an unnatural deadness of sound emerged.

Out of nervous boredom, Zane tried an experiment, testing an odd theory discussed by him and his brothers. Without dropping his vigilance, he cleared his mind and projected a deliberate thought, *"Bet you're hankering for a cigarette, aren't yah, Brother?"*

Instantly, Zane heard his brother grunt and shift. He imagined Hoyt with his rifle raised against whoever spoke in his mind.

"Easy, Hoyt! It's me!"

Zane didn't anticipate a telepathic response. Instead, he saw his brother's head lift above the thicket and look in his direction.

"Hoyt, if you hear me, shine your penlight for a quick second," Zane said, all the while paying attention to nighttime surroundings.

A pinprick of light flickered. So quick, most would have missed the luminance with a blinking eye or discarded it altogether as an imagined vision.

"I saw it," Zane said. *"Take a second to clear your head and try sending me a message."*

For several seconds, Zane stared into the starry sky and listened with his mind. For a fleeting instant, he heard a faint, tinny voice spoken through a wall of white noise, like ghostly chatter from a faraway AM radio station at night.

"I can hear you a little, but I can't understand," Zane said, sending his thought outward. *"Maybe with more practice, but not tonight."*

The wings suddenly lifted and enfolded the back of Zane's head as if creating a hollow to capture distant sounds from a particular direction. Turning his left ear to the north, unseen vehicles approached. Turning his head and shoulders in the opposite direction, three sets of yellow headlights flickered on the distant horizon, but no sound yet.

"They're coming," Zane spoke in his mind. *"Probably another ten or fifteen minutes. If you need to wet your throat or take a leak, better do it now. I'll signal Audie."*

Zane donned a voice-activated headset and keyed the microphone on his walkie-talkie in a sequence of three, two, and then one. Audie replied the same in reverse order.

Crouching low on the branch, Zane listened in both directions at the same time. Most likely, the Romero Crew would arrive first from the north. Zane understood each party would come in two vehicles for security and backup transport. He noted three vehicles conveying the Castro Gang. Since theirs was a new business relationship, both groups were antsy. Zane hoped this would work in his and his brothers' favor.

Sure enough, two pickup trucks arrived and stopped within sight of the bridge. A cloud of dust followed and enveloped the massive four-wheel drive vehicles. The drivers kept the engines idling and shutoff their headlights. Soon after, another set of trucks appeared on the other side of the bridge. Castro's third vehicle did not appear.

A single man exited from each of the trailing vehicles and sauntered to the bridge. Zane recognized the man from the Romero Crew, named Augustine Salazar. He was short and stocky with a soft-spoken voice. Zane thought he was a nice enough guy, who had three kids—all girls. Last month, he had even stopped by the store and bought jewelry for his wife and daughters.

The other man from the Castro Gang was medium height and portly. Unlike the vaquero garb of tailored jeans, collared shirts, and cowboy boots favored by Romero's men, the others wore an urban attire of baggy pants, sleeveless tee shirts, and canvass sneakers. Bandanas wrapped around their heads and slung low forced them to lift their faces to see better.

"Chrissakes! It's a goddamn Charro and Cholo convention," Zane thought. *"Now where's that third truck from Castro's Gang? Are they hanging back and watching their back trail, or are they up to no good?"*

The men met in the middle of the bridge and spoke in low mutterings. Zane heard every word, but he wasn't fluent in Spanish. He understood enough to recognize nervous pleasantries. This was a new alliance between groups of Hispanic men from different parts of the barrio. Except for a shared language, they had little else in common, but a desire for money. Zane smelled testosterone and adrenaline leaching from their bodies. Index fingers hovered and quivered over triggers of loaded weapons—safeties off.

Each man looked back at his respective group and signaled. Augustine waved his hand with fingers pointing skyward, and the other raised a fist. Immediately, another man broke from each group carrying a laden duffle. Presumably, Romero's courier had the cash, and Castro's had the drugs. Zane's olfactory sense verified the paper currency in one bag. The other emitted an odor akin to hot asphalt.

A suffocating pall fell across the night. Zane's nocturnal vision diminished along with his other heightened senses. Time slackened. The men on the bridge moved slower. Insects flitted by lazily. With a sheer force of will, Zane breathed to overcome the sudden inertia. His supernatural senses returned, albeit still somewhat lessened.

Nighttime shadow lengthened from the trees surrounding the bridge. Several of Audie's Tasmanian Devils emerged and scuttled between the shadows, drawing nearer to the gathering of men. Human forms appeared from the thicket on the south side of the bridge. Flanking the Castro Gang, two men approached from the east and two from the west, all clothed in military style fatigues, faces painted camouflage, and heads adorned with night vision goggles. They converged on the bridge, taking positions along the creek facing the Romero Crew.

"Son of a bitch!" Zane thought. *"Castro's gonna take the money. Stay down, Brother. They're packing automatic weapons and wearin' NVGs."*

Remaining hidden, Hoyt pivoted his rifle toward Castro's men.

As soon as Romero's courier reached the middle of the bridge, gunfire would ensue. Zane suspected Castro's men would fall prone and wait until Augustine and his partner were dispatched, and then bolt from the bridge with the cash while Castro's men kept firing. Zane wondered about the duffel with the asphalt odor.

"Hoyt, this isn't goin' as planned, but it might still work in our favor," Zane projected with his mind. *"It's gonna be loud and confusing. Just watch and cover me the best you can and be ready to beat feet."*

As soon as they came together, Castro's men dropped to their bellies. As expected, gunfire erupted from the south side of the creek. Rounds struck Romero's men. Augustine fell to his knees and rolled sideways over the edge of the bridge. Castro's first emissary rose to his knees, grabbed the cash duffel, and ran. The other man pulled a strap on the drug satchel and followed. A hissing and ribbon of smoke issued from the discarded satchel.

Bomb!

The wings enveloped Zane in a protective shroud as he waited for an explosive percussion to take out the bridge. Nothing happened.

Dud!

After a moment of hesitation, Romero's men spread out and advanced, aiming at muzzle flashes from Castro's men and squeezing off rounds. One man knelt and took deliberate aim at the men fleeing from the bridge with the cash duffle. He fired several shots in rapid succession. Both of Castro's men fell.

Zane observed the violent onslaught unfolding in a slowed progression. His heightened senses saw everything from his elevated vantage point. So keen was his sight, Zane could see bullets soaring through the darkness from both directions, shearing off tree branches, peppering truck bodies, and shattering windshields. Rounds of every caliber struck the dirt road at shallow angles and ricocheted, some making that high whining sound heard in western films.

From behind their vehicles, Castro's Gang fired wildly. Most were young men barely out of their teens, holding their pistols single-handed in a sideways manner. Rounds flew in every direction with no deliberate trajectory. Even though Zane was in a position above and well beyond direct line of fire, stray bullets pierced the tree canopy just below him. The men who had taken ambush positions before, ensnared Romero's Crew in a lethal crossfire.

As expected, gunfire lulled as hundreds of shell casings littered the ground. Clouds of dust and wisps of gunpowder hung in the air. Fitful bursts of gunfire sounded when a shooter found a full magazine or managed to unjam his weapon. Shouts carried from the darkness. The men were busy reloading. Zane imagined many had parched throats, ringing ears, and frayed nerves. Three of Romero's eight men were dead, dying, or wounded, and six of Castro's twelve men were in the same predicament. One of the advance men nearest Zane was down. The other was intent on something in the creek below.

The cash duffel was lying on the ground. Castro's lead men were prone and unmoving. Somehow, Zane recognized they were dead.

Flitting from shadow to shadow, the Tasmanian Devils approached the bridge.

Get ready, Hoyt. I'm going for the money.

Zane unfurled the wings. Preparing to swoop, he noticed movement below the bridge. Romero's man, Augustine, had landed on a sandbar. He was still alive and struggling to crawl for cover. Castro's advance man had taken notice and took aim at the wounded man.

With no forethought, Zane flew down and landed astride Castro's man. In a blurred motion, Zane punched him in the head knocking him unconscious. He leapt the distance to the creek bed below the bridge in a single bound. Zane kicked at the shadow creatures, which dissipated like puffs of acrid smoke. A sulfurous odor permeated the balmy air.

Having seen a winged apparition flying from the trees, Augustine's face expressed sheer terror. He scrambled to get to his feet and bound away, but his injured arm and leg prevented him. He pulled back when Zane reached down.

"Por favor, no!" Augustine begged. "My wife and children. Mi esposa y mis hijos…"

"Easy now," Zane soothed. "I'm here to help."

"No, no…el diablo!"

"Not tonight," Zane assured. "I'm gonna take your arm and get you under the bridge."

"No, no, no!"

"Si, si, si!"

Zane lifted the man up and carried him under the bridge. "I hope you remember this," Zane said, laying the man down. "You may wanna stay under cover for now."

"Muchas gracias," Augustine groaned.

Zane noticed the man's injured arm draped askew across his chest. The limb was broken and bleeding profusely. A shard of bone protruded through his shirtsleeve fabric. "You gotta nasty break," Zane announced removing a bandana from his back pocket and wrapping it around the man's arm. "I imagine this hurts like hell, but you're still breathing."

"Come on Zane, get that duffel already!"

The voice in Zane's mind was unmistakable. Somehow, his brother had breached the mental wall.

"I hear yah!"

Without another word, Zane jumped onto the bridge. In an instant, he secured the money duffle to a harness wrapped around his abdomen. As expected, it was difficult to get airborne. Though the wings negated the weight of the wearer, their magic was less effective with added ballast.

A bullet whipped by his face. The round left a vaporous contrail in its wake, its passing marked a sharp crack. Bits of bullet debris dug into the skin above his right brow. Zane ducked just in time as two more rounds sped by in supersonic flight, followed by another volley.

"Castro's other advance men!"

Immediately after, two distinct shots sounded as Hoyt's M14 rifle found two marks. Castro's men went down. In the darkness and confusion, both groups fired on the new shooter. In his mind, Zane saw his brother rolling behind the limestone outcrop.

Crouching low, Zane jumped skyward with all his might and beat his arms rapidly. The sensation was akin to swimming with one's feet bound together. Zane strained to stay aloft as he ascended with each downward stroke of the wings. Soon, he flew over his brother, who stared upward. Zane's feet and legs grazed the treetops.

"Hurry, Hoyt!"

"Right behind you."

A tremendous cramp in his right thigh threatened to ground him much sooner than he wanted. Following the access trail, Zane flapped his muscled arms as fast as his could. A quarter mile up the creek, he lost his remaining strength and glided to the ground, clipping a mesquite tree. Sharp thorns ripped into the underside of his left forearm. Zane fell the last twenty feet to the ground. The hard landing pounded the air from his lungs. For long seconds, he struggled to breathe as his injured body quaked. Zane was helpless when the Tasmanian Devils scampered nearby. Hissing and scratching, the creatures jumped at his face. Tiny claws dragged across his temple and cheek...

"Get outta there!"

Zane felt someone reaching under his arms, lifting him up, and leaning him back. Air refilled his aching lungs as he took hitching breaths. Zane lay in his brother's lap. Blood dribbled from Zane's left arm and soaked his shirt.

"Hey?" Audie called out with a hoarse whisper. "What the fuck?"

"Hold the light, will yah," Hoyt said. "I'm gonna shuck the wings and put 'em on. Should give me enough strength to carry him to the truck. Unclip the duffle."

The brothers made quick work of it. Sporadic gunfire and shouting voices still carried from down the creek. Within minutes, Hoyt wore the wings and lifted Zane in his arms. Audie led the way along the animal trail with the heavy satchel slung over his shoulder and Hoyt's rifle in his good hand. Reaching the truck, Hoyt placed his brother into the passenger seat and gave him a bottle of water.

"That could have gone better," Zane groaned. "Goddamn Mexican standoff back there."

"Quiet and stop bleeding on my truck," Hoyt scolded. "I hope you and Audie figure out a good cover story by the time we get to Wheeler."

"Take this," Audie said, handing over his holster and pistol. "Follow us to the Interstate, will yah."

"Yeah, I'll make sure no one is dogging yah back to Socorro. Hopefully, the police aren't on their way yet," Hoyt said, drinking from his canteen. "Once you're on the road, I'll circle back and see what happened before heading home."

Lightning illuminated the western horizon with a stark brilliance. Thunder cracked seconds later. Hoyt felt the leading edge of a violent thunderstorm as it pushed through the atmosphere.

"Funny?" Hoyt said. "I don't remember anything about a storm tonight."

"Never mind that. Just don't dawdle too long," Audie advised. "We got what we came for. I'll call yah as soon as I can."

Chapter 21
The Visitation of Augustine Salazar

Zane hobbled to the counter. The pain medication took the edge off, and he could still work. The past two weeks had been busy and worrisome. Zane had been steadfast in his accounting about a cousin's horse dragging him through a mesquite thicket. Although the Wheeler Police were suspicious, his injuries matched his explanation. Given the recent shootout west of Socorro, they were understandably skeptical.

The Romero Crew had escaped with little trace. On the morning of the shootout, flash floods forced Texas Rangers to wait until late afternoon before they could investigate reports of sustained gunfire the previous night. Army helicopters from Fort Hood had located the burned-out hulks of three pickup trucks a quarter mile downstream from the washed-out bridge. Lodged against a mire of uprooted trees, mud, and other flood debris, the bullet-riddled bodies of Castro's men were found burned beyond recognition. Except for a handful of shell casings, the deluge erased all sign of the shooters along with their footprints and tire tread marks.

Vehicle VIN numbers traced the truck owners back to members of a notorious street gang in Hildago. Although they were under aggressive surveillance by DEA and local authorities, those connected to the vehicles had supposedly gone to visit relatives in Mexico, their whereabouts and date of return unknown. Other than that, no one was saying anything.

The thunderstorm and ensuing floods were a Godsend for those, who had survived what the media had dubbed "The Socorro Massacre".

When the hospital released Zane, the brothers had counted the money totaling two hundred and eighteen thousand dollars. Though it was an odd amount, they didn't question their sudden fortune or their part in the shootout. The brothers rationalized that the clash would have happened regardless.

"Any calls or visits?" Audie asked.

"Nope, not since Monday," Zane answered. "We're still in the clear."

"Tell that to Hoyt, will yah. He's still antsy and wonders if Romero's Crew will tie us to it somehow."

"Aw, Hoyt's just being a pussy," Zane retorted. "Chrissakes, he's wearing the wings. He'll know if they're coming long before they get here. Besides, we're not helpless. Even me being banged up and you one-armed, we could still kick the shit outta anyone coming through our door."

"Maybe, but Hoyt's the boss as long as he's got the wings."

"Yeah, yeah, but we're not gonna be laid up for long. My stitches are healed over, and my bruises are almost gone. Even without the wings, we're mending ten times faster than normal. I bet you could take that cast off next week."

"Hmm, you could be right," Audie reckoned. "We should have another meeting tonight."

"Damn right!" Zane agreed. "Except, I gotta date tonight."

"Christ Almighty!" Audie snorted. "You mean those crazy girls again?"

"Hey, don't call 'em names! They might be crazy, but they're mine, and I don't take kindly to you insulting them. I don't go around makin' fun of the girls you're cattin' around with."

"You mean, Aubrey and Maxine!" Audie countered. "They're wild cats in bed and up for anything."

"Yeah, I bet they are," Zane said, "but I'll wager you a hundred dollar bill my gals are even wilder."

Abruptly, the phone rang. "Unlock the front door, will yah," Zane said lifting the receiver. "Earl's Pawnshop. We're buyin', if you're sellin', and we're sellin' if you're buyin'."

"Dammit, Zane! You need to answer the phone more businesslike," Hoyt scolded on the other end. "You're gonna put off the customers."

"Aw, enough already. Folks get a kick outta my greeting. Anyhow, it's not like you're working."

"That might be, but someone has to watch over the wings."

"Yeah, yeah, what do you want?"

"I'm calling because I gotta feeling," Hoyt replied. "Like you're gonna have a visitor today."

"Yah don't say. Like a customer comin' to the pawnshop?"

"Hey, knucklehead, just keep your eyes peeled! If you don't get killed today, I'll drop by the store tonight."

"Yeah, have fun taking my turn tonight!" Zane slammed the receiver. "Asshole!" He winced as pain flared throughout his body. Zane looked at the clock and wondered if he should take his pain medication but decided against it.

"Audie, maybe you could hold off going out this morning, huh?"

"Hoyt having a feeling?"

"Yeah."

Just before noon, a jet-black Chevy Silverado pickup truck with silver wheel rims pulled into the parking lot. The vehicle's waxed body gleamed, and sunlight glinted off a chrome roll bar and a series of floodlights mounted behind the cab. The truck rumbled from a set of thrush mufflers. Tinted windows masked the driver.

"Are the backdoor and windows secured?" Zane asked his brother. "Guns loaded and ready?"

"Yeah," Audie answered. "We're packin'."

Augustine Salazar hopped from the high truck. Right arm strapped across his chest, he walked with a noticeable limp.

"Do we know him," Audie asked. "He looks familiar, but I can't quite place him."

"Yeah, he's been in here before," Zane answered. "Plus, he was there that night. He's the one I pulled under the bridge."

"Shit, one of Romero's guys?" Audie whispered. "Is he alone?"

"Seems so, but why don't you go out back and watch the video monitors. I'll speak with him. Maybe it's nothing."

Audie disappeared into the back storeroom just before Augustine entered the store. Zane's right hand rested above a loaded .357 Magnum revolver under the register. He held his breath for a moment as the man passed through an inconspicuous metal detector inside the front door. Zane breathed easy when the machine didn't make a sound.

"Buen dia," Augustine said his voice tinged with a slight accent. No doubt, the man was raised in America, but most likely, in a Spanish speaking family.

"Hello," Zane greeted. "Augustine, isn't it? You've been here before."

"Si...yes."

"Well, I'm Zane in case you don't remember."

154

Augustine gazed around the store, studying the merchandise. He observed the cameras overhead as he gravitated to the display case that contained jewelry, coins, and other collectables.

"Real hot today," he said. "My friend waxed his car earlier, and the wax baked on."

"Ouch!" Zane said casually. "Not easy to get off."

Augustine grimaced as he adjusted his arm sling. "It's not all bad," he said. "His car's a piece of shit anyway."

"Were you in an accident?" Zane probed.

"Si…you could say that," he said, looking at his arm and leg. "I fell from high…on boulders."

"You don't say," Zane said.

"Hurt bad… Knocked the wind outta me," Augustine said. "Real close call, you could say."

"Sorry to hear that. Are you okay?"

"Si, I'm okay," Augustine said then pausing. "While I was laying there, I was thinking of my wife and girls… Wondering what would happen if… Then, someone helped me."

"Thank goodness for that, huh?"

"Si…it was," Augustine agreed. "Thing is…I must have been in shock or something because my savior flew down on wings."

"Like an angel?"

"No…no angel… An ordinary man…but wearing wings."

"Well, whatever he was, it was a good thing, yes?"

"Yes, I think… I'm alive, and for that, I am very thankful," he said. "You see…I can't die yet. Except for my children, I've done little good in my life. If I had died, I would have gone to unpleasant places in the afterlife. This, I am certain."

"Well, I don't know about that," Zane assured. "You seem like a nice enough fella, and we've all done things we've regretted."

"Si," Augustine said. "But, at some point, we have to atone, and I imagine it's best when we're still living."

"I suppose that would be best," Zane agreed. "Seeing you're here, is there something I can do for you?"

"Could I see that necklace there," he said, pointing to a silver pendant with chain. "It looks antique. My wife likes older pieces. She doesn't buy anything new. She believes in karma. Yah know, like the previous owners are still attached somehow."

"Never thought about it, but women think about that stuff more than men. At least, that's my experience—for what it's worth," Zane replied. "If there's such a thing as karma, it might not always be a good thing."

"No, I wouldn't think so, but my wife believes good is more powerful than the other," Augustine explained. "For me, I don't know. I just see a pretty piece of jewelry. It would seem karma would come from the person, who now wears it. Listen to me...I sound like an old superstitious woman."

"Nah, not at all. I probably wouldn't spout off about such things at my family dinner table, but still interesting stuff," Zane said, handing over the necklace. "An older gentleman, Ed Turnip from Cotulla, brought in this piece. His wife passed away two years ago. From what I gathered, she was given the necklace by a boyfriend when she was a teenager, and sometime after, he was kicked in the head by a horse and died."

"That's quite the story."

"It is," Zane replied. "Supposedly, she gave it away years ago, but he found it in her jewelry box after she passed. Though she never wore it, she kept it just the same. I usually can't read people, but Ed seemed to have mixed feelings about the piece...like he felt bad selling it and jealous at the same time. Well, I gave him a good price for it, and he went on his way, but he was tearing up by the time he left."

"Shit..."

"Yeah...shit..." Zane agreed. "And, the poor guy died a month after that."

"Really?"

"Swear to Christ," Zane said, raising his right hand. "In fact, you'd be doing me a favor buying it. It's like cutting raw onions with a fork whenever I look at it."

"How much?"

"I put a hundred and eighty on the tag, but I'm thinkin' a hundred and twenty is fair," Zane said. "No gold or diamonds, but it's old and has a good backstory."

"I'll take it," Augustine said without hesitation, reaching into his wallet. "My wife will like it anyway, but she'll love its history."

"It's a deal," Zane said, taking six crisp twenty-dollar bills. "I'll get you a receipt and a nice box."

Tucked within the bills, Zane discovered a scrap of yellow notepaper. Once pristine and neatly folded, it had been through at least one wash and dry cycle. On the paper scribbled with pencil in Zane's faltering handwriting, were Waunita and Lily's names and phone number. In an instant, Zane thought of the note tucked in his pants pocket. Blue jeans he didn't wear often but wore on the night of the Socorro Massacre because they were loose—comfortable for flying. He recalled pulling a handkerchief from his back pocket and cinching Augustine's injured arm.

Prepared for any possible reaction, Zane remained calm. Similarly, Augustine was outwardly relaxed, his hands on the counter in plain view. It was obvious the man wasn't here to exact retribution against an individual with supernatural abilities, who had saved his life.

"Well, this is awkward," Zane said. "I won't insult you with denials, but probably best we speak without...details."

"Agreed," Augustine replied. "Besides, I'm here on my own."

"Glad to hear it," Zane said. "I'm sure we can talk through any problems like gentlemen."

"Si, let us speak then," Augustine said. "It took some work to find you. I remembered you from before, but hearing your voice, I knew for sure."

"I guess that's on me, but when I was checking things out, you seemed a nice man...a good husband and father. When you were in trouble, I had to help."

"This is true I'm certain, and I am grateful. Still...my boss is angry at the betrayal. Anxious about a war...the police. Mostly, he has many questions and no answers."

"What now, Mr. Salazar?"

"Nothing...nothing at all. My boss knows nothing of you, and he wouldn't care for my tale," Augustine answered. "But, a few questions, if you don't mind."

"Given the circumstances, I may not answer all of your questions, but ask away."

Pausing, as if pondering his words, Augustine asked, "You were not responsible for what happened?"

"No, not for what actually went down," Zane answered. "I can't say what would have happened if the others had come for a straight up deal. Obviously, they had different plans."

"Then, there may have been trouble either way?" Augustine posed.

"I suppose," Zane said. "Please pardon me for saying, but I wasn't overly concerned about what happened either way."

"Comprende..." Augustine replied. "Sadly, we lost some. One was a close... Excuse me...it's difficult to speak..."

"I'm sorry to hear that," Zane said. "Please remember we didn't start it and fortunate for you and your compadres, we were there. On the other hand, if us being there caused it, then I could understand if there was hard feelings."

"Luckily for us, the others had brought the drugs, even though they still meant to rob us," Augustine revealed. "And, there were lots of guns and more cash on them. So, other than our dead amigos, my boss was pleased."

"That's good...I reckon? What about you?"

"Me? I'm mostly here to say thanks. You didn't have to do what you did," Augustine said nodding. "But, you and your compadres should take care."

"We will."

"More questions, if I may."

"Go ahead."

"What are you?"

Straightaway, Zane couldn't think of an answer. He considered the question. "Just a man," Zane answered, "who found something wonderful."

"Angel wings?"

"No idea," Zane said, a puzzled expression crossing his face. "Magic..."

"Good or evil?"

"Neither really, but obviously, we're taking care of ourselves," Zane replied, sweeping his arm around the store. "Nothing fancy, but it's more than we ever had."

"You could do many good things with such a gift," Augustine said. "If there are angel wings, then there must be GOD. No?"

"Well...I don't know about GOD. We've seen spirits and shadow creatures, but so far, we haven't seen anything like GOD."

Augustine crossed himself and muttered a prayer. "My family is very religious, but I've never thought of it...until recently," Augustine said. "What you are doing and seeing is supernatural. If there are spirits and demons, then there's something beyond death. Perhaps, GOD even…"

"Like I said, I don't know about GOD."

"But, there's something, yes?" he posed. "You should be very careful. I don't believe we're meant to possess such things. I hope for your sake it is your destiny to do good."

"Well, we did save you," Zane said. "That's a good deed, isn't it?"

"Maybe…" Augustine said, "but maybe, I was meant to die…to pay my penance for bad things I have done."

"What are you gonna do now, Augustine?"

"After some time, I will leave my employer. Maybe, go work with my cousin. He owns a sheet metal shop. Doesn't pay much, but at least, my family will have a husband and father," he answered. "For the rest of my life, I will try to redeem myself, if that's even possible now."

"Sounds like a good plan," Zane replied. "Again, I am sorry for your loss."

"Protect your magic," Augustine said. "Many would do anything to take it from you."

Chapter 22
Our Own Kind

The moon exerted an unusually powerful influence on this night. The bright orb pulled and coaxed Hoyt to ascend the celestial sky, but he was very mindful of Audie's past misfortune. Instead, Hoyt ignored the moon above and attended the earth below.

Although Audie had argued against it, Hoyt and Zane tested the wings' physical reach. Meaning, how far could one fly from home and back in a single night? The brothers assumed how the supernatural effect lessened the farther from home. Was their house the epicenter of the wings' power? What would happen if they traveled too distant?

For past weeks, they had flown defined routes, increasing distance with every outing. In little time, it was evident the wings must return home before dawn. Otherwise, their power waned, and flight was much more strenuous the next evening. After several outings, the brothers calculated time between sunset and sunrise, rate of travel, linear path, and distance to determine a reasonable radius from home. They included variables like physical and mental fortitude and weather. Regrettably, they could not factor unknowns, so Hoyt resigned himself to the likelihood of being stranded hundreds of miles from home this evening.

Somewhere west of New Orleans, Hoyt was lost. Much of the topography below was a confluence of tributaries meandering through the Mississippi River Delta. He savored the bayou wilderness rushing past. He breathed in scents wafting through the balmy air. Once, he lingered to watch an alligator ambush a large water moccasin swimming across a channel. On another occasion, he observed a cougar chasing a possum. Hoyt had heard tales of mountain lion sightings in Eastern Texas, but he had never seen one himself.

Gettin' tired... Gotta find high ground near a road. Hope to hell I can reach out to Zane.

Mustering his fading strength, Hoyt ascended for a better view of his surroundings. Several miles east, he spied the pale lights of a town that bordered another winding tributary. He changed course and paced himself.

Suddenly, a wisp of moon shadow brushed against Hoyt's back. Instinctively, he rolled and peered up and behind as he glided. Silhouetted against the starry night, another figure flew. Human eyes would not have taken notice, but Hoyt's raptor vision recognized another winged being, human in form, trailing him from afar.

"What the hell?"

So shocked by the sight, Hoyt could barely comprehend the ramifications of another of his kind. He righted himself to steady his path and rolled again. The being was closer having descended hundreds of feet in the seconds it took Hoyt to maneuver. Adrenaline coursing, his field of vision contracted as he studied his pursuer.

"Not human!"

Hoyt rolled and dove earthward. At the last moment, he pulled up and skimmed the uppermost branches of a cypress. An awful screech like an angry buzzard carried from close behind. He felt frustration and apprehension from the creature on his tail. He weaved in and out of the forest canopy. So, intent on the narrow path before him, Hoyt saw nothing in his peripheral vision. Recognizing a structure, a mile ahead, he doubled his efforts, increasing his speed. Ligaments and tendons threatened to tear as he pumped his muscular arms. Sweeping in low above the ground, Hoyt threaded a narrow gap between a set of electric cables spanning a set of poles.

A twanging noise erupted as Hoyt's pursuer contacted power distribution wires. A shower of sparks illumined his back trail. He arched upwards and pumped downward to clear the church's roof eave. Hoyt lighted near a brick chimney and drew his pistol in a fluid motion. Just as he took a defensive firing position, a winged being settled on the church steeple twenty feet away.

Smoke wafted from the singed feathers of a gangly figure. Its wings whipped against each other to extinguish smoldering embers. Unlike Hoyt, the creature's arms were untethered from its feathered appendages. If it was an angel, it wasn't the kind depicted in art and literature. Except for a long dagger of bone, sheathed in a leather holster, it wore no garment. It was smooth and hairless, absent any physical features to indicate gender. Whiter than a mottled albino, it most certainly had seen little, if any, sunlight. Though inhuman and grotesque at first sight, beautiful emerald eyes glowed in the darkness.

"Greetings, Brother! What is your purpose?" it spoke in Hoyt's head. *"I have never seen or heard of you before."*

"Hello you… I'm new…I guess," Hoyt replied without knowing how. *"I haven't met others like you until now."*

His throat parched, Hoyt rubbed his mouth with the back of his hand. Images, thoughts, and emotions suffused his mind. Created from nothingness, countless millennia before, the creature was ancient. If Hoyt's own magic wings weren't proof enough of an ALMIGHTY CREATOR, then this being was irrefutable evidence. Something unbeknownst to humankind in a tangible sense, Hoyt beheld an angel of GOD, even if it wasn't wholly what he had imagined.

"Not unusual," it said. *"I have not spoken to our brethren in years, but you are new to me. You seem just born. And, unlike what I have known. Do we continue to evolve? Have you spoken to HIM of late?"*

"Uh…no."

"No?" it said, as if puzzled. *"Surely, you are not born of the other. You are far too human in form to belong to him… Unless?"*

"Unless what?"

"Unless, you are neither?" the angel posed. *"I say again. What is your purpose? You are compelled to answer."*

Shallow breaths and pounding heart were Hoyt's answers. A fragment of thought came to Hoyt's mind, *"Oh, shit."*

In response to Hoyt's silence, the entity fidgeted. Wings rippled. Long bleached fingers curled and clenched. Its fingernails were long and serrated. Poised to act, but still taking measure, bright green eyes studied Hoyt, taking careful notice of the leather harness and straps of Hoyt's wings. *"Why you are just a lowly human!"* it hissed. *"From whom did you take the wings? Tell me now! I command you!"*

"Easy now…" Hoyt replied, with a deliberate thought. *"Let's talk and figure this out…"*

"Sacrilege!" it screamed, leaping and drawing its dagger midair.

Time slowed; moments lingered. With no thought of cause and effect, Hoyt fired several shots, hitting his attacker square in the breast. He sidestepped an instant before the angel crashed into the chimney. An explosion of bricks and mortar went flying as if struck by a bolt of lightning. Just as the angel flipped over the church roof,

Hoyt turned and leapt. Without thinking, he glided across a road into the woods.

Branches and brambles tore at Hoyt's face as he weaved a circuitous path through the trees. He lighted on the ground and took cover behind a thick oak. Hoyt changed out his pistol magazine and hunkered. He eyed the church through a gap in the canopy. The angel flew up and lighted on the rooftop. Stretching its lanky arms and unfurling its wings, the being clenched its fists and shrieked. So loud, the air vibrated. Startled from nighttime slumber, thousands of roosting birds took flight. Chirps, whistles, and caws carried across the predawn sky. Countless cicadas buzzed. Hoyt pictured nocturnal creatures fleeing the angel's fury.

Craning its head upward, the being looked around, searching for an enemy never encountered before in ageless wanderings. Turning eastward, it lifted an arm to block the view of the horizon where the faintest glow of dawn appeared. It knelt and clawed the church roof with bleached fingers. Shingles and boards sailed through the air as it vented its rage. When a wisp of smoke wafted from its feathered wings, the angel turned westward and sprinted across the roof ridge. Taking flight, it streaked above the treetops and piloted toward some darker destination.

Oh, shit…

"Wake the hell up!" Zane snapped. "You're not napping until you tell me again what you ran into."

"Can it wait 'til later?" Hoyt asked. "I'm awful tired."

"No way," Zane replied, his hands gripping the steering wheel. "This affects us all. My arm's nearly healed to fly again, and I'd like to know what to watch for."

"I dunno what it was. I've told you everything I know, but it stands to reason we're not the only ones flitting through the night skies. Between banshees, spirits, angels, and gangsters, we're really pushing our luck."

"That may be, but I'm still going out first chance."

"Good thing is, we haven't seen one before, so we might be okay if we stick to home," Hoyt figured. "We pretty much have all of Texas. We just need to stay low and watch our back trail."

"Did you hurt it?"

"Stunned…maybe… Except for sunlight, I don't think it can be killed," Hoyt said. "If it got ahold of me, it might have ripped me to shreds."

"That's just great. How do we protect ourselves against that?"

"I dunno."

"Audie's gonna have a cow," Zane declared. "He's as pissed as a hornet already, and I wouldn't be surprised if he goes after it. Maybe, we shouldn't tell him—at least for now."

"Usually, I'd agree," Hoyt said, "but it wouldn't do any good to keep it secret. He's sure to read our thoughts."

"Yeah, it's getting easier," Zane said. "How far this time before you heard me? Twenty miles?"

"At least… Good thing… No telling how long I would have been waiting. Part Pierre, was it?"

"Pierre Part," Zane answered. "I thought Marlboro was the middle of nowhere."

"Evidently not," Hoyt said. "Did I tell you about the wings?"

"What about 'em? You didn't hurt 'em did yah?"

"No, nothing like that," Hoyt answered. "When I jumped from the church roof, I forgot to palm the handholds. The wings flew on their own. They just did what I willed 'em to do."

"Damn…really?" Zane replied. "Ain't that something. Did you try again later?"

"Nah, didn't have a chance. Sun was rising…had to get under cover. Luckily, I found an old tarp. You should check it out tonight. Oh! Did I tell about the mountain lion?"

"Fuck that! The only thing that would interest me now are dragons and vampires…maybe a space alien," Zane blurted and paused. "What about the mountain lion?"

Chapter 23
Best Laid Plans

"Stop talkin' it to death!" Audie snapped, his frustration growing. "My plan can't be any worse than that Romero job. Quit acting like a couple of Nancy boys, and let's do it already!"

"All right, all right…I hear yah," Hoyt replied, his resolve eroded after much debate. "I know you wanna get back at Luther Hadley and his Samoans, but they're always watchful, so we may not catch 'em off-guard."

"Believe me, if I could trade places, I would!" Audie spat. "Besides, you've scouted Luther's place inside and out. You could probably walk through his mansion blindfolded."

"I've seen plenty through his windows, but that's no guarantee. A lot can still happen," Hoyt defended. "Just ask Zane about Socorro."

"Don't get Audie raving at me," Zane countered. "Anyhow, if Hoyt's up for it, I'm okay with it."

"All right, all right," Hoyt replied, "but I'm still the one with his ass hanging out there."

"Oh, don't be such a pussy. You'll do just fine," Audie said. "So…we're goin'?"

"Tonight?" Zane posed. "Full moon…wings will be amped, and we'll see better."

"Yeah, yeah, let's load up then," Hoyt said. "I'll follow, but take it easy. No sense gettin' stopped. Legal or not, lots of questions will be asked, especially about the arsenal in the truck bed. Hog hunting isn't gonna satisfy Joe Law's curiosity."

"Joe Law can kiss my ass," Audie said. "Until we let loose, we're not doing anything illegal. Besides, you'll see 'em coming from miles off."

"Not if I get shot, I won't. We may have some supernatural abilities, but we can still be killed. How about you, Zane? You wanna another Socorro Massacre?"

"Nope," he answered. "We'll take care. Won't we, Audie?"

"No shit!" Audie barked. "I'm not a nimrod, yah know."

"No, you're not," Hoyt replied, "but you're more fearless than careful. I'd prefer we not get killed."

***

As expected, the magic was more powerful on this evening. Liftoff usually entailed mental and physical effort to overcome inertia and gravity. Occasionally, execution was awkward since the wearer had to synchronize thought and action with the wings. There was no inherent sense of knowing how to become airborne. The act of autonomous flight was as alien to humans as breathing underwater, and if there had ever been an evolutionary connection, natural selection had bred this out of the human species eons ago. Supernatural influence was the only conceivable explanation for this newfound ability.

Since his encounter with the horrid angel, Hoyt preferred to fly low, hugging the contours of the terrain, only ascending to scout ahead. At one point, Hoyt signaled his brothers to stop when he spied a familiar pickup traveling west from Pima Reservoir. Reginald "Reggie" Tooley was the local game warden. Having cited generations of Harlan's for hunting and fishing violations, Texas Fish and Game officials were aware of the brothers. Hoyt figured Reggie would exercise his unusual stop and search powers if he observed Zane and Audie on back roads so late at night.

Fortunately, Reggie maintained a straight bearing miles north of their destination, which was a sprawling estate southwest of the reservoir. Luther Hadley was the great-grandson of Samuel Hadley, founder of Hadley and Sons Incorporated. At the outset, the Hadley Family ranched and farmed thousands of acres of fertile land throughout the county. Later, they diversified into limestone quarries, and then oil and gas. After generations of operations, hundreds of abandoned rock quarries and bared oil fields pockmarked the entire county, but dozens were still operational to this day. Although many county residents were beholden to the Hadley's for their jobs, few had kind opinions of their employer.

After the passing of Samuel Hadley III two years ago, his sole son and heir, Luther, returned from parts unknown. Luther was a lanky man with long greasy hair, pasty skin, and an angular face. Although raised by a domineering and disapproving father in an affluent family, no one could explain Luther's peculiar nature. However, some theorized his mother's disappearance when he was an adolescent stunted his mental stability. Occasionally, he appeared on job sites unannounced and fired longtime employees without cause. He enjoyed harassing his transient laborers, mostly Hispanics, who had traveled far to toil in dusty quarry pits for minimum wage.

Thankfully, Luther was away much of the time. Although many of his employees were not interested in his whcreabouts, some thought he patronized murky places in Central and South America. Whenever Luther was home, three nameless men always accompanied him, presumably acting as personal bodyguards and purveyors for their employer's depraved wishes. Otherwise, Luther remained ensconced at his estate, hidden behind hundreds of acres of cedar and oak woods, and fenced off by miles of nasty razor wire fence. Except for out-of-state contractors, foreign domestics, and laborers, few county residents had actually seen the Hadley's sprawling plantation-style home.

***

Having reconnoitered the estate in the weeks before, the brothers had mapped the locations of dozens of video cameras. Hoyt had found a coaxial cable connecting a series of cameras that marked their approach to the mansion.

Hoyt lighted on the ground out of sight from the video feed. He breathed deep, savoring nightly scents. Closing his eyes, his sixth sense spread outward like ripples from a pebble tossed into a still cow tank. Nocturnal images appeared in his mind: an opossum hidden in night shadow, an armadillo grubbing a rotted stump, a moccasin swallowing a frog. Then, he envisioned his brothers pulling off the road alongside a phone company pedestal, and Audie jumping out with a heavy-duty padlock cutter. Hoyt's perspective ascended into the starry sky, probing for the presence of others. No lights shone; no voices spoke. He sensed people in the Hadley mansion, but no coherent thoughts, only muddled dream imagery and insentient emotion.

Are you ready? Hoyt asked, his mind projecting a message over an unseen communication medium. He removed a set of wire cutters from his abdomen pack.

I hear yah. Audie answered. *Now?*

Count of three…one, two, three.

Mental thoughts coordinated, Hoyt and Audie cut their respective cables.

With phone lines and video out of commission, Audie crossed the dirt road and clipped six taut strands of barbwire. He stood aside

167

as Zane plowed through a barricade of mesquite with his pickup. Long, thick thorns were no threat to the truck's knobbed tires.

Wearing a black patch over his left eye, Audie followed on foot. When the truck came to a stop, he clambered onto the bed and tapped the cab roof. Audie held tight to the roll bar and kept his knees bent to absorb the worst of the jarring ride. Coming upon a flattened cattle trail, Zane flipped a heavy-duty electrical switch under his console. Truck lights extinguished, the nighttime darkness vanquished their sight. As soon as they removed their eye patches, their already enhanced night vision returned.

Watching his brothers below, Hoyt circled the mansion. Given the hour, he figured Luther's security staff wouldn't react straightaway—if at all. So far, it was quiet.

Parked behind a stand of cedar, Zane killed the engine. Leaving the door open and keys in the ignition, he donned a Kevlar vest and clipped on a small tote laden with ammo. He also grabbed a 12-gauge semi-auto shotgun preloaded with five shells alternating between double-aught buckshot and slugs.

Similarly equipped, Audie had Hoyt's M14 rifle with night-scope. Both carried .45 caliber automatic pistols and spare ammo magazines. Within seconds, they had taken positions in the trees, covering three sides of the mansion.

Sit still for a sec', Hoyt said.

A tentative chirp called from the brush, followed by another, then another, until a cacophony of crickets permeated the silence. Hoyt strained to hear beyond the walls of the stately mansion. Still, no discernible human voices issued. Instead, heightened olfactory senses sniffed delicate currents, smells of male deodorants, musky sweat, and stale cigarettes. Hoyt's nose crinkled against the odors of soured farts and an unflushed toilet. Although a lessor smell of a feminine presence pervaded, it wasn't of perfumes and soaps. He smelled scents that were harsh and pungent, metallic and cloying, adrenaline...

Something doesn't feel right.

What's that? Audie asked.

Not sure. Just...something's off...maybe.

Keep going? Zane offered. *Be a shame to call it off now.*

Let's stick to the plan, but be mindful.

Make sure you disarm the panel and open the door for me, Zane reminded.

Let's hope Audie's buddy came through with the code.

It's good...guaranteed, Audie interjected. *Hasn't been changed since it was upgraded two years ago. If not, Sidney knows he's gonna get beat within an inch of his life.*

Unfortunately, we might spend time finding our way, and if the door's locked, we're gonna have to improvise. It may come to a fight.

Fuck it, Audie thought. *We'll just take 'em out. They're assholes—plain and simple.*

I agree, Zane replied. *Give 'em no quarter.*

Okay then. Don't forget your masks and gloves. I'll signal soon.

Arms no longer tethered, Hoyt lifted skyward and lighted on the rooftop next to the tower. Sliding over the railing, the floor timbers creaked, but imperceptible to normal human ears. Hoyt crept, his old canvass Nike's quiet as a well-worn pair of leather moccasins. The wings lessened gravity's effect and enhanced the wearer's stealth.

Even with raptor vision, it was dark through the windowed door. Hoyt stared into the gloom searching for traces of infrared light from a motion detector. Taking off a glove, he touched the door feeling for a tingle of electrical current coursing through hidden wires and magnetic contacts. As expected, there was no sign of an alarm system in the belfry. Surprised by the absence of security appliances, Hoyt figured it made sense since a typical thief couldn't enter the residence through the rooftop.

The unlocked door latch turned. Hoyt sniffed the refrigerated air wafting outward. Except for the mansion's inhabitants, he detected nothing that concerned him. He stretched a black thin-knit cap over his face. His six senses attuned to unfamiliar surroundings, Hoyt descended a spiral staircase. Only a vague shadow gave away his presence. He reckoned his dusky appearance might inspire dread in those who encountered him.

The central part of the mansion was an open expanse connected by an impressive circular stairwell. House lights cast a dim radiance. The high vantage point offered a view throughout the home. Many rooms bordered the second and third floor landings, protected by hardwood railings. High, narrow doors concealed dangers within the rooms. Hoyt heard snoring and slumbering sounds from the master bedroom and another bedroom on the floor below. He sensed two men in each room.

All told, Luther and one of his guards are in the master bedroom, the other two on the second landing across the way, Hoyt projected. *We're sure no domestics are staying over?*

None, Audie replied. *Three to five women come every day to cook, clean, and run errands, but none living in the house...for now.*

Hoyt was tempted to vault over the railing to the ground floor. Even without aid of the wings, the brothers had proven their lessened mass by jumping from trees and bridges. Just how high a distance their bodies could tolerate, they didn't yet know. Until his accident, Audie had continually tested his bounds. Zane was less daring, preferring to use the wings as intended.

Arriving at the landing, the wings quivered. Hoyt stepped into a shadowed nook and unsheathed his treasured *Knuckle Duster* trench knife with its long, pointed stiletto blade. Clicking noises carried from the ground floor. Two dark bulky shapes appeared from around the edge of the lower stair railing. Crimson eyes glowed.

Good boys... Better than any alarm system money can buy...

As Hoyt ambled down the stairs, the canine beasts sat on their haunches and waited. In any other scenario imaginable, the dogs would have mauled a stranger. Another unique power, courtesy of the wings, bestowed sway over beasts—wild and domesticated. Hoyt put away his knife and reached into a pouch attached to his waist. He presented two pig hooves to the dogs, who accepted with gentle appreciation.

Back to your beds and stay until first light—no matter what you might hear.

The Rottweiler's obeyed dutifully. Undoubtedly, a familiar clicking of toenails on the hardwood floors would not awaken Luther and his minions. Soon Hoyt spotted a keypad near the main entrance. Backlit with a red LED, the alarm system was armed. Hoyt heard Zane's shallow breathing from the other side of the door.

All right guys, let's hope this code was worth the money. Six, nine, six, nine, six, nine, six, nine...OFF.

The keypad turned green. Hoyt turned three separate deadbolts and opened the door on silent hinges. Zane entered with his shotgun at the ready. Safety off, his finger hovered outside the trigger guard. His footsteps were loud in Hoyt's ears.

What's the deal?

All asleep where we expected.

Dogs?

Settled down in the back.

Good. Then I'll hit the safe while you keep watch.

Will do, Hoyt replied, his attention drawn down a darkened corridor. *You do your thing while I go down the hall for a sec'.*

Okay, but don't go too far. Zane cautioned before slipping into the den leading to the library.

At the end of the hall, a glass-paned door marked the entrance to a grand dining room. Hoyt glimpsed a long table, gaudy chairs, and antique furnishings. He turned right and crept down a shorter span of corridor that veered to the left. All the while, an increasing static of gloomy imagery and adrenaline emotions suffused his mind.

Something...not right, Hoyt thought to no one. *Gotta know.*

At the end of another hallway was a low-hung window with red drapes. On the right was paned door to a utility room of sorts. To his left, was a closed door, thick and solid, with recessed hinges and a sturdy keyed dead bolt. No latch or knob protruded. Hoyt removed a glove and touched the door with the tips of his fingers. Beyond the hardwood panel, his mind sensed a narrow stairwell to the left descending into darkness and a set of stairs rising in the other direction.

Hoyt's disembodied psyche descended the stairs to the left, passing through vaulted doors and walls, drifting through oppressive environs. Suddenly, Hoyt envisioned two girls bound in a tiny room, airless and dark. Unwashed and unclothed, raped and beaten, they no longer thought of escape—only of merciful death. Emotions stirred as Hoyt thought of what they had suffered. He had a powerful urge to inflict sadistic punishments on the perpetrators.

Hoyt, what's happening? Audie interrupted. *What are you seeing?*

What? Zane added.

With little effort, Hoyt conveyed what he had seen in his mental wanderings. He awaited his brothers' reactions.

Let's just storm the house and fuck those bastards up! Audie raged. *I knew something wasn't right when I was there!*

Shit...yeah, I'm with Audie, but let's not run in there shootin' blind, Zane said. *Whadda you think, Hoyt?*

171

Beyond this thick door is a set of stairs going down and another going up…to the third floor…I think. Must be another stairwell going to the second floor? Kinda odd, don't yah think?"

Maybe not, Zane said. *The old Marlboro Depositary building had false stairwells to thwart robbers.*

That could be it. Anyhow, it's a damn solid door. I could get a handhold if Zane punched a couple of holes through it with the shotgun, but that'd be pretty stupid.

Yeah, it would.

"Fucksakes! You two gonna keep yackin' or what?" Audie interrupted their mental exchange. *"Hoyt, get to the third floor and find the back stairwell."*

"All right…I'm goin' already, Hoyt answered. *Zane, knock off what you're doing and get back here.*

More assured of his stealth, Hoyt made his way upstairs in little time. After a few moments of reconnoitering, he figured he would have to go through Luther's bedroom to get to the rear stairwell. Hoyt touched the door with his fingertips. Inside, both men were sound asleep. So much so, he presumed they had imbibed heavily on alcohol and drugs before bedtime. A dim shaft of light shone as the door swung inward. The wings retracted, allowing Hoyt to slip into the room without opening the door wider.

A shag carpet cloaked Hoyt's soundless footfall. He stepped over and around clothes and shoes. Odors of men and marijuana were pervasive. Hoyt took shallow breaths. The moon cast a pale light across the bed. A large naked man, presumably Eloni, lay across the backside of a tall lanky figure. Beer bottles, a wine decanter, and assorted pills littered the nightstands.

Where's that stairwell?

As if hearing Hoyt's thought, Eloni stirred. Hoyt melded into the darkness and stood silent, his hand clasping his knife. The Samoan rolled over, staring at a walk-in closet. Hoyt's hand relaxed. He recognized the comatose gaze of a person sleeping with eyes open. The closet door was ajar. Hoyt entered. As Luther's garments brushed against its feathers, the wings trembled. Hoyt spied a small door at the end of a wide lane of hung garments. Except for a stout slide lock, the door was otherwise unsecured. He slid the bolt. Unlike the other doors encountered, raspy hinges protested. The creaking was loud in Hoyt's ears in such a confined space.

Son-of-a-whore!

Hoyt listened for the sounds of rustling bedspreads but heard nothing. As suspected, the stairwell bypassed the second-floor landing entirely, continuing to the first where Zanc waited.

I'm here, Hoyt announced.

No mental voice answered. Hoyt turned the deadbolt knob and opened the heavy door, but his brother wasn't on the other side.

Zane, you dumb shit!

Don't get your britches in a bunch. I kept with the safe while you were gallivanting. Audie, you were right about the combo! You should see it! Wads of cash...lots of dope... Holy shit! Look at the jewelry! You'd think Liberace lived here for Chrissakes!

Zane, take the cash and leave the rest. I need you watching our back trail.

Go ahead. I'll have eyes on the landing in a sec'.

You better!

Like a mine tunnel at midnight, Hoyt's raptor vision couldn't penetrate the darkness. For some inexplicable reason, there was no light switch anywhere. Fishing a penlight from his pocket, he illumined another steel door at the bottom of an exceedingly long and steep stairwell. Hoyt descended and upon reaching the door, he pulled a thick slide bolt. The heavy door swung inward on a single, well-oiled hinge and rod that ran the length of the frame. Hoyt ducked his head to avoid a thick slab of steel-reinforced cement.

On the other side of the door, it was cool and dry. Hoyt found a switch. A loud hum preceded a blinding light. The wings opened in response to shield Hoyt's face. Eyes squinting, he gazed upon a subterranean room much more expansive than the mansion above. Not accustomed to cellars in southern states, Hoyt became claustrophobic. He took a moment to breathe until his head cleared.

Something odorous and rank permeated. Hoyt winced and crinkled his nose. Faraway screams sounded in his mind. Fear and pain... The bunker grew dim. Shadows appeared from the darkest recesses. Shapeless and vague, they drew near. Hoyt's jaw clenched, and his nostrils flared. The wings unfurled and spread wide in response to a terrible feeling that pervaded. The smoky figures fled at the sight of an archangel. Hoyt's mind cleared, his confusion dissipating.

A grid of electrical conduits and water pipes ran along the cement walls and ceiling. A maze of ventilation shafts hung low. Lengths of steel-framed shelves held containers of every shape and size stenciled with words like crackers, cakes, and candy. Two large, galvanized tanks labeled *POTABLE* lay on Hoyt's left and right. A long row of metal bunks ran down the middle of the room. A pile of olive military fatigues lay on one of the lower bunks. Farther along the wall on his right were open shower stalls, basins, and toilets. One showerhead dripped water. Arranged in a floor depression were a series of drainage grates. Folded tables and chairs were stacked. On the far wall was a metal door marked *GENERATORS*.

Farther along on Hoyt's left was a long-barred cage that housed an arsenal of rifles and pistols along with many cases of ammunition. Though there were several weapons he couldn't identify, Hoyt did recognize M1 rifles and M1911 pistols lining the cage. He noticed an absence of more modern weaponry like AR15s. Given the cellar's controlled temperature and humidity, the arsenal was well preserved, though a thin layer of dust covered every oiled surface.

Luther's daddy or granddaddy must have built a bomb shelter way back. Zane and Audie would have a field day...

So, caught up with the bunker and its trappings, Hoyt almost forgot his purpose. There were more unidentified doors constructed of thick riveted metal plates, but only one latched. Outside were two yellowed mattresses. Hoyt noticed traces of dried blood and other bodily fluids smeared into the fabric. Dirty clothes and tissues littered the floor. Hoyt approached and placed his hand on the door. The girls were there...awake and fearful.

Hoyt got on his hands and knees and spoke in a low, gentle voice, "Hello there, my name is Hoyt. My brothers and I are gonna get you outta here."

Straightaway, the girls answered, their muted voices shrill from behind the door, "Por favor apúrate, por favor apúrate! Antes de que vengan!"

If the girls hadn't understood his words, they comprehended the sincere tone of his voice. Hoyt's Spanish wasn't as good as Zane's, but he understood their anxious pleas. Still, Hoyt didn't unlatch the door straightaway.

Girls, when I open the door, please don't be frightened. Regardless of how I look, I only mean to get you outta here...somewhere safe...back to your familias. Okay?

As part of his message, Hoyt provided a vision of himself with black cap over his face and the magic wings strapped to his back. He imparted a feeling of benevolence. Surprisingly, the girls didn't flinch in reaction to his voice speaking in their heads. Hoyt provided no further explanation, not wanting to reveal his identity. He pulled down his mask and hauled on the heavy door.

"No tengas miedo..."

Gaunt faces appeared from the darkness. Tentative at first, the girls came out, naked and dirty, bruised and scabbed. Shielding their eyes against the fluorescent lights above, they didn't hide their nudity. Because of their physical condition and all they had been through, Hoyt couldn't estimate their age, though they couldn't have been out of their teens yet. He averted his eyes.

"Follow me," Hoyt motioned. "Por favor..."

Hoyt searched through the fatigues until he found two oversized jackets and green wool socks. While the girls dressed, Hoyt rinsed out a dusty glass and filled it with water. The girls took turns, emptying the glass. One of them returned to the spigot to refill it. The other looked Hoyt up and down, studying him.

"Me llamo, Maria," she spoke softly then pointed. "Anjelita..."

"I'm Hoyt."

"Eres un ángel?"

"Me? No, no... Sólo un hombre..."

"Wings...alive...jes?"

"Si, can't explain... Must go now."

After another drink of water, Maria and Anjelita followed behind as Hoyt ascended the stairs. The wings quivered as the girls touched the feathers. Approaching the landing, Hoyt tensed. His nostrils flared as the terrible feeling and awful odor returned.

"Wait up there," Hoyt whispered, pointing to the landing above. "I'll return soon."

The girls brushed past without question. It took a sheer force of will for Hoyt to descend the steps. Fluorescent lights flickered. Hoyt tried to make spit and wet his throat, but his tongue wouldn't obey. When his boot heel touched the floor, his other foot felt cemented to the last step. Hoyt had to pull on his pant leg to make his foot move.

175

At the far corner of the bunker, beyond the vault where the girls were interred, a fathomless darkness filled with flitting shapes. This time the wings remained furled against his back. Hoyt walked slowly, his right foot dragging across the floor. He approached, the gloom parting on both sides. Ahead, framed into the cement wall was a thick steel bulkhead door. Stark and windowless, its only feature was a large wheel that retracted two pinions on the right side.

Don't wanna go in there... Don't wanna...

His hands reached out with no deliberate will whatsoever. Hoyt was relieved when the wheel refused to budge, as if closed tight for years. However, his supernatural strength overcame the wheel's inertia. The pinions slid open begrudgingly. As he had dreaded, the doorway had been sealed. A noxious stench emerged. So powerful and terrible, he nearly bowled over. If not for a feeling of omnipotence bestowed by his feathered appendages, he might have fled. The wings fluttered in such a way to deflect the foulness that polluted the stale air.

Although an irresistible force urged him to go inside, Hoyt remained still. A shaft of light spilled through the open doorway revealing the most horrendous sight imaginable. Naked bodies of women and children lay in a pile of putrid corruption. Black mildew and hoary mold covered faces once pure. Sickening gore oozed from open eyes that belied the horrors inflicted. Innards protruded from bloated bellies. Skin pulled taut over grimaced skeletal expressions.

If only I had known... I would have... What have I been doing with my gift?

Despite his revulsion, tears streamed down Hoyt's face, but in little time, his wretchedness transformed into a great resolve. The heinous perpetrators of these murders were within his grasp. No trials, no pleadings, no mercies... A cruel vengeance was forthcoming. Hoyt closed the door, shutting out the grim scene forever burned into his memory.

Hoyt's jaw and fists clenched. Sinewy muscle rippled. Fully extended, the wings quivered as if waiting for a draft of rising air to go aloft. Setting aside any façade of stealth, Hoyt marched up the stairs. At the landing, the girls sensed a severe change of temperament and stood aside.

Zane!

Where you been?

Never mind that! There are two girls you need to take from here—now! Go out the back and leave the door open for the dogs. They won't bother you.

I'm here, Audie spoke.

Audie!

What the fuck! One moment you're there and gone the next!

Get over it! Just help Zane and get the hell outta here!

What's up, Brother?

Just a single image of the horrific scene was enough to explain his fury. Hoyt unsheathed his trench knife and stomped up the main stairwell. His heavy footfall echoed. Fearful Rottweilers howled. At the top of the second-floor landing, he heard a flurry of movement from the bedroom where Luther's Samoan henchmen had been sleeping. Hoyt didn't hesitate. He bounded across the foyer, his winged form silhouetting the doorway.

From the dim room, two burly forms stared as if dazed. Before they reacted, Hoyt swept across the room as the wings operated autonomously. He slashed one man across the face. The stiletto blade cleaved skull and cheekbone. A shrill scream issued. The other man rushed ahead and tackled. Hoyt stood steadfast as if buffeted by a stiff wind. He thrust the knife upward. The blade tip penetrated under the attacker's breastbone perforating the heart and a lung. A spray of dark blood covered the length of his right arm. Hoyt lifted with the knife. The blade buried deeper. Hoyt's closed hand entered the man's chest cavity. Like a sack of dirty laundry, Hoyt lifted the massive man over his head and threw him through a bedroom window.

Without thinking, he turned and weaved just as a loud percussion sounded from his left. Hoyt felt a large caliber bullet pass within inches of his face. The man he had slashed held a large revolver. Hoyt's hand reached out, wrapping his fingers around the gun cylinder before it could rotate far enough to drop the hammer. A standoff ensued as the large man grasped the pistol and squeezed the trigger. Hoyt's grip was unyielding. Slowly and purposely, Hoyt piloted his knife in the Samoan's direction. Veins appeared on the man's large, sweaty face as he redoubled his efforts to discharge the weapon. Despite the man's struggles to pull away, Hoyt remained fixed. It was a silent combat interrupted only when the revolver's trigger suddenly snapped off.

177

At that instant, the man lunged. In the blink of eye, Hoyt thrust the blade tip into the Samoan's throat. The man made a gurgling sound and grabbed Hoyt's wrist with beefy hands. Within seconds, he dropped to his knees, head lolling. Hoyt pushed out with the flat of his booted foot. The man's limp body slammed against the far wall.

Suddenly, a hail of gunfire erupted from the landing above, spraying into the bedroom. Bits of plaster and wood lath peppered as bullets tore through the walls. Hoyt threw himself to the floor, taking shelter behind a low shelf crammed with hardbound books. The wings enshrouded him. Hoyt waited knowing the shooters would have to reload soon. In the meantime, he just hoped a bullet didn't find a gap between the thick books behind him. All at once, a volley of gunfire sounded from the lower landing.

I got yah covered, Hoyt! Get ready!

Audie...

As expected, the shooting above stopped as Luther and Eloni hurriedly reloaded. Audie kept firing away, taking deliberate aim. Hoyt bounded from the bedroom and launched himself upward. The wings spread and swept downward with powerful strokes. For a moment, Hoyt hovered before the dumbstruck men. He grabbed a patch of hair on each head. The wings propelled him backward pulling the men. They plummeted headlong past the second floor, struck the first-floor stairwell, and tumbled down the hardwood tread. Luther and Eloni came to rest at Audie's feet.

Hoyt lighted beside his brother and stared. Eloni was silent. His large head askew, his stout body trembled. Luther groaned. His legs and torso lay on the steps above his head. Both of his arms were broken. Ashen bone protruded through the skin on his bare forearms. Blood sieved from a deep gash on his head.

"I know you... You're Audie...Audie Harlan," Luther croaked. "Oh...I'm hurt real bad. Why...do this?"

"Yeah, you know me," Audie replied. "You'll also get to know some other psycho assholes where you're goin'."

"Chamber of horrors you have in your lair," Hoyt spoke. "I'm thinkin' you deserve a final earthly reckoning for what you did to those poor women and children."

"I got a better idea," Audie said, as he grabbed ahold of one of Luther's legs and started dragging.

178

Luther shrieked in agony, "Please...no! I have money! I'll confess. Just don't...!"

Undoubtedly, it was a tortuous journey for Luther as his injured body was dragged to the bunker. Hoyt and Audie didn't care, and they made no pretense about Luther's fate. At the threshold of a nightmarish dungeon, Hoyt threw Luther atop dozens of murdered women and children.

"Have a nice time in hell, you sick son-of-a-bitch!" Audie shouted.

Hoyt held the door handle and paused while black creatures flitted from the shadows and poured into the room. Luther's shrieks continued long after Hoyt shut the door and clamped it tight.

***

The heat was unbearable as flames climbed higher and higher. The mansion engulfed, Zane and Audie left the girls hidden near the road. Hoyt stayed with them until he heard sirens in the distance.

"Please repeat your story," Hoyt instructed. "Remember, tell about everything that happened to you until tonight. After that, just keep it simple and hold to your stories."

"Masked men came, let us out, and led us away. Five of them, we think... They were nice to us...gave us food and water. They spoke Spanish but didn't say much. They left us here and said they would call the police."

"I am so sorry for all that has happened to you girls," Hoyt said, wiping his eyes with the heel of his hand. "I wish we had known, so we could have come sooner. We have your home addresses, and we'll get money to you somehow. I promise."

The girls sobbed and hugged Hoyt, thanking him. Just as strobe lights appeared, the wings spread wide. He knelt and leapt into the night sky. At the supernatural vision, the girls fell to their knees and shouted praises to GOD.

Chapter 24
Bother the Day

For several nights, there were no flights. The brothers kept to the house and pawnshop and watched the news. The happenings in a small Texas town of Pima had captivated the entire nation. Masked bandits had freed two teenage girls from a den of horrors. Heir of a wealthy family, Luther Hadley and his Samoan henchmen, had raped, tortured, and murdered dozens of women and children over the years. In an immense bunker built for the next Armageddon, firefighters had discovered Luther's corpse atop a pile of his victims.

Maria and Anjelita told law enforcement agencies a disturbing tale. Lured from Mexico with promises of work as household servants, the girls came from poor circumstances. Luther had flown them into the United States aboard his private plane, having bribed local customs officials to overlook the extra passengers. Upon arrival at the Hadley Estate, Luther's men had taken them prisoner. For countless weeks, the men had forced the girls to satisfy their depravities.

When they first arrived, there were three others including a boy and his mother, Juan and Carla, and a teenage girl, Delfina. Sometimes held together and sometimes separately, there was no delineation between night and day, only long periods of isolation and bouts of fear and pain. Eventually, Delfina did not return, and shortly after, Juan and his mother died. Unable to endure further torments, Carla smothered her son with a filthy pillow. Immediately after, she strangled herself with a cloth strip.

The girls had survived their nightmare by capitulating to the wishes of their tormentors. No matter the act, they tried to gain trust in hopes Luther and his men might become complacent. Regrettably, this worsened their situation as the men preferred their victims afraid. Near the end of their captivity, they were ready for their own deaths. Anjelita vowed to bite hard the next time one of the men forced himself ...

Except for descriptions of their saviors as avenging angels, the girls kept true to their rehearsed story.

"Fuckin' house of horrors," Audie said. "I should have known. I should have done something sooner."

"Don't beat yourself up, Audie. Who the hell could've known," Hoyt replied, as he helped his injured brother don the wings. "You want me to cinch the straps for yah?"

"Nah, that's okay. It's enough just to wear 'em. They help with the healing," Audie said, flexing his arms. His ribs still ached, and it was sometimes hard to breathe, but he was getting better. At the rate he was convalescing, Audie figured he might fly again within days.

"Maybe…but it seems a waste not to use 'em," Hoyt opined. "I could be flittin'."

"Oh, give me a break. You've been gallivanting all over Texas on my dime. Like I said, it helps with my healing. Besides, you need to spend more time helping at the pawnshop. Don't tell Zane I said it, but he's been busting his hump. What's the matter with you, Big Brother? Your head's clear. Your body's strong. Why aren't you going out? You got your license back, and there's always wheels in the driveway now."

"I dunno? I worked at the store today…working most days now. Yah know…minding the books and keeping inventory. Sometimes, I even do sales when you aren't around. Little steps, I guess?"

"Little steps, hell!" Audie countered. "You're a warrior angel for chrissakes! Even without the wings, you're faster and stronger than the baddest hombre around. You could have any woman hot and bothered with just a few words. Shit…I have to go outta my way now to avoid the ladies. When they start gettin' flirty, I get aroused down below. And, the silver-haired ladies are the most randy."

"Whadda mean? Have you been…?"

"Well…a few… They're the horniest…up for anything."

"For cryin' out loud, Audie. You're worse than Zane. Hump a knothole if it was drippin' sap."

"Screw you! Some of them ole biddies are pretty hot! Anyhow, Maxine and Aubrey are always up for it, or I'd explode."

"More information than I needed."

"Hell with that," Audie said. "Zane and I got together and did something for yah."

"Whadda mean? What are you two up to now?"

"You remember Shelia from Buck's Hardware?" Audie asked, still flexing his arm.

181

"You mean the lady, who works behind the counter? The one with the...?" Hoyt asked, holding his hands apart near his chest. "The lady with the red hair...wears a lot of makeup?"

"Yeah, the one with the big tits and round ass," Audie replied. "Anyhow, Zane talked you up. How you were a business owner now, and you being single and all. She noticed you in the store last week. Said you looked buff in your tee shirt and jeans. Heard you were a real outlaw...a badass."

"He shouldn't have done that," Hoyt said, his voice trembling. "What do I say to her now? I can't go back there."

"Well, you better figure it out, Brother, 'cause she's comin' over tonight. She's gonna do a real job on yah."

"Whadda mean, comin' over?"

"She's gonna be here in the next hour. Bringin' yah supper and a six-pack."

"That's not so," Hoyt said, his eyes darting around the house. "I've never had company here. Haven't had a chance to straighten up."

"House is clean as a nun's twat. I made sure of that earlier today. All you gotta do is take a shower, dab on some cologne, and wear a nice shirt. How 'bout the blue western shirt buried in the back of your closet?"

"How am I supposed to act?"

"Just be yourself," Audie answered. "Except, don't mumble. Speak in complete sentences. Compliment her on her shoes... Hell, I don't fuckin' know! Zane's already paved a path for yah. Shelia's been around the block a few times. She'll make it real easy for yah."

"Shit..." Hoyt said.

"Wished you had given me warning, is all." "Hoyt, just remember who you are...not who you were," Audie explained. "You're different now. No need to get all nervous."

"I guess..." Hoyt muttered, rubbing his whiskered face. Carnal urges coursed. His body trembled with anticipation.

"I left a box of rubbers on your bureau," Audie said. "I'll be hunkered in the backyard."

"What are you gonna do?"

"Oh, don't you bother none about me," Audie ordered. "I'm gonna let my mind wander through the neighborhood. Peek in a few windows. Let my body heal. Hell, that'll keep me busy enough."

"Okay."

"Just get Shelia outta the house before daybreak, and remember, you can't trust anyone, especially loose women. Go out with her all yah want. Fuck her brains out, but don't get too close."

"You're a real dream date, aren't yah, Audie?"

"I'm just saying. You start goin' on about magic wings, and assholes with badges will kick in our door. You can count on that."

"I don't doubt it," Hoyt admitted. "No worries. I won't try to impress anyone. I like things the way they are."

"Go shave and shower and brush your teeth. I'm gonna be out back perched on a tree limb."

Although hurried, Hoyt was thorough with his personal grooming. He had just finished buttoning his shirt when he heard a car. Hoyt turned on the back light and sauntered outside. In the driveway, an older model El Camino idled. Acrid exhaust wafted through the evening air. Hoyt winced at the odor. When the driver turned off the ignition, the engine continued to diesel for several seconds.

"Hi, Hoyt! I brought yah supper!" a woman hailed, getting out of the car. "Well, look at you. I don't think I've ever seen you all cleaned up before."

Shelia May Nelson was a busty, auburn-haired woman, somewhere in her mid to late thirties. She wore a generous coating of makeup, including a shock of blue eye shadow and dark liner. Ruby lipstick and pink rouge adorned her pale face. A blue dress clung to her shapely figure.

Hoyt blushed when Shelia wrapped her arms around his neck and kissed him on the cheek. His body stiffened against her yielding figure. An aroma of perfume and stale cigarette smoke overwhelmed him. For a fleeting moment, Hoyt wanted to push away—the sensation so abrupt and unfamiliar. Instead, he embraced her in return, savoring the physical closeness of a woman he had fantasized about so many times.

"Hello, yourself," Hoyt sputtered. "I was surprised to hear about you coming over. My brothers have been playing matchmaker for a while."

"Well, I hope they're no good at that," Shelia said. "I went all out to make you supper and get gussied up for yah. Zane's been telling me all about you. How you went into business and getting into shape."

"Yeah..." Hoyt stammered.

"He was telling the truth," she said, her fingers running down his arms. "All hard and muscled, aren't you? My goodness... Feels like you've been working out down below too."

His manhood engorged and throbbing, Hoyt pulled back, "Oh...sorry 'bout that, Shelia. I didn't know."

"That's okay, Sweetie," she said, her hand gliding down and rubbing. "Damn...you are a big boy, aren't yah? Hard as a hammer... You could pound nails with that thing, couldn't yah?"

"I sure...could..." Hoyt grunted, pulling her close. Placing his mouth against hers, Shelia's tongue swept inward flicking and probing. Hoyt pressed a hand against the small of her back while his other roamed across her backside, feeling every curve of her buttocks.

A light illumined from the house across the driveway. Mrs. Sanchez's stooped figure was silhouetted on the other side her blinds. Shelia hesitated, pushing back. "Let's go inside," she whispered breathlessly. "I don't wanna audience."

"Can't stop now," Hoyt uttered, his fingers sliding between her upper thighs. He ground his pelvis into hers. Hoyt's entire body was flush. As he erupted, he felt Shelia tremble at the same time.

'What's happening out there?" Mrs. Sanchez called out. "Hoyt, what are you doin' with that, *senora*?"

"For cryin' out loud, Mrs. Sanchez! Mind your own business for once. I'm gettin' intimate with a lady friend."

"It's all right, ma'am," Shelia said, her voice winded. "Just grownup stuff. Sorry for disturbing..."

"Oh..." she said taken aback. "You're making so much noises."

"Yeah, yeah," Hoyt replied. "Now, go away!"

"Rude!" Mrs. Sanchez hissed, as she closed her kitchen window.

"I'm so sorry, Shelia. I couldn't help myself. You being so close...and desirable..." Hoyt whispered. "Are you okay?"

"I'm okay, but I'm not like that...usually," she answered. "I don't think I could've stopped yah. A little scary...but hot."

"I hear yah," he said. "Wanna come in? I'll mind my manners...unless you wanted...that is."

"Look at me...look at my dress!" she said pulling her thin garment from her belly. "Look at what you did! Soaked through your britches all over me... Not very gentlemanly. Not at all! You're gonna have to pay for this!"

"Aw hell...so sorry..." Hoyt stuttered. "Just...it's been so long since last time... It's no wonder..."

"What the fuck!" she snapped.

"Again...so sorry," Hoyt pleaded. "Let me make it up to you."

Her anger subsiding, Shelia paused and deliberated.

"Oh shit!" Hoyt thought, *"She's gonna make me pay big time."*

"I hear you sell jewelry at your store," she said, her voice lowered. "We do. Say...how 'bout you come out tomorrow and pick yourself out a piece. It's the least I could do...and money to buy a new dress. Anything you want."

"Well...maybe..." Shelia said. "I suppose you really couldn't help yourself, could yah?"

"No...no, I couldn't," Hoyt said. "You're a sexy lady, Shelia. I've thought about you a lot over the years. The things we've done in my dreams... Probably best if you don't have anything to do with me."

"I understand," she said as if chastened. "A lot of men have hit on me in my life, so I shouldn't be surprised if, once in a while, one of 'em can't control himself."

"That's right," Hoyt said. "Thank you for understanding...and I'll do anything for a second chance. Treat you like the lady you are."

"Take me to lunch tomorrow, and we'll talk about it," she said, waiting by her car and saying no more.

"Oh...sorry!" Hoyt uttered and opened her door. "You're gonna have to help me with my manners, Shelia."

"We'll see," she said, sliding into the car seat. "You're a rough gem that needs a lot of polishing."

"That I am," Hoyt said. "I look forward to knowing you...proper like."

"How 'bout taking your food from the passenger seat, Baby," Shelia directed. "You might as well have dinner, since you've already had dessert."

"Okay...smells real good," Hoyt said, running around to the other side of the car. "Thanks, Honey."

"Uh huh," she replied. "I'll drop by your store tomorrow sometime between eight and twelve."

"I'll be there," Hoyt said. "Sweet dreams…"

An engine belt squealed as Shelia started her car. Backing out of the driveway, she clipped the mailbox and scraped the car's undercarriage on the curb. Shelia drove away trailing a plume of black exhaust.

As Hoyt hoisted a casserole tray and trudged back to the house, Mrs. Sanchez called out from behind drawn blinds in a high mocking voice, "Sweet dreams, Hoyt."

"Not very ladylike, Mrs. Sanchez."

"I'm not one *el sexo* in drive. Red-haired *senora…la puta*. You do better. *Si. Senora* too old for you."

"Maybe, but I haven't dated in a while…ever actually, Mrs. Sanchez. Little steps, yah know. Gotta learn to saddle a horse before I can ride."

"You get clean, Hoyt. S*enora* give you *las ladillas*."

"I'm sure she didn't give me the crabs, Mrs. Sanchez."

"And tell Audie go inside. Why he hide in backyard dressed like *el pallo*…chicken?"

"I dunno, ma'am. Yah know, Audie. No tellin' what he's up to."

"Si…all of you *loco* since boys, but much stranger things lately."

Hoyt stopped and turned, thoughts running through his mind. "How 'bout me and my brothers clean out your backyard and replant your flower and garden beds," Hoyt offered. "You've always been a good neighbor to us. It's the least we can do."

"*Si*, I like that," she replied. "Maybe fix front steps…move couch. Maybe, I not see strange things."

"*Si, Senora* Sanchez," Hoyt sighed, knowing this was the beginning of an unending line of chores. With the sound of a window sliding shut, Hoyt turned back to the house.

Probably just as well to have an understanding with our neighbor. She's put up with a lot of shit from us over the years, and no telling the things she's seen lately. Yep…keep on her good side…

"Sweet dreams, Hoyt!" his brother called out from the blackness of the backyard. "Who's the dream date now, huh? Hee hee hee!"

Oh shit! I'm never gonna live this one down…ever…

186

Chapter 25
Shelia's Revenge

"Did what?" Zane asked, cradling the telephone handset. "Dry humped her in the drive with Mrs. Sanchez watching? What the hell...! She's what! Coming over today! For what? No, she isn't... Well, it's comin' outta his pay!"

Waiting for Audie to continue a descriptive narrative about Hoyt's date, Zane looked out the front window. Still early, the pawnshop hadn't opened yet. Brilliant sunlight streamed through the metal bars that secured a thick pane of protected glass. The brick-and-mortar building was a fortress, safeguarding the store's valuable inventory.

"Nope, not yet, but should be here soon," Zane answered, and then paused. "Yeah, I'll beat on him good today. Yep...good enough... Don't worry. I'll be home in plenty of time."

Seeing movement on the video monitor overlooking the rear parking lot, Zane spied his older brother circling in his truck. It was a routine maneuver before entering through the back entrance. More than a dozen times over the years, thieves had attempted to rob the pawnshop. Unfortunate for them, Earl Pomeroy didn't tolerate thievery kindly. Three times, he had shot men trying to storm his premises. Always vigilant, always distrustful of strangers, the shop's former owner imparted his security protocols. Regardless of electronic alarms and video monitors, nothing could substitute for always being mindful of one's surroundings. Although the brothers held great advantage in this area, they appreciated Earl's experience and advice in such matters.

Getting out of the truck, Hoyt looked about and waited a minute. Satisfied no one was watching him, he walked across the lot to the rear entrance. Before unlocking the heavy steel door and entering, Hoyt buzzed to give his brother a heads up.

"What's goin' on, bro'?" Zane called out.

"Oh...not much..." Hoyt answered, wandering into the back office. "Coffee pot on yet?"

"Yeah, fresh brewed. So...?"

"So what?"

"How was your date with Shelia?" Zane asked. "Did yah make her acquaintance?"

"Yeah... I imagine Audie's already given you a blow by blow."

"Well, he mentioned a few things, but thought I'd make you feel more uncomfortable than you already are," Zane admitted. "Grab a cup of coffee and tell me about it. Got a half-hour before we open."

For several minutes, Zane subjected his brother to a series of rapid-fire questions, which Hoyt answered reluctantly, but openly. As much as Zane wanted to tease, he held back. He suspected his eldest brother had never been physically intimate with a woman, much less ever had a girlfriend. He also knew that Shelia May Nelson was too old and far too worldly for his inexperienced brother. Yet, Zane thought his brother needed a casual fling with a mature woman.

"No worries, Hoyt. First time's always awkward. Hard to believe, but I wasn't always a stud. Just between you and me, I wasn't gettin' any at all until the wings came along. Now, I'm irresistible to the ladies. Wish I could say it's because of my natural appeal, but no doubt, there's magic afoot," Zane explained. "For now, I'm gonna get all I can 'til there's no more. Hopefully, if that happens—and it probably will—some of it will have rubbed off on me. My worst nightmare is goin' back to what was."

"So, you're not bothered that Shelia's dropping by for an apology gift?"

"Oh...fuck yeah I am," Zane retorted. "Mrs. Sanchez is right. Shelia's gonna pussy whip you bad. I just hope the wings can protect you from that."

"Aw, hell...here she comes," Hoyt stammered. "Shit...whadda I do now?"

"Unlock the door, and let her in. Kiss her cheek. Compliment her on her shoes. Don't mumble. Yah know...just be yourself," Zane advised. "Remember...you're an angel warrior with a big pecker. Shelia doesn't stand a chance."

"Yeah...I'll jot that down in my journal..." Hoyt replied, holding the front door open. "Hey there, Sweetie! Come on in."

"Hey yourself," Shelia greeted, giving Hoyt a kiss on the mouth. "My, my...nice little store."

"Hey, Shelia, welcome to our awesome pawnshop," Zane said, waving from behind the counter. "I hear Hoyt's gonna give you a treat—jewelry that is."

188

"That's what he told me," she said, staring at Hoyt. "Taking me out too, aren't you, Honey?"

"I am," Hoyt answered, taking Shelia's hand and leading her to the middle of the floor. "Let me show you around before customers start crowding through the door. From here, you can pretty much take it all in. Appliances are on the right, and musical instruments are on the back wall. Hunting and fishing gear are along the front aisle, and coins and jewelry behind the counter. Gets busy most days, so there's always two of us here."

"Lots of nice things," she said, looking around. "Making good money?"

"No regular pay yet. Still renovating…making the place nicer. The former owner let it go some, so we have work yet, but it's comin' along. We're figuring out the business."

"That's good," she said. "So, what do you have that's really nice?"

"Rings, bracelets, necklaces, earrings…we have it all," Hoyt declared with muted enthusiasm. "Come over and have a look."

"I hope you have lots of time, Darling, because I like what I'm seeing," Shelia declared, pointing a manicured finger. "Let me look at that one."

For the next hour, Shelia tried on dozens of pieces all the while looking in the mirror. At the same time, Zane handled a stream of customers, who bought, sold, or pawned items. In the end, Shelia sweet-talked Hoyt out of a ring and two necklaces worth several hundred dollars.

"You're quite the gentleman, Hoyt," Shelia said. "Are you ready to take me out for dinner? I hear there's a new restaurant downtown. Do you have a dress shirt and slacks…maybe, a nice pair of shoes or cowboy boots?"

"Sorry, Shelia. All I managed today was a clean shirt and blue jeans, and I don't have any dress clothes here at the apartment."

"Okay…we'll go someplace casual then," she replied with a palpable tone of disapproval. "Afterwards, we can go to the mall, and you can buy me a new dress."

Hoyt sensed irritation from his brother, who presently handled three customers at once. "How 'bout midafternoon, Honey," he suggested. "It's awful busy right now, but it'll slow down after lunch.

I'll give you money, so you can buy a pair of shoes to go along with your new dress."

For the briefest moment, Shelia glared until offered a monetary inducement, her expression softening. "It's okay this time, Honey, but I'm not a lady to put off," she warned, taking the money. "I expect you'll be ready to go when I get back?"

"Yes, ma'am, I will," Hoyt soothed. "Just you and me on the town." Again, Hoyt felt his brother's annoyance.

***

"A glass of red wine for both of us," Shelia told the server. "And, don't dawdle, Sweetie. My boyfriend and I have places to go."

"Yes, ma'am," the young woman returned. "I'll get your order in right away."

"I swear...these young ones nowadays..." Shelia said. "Slow service everywhere I go. Don't you dare tip her more than ten percent...maybe less."

Hoyt breathed deep. Although he hadn't smoked in months, he now yearned for a cigarette. In spite of lustful urges for the auburn-haired woman with the pouty lips, generous breasts, and shapely derriere, Hoyt's desire waned. He wondered if he could tolerate Shelia for the time it would undoubtedly take to bed her proper.

"What's the matter, Honey? Cat got your tongue?"

"Oh...no," Hoyt hesitated. "I'm just taking you in... You're so gorgeous and sexy I can hardly concentrate on what you're saying."

"Well...I suppose I can overlook your inattention with that excuse," she said. "You'll come over to my place tonight. Since you're really into me, I expect you to do certain things for me. If you do it right, it'll be worth your while. So, what do you like...in the bedroom?"

"Uh...I don't really know..." Hoyt said, images coming to mind of things he had seen in magazines, porn videos, and fantasies of Regina. "Everything... I wanna do everything with you."

"My... You're like a block of Play-Doh, aren't yah," Shelia said, her voice sounding hoarse. "Bet I could make you do anything, couldn't I, Big Boy?"

"Yeah...you could," Hoyt uttered.

"So, we don't have any misunderstandings later on, I'm gonna tell you how it is. First...if you're a good boy, I'll go down on you, but nothing nasty. Belly is okay but nowhere else," she affirmed.

"Second...don't think of doing me from behind, so get that outta your mind right now. Got it?"

"Really?" Hoyt said. "But...I was looking forward... You have such a fine backside."

"Absolutely not!" Shelia affirmed. "I'm a lady...not some skank."

"Right..." Hoyt sighed. "Nothing like that."

Lifting a glass of water, Hoyt discerned a slight tremble in his hand—not that he cowed by Shelia's brusque manner. He tugged at his shirt collar. "Is it hot in here?" he asked, taking out clean handkerchief and wiping his brow.

"Not at all," she answered, peering into a purse mirror and applying bright red lipstick. "Sex talk is making you horny. You men are all the same...every one of you."

"Yeah, that's it... I hope I don't have to get up anytime soon," Hoyt said, looking around. Thankfully, the lunch crowd had thinned out.

"Little worked up, are yah?" Shelia murmured, snapping her mirror closed and glancing at Hoyt's lap. "Why...you are excited, aren't you?"

"Yeah...guilty as charged," he chuckled, trying to redirect Shelia's attention elsewhere. "I hear the steaks here are good."

"What I'm seeing looks good too," she said, staring noticeably, her hand drifting down. "That big thing of yours needs a lot of care, doesn't it?"

"Uh...yeah...if you think so..."

"Oh...I know so," she whispered, her eyes darting around the restaurant. "I like 'em big. Sometimes, I like it to hurt some—but only if I say so."

"Glad you think so," Hoyt said. "Maybe, we oughta talk about something else, or I'll never get back to normal—if yah know what I mean."

"Oh, I know what you mean," Shelia said as if snapped out of a trance. "Just know your place. If you want my lovin', you're gonna have to mind. Got it?"

Abruptly, Hoyt became incensed at the thought of that prospect. He remembered Audie's comment; "You're a warrior angel...you could have any woman hot and bothered with a few words." The notion took hold, and Hoyt acted on it.

He stared into Shelia's green eyes, which bore into his own like pinpricks of noonday sunlight. Hoyt sensed a range of emotions built upon a foundation of ruinous behaviors. Shelia had always been pretty and alluring, and a lifetime of masculine attentions—wanted and unwanted—had shaped an inflated sense of self. So much so, she had never known the friendships of other women deemed competition. However, relentless time was corrosive, and Shelia's already thin veneer was slowly wearing away.

"Darling, you are a sexy woman, and I have carnal urges only you can satisfy," Hoyt spoke in a hushed voice, leaning across the table and taking her hand. "But, you will not dictate terms. As with any romantic coupling, there's give and take. I'll do those things you wish me to do for you, but you will in turn do the same. Right now, I'd love nothing more than lay you right here."

Shelia's mesmerized expression was proof enough of Hoyt's newfound influence over others. Under the table, her hand rubbed against his manhood. Hoyt felt sexual heat rising from her voluptuous body.

The young waitress stood beside the table with two glasses of wine and a mortified expression. "Excuse me… Your wine…" she said. "Sorry… I didn't mean to interrupt."

"Why you little busybody!" Shelia hissed in a low tone. "You like spying on folks? Bet you got an earful, didn't yah?"

"Easy, Shelia," Hoyt coaxed. "Not her fault…"

"Whadda mean, not her fault," Shelia blurted. "Look at her standing there. Why, she's a little sneak…barely outta her teens…traipsing around in her short-shorts…"

"Shelia, shush now…"

"I don't see why you're taking her side. Do you like 'em young? Is that it?"

Clasping her hand firmly, Hoyt stared into Shelia's eyes and soothed, "Calm yourself, Honey. You're a beautiful woman with few equals, but behaving the way you are at this moment, makes you ugly."

"What…?" Shelia blurted. "What are you saying?"

"We'll talk later, somewhere less public. Now, you go to the car, and I'll settle the bill."

"But…we could still…"

192

Hoyt squeezed her hand and fixed his gaze into her green eyes. "Not here," he said. "We're well past that now."

As if transfixed, Shelia's demeanor relaxed, her face less flush and more serene. "Okay...not here then," she complied. "I'll wait in the car." Ignoring the embarrassed server entirely, Shelia stood up, straightened her dress, and sashayed past empty tables.

"Young lady, my heartfelt apologies... My girlfriend and I behaved terribly," Hoyt said, handing over a role of twenties. "I assume this will cover the tab and leave a generous gratuity."

"Uh...yes...it will," she replied. "Say...what you said...was really hot... I go to college here... If things don't work out...yah know...come back. I work afternoons...Tuesdays and Thursdays. Just ask for Rita—that's me."

Not knowing what to say, Hoyt grinned. "Thank you, Rita, for making my day. I'll consider your invitation. I hope the rest of your day is more pleasant. Bye now."

***

"Why, you're no gentleman at all!" Shelia fumed. "Got me all hot and bothered, and you're not interested any longer! What's your fucking problem?"

"I can only apologize and say you'll do fine without my company," Hoyt tendered. "You need a man, who will cater to your every whim. Regrettably, I'm not up for the job. Besides...you can do a lot better than me."

"You better believe it!" she raged. "Get outta my car...fuckin' weirdo! Yeah...I know about you...fuckin' crazy asshole... Who needs yah!"

Before he could shut the car door, Shelia peeled rubber across the parking lot. Hoyt pulled his hand from the door handle just in time to avoid injury. Shelia drove recklessly, grazing an asphalt curb and clipping a shopping cart. Hoyt watched her, hoping she didn't kill someone. After a few near misses with other vehicles, Shelia disappeared.

So...that's what a bad breakup is like. I hope that's the only one for a while...

Chapter 26
Brothers Asunder

Audie headed in a southerly direction. The Brazos River snaked across the earth below. Pain coursed through Audie's arm and settled into his ribcage. Sweat beaded and dribbled down his face and chin as he scanned for a place to light. After weeks of recuperating from debilitating injuries that usually took much longer to heal, it was exhilarating to fly again. Nonetheless, Audie's stamina had diminished considerably.

Southwest of Hart, a winding creek named Little River emptied into the Brazos. Audie landed on a sandbar at the edge of a narrow strip of wooded bottomland. Both waterways converged into one on both sides. Audie released his arms and slumped to his knees on the warm sand. Several feet away, a large water moccasin rested on the shoreline with its elongated body half in the water. Its tongue flicked the night air for scents. The creature exhibited no agitation or aggression toward the wearer of the wings. In fact, Audie could handle the serpent without fear if he desired to do so.

Rising from his knees, Audie stretched. His arms quivered from fatigue. He spat into the quiet water and wiped cold sweat from his brow. He closed his eyes and breathed deep until no longer winded. For the umpteenth time this evening, he cleared his mind and concentrated. With some hesitation, the wings obeyed his mental command and unfurled. Audie instructed them to sweep downward and raise him from the ground. The wings fluttered with awkward locomotion. His body quaked, and his heels lifted slightly, but his mental energy waned rapidly. Audie ceased the exercise. The wings enfolded against his back.

If I had as much practice as Hoyt, I would have figured it out by now. Hell with it! Rather bulk up my arms anyhow... Chrissakes! Why did I light here?

For the most part, Audie didn't question his instincts, figuring he had commonsense enough to foresee probable outcomes for every action. However, here he was, in a shallow bowl surrounded by woods and eroding banks. Now accustomed to viewing the world from a high vantage point, he felt vulnerable, especially with the Tasmanian Devils lurking in night shadow. Using his six senses,

Audie breathed deep, sniffing and tasting the balmy air. His neck on a swivel, he pursed his eyes and peered through the twilight radiance. His ears took in every sound, and his skin tingled from the sensations borne by sluggish wafts of air. He sensed the usual nocturnal creatures that walked, crawled, flew, and swam during the night.

Audie willed his mind to venture upward and outward from his body, but only for short distances. Other than a far away vehicle heading in his direction, he distinguished nothing that threatened. Curious about the night traveler approaching, Audie lingered.

Drinking from his canteen until emptied, Audie wandered to the wooded fringe to take a leak. Although the pain had subsided to a dull ache, he wondered if he had enough strength to make it home. In his mind, he pictured a payphone outside Dooley's Mercantile Store where he could call home and have Hoyt come get him.

Probably still up, waiting for me. Awful selfish with the wings since he's been the only one able to...

A vehicle crested the bluff across the river to the west. It was a white van covered in a layer of reddish dust. No headlights illumined its path as it traversed a narrow dirt road ending at a sandy shoreline. Coming to a squealing halt, no crimson brake lights shone in its wake. The driver opened the door on creaking hinges. A squat man emerged. He wore a cap. Reaching in the van, he removed a Coleman lantern and short-handle spade. He walked under a cluster of cedar and lit the lantern. An eerie light glowed from behind stout trunks and low brush.

Willy Gallison, what are you doing out here so late? Checking a trotline maybe?

Hidden in shadows from across the way, Audie watched and listened. Although he heard diggings in the loose sand above the flood plain, he couldn't see. Audie sensed another person—a woman—in the rear of the van, but she made no sound.

What the fuck, Willy!

Letting his mind drift to the far side of the river, Audie probed the van. The poor woman was dead, but dreadful feelings lingered. Her last peaceful memory was of going to bed with her husband before awaking in the back of a rattling vehicle, bound, gagged, and blindfolded. Confused and panicked, she could not comprehend her plight.

After a while, the vehicle had stopped. Seconds later, a vulgar man straddled her prone body. He had removed a woolen hood from her head, so she could see his face. She had been helpless as the man raped and sodomized her. After hours of torture and semiconscious thoughts, she had surrendered and prayed for death. The man granted her wish by strangling her with his bare hands. Her final thoughts were of her husband and children and not knowing what became of them...

And, there were others here—dozens more—interred under the cedars where the ground was loose and digging was easy. Clenching his fists, Audie's adrenaline flowed as he pondered reckoning. Without the aid of his arms, the wings lifted Audie into the murky night and sailed him across the river.

Dammit, Willy, you sick son of a bitch! Those poor women... Now, I gotta put you down! Look at you over there...no thought of what you've done. Daddy's been visiting you all right. Trying to get you to stop...

After a while, Willy finished digging. It wasn't much of a hole—four-feet deep and wide. He tossed his spade onto the ground and clambered out.

Picking up the shovel, Audie waited. The wings unfurled and trembled.

"Audie...is that you?" Willy stammered. "What are you doing out here? What are you...?"

"Don't mind that, Willy! I wouldn't have believed it without seeing it with my own eyes. So, you're the one responsible for the missing women all these years."

"No use denying it," Willy said, still staring at Audie's garb. "I've done bad things since I was a teenager."

"How many?"

"Uh...can't really say. So many now...all mixed together," Willy answered. "I used to bury 'em deep but ran outta ground years ago. Now stacking on top of another...like graveyards in Europe."

"You were my Daddy's best friend," Audie said. "Did he know?"

"No! Your Daddy was...is a good man!" Willy blurted, sweeping his hand around him. "He'd never abide this."

"Why, Willy...why?"

"Can't help myself..." Willy explained. "It's a sickness...plain and simple...something I was born with. It'd be easier to stop breathing than stop killing… It's the only time I feel good. Doing with women what I want…"

"Maybe, you really couldn't help yourself, Willy, but you knew what you were doing. You just didn't care," Audie said. "You ever heard of *empathy*, Willy?"

"Uh…I've heard the *word*, but I dunno what it means exactly," Willy answered. "What's it got to do with me?"

"Nothing whatsoever, otherwise, we wouldn't be here," Audie said. "You see…*empathy* is a core emotion of caring people…the capacity to feel what others feel. It's usually absent in psychopaths. Yah know…the wicked. Imagine a world of sadists. People acting on their basest feelings…doing whatever they wanted without any regard for others."

"But, that ain't me, Audie. I was friends with your Daddy. Wasn't I always kind to you and your brothers?" Willy argued. "Like I said…I can't help myself. It's an itch that needs scratching…"

"I reckon, Willy, but you evidently have a fetish for torturing young women," Audie posed. "Good thing I didn't have any sisters, huh?"

"That ain't so, Audie. I'm a good ole boy. I have a sickness is all…like Hoyt."

"You're nothing like my big brother!" Audie raged. "Hoyt cares about people, especially women and children. Don't ever compare yourself…"

A loud percussion sounded. Audie turned his body so fast the human eye could never register. The palm of his left hand burned. In the next instant, Audie kicked, striking Willy's hand. A revolver flew through the darkness. Willy yelped and fell backward into the hole. Audie followed and straddled his prone body. He opened his left hand, which held a bullet. Audie had captured the projectile without thinking.

"Here I was trying to figure out what to do with you, and you shoot me!" Audie fumed.

"Sorry, Audie! I'm scared, is all! Please don't kill me! I'm sick!"

"Oh, I won't kill you!" Audie snapped. "You'll care plenty soon enough. What you did to those poor women… Their last moments in this world…"

"Whadda mean?" Willy beseeched. "What are you gonna do?"

197

Audie's face grimaced as he absorbed remnant memories of those interred in this desolate place. Scalding tears flowed. He experienced every horrid moment inflicted …the desperation felt by parents and husbands…the longing of grieving children… "Willy, since you've never felt *empathy*, you may find this very unsettling. Don't fight it. Just let it come," Audie cried, placing splayed fingers upon Willy's head. "See them? Do you feel their pain?"

"Please stop! Too much…!" Willy moaned and blubbered, a torrent of images and emotions inundated his mind…his soul. "Oh GOD, what have I done?"

Audie departed before dawn. Still breathing, Willy lay at the bottom of a makeshift grave. His blank expression belied thoughts reeling in his mind. Until his dying breath and release from this world, Willy would experience and re-experience his victims' final moments.

***

"Willy Gallison…" Zane said, watching the television. "Hard to believe."

The evening news was abuzz about an anonymous tip leading to the discovery of a grisly scene along the Brazos River southwest of Hart. Also, found was a van with the body of a dead woman, and dozens of shallow graves in the vicinity. A possible serial murderer, Willy Gallison was found, sanity lost in a comatose miasma.

Many questions arose. Was the man responsible for the many murders of local women over the years? Did someone happen upon the scene and mete out retribution? Initial theories alluded to the latter scenario, but what exactly did the vigilant do to Willy? Law enforcement officials questioned nearby ranchers and farmers.

The brothers took care and avoided the area. It was unlikely police would trace the incident back to them, and even if someone else was suspect, he or she would likely be feted as a hero and never prosecuted due to lack of evidence.

"Can you lift your arm any higher?" Zane asked as he bound a bandage around Audie's chest.

"Nah…hurts…" he replied, his reddened face wincing. "Of all nights for that asshole to come along. I knew I ripped something when I caught that bullet."

"Sure enough, but now, we're both laid up again," Zane agreed. "Hoyt's having a good time at our expense. Not a scratch on him…like he's covered in titanium. Seems he's real careful with his own skin while we're gettin' beat on."

"You think so? I mean…he put himself out there at Luther's… Nearly got killed…"

"Fuck that! We had his back on that one."

"Seems so…but I can't blame him for my accident," Audie said. "I really pushed myself."

"Yeah, maybe, but he was there when I nearly took a bullet in Socorro. Sometimes, I can't help but wonder if he held back some. He was quick to get the wings off me, and he's pretty much had 'em since."

"Just remember, you didn't actually get shot, so it isn't likely he held back. But, he gives me a hard time when I just wanna wear 'em. Yah know…to help with the healing and everything."

"Same with me. Always going on about not wasting the magic by keepin' 'em inside," Zane complained. "He's gettin' too comfortable with 'em, I tell yah. I'd probably be healed up fine by now if I could have wore 'em on my nights."

"Won't be long before you're okay to fly again."

"That may be, but we need to set new rules, so we don't get screwed."

"He's having a time tonight with a full moon and all…" Audie said. "Yeah…I'm thinking you're probably right."

Chapter 27
Lunar Sway

His arms no longer tethered, Hoyt commanded the wings with little mental effort. Like a bodily appendage, they followed suit, climbing, banking, and diving. A super moon filled the night sky. So bright, Hoyt couldn't look at it directly. Supernatural power surged through feather, tendon, and bone. The chest harness strained as leather fabric flexed and creaked. Though flight was no longer physically laborious, his mind tired from continual use. At times, he alternated using his arms to rest his mind.

Hoyt thought about his brothers and their growing resentment. At some unconscious level, they blamed him. Logically, it made no sense. He had no control of events leading to their current circumstances. Audie had been foolhardy, and Zane might be dead if not for him.

With the moon overhead, the wings pulled him in no direction. So far this evening, there were no innocents in peril, no psychopaths with murderous intent, and no drug deals to intercept. Perhaps, he'd drift to Port Odessa. Maybe, sit on the white sands of Matagorda Island and savor the Gulf breezes. If the mood struck him, he'd fly over Hildago on the way home.

Something passed between Hoyt and the moon. Rolling on his side, Hoyt discerned several shapes. Recognizing the forms, he dove toward the dark woodlands. Exiled angels patrolled for him. They had not seen him, but knew he was near. Hoyt admonished himself for not staying closer to home. Now, these beings knew of his range. How long before they converged on Marlboro and laid siege to his home? Though he didn't yet know their true intentions, Hoyt suspected capture and interrogation, and in the end, a drawn-out death for donning the shorn wings of one of their brethren.

He and his brothers were in mortal danger and could no longer go about their business, but perhaps Zane and Audie were still unknown to the creatures. Hoyt hugged the flat contours of the earth below, staying in shadow. He searched until he found a place where no harm could befall him.

Main door unlocked, Hoyt entered the little Baptist church. Taking shelter among the pews, he watched the night sky through a window. For a long while, figures flitted past the moon as the angels circled. Fortunately, none descended from the high altitude seeking him out. Hoyt relaxed as he breathed in the smell of hymnal texts. As he reclined across a hardwood pew, the wings wrapped around his body like a snug blanket. Hoyt closed his eyes and dreamt.

***

Before sunrise, angels gathered in a shadowy bayou. Hairless and gaunt, some clung to the branches of giant cypress trees. Others perched upon uprooted trunks and roots. A few sat in the muck, not caring about the filth that sullied their wings. None spoke in voice, but they said much in an exchange of mental currents incomprehensible to the human psyche. Many in attendance voiced blames and grievances against Belial, the one who had first encountered the human with the wings.

You failed to slay the human!

Where is this man?

Belial, you are a known purveyor of lies. Why must we believe you?

Zambrim, what is your decree?

Zambrim was the undisputed ruler of fallen angels. Unlike the others, he was the most human in appearance, except he was much larger than any man that had ever walked the earth. His skin was as black as night at the bottom of the deepest ocean. When his wings unfurled, he looked as fearsome as any dragon imagined in the mind of men. Zambrim's eyes shone at night like glowing emeralds, and his teeth were ashen like bleached bone.

We shall seek this human and know what he knows. It is blasphemy for any man to know our power. Humans shall always be inferior to us—although our FATHER favors them for unfathomable reasons. Let it be known, Belial! If you have told us lies, I shall punish you.

Please, Zambrim...my brothers... I lie not for it is true! It was a man, who wore the wings of one of our brethren. Not one of the fallen, but of another not cast from heaven. Perhaps, FATHER may look upon us favorably if we capture this human.

Enough, Belial! We shall do this and mete out our own reckoning. Our FATHER will have no part. We shall rest and wait for night. If Belial is truthful, this human is near.

201

The gathering ended with a round of hisses and growls as wings enfolded the skeletal bodies of stricken angels. Protected from the terrible sun within their feathered cloaks, they slept and dreamt of redemption and reascendance.

***

"I'm tellin' yah. There's a hive of these creatures drawing near," Hoyt explained. "I'm damn lucky they didn't spot me last night, but they're closing in on us. One of them was a handful; I can't imagine taking on a bunch of 'em."

"Well, why haven't we seen 'em?" Zane said. "We've been traipsing all over Texas like you, and we haven't come across anything like what you described."

"Why would I lie about such things?"

"Maybe, you wanna scare me and Audie from flying... I don't know. You don't seem right in the head lately. Like your melancholy is coming back..."

"Granted, my thinking has been a little unclear lately, but I've seen what I've seen," Hoyt said. "Believe me or not, we're in serious shit here."

"What are we supposed to do then?" Zane posed. "I don't wanna give 'em up. I don't wanna go back to before. I'm not doin' it."

"Whadda propose then?" Hoyt asked. "Keep goin' like nothing's happening?"

"I gotta see 'em for myself!" Zane snapped.

"Chrissakes!" Hoyt sputtered, his face growing flush. "What about you, Audie? Any opinion?"

"I haven't seen what you described," Audie said. "Yeah, there's lots of strange shit out there, but I'd like to know more before we put the wings away and go on like nothing ever happened."

"Dammit! We got the pawnshop and can make a good living if we work hard and stay outta trouble. Yah know...lay low... That's all I'm saying..."

"I dunno..." Audie said. "I'm afraid the depression will come back. I'd rather die than..."

"Oh, you'll die all right!" Hoyt suddenly raged. "Those creatures will root us out and come swooping in here one night. We'd be lucky if they killed us outright, but I saw their thoughts...twisted and venomous. They'll torture us until we go insane, then keep us alive and do it over and over. You won't covet the wings so much when a demon with a barbed pecker rapes your ass."

"That's bullshit!" Zane shouted. "You're just trying to scare us off, so you can have the wings for yourself! That's what I'm thinkin'!"

"Is that right?" Hoyt said, knowing further reasoning wouldn't sway his brothers. "If you wanna see 'em for yourself, then go right ahead."

"Oh, I will…tonight!" Zane said. "I'm feeling okay now."

"Just go easy, Zane, and watch yourself," Hoyt warned. "There's a shit storm brewing."

Chapter 28
All Things Must Pass

From the rooftop of an adjacent building, Zane watched Waunita and Lily through the window of their dorm room. Although the lights were dim, Zane observed them having sex with three men. Tall and brawny, the men were football players from Tyler University. One was atop Lily, her milky legs spread wide to receive his thrusting pelvis. Another pounded Waunita's tan backside while she pleasured the third man with her mouth. Young, healthy, and uninhibited, they enjoyed themselves.

Bowing his head, Zane struggled with his emotions. All at once, he wanted to kick in their door and pummel the men, breaking bones and derailing football careers. Afterwards, slap the girls around, make them beg for forgiveness and make promises of unerring fidelity. His face grimaced as tears flowed. Anger turned into heartache. Rage, sorrow, and sexual arousal were a potent blend. Zane's insides churned. Unable to stifle the awful feeling, he vomited until there was nothing left to purge.

Rinsing his mouth with a drink of water, Zane closed his eyes and recited a chant, hoping for relief, so he wouldn't act on dreadful thoughts.

Please wings...make these feelings go away...make these feelings go away...

Although he was doubtful of any helpful effect, powerful emotions diminished as if time elapsed rapidly in his mind. Gradually, he disconnected from a wretched memory that had occurred just minutes before. Zane's relief was immense. When he opened his eyes, he was now immune to the view through the window. Zane no longer begrudged Waunita and Lily, or even the men.

"Goodbye, girls," he whispered. "It's been nice, but I guess all things must pass."

Ascending into the darkness, Zane flew high seeking cool air. Eclipsed by earth, the moon was a bright fingernail of light shrouded by wisps of clouds. He thought of other women. Since he had dedicated most of his sexual energies to Waunita and Lily, he would have to search for other female dalliances. Regrettably, none came to mind, but he figured a jaunt to Hildago or Denton. He wondered about Francine and if Clyde Rush was ever successful in his romantic attempts. With his powers, Zane figured he could seduce…

Faraway shrieks and howls carried from somewhere ahead. Zane searched the night sky for the source of the terrible sounds. He spied winged beings descending in his direction. Too many to count, Zane discerned unnatural outlines. Skeletal and bare-skinned, some had spiked horns, pointed ears, and clawed feet. The creatures were enraged. The brief image convinced Zane of his brother's veracity.

Oh, fuck!

Zane somersaulted and plunged toward Wheeler, sensing he might cloak himself in the glow of city lights. At the same time, the angels might avoid peopled places for fear of revealing themselves. Zane angled to a railroad bridge spanning the Brazos River. Tonight, a crowd gathered for the annual Cinco de Mayo Fiesta in the city square. Zane weaved in and out of the rusted bridge trusses, trying to thwart his pursuers.

Lighting near the shoreline, the wings folded against Zane's back. He cleared his mind and willed himself invisible to those around him. He emerged from the shadows calmly walking into the crowd, who didn't take notice. It was an opportune event since many were dressed in outlandish costumes. Even if observed by others, he wouldn't necessarily appear out of place. Along the way, he saw a man wearing a Mexican poncho and Sombrero and downing a bottle of Corona.

"Buena noches," Zane said, walking up. "Venda su sombrero y el poncho?"

Though somewhat inebriated, the man noticed a roll of crisp fifty-dollar bills in Zane's hand. "How much?" he asked in perfect English.

"Three hundred and fifty, si?" Zane offered. "It's all I got on me."

"Sounds good. Here," he replied, setting aside his bottle, handing over his Sombrero, and shucking the poncho. "Excuse the smell. It hasn't been washed in a while, but not a cheap copy…hand-woven."

"Very nice," Zane said, paying the man. "Have a good evening."

Just as he donned the hat and garb, Zane felt the angels congregating under the railroad trusses. Walking away unhurriedly, he blended into the throng, taking a meandering path behind tents and concession booths to lessen his exposure. Zane willed himself not to look back, knowing they would see him if he showed his face. The crowd thinned as he trekked farther from the square.

"Hola, Zane!" a man greeted.

Augustine Salazar stood with a woman and three girls—presumably his wife and daughters. They nursed snow cones. Mouths and teeth stained purple, the girls smiled.

"Hola, Augustine," Zane said, feigning nonchalance. "Your wife and daughters?"

"Si, my wife, Maria, and my girls, Noa, Elisa, and Luna," he introduced. "Maria, this is Zane Harlan. He and his brothers own Earl's Pawnshop."

"Yes, I know your store well," Maria said, extending her hand. "I've bought pieces of jewelry from there. Mr. Pomeroy is enjoying his retirement?"

"Nice to meet you, and yes, he is," Zane said, shaking her hand. "You and your girls are very lovely. Augustine is very fortunate."

"Gracias," Augustine said. "Are you enjoying the fiesta?"

"I am," Zane said. "I was just heading out. Gotta get up early tomorrow."

"Bird!" Luna squealed, reaching out to stroke the feathers protruding from beneath Zane's poncho. Her sisters tittered and did the same.

"Oh, yeah…a costume," Zane said. "I just won the ugliest chicken contest."

Maria and the girls laughed. Augustine chuckled, but he appeared puzzled.

"Honey, could you take the girls to the lady doing the face paint," Augustine asked. "I must speak with Zane."

"Okay, girls," Maria said. "Who wants their faces painted?"

"Me!" they all clamored.

"Say goodbye to Mr. Harlan," Maria instructed as she herded them away.

"Bye, Senor Birdman! Don't fly away! Look out for foxes!" they said at once.

"Bye, bye, Little Ladies," Zane grinned and waved.

When his wife and daughters were no longer within earshot, Augustine said, "Something the matter, Zane?"

"There are creatures on the bridge," Zane said, nodding toward the river. "Don't look directly at them."

"Creatures? What kind?" Augustine asked, looking everywhere but the bridges. "I see things on the trusses…like smudges. Too dark to see clearly…"

"Bad angels…like demons," Zane said. "They're after me and my brothers. Evidently, they hate humans, especially ones with wings."

"Maldita sea!" Augustine uttered. "I've been reading the papers about the Hadley son…the serial killer… Were you and your brothers involved somehow?"

"We've been trying to do good," Zane answered. "Seems, we're drawn to bad things. If they see me, no tellin' what they might do…even with all these folks around… Anyhow, I have to get outta here."

"Take my car," Augustine offered straightaway. "Red Taurus parked in the lot behind the big tent. Just leave it behind your shop with the keys on top of the rear tire."

"What about you?"

"No problem," he said, handing over his keys. "Here…go."

"Muchas gracias, Augustine."

Zane felt eyes searching for him in the crowd. He kept his own thoughts in check, lest the angels sense his presence. Zane sidled up to the car behind the tent. He slid into the driver's seat. The wings shifted to accommodate. Zane started the engine and drove away as if he was just another person without a care. On his way home, he scanned the skies for pursuers. Especially unsettling was the rural stretch between Wheeler and Marlboro where darkness cloaked the fields and woods for miles. At any moment, Zane expected an aerial assault.

***

"Believe me now, dammit!" Hoyt scolded. "They're zeroing in on us. Won't be long before they're roosting in the oak tree out back."

"All right!" Audie snapped. "Heard yah the first hundred times!"

"Sorry for not believing you, Big Brother," Zane said. "What the hell we do now? Nasty lookin' sons of bitches, and there's too many of 'em."

"Could we talk with 'em?" Audie posed. "Yah know…reason with them…"

"Nope," Hoyt said.

"They're real pissed," Zane added. "I heard 'em in my head. Made my nut sack shrink to the size of a raisin. Real scary shit…"

"They were exiled from heaven long ago. Not damned to hell, mind you, but banished to earth with only their thoughts," Hoyt explained. "I feel kinda sorry for 'em actually. Imagine lingering for eons…unable to go home. Once loved and favored by their FATHER until humankind came along. So angry, they would slay every man, woman, and child, but they're forbidden. Otherwise, they'd be sent to an even worse place…or even wiped from existence altogether."

"Well…that's just fuckin' great!" Audie barked. "Some real Daddy issues if I ever heard…and whadda think HE's gonna do to us… I can't imagine he'd approve of what we've been doin'!"

"Shit…never thought about that," Zane groaned. "Not like we've been Boy Scouts or anything."

"Guess not," Hoyt opined, "but, we gotta deal with the present situation, and worry about that later—whatever that might be. Stow the wings and put 'em away for now. We may wanna stockpile guns and ammo…"

"We can't fight 'em here," Zane interrupted. "They'll kill everyone around."

"No. They can't harm others…just us," Hoyt replied. "Most likely, they'll keep searching until they find us…surround the house at night…bed down nearby during the day. For some reason, the wings are attached to the house, so we can't move 'em without losing their magic. They'll wait us out…or sweep in when no ones' looking. Maybe, set the house ablaze and smoke us out. Or, even wait for cover like a tornado or hurricane or flood. Doesn't happen often, but they got all the time in the world."

"We could shoot at 'em at night…" Audie posed. "Put silencers on our rifles…"

"Just piss 'em off more," Zane said. "They'll go away, heal, and come right back. Besides…we'll just bring the law down on us…put us in jail where we can't fight. Then, someone else will find and take the wings."

"They haven't found us yet, so we still have some time to plan," Hoyt soothed. "Let's just keep brainstorming…no idea too farfetched. Agreed?"

Chapter 29
The Seraph Siege

"Holding up?" Hoyt asked, closing the backdoor.

"What kinda smartass question is that?" Audie snapped. "I haven't slept in days. This shit is gettin' old. How much longer we gotta keep doin' this?"

"I hear yah, Little Brother, but we have to lay low…for as long as it takes."

"Pawnshop, house, pawnshop, house… It's the same ole thing…day in, day out."

"Better than dead, isn't it?"

"I don't know about that," Audie retorted. "Daddy was doin' just fine on the other side."

"I'm not sure what to say to that," Hoyt admitted, "but I'm sure we wouldn't get there soon enough if captured. They would make us suffer a long time."

"Yeah, yeah, all the while torturing and raping the shit outta us," Audie said. "You're like a record skipping on a turntable."

"Unfortunately…unless…uh, never mind," Hoyt spoke without finishing.

"Unless what?"

"Nothing… Just a random thought not worth mentioning…"

"I'm not buyin' it," Audie countered. "Zane will be here soon. We can talk about it then."

"Talk about what?" Zane asked, walking through the door. "Did Hoyt have an idea?"

"He's thinkin' on something all right," Audie said, combing his unkempt hair with his fingers. "Probably what we figured he might do eventually."

"What have you all been talking about?" Hoyt asked. "You shouldn't be talking without me."

"We talked about how you might play hero. Yah know…take 'em on by your lonesome."

"Well…that would be dumb," Hoyt said. "How exactly would one do that…hypothetically?"

"Take the wings and draw 'em away," Zane offered. "Bring 'em in close and blow 'em to bits."

"Sounds like a half-ass idea to me," Hoyt said. "Too many things could go wrong, and you'd have to get 'em all at once, which could leave you two fighting the rest."

"Uh huh...just don't do anything on your own, got it?" Audie cautioned. "I ain't ready to handover our wings without a fight."

"Same here," Zane added. "Don't do anything reckless...not just yet. Besides...we should draw straws or something if it comes to that."

"Okay then," Hoyt replied. "Sunset in an hour, so you better eat and get cleaned up. Who's first watch tonight?"

"Me," Zane said, looking at the kitchen walls. "I tell yah...the house looks like hell."

In past weeks, the brothers had worked feverishly to secure their home. Metal bars had been placed over all windows, and the outside entrances had new security doors. Inside the house, they had covered the exterior walls, floors, and ceilings with thick sheets of plywood fastened with heavy-duty lag bolts. The brothers had cut ports into the sheets covering the windowsills to see outside, and if necessary, fire their rifles. They had stockpiled dozens of guns and thousands of rounds of ammunition around the house along with an arsenal of bladed weapons. Since a nighttime siege was the likeliest scenario, they kept flashlights and fresh batteries on hand.

As expected, Mrs. Sanchez asked many questions while they fortified the house. Hoyt provided plausible explanations for all questions, but she was having none of it. With no subtlety whatsoever, Mrs. Sanchez said she wanted to go visit her sister in New Mexico, but she didn't have the money to do so. If Hoyt and his brothers provided sufficient monies, she would make herself scarce, so they could carry on without her presence. Without further discussion, Zane delivered Mrs. Sanchez to the nearest airport with ticket in hand along with three thousand dollars in cash. When things settled, they would call her.

***

"Comfortable?" Hoyt asked, helping Zane with the wings.

"More so, if I could go out instead of staying holed up in the kitchen," he answered. "What went wrong? Things were so awesome."

"I know, but let's keep plugging away and see what happens" Hoyt said. "How's it goin' with your mind's eye?"

"Good, but still can't go as far as you two. Gives me an awful headache when I push too hard."

"Your mind won't have to travel far. You'll feel 'em. Just be ready to pull back quick, or they might find you."

"Gotcha," Zane said. "Go to bed. I'll get Audie up at midnight."

"Sleepin' away, he is," Hoyt observed. "Nothing upsets his sleep...not even demonic angels."

Except for the sounds of muted snoring and an occasional creaking of bedsprings, the house was silent as the wall clock approached midnight. Zane sat cross-legged on the kitchen table, hands on his knees, eyes closed. Like a spectral eye, his mind roamed the neighborhood, scanning the night sky at regular intervals. Especially worrisome, was an absence of sound from nocturnal insects.

Zane ascended, gaining a higher vantage point from which to see. He discerned nothing to cause alarm. Streetlights shone through a canopy of treetops. Except for a blinking of faraway communication tower lights and the glow of Wheeler's cityscape, the horizon was clear. However, Zane was still uncertain, not knowing what to expect.

"Zane," Audie said. "Come on back."

Whenever a mental journey was disrupted, the mind's eye withdrew to its host instantaneously. In the beginning, the abrupt change caused a wave of vertigo, which made Zane lightheaded and sometimes nauseous. Now, he recovered with little ill effect.

"I'm here," Zane said, opening his eyes, his body slumping. "It looks clear, but I feel awful anxious. I don't think they'll come all at once. Likely, one or two at a time will come, flying from tree to tree, shadow to shadow. They'll hide during the day in mesquite thickets, swamps, and abandoned buildings. Then, some night, they'll converge, lighting on the roofs and treetops in our neighborhood, surrounding us. What then? I don't know."

"Thanks for that prediction," Audie grumbled. "Let's trade places, and I'll give it a try. Maybe, I'll see something you didn't."

After his brother went to bed, Audie perched upon the kitchen table and performed a feat Hoyt and Zane could not yet do. He cleared his mind, filtering extraneous clutter from his thoughts. As his mind's eye detached, he willed his body to levitate. Hovering several inches above the table, Audie's nerves calmed, and his mental energy amplified. With the house boarded up, the air was leaden, stale, and odorous. Once his mind departed the house, Audie's body breathed in fresh, cool night air.

Unlike his brothers, Audie didn't linger near home. He traveled outward seeking contact with other unworldly entities. The Tasmanian Devils were about flitting between shadows, but they never spoke. Instead, their minds were a mass of nasty mutterings. Perhaps, natural selection had bred them to absorb the lethal excesses of human evils, which is perhaps why they were attracted to places of violence and death. Maybe without them, people would mindlessly destroy one another until extinct.

Apparitions were mute altogether. Most were simply spectral images of past lives that played out cyclically. Then again, some were wholly aware of earthly surroundings and could interact with mortal beings, but chose not to or were forbidden from doing so. Audie figured any cognitive communication between spirits and people was accidental or occurred through an amalgamation of rare environmental conditions. Thus far, Audie was unable to coax a ghost into a two-way conversation.

On the other hand, intelligible transmission with banshees was possible, albeit unpredictable. From what Audie and his brothers had gathered, they were disembodied souls unable or unwilling to pass to the next realm. Audie sensed many were troubled during their corporeal existence. Since Audie had much experience with crazy people, he recognized the psychopathy of personalities. Thus, normal dialog was oftentimes akin to running barefoot across a yard full of sticker burs. Occasionally though, he encountered one coherent enough to answer questions.

His mind's eye searched the skies for wavering charcoal masses. Whenever, Audie spied a banshee, he pursued and listened. Unfortunately, he heard senseless discourse from most until he met one quiet entity.

"Hello there," Audie probed.

"Who's there?" a feminine voice replied. *"What do you want?"*

"My pardons, ma'am. I don't mean you any harm."

"Who are you, and what are you?"

"My name is Audie Harlan. I'm just a good ole boy from Texas."

"You are still living?"

212

"Yes ma'am, I am...for the time being. If it's no bother, could I ask you a few questions?"

"You happened upon me at an opportune time, Mr. Harlan. Presently, my mind is lucid. Ask your questions, but I do not guarantee truthfulness in my answers. I have lost my way, you see."

"I'm sorry to hear that, ma'am, but I understand. May I ask what your name is?"

"Sadly, I don't remember. I was once a girl, then a wife and mother. Little else..."

"Do you remember horses, trains...automobiles?"

"Horses, trains, yes. Auto...mobiles...no?"

"Where were you born and raised?"

"The South. I believe... My memories are hazy. Perhaps, you should ask your questions posthaste."

"Ma'am, have you seen angels hereabouts lately? Winged beings...nasty lookin' things."

"Yes...more than ever before. Foul creatures...hateful... I shy from them, though they cannot harm me."

"Are they near?"

"Yes...they congregate in bottomlands, near a snaking river."

"Thank you, ma'am. That's very helpful. Is there anything I can do for you? I'm not sure what exactly, but I can try."

"Yes...please tell my dear children I miss them terribly. Please tell them how sorry I am for what I did. It was no fault of theirs..."

Like flicking the off switch on a radio, all sensory contact severed. The banshee flitted away too fast even for his spectral eye to match.

Audie perceived tremendous guilt from the forsaken spirit for an awful act committed long ago. Like many banshees, Audie suspected most were not wholly responsible due to mental disturbance. Minds cleared upon death, the reality of their misdeeds reopened wounds to their psyches causing self-imposed exiles in purgatory. Audie couldn't help but question the justice of it. If there was an ALMIGHTY CREATOR, why perpetuate this cycle? Since nature and nurture shaped human character, were we entirely blameworthy? Was there actually such a thing as freewill? Why subject the female banshee to further torments? Where was forgiveness?

"Rise and shine, Audie."

The return of the mind's eye jolted Audie into consciousness. His suspended body dropped to the kitchen table with a thud. Face grimaced and flush, Audie sobbed uncontrollably.

"Rough night?" Hoyt asked, handing over a damp handkerchief. "Banshees can be an awful pitiful bunch."

"Poor woman..." Audie said, wiping his face. "Anyhow...they're here...the angels. They're roosting in the High bank Creek bottomlands. If they don't know we're here already, they'll know soon enough."

"Not unexpected," Hoyt said. "It'll be daylight in a few hours. I'll take the wings. You go back to sleep."

"We need to plan and act soon," Audie said, stretching his arms and yawning. "Not much time left."

After his brother fell asleep, Hoyt slipped into the backyard, knelt to the ground, and meditated. Instead of allowing his mind to communicate over the entire wireless spectrum, Hoyt focused on a narrow sliver in the very low frequency range. Using finite psychic modulation and encoding elements, he opened a channel typically occupied by earthbound angels. Any human listening on this band only heard bits of static over white noise.

"Greetings! I hear you're looking for me."

Immediately, a cacophony of voices answered. Hoyt winced in response. Countless images roiling with hateful, enraged emotions flashed in his mind, imparting a dissertation on angelic history. Hoyt was both fascinated and repulsed.

Conceived as companions for their CREATOR, angels were also the eyes and ears throughout HIS given territory of the celestial universe. Left to evolve without outside influences, worlds and civilizations were born and died. The souls of all things once living continued into farther realms, always progressing to a higher state of being. In this regard, angels resented their predetermined existence, but served faithfully without grievance. They considered their place vital in the furtherance of life—that is, until the arrival of humans.

On a backwater world in the farthest reaches of a relatively unremarkable galaxy, lowly hominid creatures had come into existence. These beings bore a passing physiological resemblance to the CREATOR, which piqued HIS curiosity. So much so, HE dabbled in their evolutionary development. Since even the ALMIGHTY was not perfection, humankind was also imperfect, but this only made HIM love them more, leading to the rebellion and exile of some of his eternal companions.

"*Silence!*" a singular voice commanded. "*I will have silence, so I may speak with the human!*"

After a prolonged quiet, Hoyt spoke, "*I feel your anger for what you perceive as a damnable affront to your kind. It was not my intention to enrage you so, especially since I did not know of you.*"

"*How did you acquire the wings, human?*"

"*I happened upon a set of shorn wings. In my ignorance, I wore them and coveted their power. Until now, I received them as a great gift to further myself, and hopefully, help others.*"

"*You know not of the original possessor?*"

"*I do not.*"

For long seconds, there was no response, but Hoyt knew a raucous discussion ensued. Since their hatred against humans was so entrenched, Hoyt held no hope for a remotely favorable outcome. All he could do was carry on a pretense of dialog.

"*Very well, you speak truth. Still, your ignorance does not excuse your transgression, and you will appear forthwith before us to receive punishment.*"

"*What punishment might I expect?*"

"*Human, your punishment is no longer of concern to you. You will simply obey.*"

"*I hear yah. Perhaps then, we can drop the façade now and speak frankly.*"

An emotion of immense vexation permeated the airwave used for this transmission. So tremendous, the white noise undoubtedly intruded upon adjacent frequencies.

"*We shall exact a drawn-out punishment upon you no human has ever suffered! We shall inflict tortures, which pale to those most horrid carried out during the darkest of human times! Your family— yes, we know of your brethren—will endure similar agonies.*"

"*Yeah, yeah, yeah… The most horrible pain ever experienced by a mortal man. Enough already! I get it!*"

"*You dare mock me, human!*"

"*It wasn't my original purpose, but your tirade was getting tiresome. I had hoped to explain myself, and maybe, reach an accord. Heck…I would have gladly served a reasonably harsh penance. I also needed to know if you were aware of my kin, which you are, so that settles a few things."*

"You cannot fathom..."

"Oh...I get it. My puny human mind understands you're really pissed, and my brothers and I are the first humans in ages you can harm. Since I try very hard to emphasize with others, I can understand how you and yours might feel. I'd be jealous too if my Daddy left me home and played with the kids down the street. I really get it. So, let me cut to the chase. You and your pussy gargoyles can go fuck yourselves! You can take all that rage and hate, roll it up into a phallic shape, and stick up your asses! You wanna go at me; you know where to find me! Nasty lookin' sons of bitches!"

The master angel did not answer. Hoyt heard a wailing of shrieks that carried over the entire radio spectrum. So enraged, the angels unknowingly revealed themselves across the airwaves. Hoyt's desperate plan was afoot.

Chapter 30
Icarus Flew

Hoyt moved aside the kitchen table and rolled up a thick scatter rug. Beneath was a sturdy trapdoor, which he had secretly built weeks before. Recessed into the floor, one wouldn't have noticed it under the carpet. Hoyt slid open two bolts and pulled on a swiveled handle. He lifted a satchel from the crawlspace.

Inside were a series of glass tubules filled with a clear, oily liquid. Hoyt had applied his newfound intellect and refined a special blend of nitroglycerin. It was an exceedingly complex task even under the most desirable conditions, but nearly impossible in a household kitchen. Hoyt had to liberate the necessary chemical ingredients during midnight forays and researched volumes of scientific journals in local libraries. When his brothers weren't home, Hoyt cooked a brew of volatile explosive. Although he was confident in its stability, he employed supernatural influences to ensure it remained inert, lest he destroy the entire neighborhood.

Hoyt strapped a handmade vest around his abdomen and bound it with padding. A wire with a metallic coupler protruded from the apparatus. A separate pocket held a detonator assembly with another loop of wire and coupler. Looking at the clock, he figured two and a half hours until sunrise.

Knew it had to come to this…

"What's happening here?" Zane barked, standing at his bedroom door in his underwear. "What's that contraption around your stomach?"

"What the fuck!" Audie added, as he trudged into the kitchen. "You're not supposed to do anything on your own!"

"Too late now, they know about us, and they're coming," Hoyt said. "It's now or never, Brothers."

"Whadda mean they're comin'?" Audie sputtered. "What did you do, Hoyt?"

"I made contact and poked 'em with a stick."

"You dumb bastard!" Zane shouted. "They gonna tear you to shreds! Here…we can take a few with us!"

"Zane, no need for all of us to die," Hoyt said. "You and Audie can still live. Work hard…get married…have kids… All the things, you've ever wanted… Everything I ever wanted…"

"No, Hoyt…you can't…" Audie said, his face growing flush. "Like Zane said, '…we can take a few with us…'"

"Don't do it!" Zane pleaded, his face grimaced, tears flowed. "We'll go together…all of us!"

"No, my mind's made up…"

Hoyt was taken aback when both of his brothers leapt over chairs and table and tackled him. For a moment, he wobbled as Zane threw his arms around his legs, and Audie pushed against him. However, he didn't budge under the onslaught. Despite his brothers' grappling, he pushed forward with the mass and strength of a dozen men. Hoyt paused at the door's threshold. Audie grabbed the doorsill while Zane tried to lift. Hoyt peeled hands from around his chest and pushed hard. Audie crashed through the screen door and tumbled into the yard. Hoyt found it much harder to extricate his other brother. Strong arms bound his legs in viselike clench.

Hoyt grabbed a can of cockroach killer from the kitchen counter. For long seconds, Zane closed his eyes and held his breath, but he couldn't withstand the noxious spray. He relented and rolled away, gagging and gasping. Hoyt bolted through the door and lifted skyward. Several times, he circled the neighborhood above and watched his brothers. They ran across the yard shouting curses and pleading for him to return. Hoyt climbed into the night sky until their cries faded.

Many miles from Marlboro, Hoyt flew a southerly course. Countless stars flickered against an inky backdrop. So clear, he could count the moons of Mars and see the miasma of Venus' atmosphere. His fingers flexed as he scanned the moonlit horizon for other winged beings. Nothing appeared but the contrails of faraway planes. Except for a passage of air, it was silent in the twilight sky high above the earth. Here and there, city lights illumined the landscape. The Brazos River snaked across the Texas flatlands toward the ocean. In the distance, Hoyt discerned the Gulf of Mexico, an unbroken expanse. Far beyond the sandy coastline, a phalanx of high cumulous clouds formed, dark and ominous, silhouetted by a bright flare of lightning.

Suddenly, the air changed. No longer cool and unsullied, a stench flooded his olfactory sense. Hoyt rolled with the ground to his back.

High above, hundreds of beings, beautiful and hideous, flew in a gathering mass. Stars winked out as dark forms filled the heavens. Filled with jealous rage and sadistic intent, GOD's fallen angels turned their attentions to the human, who masqueraded as one of them. During countless millennia spent earthbound, GOD had forbidden them from interacting with humans. The decree was absolute, and if broken, punishment was exile into the fiery nether regions—a place where Lucifer reigned over the most terrible of damned souls. Now, for the taking, was a man exempt from GOD's edict.

Hoyt turned his body and set course. He willed the wings to make haste and climbed. The Texas coastline disappeared in his wake. Soon after, winds pummeled in spite of the supernatural buffer surrounding him. A torrential rain poured. The hairs on his body raised near powerful electrical magnetic fields. The sensation was both thrilling and terrifying.

An unnatural darkness supplanted the twilight as Hoyt entered the storm clouds. No longer able to navigate, he continued to ascend, tacking back and forth to lessen drag and maintain momentum. The continual climb was exhausting until Hoyt happened upon an updraft. He leveled off and glided in wide arcs. Hoyt's hand moved to his pistol when he heard the first shrills. All around, hurricane force winds carried the war cries. Hoyt unholstered his .45 automatic and cocked its hammer.

Unexpectedly, a shape whipped past on his right. Hoyt looked all around. Other figures sailed through the storm's vortex, but too distant to pose an immediate threat. An awful shriek pierced the raging winds and thunderclaps. Hoyt rolled in time to see a terrible being diving toward him. Pale skin and veined wings outlined a figure filled with murderous intent. Instinctively, Hoyt took quick aim and fired. Inherent skill or pure luck, a large caliber round struck the angel's twisted face. Like a lead weight, it plummeted into the roiling mist. Hoyt knew he couldn't kill these beings, but they could be hurt, albeit only for a short while.

Hoyt willed the wings to spread wide and capture the rising air, occasionally flapping to correct and stabilize his path. Another shape, black and burnished, flew past at an impossible speed. Sighting Hoyt, it screeched in fury, unable to overcome its own momentum and double back. Hoyt changed course, flying into the calmer center of the storm. Flight was more arduous, but Hoyt hoped to avoid a path that offered winged beings easier flight.

The atmosphere was dense, providing more lift for the wings. Breathing deep, Hoyt ascended. His senses were awash with countless stimuli. A perceptible nattering filled his mind, like cicadas buzzing from a distant oak grove. At the risk of siphoning from his other much needed senses, Hoyt focused his attention. Voices rose from the storm's din.

Where is the human!

He is close! I smell his stench!

Where is Gazardiel! I no longer hear Gazardiel!

Gazardiel...Gazardiel...Gazardiel!

A chorus of voices clamored for Gazardiel, but there was no reply, only howling winds and percussive thunder.

Zambrim, what shall we do?

We shall seek!

What of dawn?

If need be, we slumber in the gloomy depths!

Oh...not the sea!

I hate the brine!

It burns!

Damn you, Belial, for your failure!

Silence! We shall end this, here and now! Whatever our suffering!

Yes...yes...Zambrim...oh merciful and powerful one, we obey.

"Oh fuck," Hoyt said through gritted teeth.

Before he realized, Hoyt had wet himself, so shocked by the alien voices in his head. He regretted the telepathic ability to interpret their words and emotions. Myriad images, gleaned from countless memories of eternal archangels, filtered through Hoyt's mind. He observed earth long before humankind...an endless voyage through remote galaxies...a span of absolute darkness beyond the known universe...shifting of time and space...alternate dimensions... imaginings so incomprehensible, Hoyt's mind could not fathom. So stupefied, he bellowed to clear his mind. Immediately after, he heard a surge of mental voices.

The human is this way!

Hoyt sensed a hailstorm of shapes passing him on their way downward. Fortunate for him, the vastness of dark cumulous clouds cloaked him. Hoyt knew it was only a matter of time before they found him and converged, cutting all avenues of escape, rending him limb from limb. Hoyt resigned himself to his fate, but still worked to prolong his survival...

Falling and spinning, Hoyt fought to stabilize his path. A passing angel had clipped him, and now, he somersaulted. Hoyt raged at the sight of his mottled feathers swirling in the airstream. He observed a reptilian shape with an elongated tail and bat like wings, its body covered with shimmering, emerald scales. Instead of veering off to elude his attacker, Hoyt dove headlong. Just as the being leveled out, Hoyt held his pistol with both hands and fired in rapid succession. Bullets mushroomed and shredded flesh and bone. Black blood spurted. The creature screamed before going limp and plummeting out of sight.

Hoyt suffered a wave of distinct emotions with every form that came within proximity. Fury, envy, and worry flowed through his psyche, but he didn't believe they were his own. Instead, the creatures imparted unwelcome human feelings. He now understood the original owner of the wings was the angel of melancholy. No wonder, depression had bedeviled his family—wings stowed so close for generations in his home.

"Zambrim..." Hoyt thought. *"So, you're the ruler of fallen angels...the ones who repress joy for humankind..."*

His wings shorn a few feathers, Hoyt steered toward the outer vortex to resume his ascent. He sensed a good number of enemies below him with many still poised to dive. Hoyt cast a delicate mental web into the winds, concentrating on the rising currents. He grazed the dark mental energies of dozens of archangels, never lingering long, lest they take notice of him. Onward and upward, he projected his mind, seeking the leader of this army of wicked sadists.

There you are...leading from high...marshaling your forces, but unable to find me. My humanity too alien, even for you... Well, I'm coming for yah, so hang tight...

Climbing laboriously, Hoyt sensed three entities on a collision course with him but not intentionally. He was invisible to his adversaries. Hoyt felt their presence as they swarmed blindly in buffeting winds. He turned aside just before two misshapen forms dove past, unaware of him. The third creature swerved in his direction. So sudden a maneuver, Hoyt could not evade. Human and angel collided in the slipstream. Hoyt's treasured pistol fell from his hand and disappeared into the murk.

A monster of great girth and length enveloped Hoyt in a deadly embrace. As he tried to push away, Hoyt put himself in range of sharp fingernails that raked his face. Recognizing a disadvantage of proximity, Hoyt drew in his wings and pulled in close. Grimacing against a malodorous corruption of rancid flesh and sewerage, Hoyt wrapped his hands around a stout neck of tendon and muscle and drove his thumbs into its quivering larynx. The creature's reaction was immediate. A maw filled with picked rows of yellowed teeth attempted to bite. Hoyt locked his arms in rigid repose, unyielding in the angel's grasp. Hoyt squeezed. Bone flexed then fractured. Pressure increasing, a large eye ruptured. Hoyt turned his head to avoid a spray of blood. The creature went limp and somersaulted downward. Hoyt broke free and regained flight.

Casting his mind's eye once again, Hoyt located his quarry. He skirted the outer vortex and continued climbing. Hoyt flew in gloom and mist. More figures dove past, some diminutive and emaciated, some large and muscled, all lacking human visages. None could be mistaken as mortal.

Hoyt could not see. It was far too violent inside the thunderstorm. Rain and hail threatened to overwhelm the wings' protection. Still, rain and sweat saturated Hoyt's body. He shivered as heat sieved from his trunk. His strength waning, Hoyt inhaled the moisture laden air trying to catch his breath.

Finally, Hoyt felt a presence ahead on the same level as him. Surrounded by a phalanx of guards, the leader hovered, signaling his minions to descend in an arbitrary sequence.

He can't find me…not really… Just guesswork…

Hoyt sensed the dark angel drifting in his direction. Though it was a subtle maneuver, Hoyt wasn't fooled.

He knows I'm here now. Not exactly where, but he knows. Even now, he's stopped sending his soldiers downward. He's feigning…trying to get closer…trying to pin me down…

Though scarcely perceptible, Hoyt observed a lessening of gloom. Wiping the fog from his watch, Hoyt noted the time and did a quick mental calculation. He grinned and caressed the wings with his fingertips. After a moment of deliberation, Hoyt unsheathed his shortened Calvary sword. The wings swept downward with powerful locomotive strokes. Hoyt ascended the buffeting winds. Assured of a chosen vantage point, Hoyt dove headlong with the sword held forward with both hands. The wings enfolded their master, streamlining his lanky form. Plowing through gloomy mist, the wind whistled in Hoyt's ears. Tears flowed from his blurred eyes.

Furious shrieks erupted as Hoyt whipped past surprised angels. They dove in pursuit until a screaming procession trailed him. Hoyt plummeted through thundering clouds. He did not aim for a discernable object in his vision, but a cold presence, baleful and angry.

"Hey!" Hoyt bellowed, his cry unheard in his own ears.

Instead, the single utterance surfed in the wave of air pushed ahead of him until it reverberated in the ears and mind of the ruler of exiled angels. There was no time to react, even for the most ancient of the fallen ones. The creature glimpsed a transitory image of a man wielding a stout blade before it plunged into his chest.

Colliding with a figure much larger than himself at over three-hundred miles per hour, Hoyt's final mortal thoughts were of debilitating shock and falling. Angels fell upon him, but unable to extricate him from the body of their master, they enveloped him, forming a growing mass of writhing creatures. Hoyt heard their screams and gnashing of teeth.

After many seconds, the dark cumulous clouds expelled the angel horde from the storm. Hoyt sensed bright sunlight and an explosion of blue flames as wings smoldered at the touch of sunrise. He fingered two wires and touched their ends, igniting a massive explosion heard hundreds of miles away. Hoyt felt no pain as his spirit separated from his body. Gray ash wafted downward into the Gulf of Mexico. From afar, the crew on a Texas shrimp boat watched as strange shapes emerged from the thunderstorm and erupted in the early morning sky like shooting stars.

Chapter 31
Begin the Begin

Zane and Audie waited long after sunrise, but their eldest brother never returned. By midafternoon, Zane had doubts, but he kept his thoughts to himself as he sat and stared out a window. Audie paced between the kitchen and living room, head down, forehead furrowed.

"Not good…not good at all. Even when he was far off, we could still sense him. Now, it's like he left the earth. Nothing at all. Just dead air," Audie spoke. "Should we get in our trucks and go in different directions? Conduct a grid search, maybe?"

"I hate to say this, but Hoyt's gone. No doubt in my mind," Zane concurred. "Something happened. He was over water…somewhere over the Gulf…I think. No sense even trying."

"I don't hear the angels anymore," Audie sighed and shuddered. "What do you think?"

"I don't hear 'em either," Zane said. "I think Hoyt killed 'em…somehow killed 'em all."

"What about the wings? You think…?"

"Fuck the wings," Zane spat. "Hoyt deserved 'em more than we ever did."

"We really fucked up. We should have listened. I couldn't let 'em go. Now, our brother's gone…" Audie sobbed, crossing his arms on the kitchen table and bowing his head. "Poor bastard never stood a chance in this life."

In the bedroom, Zane sat and leaned back against the bed and muttered, "…love you, Big Brother…"

Tears spent, Zane and Audie waited out the night. By morning, they accepted their loss. Zane and Audie spent ensuing evenings removing plywood from the walls and windows. Sunlight streamed through glass panes, purging the melancholy from the house.

"I can't stay here any longer, and you shouldn't either," Zane announced. "We should live in Wheeler, but not that dingy apartment at the pawn shop…some place real nice. We could fix up this house and sell it, or give it to a relative."

"Not a bad idea, but I don't wanna take a chance on another family living in misery like we did. We should burn it down."

"Seems a waste, but I can't stand the thought of the house sitting here…waiting," Zane mulled. "Too much history…too many bad memories."

"We can give the lot to Mrs. Sanchez," Audie suggested. "She's put up with a lot of shit from us over the years."

"She sure has," Zane agreed. "I'll call the town office. Fire department might torch it for a training exercise. Afterwards, I'll get a contractor in here, fill it in, and landscape it nice. Maybe, put up a new fence and plant some flowers."

"What about Hoyt?" Audie posed. "I mean…how do we settle his affairs? Shouldn't we report him missing? Won't the V.A. come asking around?"

"No," Zane answered. "Hoyt gave up his disability claim a few months back, so there's no one left to ask about him."

"No…really?"

"Except for us, no one's gonna miss our poor brother. Not sure where exactly, but Hoyt's with Daddy now," Zane offered. "It's just you and me now, Audie. We need to stay together and get along. Anyhow, who else are we gonna talk to about all this?"

"Yeah…time to grow up," Audie admitted, wiping a tear from his eye. "Hoyt would want that."

Although they grieved for their eldest brother, Zane and Audie no longer felt the wings tugging at their thoughts and emotions. With time, they became convinced the feathered appendages had been the source of their family's wretched legacy. However, for the rest of their lives, they yearned to relive the thrill of magical flight.

***

The fairground was awash with colored lights and music. Marlboro residents jammed the lanes and formed long lines for the rides. The air was balmy but comfortable if one didn't move too fast. Audie breathed in the scents of popcorn and cotton candy. Alone this evening, he kept to himself, cloaked in the festivities surrounding him.

"Audie…Audie Harlan!" a woman's voice called. "Over here, Audie." From the crowd, a tall, slender woman emerged. Wearing cutoff jeans and a halter-top, her dark skin glistened with sweat.

"Kaneesha Mack! What could she want?"

"Audie, how are you?" she asked, holding out her hand.

"Uh...I'm okay," Audie answered, taking her hand. "Long time no see, Kaneesha."

Although she had never been friendly with him, Audie always thought Kaneesha was sexy, and he had fantasized—many times—of having angry sex with her. He maintained his guard, lest she had an ulterior motive for approaching him.

"Audie, could I speak with you?"

"Sure," he said, finally letting go of her hand. "Under the oak where it's less noisy."

Despite himself, Audie couldn't help noticing her long legs. In high school, she was the fastest runner he had ever seen. He imagined if she had had a better attitude, she could have been an awesome track and field competitor. He supposed her father dying in a construction accident during her sophomore year might have had something to do with her bitter nature.

"I wanted to say how sorry I am for causing you so much trouble," she began, her eyes looking down. "It was me, who told Big-Mart managers about your juvenile record. I don't know what I was thinking, doing something like that. Angry 'bout getting passed over for a promotion... I'm ashamed about it, and even more for taking so long to say *I'm sorry...*"

"Well..." Audie sputtered. "I have to admit I was angry, but I'm over that now. Just as well... They would have found me out eventually, so don't feel too bad. I've been doing okay since."

"Yeah...you and your brothers own a pawnshop in Wheeler," she said. "I've stopped there a couple times, but you're always out."

"Yeah, I'm traveling lately. Lots of estate auctions and such...buying stuff for the store."

"More fun than stocking aisles at Big-Mart, I imagine," she said. "I'm glad you're doing okay, but I'd feel better if I could do something for you. Make up for it...if you know what I mean."

"Well...I learned long ago not to assume anything, so you may wanna tell me *what you mean.*"

"My mama and sister went home and left me stranded," she said, taking his arm. "Why don't you ride on the tilt-a-whirl with me, and we'll think of something."

Though Kaneesha was several inches taller than him, Audie didn't mind. He was young, healthy, and thoroughly aroused, and she was hotter than new asphalt on a summer day. Wrapping a hand around her narrow waist, Audie Harlan and Kaneesha Mack spent the rest of the evening at the Marlboro Fair.

***

Zane figured it had been a year or more since he had been to the Marlboro Diner. He remembered the circumstances of his last visit quite well given the incident with Clyde Rush. However, his experiences over the past year trumped that humiliating encounter, so he had nearly forgotten it altogether—until now. Zane thought back to that exchange, but no emotion stirred, the memory so trifling in comparison. He smirked.

There were few patrons in the diner since the lunch rush dwindled. The staff prepared for the dinner crowd. Midmornings and midafternoons were Zane's preferred times to go out to eat. He didn't dislike people, but the white noise of a crowd bothered him. When people congregated, voices amplified in response to disparate conversations. If only folks realized the effect and spoke accordingly.

So far, Zane had not seen Francine, nor did he even know if she still worked at the diner. He heard she and Clyde dated for a while. No explanation was forthcoming about their fractured union—if it was just a casual affair, or if there had been an acrimonious uncoupling. Zane suspected Clyde was an asshole on most days, so it was just a matter of time before she realized it. She always had an abundance of commonsense.

Anyhow, Zane's curiosity overwhelmed his resolve never to return to the cafe, so here he was with so many wonderful and terrible events behind him. A rumbling sound carried from down the street becoming louder. Zane recognized the truck before he even saw it.

Oh, you gotta be kidding me! Not that douchebag! What the hell is he doing here?

Not bothering to watch Clyde Rush pulling into the parking lot, Zane sat back and ate his meal. Determined not to put himself in an indefensible position again, he read the Marlboro Gazette and ignored the man lumbering through the door. On this occasion, there was no pronouncement of his arrival. He headed straight to the counter and called out to the owner of the diner, Ned Randall, who was in the kitchen.

"Where is she! I told you to give her a message for me, and I'm not leaving until I speak to her!"

"For crying out loud, Clyde!" Ned replied, walking out from the kitchen. "I told you already, she don't work here anymore."

"Get your skinny hide out here, Ned, or I'll come back there and beat you!"

"No, sir, I'm okay right where I am," Ned said, folding his scrawny arms and standing his ground. "You need to stop coming over here, raising your voice and scaring my customers."

Looking around the diner, Clyde's eyes passed over Zane. "You ain't got no customers," Clyde blustered. "Just Little Hoss, and he don't mind me being here. Do yah, Little Hoss?"

Zane licked his thumb and turned the next page of the newspaper. He picked up his coffee cup and sipped. "Actually, I do mind. I'd like to enjoy my dinner without your bawling like a bitch," Zane replied, setting the heavy mug on the table. "How's my steak coming along, Ned?"

"What dah...?" Clyde sputtered, as he lurched ahead. "You little shit... Why I'll..."

In a blurred instant, Zane flew from his seat and stood in front of Clyde, who was massive in proportion to an average man. "You'll do what?" Zane said, looking up. "You know what? I think you're full of shit...nothing but a big croaker sack of turds."

For a moment, Clyde bowed backward as if giving way to a tremendous wind. Prepared for any scenario, Zane was content to stare the big man down. Though he no longer possessed the wings, remnant powers still flowed through his slight frame and agile mind. If the standoff hadn't been interrupted, Zane was certain Clyde would have back peddled out of the diner without any altercation whatsoever.

Zane, whadda you doing?" Ned cried. "Don't do it. He's big as an ox. He'll walk all over yah, boy."

Thanks a lot, Ned.

His ego suddenly stoked, Clyde made a fist, drew back a stout arm, and delivered a clumsy, but powerful, roundhouse punch.

Zane saw the blow coming and could have easily sidestepped it. Instead, he stood and let it come barreling across his left cheek. Clyde's fist and knuckles connected fully with Zane's face. The natural laws of momentum and energy ceased to exist in that instant. An audible cracking sounded as bone shattered, except it wasn't Zane, who howled in agony.

Clutching his broken hand, Clyde stared dumbfounded until the initial shock subsided, and pain flared from his fingers to his shoulder. "Oh fuck! My hand...! What did yah do to my hand, you little shit..."

In answer, Zane slapped the man hard across his cheek. Clyde fell to the linoleum floor as if kicked in the face by a shod mule. Knocked senseless, the prone man curled into a fetal position. Zane wrapped a splayed hand around Clyde's enormous face, and squeezed, fingers digging into flesh and muscle. Zane dragged him across the floor and through the diner door.

Out in the parking lot, Zane rapped a knuckle against the driver side window of Clyde's truck. Glass smashed and flew into the cab. Zane pulled the lock, opened the door, and then lifted Clyde's limp two-hundred and fifty-pound body from the ground by his face. Clyde grappled Zane's wrist with his uninjured hand.

"Let me go!" Clyde pleaded, through unyielding fingers.

Zane leaned the man against the cab and spoke in a low voice, "Listen close, Big Hoss. As you can see, I'm not what I seem."

"What are you? You ain't normal."

"That doesn't matter!" Zane snapped. "Just know I could do much worse if inclined, so I'm gonna give you one chance—one chance only." Zane released his hold and stepped back.

Clyde slumped to the pavement, five distinct divots appearing on his face. "Whadda want, you fuckin'..."

Though not as hard as the first slap, the open-handed blow stunned the man into submission. "Are you naturally stupid, Clyde, or did you get brain damage when your mama squeezed yah outta her asshole?"

"Sorry...no more...please," Clyde begged, drawing his hands to his face.

"Chris sakes, you'd think you'd wanna hear what I had to say before you got mouthy," Zane said. "No more misunderstandings, Clyde, or I swear..."

"Sorry...sometimes, I don't think before I speak."

"Uh huh," Zane said. "First of all, leave Francine alone. Don't look at her; don't speak to her; don't even think about her. Second, don't come back to the diner...ever. Thirdly, if you see me coming in your direction, you beat feet. If not, I'll slap you down in the street

229

for everybody to see. You won't be so impressive getting the snot beat outta yah by a little shit like me."

"Yeah...yeah... I understand."

"Good! Now repeat it back to me, just so I know for sure you understood me."

"Leave...Francine alone. Stay outta your way... Oh...don't come back to the diner... Is that okay?"

"That'll do for now," Zane said. "Now, get the hell outta here."

As Zane settled to finish his meal, he watched Clyde struggle to get into his high truck. For a moment, he wondered if he should have helped Clyde up, but that sentiment passed when he thought of the grief the man had inflicted on Francine.

"Dessert's on me," Ned said, placing a bowl of peach cobbler pie and a scoop of vanilla ice cream on the table. "I've seen lots of scuffles and been in a few myself, but I never seen anything like that. Like you were made of cement. Shit! You barely got a mark on your face. How did...?"

"Thanks for the pie, Ned," Zane interrupted. "Thankfully, no one was around to see that. Otherwise, that would have been awkward."

"Yeah...sure, sure," Ned agreed, his Adam's apple bobbing up and down. "Well, no harm, except for that big dipshit. He won't come back here...right?"

"Nope...he won't," Zane answered. "I've got a good sense about such things."

"Francine's dropping by to help out with the dinner crowd. She should be here real soon," Ned said. "Why don't yah stick around. I'll tell her what yah did."

"Why would you tell her that?"

"Come now, Zane. I only got one good eye—cataract and all— but I know you've been sweet on that girl a long time," Ned said, wiping his hands on his grimy apron. "You and Francine are too shy for your own good. Well, not you any longer...it seems. But, you'll have to talk her up if you wanna get to know her. She's a good girl."

"What happened with her and Clyde?"

"Oh...that? No worries there," Ned replied. "That ended after a couple of dates, but it didn't sit well with that big dipshit. He's been hounding her goin' on a year now. Like I said, if you wanna know her, you'll have to do some work. Why, hey there, Francine! How yah doing girl?"

"I'm okay, Ned," she said, walking into the diner. "Ready for work."

"That's good to hear," he said, nodding to Zane's table. "Say…look who turned up after all this time."

For a fleeting moment, Zane cringed, but recovered straightaway when Francine looked at him.

Smile appearing on her face, Francine said, "Why hello, Zane. I've…we've missed seeing you around," she said. "Where have you been? What have you been doing? It's like you fell off the face of the earth."

"Hello Francine," Zane said, setting aside his newspaper. "I've been busy doing all sorts of things, but I finally fell back to earth."

"That sounds real mysterious," she said. "How about I pour you another cup of coffee, and you tell me about it?"

***

After Hoyt's disappearance, the world changed in ways so subtle and gradual, it took a while for humankind to take notice. Depression and anger subsided along with violence. Cooperation and goodwill became the norm between countries. War and strife ended. A great contentment settled across the world. Many theories evolved, including scientific and religious, in the years since the beginning of *The Great Peace*, but only a handful of people knew the real truth, and they weren't saying. Besides…who would have believed—who could have possibly believed.

Epilogue
The Risen

Pious heard the locomotive long before it crested the hill. Soon, the lumbering train gained momentum as gravity exerted its influence. Even if doubt intruded now, it was far too late. From a telegraph pole on the other side of the track, a length of taut chain ran to a metal ringlet on his back. Thick rope bound him to a pole on his side of the track. Pious hugged the wooden post tight as the feathered appendages attached to his back flapped madly. An eternity passed before the cowcatcher contacted the chain.

As imagined in his darkest nightmares, the wings did not tear from his body in a single excruciating instance. Instead, the chained links strained against the exorbitant force of the locomotive stretching and bending to their breaking points. In an instant before the far telegraph pole sheared off, the wings ripped from his back.

The locomotive engineer took no notice and continued staring down the track as if in a trance. The sleeping passengers stirred as if a shadowy demon appeared in their dreams, but their agitation waned as the train traveled farther away.

Disembodied wings shuddered on the tracks, dirt clinging to a patch of ashen bone and flesh. Pious slumped against the pole. Black in the dim moonlight, blood poured from deep hollows in his back. He stared into the night sky and pleaded for swift death, even if absolute.

His time before had been bleak beyond imaginings. Despite centuries of pleadings and repeated attempts to destroy his being, Pious could not sway GOD to take away the burden of human misery. Since melancholy was the most powerful weapon in Satan's arsenal, the ALMIGHTY decreed that Pious carry this human emotion, so HE could know its sway over humanity.

Desperate after millennia of despair, Pious fled from heaven to earth where he lived among humans. Pious hoped he might experience a myriad of other emotions present among their kind. Regrettably, his misery was a plague wherever he journeyed. Some committed suicide to escape their depression while others spread their wretchedness unto loved ones. Others committed heinous acts to supplant the emotion.

So overwhelmed by guilt, Pious resorted to self-mutilation. Fulfilling his penance, he longed for death. For those of his kind, death was the ultimate finality. Unlike humans, who passed from one state of being to another, angels existed in a singular realm to serve the edicts of their CREATOR. If their intended purpose ended, they ceased to exist altogether. For Lucifer and his brethren, this eventuality was so distressing, they conspired against the ALMIGHTY for the same fates as humans. When found out, HE cast his lesser angels far from heaven, so they could not corrupt others, and unbeknownst to them, might serve another divine purpose.

Though hidden from sight, GOD had followed Pious throughout his earthly tribulations, and through his tragic angel, the ALMIGHTY experienced the enormity of melancholy and aloneness. So moved by Pious' sacrifice, HE transformed him into a human. Even in his final moments of mortality, Pious felt bliss for the first time before his corporeal vessel vanished in a flash of light, and he passed into the province of human souls. Under a Texas moon, GOD left the angelic wings quivering on the ground to await another worthy soul.

The End

10259368R00142